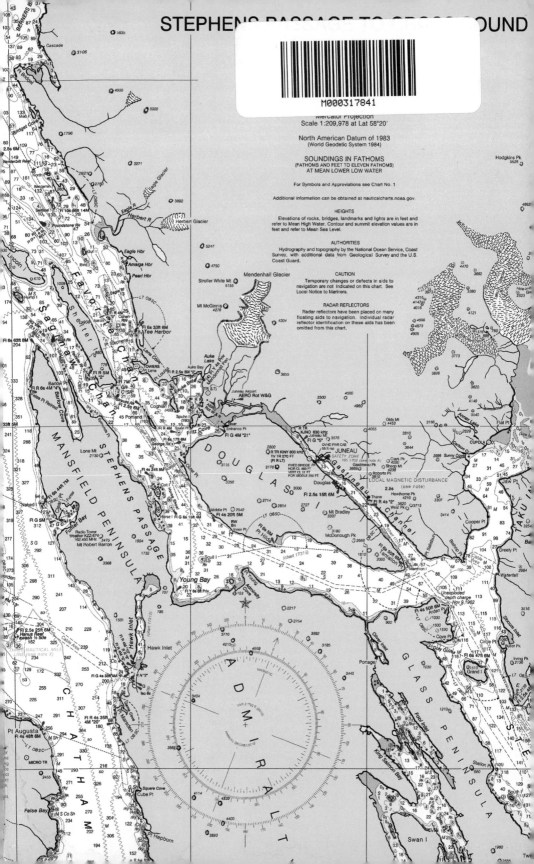

Mercator Projection
Scale 1:209,978 at Lat 58°20'

North American Datum of 1983
(World Geodetic System 1984)

SOUNDINGS IN FATHOMS
(FATHOMS AND FEET TO ELEVEN FATHOMS)
AT MEAN LOWER LOW WATER

For Symbols and Appreviations see Chart No. 1

Additional information can be obtained at nauticalcharts.noaa.gov.

HEIGHTS
Elevations of rocks, bridges, landmarks and lights are in feet and
refer to Mean High Water. Contour and summit elevation values are in
feet and refer to Mean Sea Level.

AUTHORITIES
Hydrography and topography by the National Ocean Service, Coast
Survey, with additional data from Geological Survey and the U.S.
Coast Guard.

CAUTION
Temporary changes or defects in aids to
navigation are not indicated on this chart. See
Local Notice to Mariners.

RADAR REFLECTORS
Radar reflectors have been placed on many
floating aids to navigation. Individual radar
reflector identification on these aids has been
omitted from this chart.

CLEAN SLATE

McKie Campbell

ISBN: 978-1-57833-743-9
Library of Congress Control Number: 2019916462

Clean Slate

Book Design: Carmen Maldonado, 𝕿𝖔𝖉𝖉 𝕮𝖔𝖒𝖒𝖚𝖓𝖎𝖈𝖆𝖙𝖎𝖔𝖓𝖘
The typeface for this book was set in Cambria

Cover art: "Southeast Sunset" by Byron Birdsall (1937-2016). Birdsall was one of Alaska's preeminent artists and most renowned watercolorists.

First printing January 2020

Printed in China
through **Alaska Print Brokers**, Anchorage, Alaska

Published by:

BlueWater Press

McKie@McKieCampbell.com

Distributed by:

𝕿𝖔𝖉𝖉 𝕮𝖔𝖒𝖒𝖚𝖓𝖎𝖈𝖆𝖙𝖎𝖔𝖓𝖘
611 E. 12th Ave. • Anchorage, Alaska 99501-4603
(907) 274-TODD (8633) • Fax: (907) 929-5550
with other offices in Juneau and Fairbanks, Alaska
sales@toddcom.com • WWW.ALASKABOOKSANDCALENDARS.COM

For Barb,
Every step of the way

1

When he got back to the room, it took thirty-five minutes to shower, change and throw everything he had into his duffel. He kept glancing out the window as he packed. The room was on a week-to-week lease, cash in advance. The manager would do no more than shrug when she found him gone. He moved the refrigerator and retrieved his cash from behind the baseboard.

It was dusk when he pulled onto I-5, merging the old pickup into the long lines of headlights heading north on the ebb of rush hour. As he drove, he kept watch on his rearview mirror. North of Sylmar, the traffic began to thin and he turned on the radio. The Doors were on, *Riders on the Storm*. It had come out on their *L.A. Woman* album a couple of years before. The afterglow of the sunset gave the smog an evil gray-orange cast, and in the east, in the gathering darkness over the San Gabriels, heat lightning flickered. He'd always liked the song, but it sounded different now.

Northward momentum and the need to be far away carried Pete through the night. He was thinking about one of Dale's countless stories. Those were the glory days of the king crab fishery in the Bering Sea. Dale had talked about how much money a guy he knew made commercial fishing up there. Dale's stories were always about big money and easy scores. Pete was thinking the Bering Sea was a long way from Los Angeles.

The brakes gave out on a steep hill on Pine Street in Seattle. He limped to the Alaska ferry terminal and boarded the *Columbia* using first gear and the emergency brake to ease himself down the ramp. The *Columbia* carried him up the coast of British Columbia and through Southeast Alaska, a little over a thousand miles north to Juneau. Pete planned on fixing the brakes in Juneau, catching another ferry north to Haines, and driving to Anchorage. In Juneau, he found that to drive to Anchorage required crossing the U.S. - Canadian border twice with attendant checks of I.D. at the Customs stations. He sold the truck and purchased an airline ticket from Juneau to Anchorage.

The Alaska Airlines jet to Anchorage was packed with tourists. It was his first time on a plane since the return flight to the States. As cramped as he was in a window seat in the back of the plane, it was far more comfortable than the military transport he had flown back from Da Nang. When his eyes closed, the sound and feel of the jet brought memories rushing back, almost overwhelming him. When he opened his eyes to the tightly packed cabin of silver hair and bright pastels, expectant chatter and pretty stewardesses, he felt an almost lurching disorientation.

From Anchorage he was on Reeve Aleutian Airways to Dutch Harbor, but the flights were delayed for a day and a half waiting for weather in the Aleutians. The chain, as he heard the others waiting with him call the string of islands, stretched from the tip of the Alaska Peninsula, almost all the way to the Kamchatka Peninsula of Siberia and formed the boundary between the North Pacific and the Bering Sea.

Most of the crowd waiting for this plane were young fishermen, lots of long hair and beards, jeans, Carhartts and wool shirts, Uniroyal rubber boots with the tops rolled down or expensive cowboy boots. A few government employees, also in jeans but neater and carrying briefcases. The big processing plants in Dutch Harbor were owned by the Japanese, and several Japanese businessmen in suits, wary of the boisterous fishermen, stepped politely over those on the floor sleeping off their celebrations. Pete found a corner and tried to blend into the background.

A young man seated near Pete kept pestering the gate agents and announcing to the group at large, "Don't leave, fly Reeve!" It was funny the first time or two you heard it, but you could tell that had been a long time ago for the young women at the desk.

To give the ticket agents a break and stop him from constantly drawing attention to their vicinity, Pete started asking the guy a few questions. He learned that the young man's name was Bob; he was from Bellingham and had been crewing on a crab boat for two years, which rendered him an expert. Bob was eager to share his wisdom about crab fishing in the Bering Sea, about "Dutch" as he called it and Unalaska, the Native village of Aleuts that lived side-by-side with the booming fishing port.

Bob talked of the weather, worst in the world he claimed, 60 to 90 mile per hour winds blowing straight down from the Arctic, gusts to 130, waves big enough to break over the bridges of 120-foot boats. He told of days without sleep when you were on the crab, or times when the temperature plunged and freezing spray formed ice on the superstructure, the desperate race to pound it off with hammers and baseball bats to keep the boat from growing top-heavy and capsizing. He also talked of the money to be made, crew shares of seven percent, more money per trip than most folks made in a year, and of the good times between the seasons.

Bob told Pete how hard it was to get a job on a crab boat and the names of some good boats and skippers and a few to avoid. He told him he would be lucky to find anywhere to stay in Dutch and that if he didn't have a sleeping bag he was in trouble. Pete was glad he had stopped at the R.E.I. store in Seattle and found a bag big enough to fit him.

A fisherman next to them, who Pete had thought was asleep, pushed his ball cap back from over his eyes and stretched. "Our Bobby here is generally full of shit, but he seems to be mainly telling you the truth. Unusual for him. Except that Bobby hasn't been up long enough to see any really bad weather. It can be a lot worse than that."

They gave him advice on finding a spot on a crab boat, "Walk the harbor, ask at every boat you pass that looks like it can stay afloat. Everyday go back and ask them all again. Things change, guys get hurt, sick, go crazy, or just can't take it anymore and quit. The Elbow Room at night. When the boats are in port, that's where the crews are. Listen to the talk. Which skippers are good, which are bad, who's just lost a crewman. Ninety-five percent of what you hear will be bullshit, but you'll still learn. If you see guys get hurt in a fight, get cut, or get so drunk or stoned there's no way they can work the next day, find out what boat they're on and show up the next morning and ask if they have a spot. If you're in the Elbow Room and somebody offers you a job while they're drunk, show up the next morning, but don't count on them remembering or still thinking it is a good idea even if they do."

The other fisherman gave Pete an appraising look and offered a final word of advice before pulling his ball cap back down over his eyes. "Your size you're not likely to fit into the survival suits on most of the boats. Lots of them are in crappy condition anyway. If you can afford it and get on a boat, first thing go to Alaska Ship Supply in Dutch and buy yourself a suit you can get into in a hurry if you need to. No need to do a lot of talking about it, but do it and have it."

They came down to Dutch through the clouds, buffeted by the winds, the plane giving little lurches and drops. The stewardesses, balancing up and down the aisle, collected the last of the drinks just before the tires skidded onto the runway. Pete's first impression of the Aleutians, as soon as he stepped out of the plane and down the steps on to the tarmac, was the wind. The wind here was a constant living presence; it forced you to lean against it, to hold onto your cap or anything loose. When you looked around the island it was obvious that the wind here was king. It sculpted the hills, refused to let trees grow, and kept the buildings squashed low into the land. Even when he walked inside what was rather grandly called the terminal, the wind provided an unceasing low background moan.

After several days, he found a tiny room with a shared bath at an exorbitant price. He realized later how lucky he had been to find that. He liked walking the harbor, but hated asking anybody for anything. Day after day, he forced himself to walk along the rows of boats and ask every boat if they had any jobs open. He wasn't good at asking and knew it, but found in his walks that he would run onto crews wrestling with crab pots, or hawsers, or engine parts, or any of the hundreds of other heavy things that had to go onto or come off of the boats. If it looked like they could use a hand and he wasn't intruding, he would stop and without saying anything, help. He didn't get a job this way, but he developed a number of acquaintances who would give him a wave on the docks or drink a beer with him in the Elbow Room at night and offer him tips on job possibilities.

The Elbow Room, when the fleet was in, was a solid pack of humanity, fifty men for every woman, half a dozen deep at the bar, every table packed, fishermen pissing in the sinks in the restroom because the line at the trough was too long. A dense fog of smoke hung throughout the bar and the roar from everyone shouting to be heard, the drum of excitement of a boomtown overwhelmed even the sound of the wind outside.

Pete, who hated crowds, skipped many nights to stay in his room and read, but sometimes he found solace in the anonymity of the crush and roar. This was a crowd where he didn't stick out. He was in a corner one night, nursing a beer, when a guy he'd met fought through the crowd. "Hey, Pete, see that stocky blond guy over there, the one with the tequila shots? That's Mike Reredon, skipper of the *Suzy Q.* She's a good boat, just got in from Bellingham. I heard one of their deckhands broke his arm when they were coming across the gulf in heavy weather. Might be a chance."

Pete thanked him and after a minute of mental bracing pushed his way through the crowd. "Howdy. I'm Pete McLaughlin. I heard you might have an opening on your boat?"

The crew wedged around the table all turned to look. The skipper studied him through bloodshot blue eyes. "My experience, you big guys are mainly lazy shits who eat more than you're worth and then spend most of the time hanging over the rail puking it back up. I got no time for lazy shits and

I hate people who puke on my boat. What boat you work on last?"

"I haven't been on a boat yet, but I work hard and I don't get seasick."

"Everybody gets seasick, and what the fuck would I want with a greenhorn? Can you even tie a carrick bend?"

"Yeah, I can." Pete inwardly thanked the guy on the dock who had showed him how. Pete had spent a number of evenings in his room with a length of rope, practicing it and other knots he'd been told were essential.

"Ron, give him that half-assed piece of rope you're using for a belt. You're sitting down; your pants aren't going to fall off. Now give it to him."

Pete tied a good carrick bend in the slightly greasy rope in three seconds and handed it back to the skipper. The skipper studied the knot and then Pete. He downed another of the tequila shots sitting in front of him and then grinned slightly. "You might do. You know our boat, the *Suzy Q*? You get your stuff and go down there. Lars is on the boat. You talk Lars into letting you on the boat and you still want to go fishing, you have a job, one trip only, one quarter normal crew share. Lars won't let you on the boat, you hang around and I'll see what I think about it when I'm sober tomorrow."

Pete thanked him and started shoving his way through the crowd. As he left he heard the drunk with the rope belt say, "Asshole. Wait till he meets ol' Lars. Ol' Lars hates everybody."

He stuffed his gear in his duffel bag and headed down to the harbor. It took him a while to find the *Suzy Q*, a good looking boat about 110 feet, side-tied outside an older, slightly smaller, crab boat. There were no lights inside either boat, and he didn't want to wake the guy, but the skipper had been explicit.

Pete climbed carefully across the deck of the first boat and paused before crossing to the *Suzy Q.* He called, "Hello the boat!" but nobody answered and he tried again several times. Pete's eyes were adjusting to the dark, and he could see a little better in the shadows. He decided he should climb on the boat and knock on the cabin door. If that didn't wake this Lars up, at least he would be on the boat and would wait there until the crew staggered back.

As he swung one leg over the bulwark, there was a snarl and a dark shape launched itself out of the shadows. Pete swung his duffel bag in front of him to block the lunge, but the force knocked him backward off the *Suzy Q.* He rolled backward into a crouch and saw there, still on the boat, the meanest looking dog he'd ever seen. Pete knew dogs, but he couldn't figure out for sure what this one was. Maybe one of those big hounds; Irish wolfhound or Norwegian elkhound, part Airedale, maybe part Chesapeake, all parts big and mean.

The dog was rigid on the other side of the rail, lips drawn back in a snarl, a low growl thrumming from its throat. "Hello the boat! Hey, Lars, you in there? Can you call off your dog? Lars, you there?" The second time he hollered the name Lars, he noticed that the dog, without ever stopping its snarl, cocked its head several degrees.

"Lars? Lars? Is that you, fellow? Is your name Lars? You old Lars who hates everybody? You who I'm supposed to be having my job interview with?" The dog continued to growl, but cocked his head several more degrees and looked slightly confused.

"Lars, I need this job so I'm going to get on the boat. It'd be a lot easier if you'd let me. We're going to get along fine. I'm not too good with people these days, but I get along with dogs just fine. You know what they did with dogs over there, Lars?

They ate them. Don't worry. It wasn't a habit I picked up. You going to let me on now?"

Pete slowly extended a hand toward the dog, but the instant his fingers crossed the rail the dog snapped. Pete jerked back in time and began talking to the dog again. He talked softly and steadily and smoothly and tried telling the dog to sit or to lie down. None of it had any appreciable effect. Several times he tried to offer a hand to be smelled, but each time, the moment it crossed the boat's rail the dog would snap forward.

"Lars, I appreciate you staying on your boat and I realize you could jump over here real easy and try to chew my throat out, but I'm going to get on there with you now. OK, easy boy, here I come. Honest, we're going to be friends."

Pete braced himself and shoved the dog back with his duffel. The dog immediately figured out what he was trying to do and tried to come around the duffel at him, but Pete used the bag as a battering ram, sometimes knocking the dog backwards off its feet. He managed to get both legs swung over the bulwark, but as soon as he advanced on to the deck the dog began to circle him, trying to get past the bag, to chew on his throat. After the twentieth or thirtieth circle, the dog quit circling and settled on a strategy of eating its way through the bag to get to him. The dog was biting into the bag, tearing out big hunks of heavy canvas. Pete didn't mind holes in his underwear, but hoped it wasn't the end with his books or new foul-weather gear.

The dog's teeth hung for a moment in the canvas and Pete grabbed it by the skin and hair at the back of its neck with his right hand. Instantly the dog was trying to twist around to bite his hand, but Pete lifted it clear of the deck and shook it. He managed to get his left hand around the dog's muzzle and wrestled the dog onto the deck and onto its back. He knelt over the dog, knees and elbows on the deck, his weight on the dog's chest and stomach, pinning it, both hands holding its muzzle closed and stretching the dog's head back so he could put his face in its throat and talk to it.

He was still panting a bit, whispering to the dog when he heard a soft throaty chuckle, and a woman's voice said, "I need to thank you for the most entertaining evening I've ever spent in Dutch. Mike send you down to ask Lars for a job?"

Pete was so startled he almost lost his grip on the dog, and he blushed a deep red. He thanked the darkness and strained his neck up to try and see who was talking to him. "Yeah he did. Uh, excuse me, but where are you, and who are you?"

"Just a minute." Pete could now tell that the voice came from an open port on the boat the *Suzy Q* was rafted up to. In a moment, a light came on inside that boat, and then a woman in her early thirties, dressed in jeans and an oversized gray sweatshirt came out on her boat's back deck.

"Mike's not a bad skipper, but he's a mean drunk. Sending people down to ask Lars for a job is a favorite trick of his when he's drinking. You get bitten?"

"I don't think so, but I'm not sure I'm ever going to be able to let go."

"You know, when he started chewing though your bag I thought I was going to strangle, not laughing out loud."

"In another life, did you enjoy going to the Coliseum to watch Christians be thrown to the lions?"

"Aw, you were OK. If he got to you, you would have jumped off the boat. Lars doesn't leave the boat."

"Doesn't Mike worry about somebody hurting his dog?"

"Nah. He hates Lars. Besides, you're the first person I've

ever seen fool enough to actually try and get on the boat with him. I never thought I would see anybody pick him up though, much less with one hand." She walked over to the edge of her boat rail and the light from the dock lights fell across her face. She gave Pete a very level stare, straight into his eyes. "If you tried to hurt him, I would have stopped you."

There was something about the look that made Pete not doubt her for an instant. "If he doesn't like Lars, why does he have him on the boat? I never heard of dogs on boats anyway."

"Not his dog, not his boat. They both belong to his father-in-law. An old Norwegian, Sig Petersen. Been one of the best captains up here for years and years. The family has three boats. Mike married one of the old man's daughters. The old man trusts Mike to be hell of a good skipper when he's out on the water, but he doesn't trust him not to cat around when he's in port. Insists that Lars goes along on the boat, to 'look after his share' he calls it. Thinks Lars won't let anyone on the boat who the old man hasn't introduced him to. Supposed to keep strange women off the boat."

"Does it work?"

She tilted her chin up a little and gave him another of those level stares. "Not always. When you were trying to tell Lars to sit or lie down?"

"Yeah. You heard that huh?"

"Sure. I was lying there just dozing off when you came down the dock. I've known Mike long enough to figure what was happening. One reason you couldn't get Lars to respond is that he only understands Norwegian."

"You don't happen to know a little Norwegian do you? Something you could say to Lars so I could get off of him?"

"I know a little when I need to. But if you're going to work on Mike's boat, it's probably better you and Lars work it out on your own. If the two of you can avoid any more yelling and growling, I'm going back to bed."

"Wait a minute. You're going to leave me here?"

"Yeah. I heard you tell the dog your name is Pete, is that right?"

"Yeah, it is."

"Pete, my name's Helen, and I'll leave you with a couple of observations. The first is that that I heard you tell Lars you were fine with dogs, but not too good with people these days. You seem OK with people to me. The second is that I hope you figure out a way to get off Lars before morning comes and people start walking by. With so few women up here, a lot of these guys get sort of desperate, and people who didn't see how you got in that position with that dog might come to the wrong conclusions. Good night."

She went back into her cabin, leaving Pete blushing scarlet again. He realized that during their conversation the tenseness had gone out of Lars' body. He slowly eased his weight off the dog and then cautiously released his muzzle. Lars rolled quickly to his feet and retreated a short distance away.

Pete leaned back against the cabin to wait for the return of the crew and find out if he really had a job. He kept his duffel handy in front of him, just in case. He and Lars sat there in the dark, about ten feet apart, watching each other. He reflected that, on the deck of a crab boat in the middle of the night in Dutch Harbor, sitting on an upside down dog, he just had the longest sustained conversation with a woman, almost with anyone, since his family was killed.

2

Days of gray. Weeks of never seeing the sun. The constant throb of the diesel and the high moan of the hydraulics. Nights when they were on the crab, of never getting more than three hours of sleep. Days when the sea stretched flat and oily as far as you could see, and days when all 110 feet of the *Suzy Q* raced down the backs of waves taller than the boat, into troughs you never thought you would climb out of, the boat shuddering under the weight of tons of green water. Tanner crab and king crab. Quarter share, half share, and then a full seven per cent crew share.

Helen had been right. Mike was a good skipper. Hard, but careful, he made sure Pete learned, because that made the boat money. Pete could handle the social graces of the ship; work hard, don't complain, and stay out of the others' way. He welcomed the unremitting brute labor that dropped you straight into brief hours of dreamless sleep. Sliding the 700-pound crab pots across the deck, catching the roll of the ship so it helped you, reminded him of playing line in football.

Pete learned to work the pot launcher, to coil line fast enough to keep up with the hydraulic blocks that pulled in the pots, to handle his watches on the bridge when they were traveling.

He learned to always watch for the wave out of sequence, the one that would wash you over the side in a heartbeat if you were not able to grab and brace before it hit. He learned never to raise the soles of his boots from the deck when they were launching pots, lest an errant coil whip around your ankle and suddenly plunge you to the bottom, 600 feet below, tied to a 700-pound crab pot.

Mike really did hate the dog. Many times in that first trip he repeated that he would have never given Pete a try if he could have gotten an experienced fisherman on board without waiting for his father-in-law to get into port to make his Norwegian introduction. All the crew gave Lars a wide berth and Lars snarled at anyone who got close. Twice more Lars tried to go after Pete and each time, with only minor bites, Pete was able to grab him up by the scruff of the neck and dangle him above the deck until he quit snarling and biting. Then carefully holding his muzzle closed, Pete would cradle him in his arms like a baby and talk softly to him until he could feel the tension slowly drain from the dog's muscles.

Mike would have found a way to shove Lars overboard, but Sig, his father-in-law, had made it abundantly clear that though he only had three boats, he had five sons-in-law. If anything happened to Lars, regardless of why, one of the others with a little less fishing experience, but no questions about faithfulness, would take over as captain.

Pete fished through the boom years of king crab in the Bering Sea on the *Suzy Q* and other boats. The king crab fishery back then, before rationalization and Individual Fishing Quotas, was a derby fishery, open for three to five days at a time for as much as you could catch, come hell or high water. Instead of joining his crewmates flying to beaches in Thailand or Hawaii in between the openings, Pete worked on limit gillnet boats in Bristol Bay, and herring boats in Norton Sound, developing a reputation as top notch crew. "Yah, big guy, strongest son'a bitch I ever seen. Doesn't talk hardly, but hell of a good worker. Got good sense and knows what needs to be done before you tell him. Sure reads a lot though. I never could figure what he saw in reading all that much," was the assessment one skipper might give to another in a bar in Dutch or Dillingham, Sand Point or Kodiak.

When he wound up in a port at the same time as the *Suzy Q* he would stop by the boat to say hi to Mike, but mainly to visit Lars. To the astonishment of new crew members, Lars would come over and lean against Pete. Pete would scratch the dog's ears and have long quiet conversations with him. Sometimes he would wind up in a port at the same time as Helen, and they would talk. She was about ten years older and seemed to think of him as a younger brother.

At a time when many of the other fishermen he worked with were pissing away their money on cocaine and alcohol, hand-tooled cowboy boots and gold nugget watch bands, thousand-dollar nights in Anchorage with the strippers at the Bush Company and condos in Mexico, Pete stuck his money in a savings account, not out of frugality, but rather from lack of caring enough to spend it.

The Sitka sac roe herring fishery brought him back to Southeast Alaska. It was a mad rodeo where the entire season's opening might last only a half hour and a slight mistake or just bad luck could make the difference between a dry haul and a catch worth hundreds of thousands of dollars. He had liked

Southeast when he had passed through Juneau the first time. He liked it even more now. When he was little, he always wanted to live by the ocean or in the mountains, and here were both, the myriad channels of the inside passage swirling around the mountain islands that made up the Alexander Archipelago.

Helen's boat was lost in a massive spring storm. The search found only a few pieces of floating debris. Fishermen were lost every year, men he knew, but when he heard about Helen, he decided he needed a break from fishing, a break from running into other fishermen anxious to tell their tales of the storm. He looked around Sitka for some property, a place where a person could maybe build a cabin and have a little land around him, but he found that most of Southeast was part of the Tongass National Forest, and larger chunks of private land were scarce and expensive.

He knocked around some of the other Southeast communities: Petersburg filled with Norwegian fishermen who reminded him of Mike's father-in-law; Ketchikan, half fisherman and half loggers and mill workers; Wrangell at the mouth of the Stikine River and Haines and Skagway at the top of Lynn Canal.

Finally, on the road north of Juneau he found a chunk of land for sale. It was about nine acres, wedged in between the road and Lynn Canal. It had originally been a series of mining claims. A little creek ran through the property and cascaded down the small cliff above the rocky beach. During Juneau's gold rush, prospectors had panned a little color from the creek, and following the creek up, found a promising vein of quartz in the country rock. They patented their claims and had broken their picks, their backs and their hearts chasing ore veins that all gave out. Pete admired their work and perseverance, and felt slightly disloyal to their ghosts for being glad the gold had played out before they had cut down the huge old spruces.

After he closed on the land, Pete spent the next several weeks camping out there, studying how the sun hit the land, what angles gave the best views, and where the terrain offered protection from the wind. It all came together in a site above the cove. It was high enough to be safe from the winter storms that roar down Lynn Canal, and a short, steep path led down the cliff to the cove where he could keep a skiff on an outhaul.

Pete logged out a narrow drive, curving it to follow the natural contours for the easiest slopes. He cut the smaller trees into firewood and saved the large ones to use when he started to build. He graveled the drive and parking pad above the site, built steps from the parking pad down to the site and improved the steep path down to the beach. He bought an old travel trailer and hauled it out to the pad to live in while he drew and redrew house plans.

He knew that working by himself, digging the foundation down to bedrock and drilling the rock, running rebar and building the foundation forms so when the concrete was poured, the foundation would be tied to the bedrock, building the house the way it had taken shape in his head, was going to be a long haul. There was a joke his father used to tell that Pete couldn't quite remember, but the punch line had been, "Yeah, but what's time to a hog?" Pete would tell himself that sometimes at the end of a long hard day. It didn't make much sense without the rest of the joke, but on some evenings he could hear his dad's chuckle and he would feel less alone.

Weekdays and weekends all blended together without differentiation, Pete worked them all. His social life consisted of the free cookies at Valley Lumber and talking with the guys who worked the counter or helped him load his pickup. After a year, he felt good about the progress on the house, but knew he was getting stranger, feeling even less comfortable around people.

He started eating a meal out here and there, forcing himself to go to small family places where they remembered you after the second or third time. He'd always frequented the bookstores, but began to talk to the clerks a little, asking their opinions or ordering books. He would go to the community swimming pool and swim or lift weights and then sit in the sauna, where the conversation swirled around you without requiring participation. He named his course Remedial Human Interaction and decided for now it was best if he judged himself on a pass/fail basis.

He began to attend church on an irregular basis. He would usually arrive just after the service had started and slip into a pew in the back. He always left just before the end, so he didn't have to talk to anyone. The liturgy and service, remembered from his youth, were comforting and sometimes meaningful to him.

He worked fiercely, trying to keep himself lost in labor and the challenge of thinking through each step, how each part of the house worked with the rest, how to do things he had never done before. He was pleased with the house when he was able to move in, the smell and feel of the wood he had hewn himself, the fit of the rocks that formed the hearth and chimney, the way the constantly changing views filled each room.

The results of his efforts with people were less clear cut. He could have casual conversations with people, could respond without much difficulty to comments about the weather or all the other meaningless interchanges that allow everyday life to function. When he had to go downtown, he made himself smile and nod and say howdy to familiar-looking folks he passed on the street.

When he had been totally withdrawn, he had mainly felt grim and fierce or just not felt at all. It wasn't much fun, but it was tolerable. Now, as he forced himself to open up even a little bit, to admit that he needed other humans, he found himself sometimes struggling with periods of intense sadness, with an ache in his chest and the back of his jaws that he had not allowed since the moment the young policeman had first told him the news. His response was always to throw himself into furious physical labor, hauling large rocks up from the beach, moving logs, digging out stumps, or other tasks that he could work on past exhaustion.

As the house neared completion, he began to wonder what came next. The land and house had eaten up most of his money, and he knew by the time he got the garage finished, he would have to get back to work. Of more concern than money was what he would find as a focus for living once the house was finished.

He flew back to Michigan, and after three transfers, wound up sitting in front of his old house in a rental car, watching a young father laughing and raking leaves in the slanting sunlight while a little girl romped in the leaf pile, undoing his efforts. He had thought about seeing some of his old friends, but sitting there watching, decided he couldn't go through with it. His father had been the county's Sheriff for years and he had grown up with some of the deputies acting as an extended band of uncles. There were some of them he would have liked to talk to, but decided that would be a particularly bad idea. Pete rented a U-Haul truck and cleaned out the storage unit where he had been keeping the stuff he had saved from his folks' estate sale. He drove for over twenty-four hours before pulling into a rest area and crawling into the back of the truck to sleep.

Several months after Pete was back, Mike and a couple of his old crew from the *Suzy Q* got stuck in Juneau on a weather-diverted flight. He met them and had a few beers and they all drank a toast to Helen. They tried to talk him into coming back with them to fish, but he knew it was no longer the right thing.

During his travels, he'd always kept an old fly rod handy and now he began to fish and hunt more, feeling a connection to his youth and his father. He bought a used ocean kayak and read four books on kayaking before hauling it to Twin Lakes on a nice day and nearly drowning himself while learning the Eskimo roll.

Time spent in the wild was therapeutic, but more and more, he found himself pushing the limits, hunting in the alpine of Admiralty Island until dusk and then hiking out through the woods in the dark, running the skiff or paddling the kayak in weather in which no one should be out. Pete thought about his motives long and hard after the skiff almost swamped coming back from St. James Bay in heavy weather.

He went to Costco and bought a computer program called Family Lawyer. He made a will, leaving his assets to the Glory Hole, Juneau's homeless shelter. Then he took the kayak and went paddling into the teeth of a full gale that was whipping down Lynn Canal.

Out there, bursting through the tops of waves, surfing down their backs, even being rolled a few times and clawing his way back up, bellowing, water streaming from his hair and mustache and paddling jacket, he felt more alive, more keenly interested in staying alive, than he had for quite a while. He stayed out though, heading into wave after wave, well past the point of cold and exhaustion. He made it back to his cove, barely able to pull the kayak on shore and climb up the path from the beach.

Three weeks later, he was surprised to hear a pickup rattling down his driveway. It was Don, one of the guys from Valley Lumber. "You sure live way to hell and gone out here. The delivery guys drew me a map, or I never would have found this place. Looks like it's come together pretty well. That metal roofing wound up looking good."

"Hey, Don, what's happening? What brings you out here?"

"Alaska Airlines Cargo called us. Somebody sent you a dog and told them they could get ahold of you through us. They're sure anxious to reach you. Can't believe there are people who don't have phones."

"A dog? You sure? You sure it's me they want?"

"Lady said the address read, 'Pete McLaughlin. Big guy with a mustache, building a house out the road. Reach him through Valley Lumber.' Sure sounds like you to me. She wasn't real happy about it. Said Seattle should never have accepted the dog without better arrangements. Anyway, I was getting off work so I thought I'd drive out. Was kinda curious to see this place anyway, see where all our stuff's been going. What'n the hell is this drive like in the winter? "

"Four-wheel drive and chains on the truck. I can usually make it. The dog's from Seattle?"

"That's what she said. Instead of asking me questions I don't know, why don't you give me a quick tour and then get in your truck and drive in there? The cargo office is open late."

Hector was just a puppy then, huddled in the back corner of his sky kennel, looking tired and scared about the whole process. Pete put his hand in and let the pup sniff it thoroughly before he gently picked him up. The pup licked Pete's face as Pete nuzzled him close, talking softly. The woman at the desk told him she should yell at him for being so hard to get in touch with, but they had all been playing with the pup and didn't want to let him go.

There was a letter taped to the top of the sky kennel and when he opened it he was surprised to see it was from Sig Petersen, Mike's father-in-law, and the owner of the *Suzy Q.* He had only met Sig a few times and would never have dreamed that Sig still remembered him. The note was in a large, all caps scrawl.

"LARS DIED LAST WEEK. OLD AGE. HE WAS A DAMN GOOD DOG. YOU AND ME WERE THE ONLY TWO PEOPLE HE EVER LIKED. MIKE AND SOME OF THE BOYS WERE THROUGH JUNEAU A WHILE BACK. SAID THEY SAW YOU. SAID YOU DIDN'T SEEM TOO GOOD. THIS PUP IS LARS' GRANDSON. 8 WEEKS OLD. THE OTHER PARTS ARE ALL CHESAPEAKE. HE IS GOING TO BE A DAMN GOOD DOG TOO. YOU TAKE GOOD CARE OF THIS DOG. YOU WERE A PRETTY GOOD FISHERMAN. YOU EVER WANT TO FISH ANYMORE, YOU LET ME KNOW. YOU CAN BRING THE DOG. WE'LL TEACH HIM TO BITE MIKE IN THE ASS."

3

The shift started badly for Annie. A drunk the police brought in fouled himself while passed out and then came to and began a nonstop stream of obscenities and abuse. A badly frightened and slightly hurt ten-year-old had fallen off her skateboard and been slapped by her mother for her clumsiness. Annie never doubted her choice of professions when she was dealing with a crisis, but today she was having trouble having the proper degree of sympathy for the usual run of illnesses and minor injuries.

Annie had finished her master's in emergency medicine and was working for an agency that provided nurses to hospitals with staffing shortages. She kept promising herself she was going to stop and settle down sometime soon, but she enjoyed the travel, enjoyed seeing different parts of the country, and seemed unable to control the itch to move on. Juneau and Alaska had sounded exotic and she'd come up on the ferry at the beginning of the summer.

The night before, the owners of the condo she was house sitting called to tell her they were returning sooner than expected. She had less than a week to find somewhere else to live in a town where housing was so tight people watched the obituaries for possible vacancies.

She'd just finished cleaning and bandaging the girl's abrasions and having a very firm word with the mother about the need for helmet, pads and motherly concern when she saw the aging pickup pull into the "Ambulances Only" zone. She shot out the door to catch the man. "You can't park here! There's parking around the side of the building."

The big man shut the truck off and got out without paying any attention to her. "This is ambulances only. Please move your truck right now or I'll have to call . . ." She rounded the front of his truck and saw him fully.

He had a look of fierce, clench-jawed determination and sweat was beaded on his forehead. He wore an old wool shirt with the sleeves cut off below the elbow, like the commercial fishermen she saw around the harbors, and a pair of faded brown Carhartt work pants. There were wood chips on his shirt and dirt down his left side and on his right knee. He was coming at her, leaning on the pickup, hopping slowly on his right foot. His left pants leg was soaked a dull red below the knee and sticking through the canvas of the jeans, shining pearly white, was his shin bone. The jagged end had dirt and moss and a small red leaf impaled on it, as though for decoration. With each small hop the muscles of his face spasmed.

"Stop. I'll get you a stretcher. Can you hold on there for just a second?" He nodded. She ran back to the door and yelled inside, "I need a gurney out here now and some help! I have an open tib-fib with no assistance!"

They got him on the gurney with a pillow under the leg and the siderails pulled up. They rolled him inside, took his blood pressure, checked his pulse at his wrist and then at his left ankle below the break to see if an artery had been affected. They cut away the pant leg, plucked off the leaf and began to flush the dirt with sterile water.

"When did you last have a tetanus shot? Allergic to any medications? Are you currently taking any medications? When did you last eat? How did this happen?"

He had been answering with nods or shakes of his head or terse answers, but to the last question he said, "Got downhill of something much bigger than me." He saw her look and elaborated, "A log fell on it."

"An admitting clerk is going to get some information. We're going to take a little bit of blood for a blood test and start an I.V. of Ringer's lactate with a drip of antibiotic. You'll go to X-ray, and then to surgery to set your leg. Are you understanding me? OK, I'll be back in a minute and give you something for pain."

"I need to ask a favor." She'd started to turn away, but he reached out and took her wrist, his hand totally wrapping around her forearm. He wasn't squeezing, but when she instinctively tried to pull away, nothing moved. She had the momentary thought that it was as if she'd tried to move a portion of the building.

"I'm sorry, but I don't have anyone else to ask. I tied my dog up so he would stay out of the way while I was hoisting the log. He's just a pup and needs to be untied. Could you check on him for me?"

"I'd be happy to call a neighbor for you."

"There aren't any neighbors. I was thinking maybe the vet or the humane society or somebody could board him till I get out," he paused, taking several deep breaths to shove back the pain, "Maybe someone might be willing to house-sit. I'll pay you for your time and gas."

"Where do you live?"

"Out the road, past 37-mile on the left. About 5 miles past the 'No Winter Maintenance' sign where the pavement ends. Maybe if you could lock up my house, also? The key's on the ring. I left them in the truck."

"Listen, I get off at 3:30, and I'll drive out and do something about your dog. O.K.?"

"Thank you. I don't like to ask for favors. His name is Hector. "

"O.K. I'll figure out something about Hector. Now if you'll let go of my arm, I'm going to get you a shot of Demerol."

Annie drove along the two-lane blacktop, or "out the road" as it was called by the locals. Before she came to Juneau, she used to pile into her car on her days off and head out, often with no clear destination in mind. This road curled along the eastern shore of Lynn Canal until it dead-ended north of Juneau. When she first heard the locals talking about Lynn Canal she had envisioned a manmade trench big enough for two ships to pass. Instead Lynn Canal had been gouged by the retreat of ancient glaciers and was over twelve miles wide and thousands of feet deep. It was dotted with small islands, and the peaks of the Chilkat Range reared up on the far side, sparkling in the sunshine. The drive was spectacular, through thick forests of spruce, hemlock and cottonwood and along the top of rocky cliffs overlooking the ocean. She drove slowly, pulling over often to look at the views.

She shook her head at herself. She should be home on the phone, tying to find another place to live. She'd promised to drive out here without thinking it through and was now trying to analyze it in her mind. He'd mentioned the possibility of house-sitting, but she didn't hold out much hope for the place. She'd seen too many cabins and trailers stuck on little lots in the mud. There was something about him she liked, and even made her a little bit curious, but it probably came down to her soft spot for dogs. The thought of the tied-up puppy bothered her.

Past twenty-mile, the houses thinned. About twelve miles farther, the blacktop ended and a sign announced the road was not maintained in winter. The wash-boarded dirt rattled her car and made it plain not much maintenance was done in the summer either. She watched carefully and eventually spotted a narrow, pot-holed dirt driveway that cut off to the left, marked with a "Private, No Trespassing" sign. With gathering misgivings, she turned down the driveway, branches brushing the side of the car, bumping along slowly. After the first twenty-five yards, there was a sharp turn, and the drive suddenly got better. The branches were trimmed back, the drive covered with a smooth layer of crushed green gravel.

Down the drive, she began to see a glint of water through the trees. She pulled onto a parking pad in a small clearing where Pete had been building a garage and shop. The walls were up slightly above her head, constructed of cants, large logs cut into square beams. Outside each corner a vertical log, or gin pole, was set in the ground and guyed with ropes. There were block and tackles at the top of each gin pole for lifting the cants into place on the walls. The front left gin pole was partially pulled over and still had one end of a cant attached to it. A broken pulley dangled from the back left gin pole. Annie turned the car off and got out.

From the far side of the garage, a puppy was barking. She went around and found the pup, a Chesapeake Bay Retriever about four months old, wagging his whole body and redoubling his barking at the sight of her. She knelt down and laughed as puppy kisses covered her face. "So you're Hector, huh? What a nice pup. Come on, we'll get you some water."

She untied the pup. She could see where the cant had broken loose from its lifting tackle and knocked Pete down the slope. Annie dealt with injuries every day, but looking at the bloodied track Pete made crawling back up, thinking what the crawl and the drive in to the hospital must have been like, made her stomach queasy.

"Come on, fella." At the edge of the parking pad, a covered stairway led down toward the water. Annie started down the steps and realized that she was looking at the roof of the house. It was bigger than she had expected, also made of massive log cants, with a blue-green metal roof. The door was unlocked, and she stepped in through a small enclosed porch and stopped, amazed. The sun danced on wavelets in Lynn Canal, and across the canal, snow topped the peaks of the Chilkat Mountains. Picture windows made up the far wall, and the view seemed to fill the room. This was definitely not what she had been expecting. Wide plank wood floors with faded orientals, a two-story living room with clerestory windows that captured the light, a fireplace with a stone chimney to the ceiling and a giant old sword hung above the mantle.

The room was sparsely furnished, but there were books everywhere; floor to ceiling bookshelves with an attached ladder on rollers, bookshelves built into seats under the windows, books and magazines on a coffee table. Hardbacks and paperbacks intermingled, novels, mysteries, history, politics, biographies, science fiction, fishing, hunting and nature books, a whole shelf on log construction and do-it-yourself home builder books.

Annie had always been a reader; libraries had been her retreat through all the moves of her childhood. Now books were her escape from the pressures of the ER; they were friends available in each new town as she moved around the country for the nurse temp agency. She'd never accumulated books though. She passed them on to friends or hauled them to used book stores or the Salvation Army before each move.

She saw what seemed to be complete collections of John McPhee, Tom McGuane, Dick Francis, Robert Parker, John Gardner, Jim Harrison, William Faulkner, Joseph Conrad, Dorothy Sayers, Thomas Hardy, Andre Dubus, James Thurber, and others. There was a shelf of Isaac Asimov and a shelf of Louis L'Amour. Many books and authors were old friends and others she'd never heard of. She had noticed on Pete's admitting papers that he was a veteran and there was a shelf of military history, but interestingly, no books on Vietnam.

There was a curving open staircase that went up to a balcony overlooking the living room. Curiosity got the better of her, and she went up the stairs. There were two bedrooms and a bath. The spare bedroom was set up as an office with a desk in front of a window, a fold-out couch, a file cabinet and more bookcases. A fly-tying bench, with a small pile of newly tied flies, was beside the desk. She thought of the hand that had wrapped totally around her forearm. It was hard to imagine those hands tying these tiny creations. In the larger bedroom an old-fashioned four-poster bed was set so your first view in the morning would be of ocean and mountains. No telephone or television anywhere in the house.

She sat on the bed for a minute and Hector bounded up with her, wriggling into her lap. Hugging the dog, her cheek on top of his head, staring out at the mountains, she was still for a long time.

"**I locked up your place.** There were chainsaws and some other tools out so I got them all under cover. Hector stayed with me last night. I'll check with the Humane Society this afternoon about boarding him."

"I really appreciate it. Thanks for bringing me the books, too. It will make a big difference." She had brought him *A Rage for Falcons* by Stephen Bodio, *The Mysteries of Pittsburgh* by Michael Chabon, *Leaving Cheyenne* by Larry McMurtry and *Mirror Worlds* by David Gelernter.

"I just gathered some off the bedside table and the coffee table that looked like you were reading. I'm sorry that I can't keep Hector any longer myself, but I'm in the middle of having to find a new place."

"You have to move?"

"Yeah, I was house-sitting a condo in West Juneau and the owners are coming back sooner than expected."

"You found a place yet?"

"Not yet, but I will."

"I know it's pretty far out the road, but you're welcome to stay in my place until you find something. It would be a big favor for Heck."

"You'll be getting out of here in a couple of days,"

"The doctor said it would be at least a week and a half. They're going to do a second operation on the leg."

"Well, maybe. Maybe just for a few days until I find a place. Are you sure about this? Me staying there I mean?"

"I'm very sure."

When he came home, immaculate in fresh white plaster, he convinced her it would be a favor to him if she stayed on in the spare bedroom while she looked for a place. She agreed, just for a few days. The days had stretched in the long hours of the Alaska summer. For her, it was an odd mixture of feeling strangely at home, at peace, more than she had in years, edged with an attraction to Pete.

At first he hadn't talked much, the same polite almost diffident reserve he had shown at the hospital. She was still on the day shift. Very early each morning, she would hear the quiet thump of his cast as he went down the stairs. There was a covered deck part way across the front of the house. When she came down, he would be sitting out there, drinking coffee, sometimes reading, sometimes just gazing at the view or at things she couldn't see. Annie had never been a morning person, but she started getting up earlier on nice mornings to have a cup of coffee with him.

He told her he liked it best when there was a strong wind out of the south, making the wave-tops smoke and crash on the rocks below. She told him storms were the best time to be snuggling in for an extra half hour under the covers.

They talked, there on the deck, in the mornings and sometimes in the evenings. She made small talk about Norfolk and Tampa, San Diego and Boulder, and other towns where she had grown up or worked. She asked questions about Juneau and Alaska and little by little, about him.

She found herself telling him about growing up on a succession of Navy bases, telling him things she hadn't talked to anyone about. About her dad who was mainly gone, his returns marked by her parents' bitter quarrels. About her mother's drinking and death, and the feeling that she had been drifting all her life. About being scared she would never settle down, but at the same time getting an almost panicked drive to run anytime she started to feel emotional ties.

Several times it seemed he was going to say something. She knew he liked her as a friend, she just couldn't tell beyond that. One night she had some of her friends from the hospital over for dinner. After the last guest left, Pete and Annie cleared the remaining dishes. It had felt very domestic. It seemed to imply some type of link, some sort of couplehood. She said they had been her guests so she would do the dishes, but he insisted on helping. They stood side by side at the sink. She washed and he rinsed and dried. She'd never thought of forearms as an erotic part of the body before, but even now she could remember his sleeves rolled up to the elbows, the flex of muscles and tendons, the blue tracery of the veins, the glisten of the soap bubbles caught in the hair of his arms, the palpable jolt that seemed to run up their arms every time their hands touched as she handed him a dish. They finished the dishes and said awkward good nights. She went up to her room, and he went out on the deck. He sat there most of the night, watching the moon on the water.

She continued to look for a place to live. She was scheduled to be off work on Thursday and Friday, and she had scheduled several appointments to look at places. On Tuesday night, he asked her to have dinner with him the following night, said he would cook.

"I'm having dinner with you right now. We've eaten together most nights and you've cooked most of them."

"This is eating together because we both happen to be here and it's time to eat. I thought I would fix you a special dinner to remember me by, in case you decide to take one of the places you look at the next couple of days."

She came home the following evening to a table covered with white linen and set with good china and sterling. He served broiled medallions of venison backstrap, "organic fillet mignon with no cholesterol," he joked, and a king crab caught that day. He showed her how to get the crab meat out of the shell and assured her it was OK to eat the small green shoots of wild goose tongue he had mixed into the salad.

When she complimented him on the table setting, the dinner and the wine, he said that after his folks died, he'd placed his favorite things in storage and sold the rest. A year ago, he'd brought the things back to Alaska.

He admitted that he chose wine by selecting from labels with pictures he liked. They told each other of Heck's latest antics and laughed over Pete's description of wrapping his cast in double garbage bags and duct tape and tying a life jacket around it so he could run the crab pots in his skiff. He told her it was the first time since he had brought the stuff back that he'd used the linen and china and silver.

After a dessert of freshly picked salmonberries and wild blueberries in heavy cream, they wound up on the deck. A soft warm wind was blowing. They watched the moon illuminate the water and claim the snowy mountains' peaks for its own. She was standing at the rail with him behind her when he gently wrapped his arms around her.

They stayed like that for a long time, her cheek resting on his arm, his cheek on the top of her head. As she stood there, wrapped in Pete's arms, a phrase of her mother's she hadn't thought about in years came floating through her mind. "A safe harbor." That's what her mother used to say everyone needed. Pete took her shoulders in his hands and kissed her neck, and she didn't think of her mother anymore or anyone else.

4

"Just for the record, I'm not enjoying this anymore!" Annie had to shout to make herself heard. "Hector doesn't like it either."

Pete had to grin as he glanced at her. She had been standing with Pete at the center console, but Hector had become increasingly uneasy as the weather deteriorated and was now on the seat, trying to work his way onto her lap. Heck was six years old now and weighed a little over a hundred pounds. Annie was hugging him while trying to hang onto the seat strut.

Pete concentrated on easing the throttle back as they slid diagonally down the face of the green wave. "Tell Hector he looks silly in your lap. Doesn't he know Chesapeakes are rugged water dogs?"

They'd been out for three days over the long Labor Day weekend, fly fishing for silver salmon south of Juneau, fishing the edges of kelp beds or the mouths of different rivers or creeks every day, camping at night on small islands to avoid the bears fishing the same streams. The weather had been perfect, a rarity on this misty coast of Southeastern Alaska where three clear days in a row constitute a dry spell.

When they headed for home, Pete envisioned a smooth run back in the long twilight of an Alaskan summer evening. Instead, Stephens Passage humped up into a jumbled seascape of steep six-foot waves, their tops streaming in a wind that whistled out of Canada, down across the Taku Glacier, and threatened to catch the skiff's bow as they crested each wave. Now they were just trying to make it to the next cove where they could camp and hope this would blow itself out overnight.

Annie tightened her grip on Hector with one arm and with the other began trying to bail the several inches of water sloshing in the bottom of the boat. Pete's eyes stung from the blowing spray. The high tide had been at 2:45 that afternoon, a seventeen-footer. It would be pushing five by the time they made it to the cove. He was pretty sure there would still be enough water to make it over the bar, but if not, they had trouble.

An hour later, they approached the edge of the tide flats, and there was less water than he had hoped. The waves were breaking on the outer bar, then rushing the final quarter mile in a confused mass of peaks and valleys to break again on the shore. They would need to stay in the creek's channel through the flat or risk running aground.

Pete had a nasty vision of the boat going down into one of the troughs, the prop grounding and acting as a pivot to swing the skiff sideways, just in time to be flipped over by a wave or have the solid weight of several tons of green water come crashing over the side.

"Annie! Get up in the bow and help me find the channel.

We should be OK as long as we stay in it. Remember the big turn about half way in." Pete was shouting in the wind as Annie clambered toward the bow, over the waterproof gear bags lashed between the seats.

"To the left! I can see bottom here!" Annie was pointing, which was good because the wind was taking most of her words. "Straight now! Looks OK! Left! More left! It's shallow all across now!"

Pete sped the skiff up a little and tried to stay on top of the next wave. It was a balancing act, and twice the motor kicked bottom. Suddenly they were across the bar and into the creek that twined back into the grass flat. The wind still whipped, but here the surface of the creek was only ruffled.

The stillness felt strange after hours of up and down. Annie came back to the stern, and they stood at the center console with their arms around each other as Pete nosed the boat up the creek. It was hard to see through the surface, but he remembered calm, sunny days when every stone and weed on the bottom was highlighted, and the salmon fled from the skiff in fleets.

They headed toward a large wooded hump on the right bank. He would have preferred to camp on an island, but wasn't about to go back out until the wind had died. The creek here was over five feet deep with steep banks. He thought they would be OK camping on the mound. The bears mainly stayed on the far side of the flats, where another channel of the creek was shallower, and the riffles made it easier for them to catch salmon.

Pete and Annie unloaded the gear and bailed the boat with the smiles and jokes of released tension. Standing on the bank, Pete balanced the anchor on the bow, tied about twenty-five feet of line into the bow-eye, and then tied the line back through a ring on the anchor. He shoved the skiff out toward the middle of the creek, holding on to the line's free end. When the skiff slowed, he tugged on the line and the anchor slid off into the water. The anchor caught and the skiff hung, swinging in a small arc in the current, a slight quiver in the anchor line.

The top of the hump was no more than thirty feet high, but it gave them a vista across the flats and out over Stephens Passage. The tops of the waves still smoked in the wind, but now patches of late sunlight slanted through breaks in the clouds to play across the water and across the flats where chest-high grass shimmered in waves of their own.

"Incredible, isn't it?"

"It's beautiful, but better from here than from the boat," Annie replied.

"We need a bigger boat."

"We need to use better sense about when we go out in the boat we have. Come on, get a fire going. I want to get out of these wet clothes."

Annie set up the tent and unstuffed the sleeping bags while Heck helped Pete gather firewood, unwilling to believe the purpose wasn't to throw all those sticks for him. After the fire was going, Pete crawled into the tent to change and Annie strung up a line to hang wet clothes.

Coming out of the tent, Pete stopped to watch Annie. She'd hung the last of her clothes by the fire and was toweling dry, unaware of him. A shaft of the late evening sunlight illuminated her as she stretched into its warmth, shaking out the red-golden mass of her hair in the wind.

Pete came out of the tent, and taking the towel from her, began to dry her hair as she leaned back into him.

"I'm a very lucky man."

"We're both very lucky people."

"Have I told you what the best thing about camping is?"

Annie smiled, her eyes closed, savoring the warmth of the sun and the pull of his fingers as he combed them through her hair. "Unless you've changed your mind since yesterday, it's sleeping bags that zip together."

Inside of the tent, the low angle of the setting sun suffused them with a golden glow, painting their shadows on the tent wall.

They ate dinner by the flames of the campfire. Afterward, Annie loaded all the food and cooking utensils into two five-gallon plastic buckets and pressed on the lids. At the far edge of the knoll, Pete threw a rope over a tree limb and hauled the buckets fifteen feet off the ground. They were camping near the north end of Admiralty Island, an almost hundred mile long island whose Native name, "Kootzanohoo," meant "Fortress of the Bears."

In the tent, Annie put a flashlight by her side of the sleeping bags and placed a compressed air horn where it was easy to grab. When she and Pete were fishing creeks, the horn sometimes helped convince a bear who wanted their spot to give them time to make a graceful retreat. Pete laid a .375 H&H on the tent floor on his side of the bags.

It was a good night in the tent. The wind was blowing strongly off the water and the crash of the waves lulled them and made the tent seem particularly snug. In the morning, though, the bear caught Pete, but instead of biting or clawing, he was squeezing gently. Pete was reasoning with the bear, trying to explain why he should let go when he woke to find Hector sleeping on his chest, his head on Pete's face. Heck's lips fluttered as he growled softly in a dream.

Pete rolled the dog onto Annie and sat up, wiping a trace of dog drool off his forehead. He sat stretching, looking out at the world and listening to Annie's sleepy, muffled complaints. It was just past six, and the sun had just come up. The wind had slacked and shifted around to blow out of the southwest so the cove was now in the lee. There was a high, light overcast that gave the water a metallic sheen.

"Mmmph! Get this dog off of me and hand me something to cover my eyes."

"It's a pretty day out."

"Nope."

"There are Dolly Varden in the creek, just waiting for you to float a fly by them."

"Pete, I'm going back to sleep. You and Hector go catch our breakfast. When breakfast is ready, you bring me coffee, and I'll get up." She gave him an order to leave a few fish in the creek for her and then burrowed back into the sleeping bag.

Pete put on his clothes and pulled on a pair of hip boots. Heck was busy marking his territory on the surrounding tree trunks and Pete joined him at one before taking his fly rod from its aluminum tube. He seated the reel and threaded the fly line through the guides. He studied the contents of the fly box for a minute before choosing a squirrel hair smolt.

When he cleared the tall grass, down near the creek mouth, he saw the shape on the bar at the far side of the cove. At first he couldn't tell what it was. He had to stare at it for half a minute before he realized he was looking at the bottom of a sailboat, lying on its side.

Pete went down to the skiff, dug a pair of binoculars out of a waterproof bag, and reclimbed the hump where he could get a better view. It was a fair-sized sailboat and looked as though it had run aground on the sandbar during the night and gone over on its side as the tide ebbed. There was no sign of life.

"Annie, get up! There is a boat aground on the bar on the other side of the flat. Get some clothes on, and I'll get the skiff ready."

Annie cut the motor and tilted it up as the skiff softly grated to a stop on the sandbar. Pete stepped over the bow and pulled the boat several feet farther up on the sandbar.

No one answered his shout, and Pete tied the skiff's bowline to the sailboat's stern rail. He called out again and then climbed on the boat. "The hatch is padlocked from the outside. You see anybody?"

Annie shook her head and began checking the shoreline through the binoculars. Pete yelled a few more times and blew a couple of short blasts on the air horn. The only result was to startle some birds into flight.

"I may see something," Annie said. "Does that look like the end of a gray inflatable pulled into the grass over there? That or a rock."

Pete pushed the skiff off and Annie lowered the kicker. They putted from the bar to the mouth of the smaller creek, across the flats from their camp. A small Zodiac inflatable had been pulled into the tall grass. A broken path in the grass showed where the occupants had gone.

"How about I follow them through the flats, and you and Heck stay here in case they come back a different way? If they show up, blow a couple of blasts on the air horn, and I'll come right back."

The tracks paralleled the shallow creek. Pete whistled a badly off key version of "Teddy Bears' Picnic," his thumb on the rifle's safety, as he walked deeper into the flats. The spawning salmon were splashing in the creek, about twenty yards to his left, and he tried to decipher the sounds as he walked to make sure he wasn't hearing a bear wading. Bears don't like to be surprised, but encounters were almost always benign, as long as the person kept their senses and observed some basic rules.

The creek curved to the far side of the flats where the steep side of the mountain plunged down. Ahead, the creek had cut into the side of the mountain and flowed along the bottom of a small cliff. As Pete followed the tracks, they veered closer to the creek. Ahead of him, the cries of gulls and ravens echoed off the cliff. He cut through the grass to wade up the shallow creek where he could see better.

He waded around a small bend and a screaming group of birds flushed into flight, the gulls and crows hanging above his head cursing him, ravens stopping a short hop away to watch with quizzical eye, two eagles lumbering into flight with offended dignity. Pete instinctively crouched and froze. Where the stream cut into the cliff, a small sandbar had built up on the opposite side. The sand and grasses were violently torn. The birds had been feeding on a body that lay twisted and broken, partially in the creek. Brass shell casings, glinting in the sun, littered the bar.

The broken body, the shell casings glinting in the sunlight, suddenly even the tall grass swaying in the wind, caused old memories to come cascading, avalanching down over him, trying to yank him back almost twenty years.

Feel the wind on your face, Pete. It's a cool wind, this is Alaska. Annie's waiting back at the boat for you. Nobody is going to shoot at you. You don't have to kill anybody.

He slowly eased up to the body, finger on the trigger of his rifle, trying to see, hear, smell, everything at once. It was a man, very obviously dead. His back and neck appeared to be broken. He was clawed and ripped and his scalp was partially peeled from the skull and flapped down across his face. Holes bitten into the skull were clearly visible. Pete had read that the factor that most often determined fatality in many bear attacks was whether the bear's mouth was big enough to bite into the victim's skull without its teeth sliding off the slippery bone.

The thought made the skin on his head tighten, but he held onto the thought. It was the first solid thought of Alaska, not Vietnam, since he came upon the body. He would not let himself fall back.

The man was partially in the creek. Pete pulled him up on the sandbar and blood and bits of flesh swirled in the water and flowed down the stream. Pete had recognized the 5.56 brass scattered across the sand like old evil friends. A rifle lay in the shallow water, its stock smashed. It was a Colt AR-15, the civilian version of the M-16 that was the Army's standard issue.

He thought about Annie, he focused on how she had looked last night in the shaft of late evening sunlight. He could feel himself sliding over an edge and he grasped her memory fiercely, the touch, the smell of her. She pulled him back.

Pete looked at the tracks in the sandbar. Blood smeared the grass and soaked the sand. Pete couldn't tell if the blood was all from the man or if the bear had been shot. There was another set of human tracks in the sand that appeared to run upstream into the creek.

Pete yelled, but there was no answer. He was scared he was going to find another body and hoping he wasn't going to run into a wounded and angry bear. As he began to follow the tracks, some of the birds hopped back to the body. Pete ran back, swatting and kicking at the birds, suddenly furious at them. "A murder of crows", aptly named. The birds swirled up, and then settled back on the body as soon as he stepped away.

Leave him. He doesn't care anymore. See if there is someone alive to help. Pete talked to himself as followed the tracks around the small bend and into the creek. He had lost the tracks in the creek, and now he stopped and yelled, listening intently for any response.

There was an echo, but no answer. He waded up the creek, watching for tracks coming out on the bank. The remaining wind tossed the tall grass on the right, making it hard to watch for the bear. The small cliff still formed the left bank, taller here, the creek pooling in a long glide. There was a split in the rock, an entrance perhaps three feet wide. As he got closer, he could see the bank was disturbed, and tufts of bear hair were stuck on the rock edges.

He waded across, making sure the bear was gone. The cleft appeared to go back about six feet before narrowing to an end. A person was jammed back in as far as possible, but not quite far enough to have escaped the bear's claws. The back of the person's scalp, shoulder, hip and thigh were raked and hanging open, the inside of the cleft sticky with blood.

Pete couldn't tell if it was a man or woman. "I'm going to help you. Can you come out?"

There was no answer and Pete reached in, trying to find a place to touch that wasn't open wound. He gently grabbed the person's belt and gave a slight pull. The person whimpered and began to try to wiggle deeper into the crevice. "The bear's gone," Pete said. "I'm going to help you, but we have to get you out. The bear's gone. Do you understand? The bear's gone."

Pete pulled on the belt and slowly worked the person out of the cleft. It was a young man, perhaps in his early twenties. He was slim, and had flowing blond hair. He was strikingly handsome and his face, which had been turned inward, was unmarked, but the back of his head and left side of his body, where the bear had reached, presented a nightmarish contrast.

In the very back of the cleft, where it had prevented the man from getting far enough back to be out of the bear's reach, was a large gray and green backpack. Pete couldn't believe that he had bothered with the pack at all, or hadn't pulled it after him as a shield from the bear.

Pete carried him across the creek and laid him on the grass. Pete was talking to Annie in his head, telling her she was going to have to help him with this. He stripped off his shirt and tried to sling the young man's left arm and staunch some of the blood flow. Miraculously, no large arteries seemed to be torn, but blood was seeping everywhere.

Pete talked to him the whole time, a soft reassuring croon. "You're going to be OK. The bear's gone. I'm going to carry you back to the boat. You're doing fine. My name is Pete and my wife, Annie, she's the head nurse in the emergency room. She's back at the boat, and I'm going to carry you back, and she's going to fix you up. Stay with me now. We're going to get through this. We'll get the Coast Guard helicopter to fly you out. You're going to be OK."

"The pack."

"What? Can you talk any louder? "

"The pack."

"Don't worry about the pack. I'll come back and get it for you later. Let's get you back to Annie so she can fix you up."

"No! No!"

"I can't carry you and the pack at the same time. I'll bring it to you."

"No! Leave it! Leave it there! Promise me you'll leave it there and won't tell anyone. Don't ever tell about the pack; don't tell about me and Hal. Don't tell my mother."

"Come on, let me pick you up. We have to get you back so Annie can take care of you."

"Promise me! Promise me!" The man was struggling, trying to get up.

"I promise. Now, come on, let's get you back."

Pete was wading down the middle of the creek, cradling the man in his arms. He was watching for the bear, wondering if the man was going to make it and how quickly they could get a helicopter here.

Blood seeped down his forearms and chest and dripped off his elbows, making tiny red cumulus clouds in the creek. He told himself this was not a rice paddy he was wading through. He was no longer dead inside, carrying his buddy whose life dripped out in slow, steady crimson drops.

"You promised me, right? You won't tell anyone about the pack?" The man was conscious again, obsessed with the pack.

"Yeah, I promised you. I'm not going to tell anyone about the pack. You hang on now. We don't have too much farther to go." Pete thought about other promises he had made half a world away. Promises that everything was going to be OK, that a helicopter would be in to get them. Promises that if they could just hang on, they would be back, safe and sound in the States, a short stay in the hospital with pretty nurses and then out to heroes' welcomes. They were promises that no one could keep, and by the time the helicopter came, two days later, only he and Dale were still alive.

"Hal's dead, isn't he?"

"That's your friend's name? Yeah he didn't make it, but you're going to. You keep hanging on."

"The bear was biting him, picking him up and shaking him like a rat. I ran back and hit the bear and he knocked me down. I thought I was dead, but he left me and started biting Hal again, and I ran away. That crack was in the rock, and I thought if I could just far enough in . . ." he trailed off with tears running down his face.

"Sounds like you did everything you could. Did Hal shoot the bear?"

"I think so, he shot at it anyway. We came around the corner and the bear was right there. The bear was popping his teeth together. Hal started shooting, and then the bear had him, shaking him and biting him and shaking him. You won't tell about the pack or me and Hal right?"

The man was fading in and out. Pete tried to keep him talking to keep him conscious. Pete's leg was aching now and he focused on it, letting each step reminding him of meeting Annie, each step bringing him closer back to her.

5

"Put him down over here and get my kit out of the boat." Annie had taken charge of the man and had on what Pete thought of as her ER face; calm, caring certitude without room for an ounce of nonsense or a wasted moment. She pulled on a pair of surgical gloves and began a quick survey of the damage.

Pete filled her in. "I'm going to break into their boat so I can use their radio to call the Coast Guard. You OK here for a few minutes?"

"No. Pete, Pete! Stop a minute and look at me. You have blood all over you. Do you have any open cuts?" That spring Ryan White had died of AIDS from a blood transfusion and Kimberly Bergalis had become infected from a dental procedure. AIDS was still feared as a poorly understood death sentence, but its public perception was evolving from a disease of homosexuals to one anyone could catch.

"I've got the usual assortment of nicks and scratches."

"Before you radio, wash the blood off. There are some

alcohol wipes here in the kit. Make sure you scrub any scratches or cuts the blood could have touched."

"Annie, there wasn't time for me to worry about that sort of thing, and there wasn't any other way."

"You did the right thing. Just scrub and then go see if you can radio. This guy needs more help than I'm going to be able to give him here."

The Coast Guard sent a Jayhawk helicopter from Sitka. With the additional supplies the EMT's brought, they worked swiftly with Annie to get the wounded man stabilized and loaded. After a brief discussion they decided to pick up the dead man's body and then transport the wounded man straight to Bartlett Hospital in Juneau. Annie would fly back with them. The Coast Guard's cutter and 44-footer were both out, and their 27-foot Whaler was down with engine problems. Pete said he would bring the sailboat back to the Coast Guard dock in Auke Bay.

The helicopter lifted off, the prop wash blowing sand and flattening the small waves. Annie looked down at Pete standing beside the boat. He, the boats, the cove, all shrunk as the helicopter gained height. In a way Pete never had, he looked small and somehow vulnerable.

Pete watched the helicopter until it became a speck and disappeared. The thump of the rotors was a sound that belonged in a different hemisphere, an entirely different life. Even in this world, the helicopter was an instrument for carrying away the broken and dying. He tried to shake himself from such thoughts and memories. The tide was starting to flood, and in several hours he thought would be able to float the stranded sailboat.

The sailboat's name was *Bon Temps,* registered out of Redondo Beach, California. It was a beautiful boat, sloop-rigged, gleaming paint and varnish, about forty-five feet. Fast and pretty and very expensive, it looked far from home, resting on its side on the sandbar. It had taken a pounding, but seemed intact. He climbed back into the cockpit and down through the companionway door.

The boat was on its side, and he had to hold on as he maneuvered through it, finding places to step on the built-in cabinets and the backs of the settees. He checked that all ports on the down side were tightly closed so it wouldn't take water as the tide came back in. The master suite was in the bow, the covers and pillows fallen off a large unmade V-berth, lying in a heap on the side of the boat. As he made his way through the boat, he noticed that the other berths were unused. He wondered if this is what the mauled man had meant about, "Don't tell my mother, promise you won't tell about Hal." If so, it seemed sad, and he wondered about what the pack had to do with it.

Outside, the tide was still flooding and there was enough water that he was able to walk his skiff to the *Bon Temps'* bow. He tied the skiff to the sailboat's bow-rail and clambered back aboard the *Bon Temps,* using the pulpit and forestay to pull himself up. The sailboat had good ground tackle, a big CQR for its anchor, with 50 feet of chain connecting the anchor and the nylon rode. He unpinned the anchor and carefully lowered it into the skiff, coiling the chain and rode down on top of it.

He waded out, pulling the skiff until it was deep enough to lower the kicker, then slowly putted straight out, paying out the full length of the sailboat's rode and chain until it stretched behind him. He dumped the anchor over the side and motored back to the *Bon Temps.* He took a couple of wraps of the rode around the gypsy of the windlass and tightened up the slack until the anchor bit. He cranked the windlass until the rode near the boat rose quivering and taut from the water in a straight line to the anchor. The boat was still tilted over, but the water was floating the hull now, soft grating sounds coming from its keel on the sand. The middle two hours of the flood tide, when half the water would move, was just starting, and you could almost see the tip of the mast slowly climbing back toward vertical.

Just before high tide, Pete winched the boat off the sandbar. At first it had been one grudging click at a time and then as the keel broke loose from the suction of the sand, a smooth purr of clicks until the *Bon Temps* rested above the anchor on a short scope in 30 feet of water. After a little tinkering, the diesel clattered to life, and now several sea lions rolled in the bow wake and snorted at him as he steered up Stephens Passage to Auke Bay, towing his skiff placidly behind. The waves of the night before and the morning's breeze had flattened to an almost mirror calm, and the mountains on either side stretched up into the sky and reflected across the water.

A few purse seiners passed him heading south for a salmon opening, but it was a weekday, and there weren't many other boats out until he got closer to Auke Bay. Hector came back from the bow where he had been barking at the sea lions and stretched out beside him, his head in Pete's lap.

Pete used to watch the sailboats off the California beaches. They looked happy to him, and he used to wonder who was on them and what their lives were like. At the end of his tour, Pete, still alive to his faint bewilderment, had walked off the jet into the California sunshine without a clue as to what came next. He found a cheap motel with a kitchenette and a three-quarter bath several blocks from a beach south of L.A. He read for hours each day, lying on his bed or on the beach. He still felt dead inside, perhaps even more dead without the momentary reasons football and then combat had provided to swing open the furnace door of inner rage. Despite this, he could tell it was somehow therapeutic to watch the young children playing on the beach, full of feeling and without care.

He also enjoyed watching the young ladies in bikinis strolling past. Neither the Upper Peninsula nor Vietnam had ever been like this. Once in a while, one of the young lovelies would flash him a smile or say "hi" as she walked past. He was too unsure of himself to ever do more than return the briefest of nods, but he began to tell himself he would remember how to say "hi" back.

A couple of times, before his hair had grown out a little and while he still looked like a freshly discharged soldier, young people had taunted him about the war, asking him if he had been in Vietnam, if he had killed any babies over there. He always just stayed silent, staring back at them until they grew uneasy or drifted off to find other sport. Once, when a group of young college boys showing off for their girls got particularly ugly, he stood up, walked through them into the ocean and swam straight out. He kept swimming until he couldn't see buildings or the city at all, only the curtain of smog with the tips of the mountains behind sticking up through. He had drifted out there for hours, letting the current carry him along. He thought of Mr. Leggatt from Joseph Conrad's *The Secret Sharer*, "... I didn't mean to drown myself. I meant to swim till I sank--but that's not the same thing." Just after dusk, when the cold was all the way through him, he decided to see if he could swim back. When he reached the shore, he had to walk miles back up the beach to get home.

He had spent almost nothing while in the service and still had savings left, but he began to wonder what came next. He started to think about putting his life back together. Football and night patrol were his two main skills and there wasn't much call for the latter in civilian life. Pete studied each pro team's roster and followed the NFL college draft with more attention than he had paid to the army's, looking at which teams needed defensive ends. He began doing long runs on the beach and lifting weights in a gym, thinking about showing up at a training camp to try out as a walk-on.

Dale, one of the few remaining members of Pete's original platoon, had mustered out at the same time and was living in the area. Dale had survived Vietnam by ducking every risk possible and being lucky. He was always working an angle, and Pete had tried to avoid him as much as possible in the field. Gradually, though, through mutual survival, bonds of obligation somehow developed. Pete knew he would never try to tell anyone what it had been like, but Dale knew. Dale got a hold of him once in a while to have a beer and try to sell him on whatever was his latest scheme for hitting it big. Dale's schemes were usually dumb, dangerous, illegal, or all three. He never showed up unless he wanted something, or to boast of his latest score, but the truth was, no one else showed up at Pete's door for any reason. No one else even knew where he lived.

It was late afternoon by the time Pete brought the *Bon Temps* between Coghlan Island and Indian Island into Auke Bay. The slant of the late afternoon sun gave a golden glow to the scene and reflected blue on the Mendenhall Glacier, which flowed down between the mountains of the mainland coast. Charter fishing boats sped back to the harbor, anxious to get pictures taken, fish boxed and iced, and customers back downtown to their cruise ships.

He called the Coast Guard on the radio and talked them into sending a couple of folks down to transient moorage to catch his lines and take possession of the boat. He filled out some forms, told them how to reach him and learned they didn't have any recent information on the condition of the survivor.

Pete used the pay phone outside the harbormaster's office to call the hospital. The guy was still alive, but listed as critical. The folks in the ER gave him Annie's message that she had gotten a ride home and to call her there. A telephone at home was one of the many changes she had brought to his life.

"Hey, I'm back, how you doing?"

"I'm OK. I'm soaking in a long hot bath right now. Feels mighty nice. I brought the phone in because I was hoping you would call. Jean called from Readers'. She was wondering when you were coming in to the store. They got a shipment of books this morning. I told her you'd be in tomorrow. You OK?"

"Yeah, I got the boat back to Auke Bay, managed to dock it without causing any additional damage. The Coast Guard has it now. They're taking an inventory and trying to figure out who to contact."

"The hospital will be anxious to talk to them. So far they don't have any I.D. on this guy, he's admitted as a John Doe."

"He won't be a John Doe long, that's a very expensive boat. You should see below, how the rich folks are living. The hospital said he was critical when I called there for you. How do you think his chances are?"

"I don't know; he was in very tough shape. He regained consciousness briefly when we stopped to pick up his friend's body and totally freaked out. I did what I could, and the Coast Guard medics were good. He was in surgery when I left the hospital. One thing for sure, he'd be dead if you hadn't found him. How soon you going to be home?"

"Probably about an hour and a half if I can dodge any more paperwork and questions here. The Coast Guard said Fish and Wildlife Protection wants to talk to me for some kind of report they have to do about the bear, but I figure they can wait till tomorrow. Somehow the newspaper found out, and a reporter left a message for me, which I'm definitely not returning. The *Bon Temps* is the Coast Guard's problem now. I'm going to gas the skiff here at DeHart's and head it home."

"Assuming I don't fall asleep here in the tub, I'll have some dinner waiting for you. It will be good to have you back here, be nice to sleep in our own bed. I love you."

"I love you, too. See you soon."

Pete promised the Coast Guardsmen he would get back in touch with them tomorrow, wondering if Guardsmen could be the right term since the two who seemed most on the ball were attractive young women. He gassed the skiff and idled it out of the harbor. He cleared the floating breakwater, shoved the throttle down, a grin coming to his face as always, as it leapt up on plane. He shortcut the buoy marking the rocks in front of Lena Beach and ran a fast tight course up the coast, heading home to Annie. He stopped only once, when he spotted a bush of blueberries that had been fooled into reblooming by the sunny stretch. The white blueberry blossoms were growing from the rocky shore, surrounded by red-purple fireweed, and he picked a bouquet to take home.

Pete moved around the store the next morning, straightening the books on the shelves, reshelving books that had gotten out of place. Jean laughed at his habit; she called it his "ritual soothing of the shelves." Truth was, the books, their order, color, smell, the feel of them, all soothed him. He moved from shelf to shelf, making small adjustments, greeting old friends, making new acquaintances. He didn't work the sales floor as much these days, and though they kept a detailed inventory tracking on the computer, he felt incomplete without daily contact with the shelves. This was his favorite time, in the mornings, before Jean or Jeremy arrived, before any customers, just him and the books.

After he broke his leg, he had thumped around the house in the cast, unable to finish the garage and feeling particularly restless and useless as Annie went off to work each day. He was in Readers', one of the bookstores he frequented, when he noticed a small "help wanted" notice tacked behind the counter. When they gave him the job, it was with the mutual understanding that it was just until he got the cast off.

Working in the bookstore was different than he had expected. He not only liked it, but to his mild surprise, he was good at it. It was a more intricate business than he'd ever imagined, and he had a feel for which books would move and a knowledge and quiet, easy manner that customers liked. After the cast came off, he began to commercial fish again, picking the high-stakes fisheries with short openings, but in between he continued to work at Readers'. He became friends with Rob and Sue, the owners. A year later, they told him they wanted to retire and move south and asked if he would be interested in buying the store. He and Annie talked about it for two days and decided they did. They had to put up the house and land as collateral, but a month later, they were bookstore owners with huge gaps in their knowledge about the book business. He knew Susan and Deb, who co-owned Hearthside Books down the street, and thought they might view him as the competition now. Instead, to his eternal gratitude, they provided ongoing encouragement and wisdom, citing Portland as an example of a city where the abundance of bookstores seemed to encourage people to read more and kept people in the habit of shopping locally instead of ordering books online.

He stopped and looked at an inside display Jean had put up in his absence. Books on the tarot, astrology, runes, the occult and crystal healing were stacked around several small pyramids and crystals. When Rob and Sue had the store, Sue heavily stocked and promoted New Age books. He'd planned on phasing the section out, but Jean talked him out of getting rid of the section completely, which, as she pointed out, sold well. He continued to carry some, relying on her to do the ordering, but held firm on no more New Age windows, no more burning incense in the store, and especially, no more Jeremy wearing his sarong to work.

He had just turned on the computer and typed in the password for QuickBooks so he could check how sales had been when Annie called from the hospital.

"Hi. The store still there?"

"Yeah, looks like the order from Ingram came in and they have most of the books on the shelves already. Jean stays on top of things better than I do. She snuck in a New Age display while I was gone, though. Not a window, we're clear about that, at least."

"You probably just need to spend some time sitting under a pyramid to reach a higher plane of understanding."

"Maybe. She has a bunch of books on crystal healing out as part of the display. Maybe I should put in your health section?" After they bought the store, Annie took over the ordering of the health-related books and had made it into one of the store's more profitable sections.

"No, I'm afraid I'm not sufficiently enlightened either. Definitely keep them in New Age. Listen, I know how much there probably is to do, just getting back, but after Jean gets in, could you take a break and come out here?"

"What's up?"

"Randy is still in critical condition – "

"They found out who he is?

"Randall C. Dionne, the third. Quite the handle, huh? He goes by Randy. They got back his blood work, no blood-borne pathogens, which is good. That's not something you're officially allowed to know, by the way. Admin got in touch with his mother. She wanted to fly her personal doctor up immediately. They finally convinced her that a Beverly Hills gynecologist, no matter how ritzy, was not what he needed. She also wanted to send up her plastic surgeon, but they explained he has to get a lot stronger before they start that kind of work. She is flying up, be here tomorrow."

"From the way he was going on about her when I was carrying him out, I'm not sure that's going to be a comfort.

"He's only conscious for brief periods. Every time he comes to, he's obsessed with repeating, 'Don't tell,' and, 'Please, don't tell my mother,' though nobody knows what we're not supposed to tell her. The other thing he's stuck on is he wants to see you."

"Me? He doesn't even know who I am."

"He wants to see the big man who carried him out. He's not rational, but he's desperate about it. They even asked me to come up and talk to him, see if I could calm him down and explain to him that he shouldn't have visitors yet. I told him you were my husband and that I'd tell you anything he wanted, but he's insistent. He kept telling me you promised and he had to talk to you. He seems to be getting a little better, but they don't want to sedate him anymore than is absolutely necessary. The doctors asked me to see if you would come out and talk with him next time he wakes up."

When the ICU nurse showed Pete into the room, Randy recognized him and insisted that the nurse leave them alone. She was reluctant, but finally left with murmured warnings about staying too long or causing her patient any stress.

"Hi, my name's Pete. How you doing?"

"I've done better. I suppose I need to thank you." Randy's head and part of his face was swathed in bandages, making it hard to read the expression on his face. His voice was soft. Pete found himself leaning forward to hear.

"Hey, I'm glad we were there. Annie's really the one who made the difference."

"Annie's your wife?"

"Yeah."

"I met her, didn't get her name, though. I need to talk to you. They tell you my mother's coming up?"

"I heard she'll be here tomorrow."

"Yeah. She's going to want to talk to you. You promised me that you won't tell her, right? She'll want to know everything, but you promised me, right?"

"I'm sure that she already knows your boat grounded and that you were mauled by a bear. There isn't anything else for me to tell her."

"You promised you won't tell about Hal or about the pack. You said you won't tell her or anyone else. You promised me." Randy was whispering intensely, furiously, beads of sweat forming on his upper lip and the portion of his forehead that showed under the bandage.

"I promised, and I try to keep my promises. Things are going to be OK. You just need to work on getting well."

"I couldn't save Hal. I just want to die, too." Randy stopped for a moment and panted like a dog in pain.

"Randy, listen to me. You said after the bear jumped you and then turned on Hal, you went back and hit it to try and get it off him. I don't know if that was crazy or brave, but it sure sounds like you did everything possible to save him."

Randy was silent now, his head shaking back and forth like an agonized metronome. His eyes were squeezed shut, but tears escaped.

"Randy? Randy, can you hear me? I don't know your mother, but I bet the only thing she's going to care about is you being alive. Mothers love their children, families love each other. That's what matters. In the long run, that's almost all that matters. She isn't going to care about anything else."

"You promised about the pack. Do you keep your promises?"

"I keep my word."

"I wish to God I knew whether I could trust you, but with Hal dead, none of it really matters. I told him it was a bad idea, but he kept saying it would be like we won an all expense paid trip, like a paid honeymoon."

Randy lapsed into silence his eyes closed. Pete said his name several times without response and decided he had fallen back asleep.

Pete took several tissues from the box on the bedside and reached out to blot the mingled tears and sweat from Randy's face. At the first touch, Randy jerked awake convulsively, eyes wide and body rigid, but relaxed slightly when he saw it was Pete.

"Will you stay here with me for a while?"

"Sure," Pete said.

6

When he got home, Pete took Heck for a run. It was low tide, and they ran up the beach, careful about the footing on the cobble and broken rock. There were short stretches of sand where Heck would race in circles and bark. After several miles, he cut up into the woods and headed home on the deer trail that paralleled the water just inside the woods along the top of the bluff. He pushed himself hard so that by the time he was back to their cove, the feeling from the hospital that had lingered throughout the day was gone, replaced by gasping lungs and burning thighs.

As he cooled down, he brought a half dozen large rocks up from the water's edge and threw them on the pile at the foot of the path that led up the small cliff to the house. Anytime he was on the beach Pete tried to clear a few more rocks to make beaching his skiff easier. There was a faint path up the beach when he bought the property. Pete often thought about who might have been here before.

Tlingit, Haida and Tsimshian were all cultures that lived off the sea and they had cleared paths, beach driveways, for their dugout canoes throughout Southeast Alaska. The Russians, and later the British and the Americans, hunters and trappers, miners, and those who simply didn't fit in elsewhere had followed, clearing their own paths up the beaches. The sea indifferently followed them all, storms throwing back new stones.

The collection of rocks at the bottom of the cliff had grown until now there was a pile the size of dump truck load. Some were small enough he could throw up the ten-foot cliff, others so large it was all he could do to lift them and stagger forward. Someday he was going to bring them up to the yard to build a retaining wall to extend their yard and make Annie a garden.

Pete was in the office packing up returns, tearing the covers off the paperbacks that were strippable when Jeremy buzzed him from the front desk. "Pete, there is a Mrs. Dionne on the phone. Says she needs to speak to Mr. McLaughlin personally."

She introduced herself as Mrs. Randall Dionne, Randy Dionne's mother. She spoke in clipped tones, every word and sentence so precisely arranged that you didn't dare interrupt for fear of bumping something fragile and brittle and causing the whole conversation to come crashing down. She thanked him for rescuing her son, informed him that she was staying in the Baranof Hotel, near his store, and asked at what time it would be convenient for him to meet her in the coffee shop so they could talk. She deflected his efforts to avoid the meeting, and they agreed to meet at eleven.

"I wanted to thank you, Mr. McLaughlin. They tell me you talked with Randy during one of the periods he regained consciousness in the hospital, but I doubt that he thanked you. Gratitude has never been one of his strong points."

"Actually, he did thank me, Mrs. Dionne, though I didn't do much. My wife is a nurse, and she was the main one."

"I tried to see her this morning, but they were very busy in the emergency room. It must take great fortitude to deal with other people's trauma day in and day out. Most of us have difficulty coping with our own."

"She's remarkable. I don't think I could do it." They fell into silence as he watched Mrs. Dionne stir an Equal into her tea. She wasn't what he had been expecting, but he'd had no difficulty spotting her.

Randy had inherited his striking looks from her, though Randy's hair was a rich blond, where hers was an ash blond that suggested very expensive hair stylists. They sat there for a few moments. She stirred her tea and stared out the window into the light rain that had begun to fall. Pete took in the even tan, the cashmere blazer and tailored slacks, the thick gold chains and the diamonds in her rings and earrings. Grief had not interfered with perfect makeup and nails. He idly speculated that the clothes she was wearing probably cost more than all the clothes he owned.

She asked questions about the sailboat's grounding, the bear attack and Randy's condition when he found him. He gave her the broad outline of what had happened, carefully honoring his promise to Randy. Several times as they talked she seemed to be looking at the scabbed scratch across the back of his right hand. Finally, with a slight, but visible straightening of her back, she asked if Randy had been bleeding when he carried him back to the boat. Pete replied that he had staunched the bleeding as well as he could, but yes, Randy had still been bleeding.

"Mr. McLaughlin, my son is a homosexual. If you were exposed to his blood, I think it would be prudent to have yourself tested for AIDS. I'm sorry to tell you that, but I believe you deserve to know."

Pete was careful not to let his face show anything. "I appreciate your consideration. Annie, my wife, had advised me it would make sense to do so under any circumstances. I don't believe there is a problem, though."

They both sat there for few minutes staring out. The misting rain was getting thicker. "Mrs. Dionne, does Randy know you believe he is gay?"

"He would have to think I was completely oblivious not to, but Randy has never had a high opinion of me, so I don't know."

"I know I am being personal here, but how does it affect your feelings about him?"

"Unfortunately I have many misgivings about my son. He has never applied himself or taken advantage of how we could assist him if he wanted a career. He seems to think that hanging around minor criminals is exciting, and his lifestyle is one of many of his choices that I regret. If you are asking if I love him, though, the answer is yes. He's my son, but he needs to be willing to do his part."

"I know none of this is my business, but carrying him out, willing him to live, I came to feel like I have a stake in Randy making it. Have you considered telling him that you have known he is gay and that you love him? I think it could make a difference."

"Mr. McLaughlin you didn't seem surprised when I told you Randy was a homosexual. Did Randy talk to you about this?"

"What's important is that you talk to Randy. Is he conscious now?"

"The doctors say he should be, but since I arrived he won't open his eyes or respond. It's like when he was a young teenager and I would go to his room to talk to him. He would lie there in his bed, eyes closed, refusing any response until I left. I used to try to out-wait him. I tried other things. No matter what I tried, he would always win by refusing any response."

It had been gray and raining for over a week, the clouds sitting down so low you couldn't see the mountains. During the night, the skies had cleared, the wind switched around to bring a warm high pressure down from the interior. Annie was working night shifts, and Pete arranged to take off for the afternoon. They took advantage of the beautiful weather to troll up the coast for salmon and stopped at a small beach for a picnic. The skiff bumped gently on the sand on the incoming tide and the last wisps of smoke from their driftwood fire curled up into the sky.

"What are you chuckling about?" Annie asked.

"I was just watching Heck swim around out there. A few salmon are still jumping. Each time one jumps, he swims over to where it was and tries to find it until the next one jumps and then he charges over there. He's a little obsessed, but seems to be enjoying himself."

Pete was leaning back against a bleached log, and Annie was curled against him, her head resting on his chest. They were sheltered from the small breeze here and luxuriated in the sun's warmth. "I thought you were asleep," he said.

"I was. Every time you chuckle though, there's this low rumbling sound. Leaning against you is nice, but it's noisy."

"I can try to be more serious."

"No, I like it, but you know what it made me think about? Do you remember our first night together?"

"Annie, I have great regard for your good sense, but that is probably the silliest question I've ever heard. I'll remember it in vivid detail for the rest of my life."

"You remember us laughing?"

"I do. We had a very good time. We still have a pretty darn good time."

"I think that's when I told myself that I wasn't going to let you get away."

"Then? I might have thought it was just a little earlier during all that gasping."

"No, that was very fine as well, but it was when you started laughing. We had both just finished, and if it had been an old movie they would've switched to a scene of the biggest Fourth of July fireworks celebration ever, and it just felt so good that I started laughing, and you joined me, and we just held each other and laughed. Once there was a fellow I was seeing, a doctor, and we really seemed to like each other. This was before I came to Juneau. The first time we were actually together, afterwards I laughed, not doing anything but feeling good, and he became furious. He thought I was laughing at him and wouldn't listen to anything I tried to say."

"If I ever meet him, I'll tell him that you were laughing at him and your descriptions of his shortcomings have inspired humor among nurses across the country. I can tell that I don't like this guy."

"You big jerk. This is the first time I have ever told this to anyone. It just felt so fine with you, and I started to laugh, and then I was instantly afraid and tried to catch myself, but then you were laughing, too."

"Shoot, I thought you were laughing at me," he said. "I certainly was. If a 270-pound man, mad with desire, wearing nothing but a full leg cast isn't worth laughing at, we should all quit."

"It was a slightly awesome sight, but not funny. You know before that night, I hadn't seen you with your clothes off. I thought you were maybe a little fat as well as big."

"Just slightly awesome? And fat?"

"I thought a little fat before we got your clothes off."

"You know what they say, a hard man is good to find."

She laughed and shifted her position leaning against him, "Actually if you were a little softer, you'd make a better pillow." He thought she had fallen back asleep, when she spoke again. "Pete?"

"Yeah?"

"I'd be willing to reevaluate the slightly part of awesome tonight."

Annie resumed her even breathing. Pete sat there, his arm around her. The weight of her body leaning against his chest seemed to radiate warmth and contentment down into his bones. He stared across Lynn Canal at the tops of the Chilkats, their tops powdered with fresh snow. Out in the middle of the channel there was a pack of orcas, their dorsal fins visible, leaving white columns of mist as they traveled north. Pete said a silent and half-formed prayer of thanks. He kissed the top of Annie's head and pressed his face into her sun-warmed hair, inhaling the scent of her.

"Hey, Annie?

"Yeah?"

"I'm glad that doctor didn't laugh with you."

They watched an eagle glide up around the point and along the shoreline with an occasional lazy flap of its wings. There were three marbled murrelets fishing in the cove and as the eagle approached, the round little seabirds dove in unison.

The vanishing act happened faster than the eye could take it in, leaving only ripples on the water. The eagle circled twice and then flew on up the shoreline, looking for an easy meal washed in with the tide.

Annie thought about her doctor who hadn't known how to laugh and other men she had known and the strange branches your life can take. Her first year in grad school she had been crazy about her lab partner in an advanced biology class. He was going with another woman at the time, which normally would have caused her to steer well clear, but whenever she was with him, regardless of what they were doing at the time, she was happy. She used to have little conversations with herself in which she would say, "Annie, you're a fool," to which she would answer, "Yes, but I am."

Toward the end of the semester, they spent an afternoon and evening in the lab trying to finish a project. His car was in the shop and she offered him a ride back to his apartment. He suggested stopping for a quick bite to eat. The meal stretched on for hours as they talked about a host of little things. Afterward, they sat in the car in front of his building talking, neither quite willing for the evening to end. She was wondering if he was going to invite her in and if so, what she would do, when his girlfriend drove up. They greeted each other awkwardly, and Annie drove off, leaving them to walk inside together.

It hadn't changed how she felt about him, but it sure changed how she acted. Her internal conversation shifted to, "Annie, you may be a fool, but you don't have to act like one."

It hadn't been a big conscious decision, but for years afterwards, she made sure she didn't act like a fool. She laughed and had good times, but anytime she started to feel a little too serious about anyone, the little voice was there, cautioning her not to be a fool. Looking back, she knew it had saved her some grief and pain, but she also knew it had kept her from ever risking the degree of commitment necessary to really find out if a relationship had a chance. When she was staying with Pete after he came home from the hospital, she would tell herself she was on the edge of acting like a fool. For the first time since that afternoon in the lab, she found herself answering back, "Maybe sometime it's important to risk being a fool".

Annie drifted at the edge of sleep. Hector gave up on the salmon and swam to the beach. He gave a shake that started at his head and progressed down his body to his tail, throwing off a fine mist of droplets that caught the sun and made tiny rainbows. Pete's voice seemed to reach her from a distance, whispering to Heck not to bother her, she was asleep.

"I'm not really, just lying here feeling good and thinking about things. You getting antsy to be fishing again?"

"No this is good, and we already have plenty of fish in the freezer. What are you thinking about?"

"Just stuff. Let me ask you a question. When I was staying at the house, after you came home from the hospital, you never said anything, never made any move to indicate you were romantically interested in me. I could tell I liked you more and more, and it seemed you liked me, but I thought I was going to move out without you saying a word."

"That was a question?"

"Yes it was. What's the answer?"

"The day I first saw you, there at the emergency room, I thought you were the most beautiful woman I had ever seen. I had my shin bone sticking out of my leg but the physical feeling I was most aware of was that you seemed to literally take my breath away. You hear people say that as an expression of speech, but it was true. I could hardly breathe."

"You're very sweet, but I think the truth is, you were going into shock. It's also not an answer."

"It wasn't shock, and it is the start of the answer. I couldn't quite believe it when you wound up living at the house. Once when I was hunting, I fell asleep in the woods – "

"That's happened more than once from what I hear."

"Many times, though I prefer to describe it as my Zen hunting state. You really want me to answer your question?"

"I do, though I'm curious about how you're going to get there from sleeping in the woods."

"Normally I just lightly doze, so I can hear deer walking in the woods. This time I fell sound asleep, and when I woke up there was a doe about five feet in front of me. She was browsing on a blueberry bush, and there was a slight breeze blowing from her toward me so she couldn't get my scent. She knew there was something strange about me, but couldn't quite figure it out, so she would nibble a bit and then watch me for a while, and then nibble some more.

"Over the years I've seen many, many deer in the woods, but never one that close. I knew that if I made even the slightest motion she would be gone in a heartbeat. She wandered around there browsing for what seemed like an eternity, and then she bedded down in a little patch of sunshine. By then it felt like it was my duty to watch over her and protect her while she slept. When you were staying at the house, I felt like that, that if I made one false move, you would be gone like that deer."

"So, did you shoot her?"

"No, it was doe season, but there were plenty of other deer, and I had developed a bit too much of a bond to be able to enjoy eating her. While she was sleeping I began to hum *Brahms' Lullaby* very, very softly. She woke up and could tell something was wrong. She started to walk away, stopping every few feet to look back at me. Just then the breeze shifted a little and she caught my scent. In one bound she evaporated. She left an absence so electric it hummed."

"So if you were so worried about spooking me, what drove you to finally do something?"

"You were leaving. The next day you were going to look for a place to move. There've been times I wasn't too fond of myself, but if I'd just let you walk away, I would have had a hard time living with myself. Even now I sometimes get scared something will happen and you'll leave."

"Pete, you're my husband and I'm not going anywhere. Like you said, a hard man is good to find."

7

It was raining again when Pete drove into work. The fine mist filled the air and swirled in the wind without really seeming to fall. On a clear day, the drive in was spectacular. Today the clouds were all the way down. Everything was a soft gray, and the view was mainly the dark green of dripping spruce and hemlocks along the road.

He considered stopping at the hospital on his way in, but decided he would stop on his way home, when Annie would be working. Randy was still in a coma, and Pete had started visiting when he could, just to check on him. Sometimes when no one was in the room, he would talk to Randy, about the weather, the bookstore, Hector, fishing, whatever came to mind to make conversation. He knew it didn't make sense, but somehow he felt responsible for Randy now.

Pete came in the door, gave a shake Hector would have been proud of, and surveyed the store. Jean was waiting on a customer, and a few other customers browsed among the shelves. Only one cruise ship was in port this morning which would mean a light customer load until the lunch crowd.

"Morning," Jean greeted him as she bagged the customer's book. "A guy was here looking for you, a lawyer. He was waiting when I opened the doors. Very fancy dresser. You can tell he isn't from Juneau and isn't a tourist as soon as you see him."

"He say what he wanted?"

"No, just said it was important that he talk to you. Said he's staying at the Westmark. He'll be there until he hears from you or he'll stop back later today. Said he name was Kotkin, from the firm of Mathews, Edsall, somebody or other, and he flew up from Los Angeles to talk to you. From the price of his suit, I'd make sure he isn't going to bill you before you talk to him. Isn't L.A. where the kid on the sailboat was from?"

Jean had been right about fancy dresser. The man appraised Pete's office with a disdainful glance, looking bleak at the choice between the sagging couch Heck liked to sleep on and the rickety folding chair. He gave a quick brush to the chair and sat down. He sat with his legs carefully folded to avoid wrinkling the razor creases in the pants. The fabric of the suit draped perfectly. Pete always had trouble getting clothes that fit and was impressed and bemused with the impeccable tailoring. Pete didn't know much about clothes, but this was clearly a suit that had been custom made.

"Mr. McLaughlin, I'm Ronald J. Kotkin. I'm a senior partner in the firm of Mathews, Edsall, Hummel, & Gance. We have offices in Los Angeles, San Francisco, San Diego, Sacramento and Washington D.C. I'm here because we represent the interests of Jonathon Galvan in a number of areas. Mr. Galvan is the owner of the sailing vessel *Bon Temps*, which you recently had occasion to bring back to Auke Bay.

"Normally, we would have had an associate handle a trip like this, but Mr. Galvan is an important client and grateful, very grateful, to you for your assistance in recovering the *Bon Temps* after its grounding. Mr. Galvan insisted that I deal with this matter and personally express his thanks.

"As you are undoubtedly aware, your recovery of Mr. Galvan's ship meets the three tests in Admiralty law for salvage claims: there was serious peril to the vessel, the salvage was voluntary and the salvage was successful. Mr. Galvan would like to reach a generous settlement to dispose of any salvage claim you might have against the *Bon Temps* and compensate you for your time and effort in the recovery."

The words flowed out in a smooth, caressing flow, never a break, an uh, or a stumble. As he talked, Kotkin constantly moved his hands, conducting the flow of words, soft modulations and swelling moments. Pete found himself staring at the hands, long, smooth, perfectly manicured. Pete felt a little as though he were staring at a hypnotist's watch. Pete looked down at his own hands, veins bulging down the backs, thick callused fingers, small scars intermingled with fresher scratches and the scab Mrs. Dionne had noticed. He'd helped a friend re-bed a leaking through-hull on his power troller a couple of days ago. There was a little gray still on his knuckles from the Sikaflex.

As the voice flowed on, Pete was struck that Kotkin had not said a single word about Hal, Randy, or the bear. "Mr. Kotkin, I'm afraid you've made an expensive trip for nothing. When I turned the boat over to the Coast Guard, I told them I wasn't interested in pursuing any salvage claims against the *Bon Temps*. We help each other out up here."

"That's admirable, Mr. McLaughlin. I appreciate that as does Mr. Galvan. Unfortunately, we need to resolve two small problems. The first is that while we appreciate your declining to pursue a salvage claim, your verbal indications to the Coast Guard are not binding. I have brought with me a short written waiver of claim for you to sign.

"Second, and more serious, when you turned *Bon Temps* over to the Coast Guard, they inventoried it. I understand that is standard procedure. Since that time I have had the opportunity to make a separate, private inspection of the vessel. There was some property on *Bon Temps* that is now missing. We would like to recover that property. Perhaps it is property that somehow, in the confusion, inadvertently wound up with you. I understand you were in a small boat which you towed back behind *Bon Temps,* and I understand from the Coast Guard that they did not inspect your boat. Perhaps you don't even know you have it. Mr. Galvan is willing to make a very generous settlement of any salvage claims, but we need to recover all property that was on the *Bon Temps* first.

"I'm sorry, I don't have anything from your boat. Have you double checked with the Coast Guard or with Randy Dionne in the hospital?"

"Not mine, Mr. McLaughlin, not my ship. I'm merely representing my client's interests. With regard to Mr. Dionne, he is still in a coma. When he does regain consciousness, we will most assuredly be talking to him. I am certain the Coast Guard does not have this property. I also understand it was not found with Hal Caro's body. Unfortunately, Mr. McLaughlin, that leaves you and your wife. I am operating under the assumption you would be aware if your wife might have inadvertently found something, is that correct?"

"Mr. Kotkin, I want to make this perfectly clear. Neither my wife nor I have anything from the *Bon Temps*. We have not wound up with anything that belongs to you, either inadvertently, as you keep suggesting in your soothing way, or by stealing it, which is what you seem to be implying."

"Mr. McLaughlin, Mr. McLaughlin, please. Stealing is such an ugly word. We simply regard this as a business matter. You saved Mr. Galvan's ship. He just purchased it recently and is very fond of it. He appreciates what you did. We simply need to also recover all property that was with the ship, and then we would like to compensate you handsomely for your efforts. It's simply business."

"Mr. Kotkin, we're going in circles. Neither Annie nor I have anything from the *Bon Temps*, which by the way is a boat not a ship."

"Pardon?"

"The *Bon Temps* is a boat, or a sailboat, or if you want to be formal, a sailing vessel. Pretty as it is, I guess you could call it a yacht, though that sounds a bit pretentious. It's not a ship, though. A ship carries more than one boat, like a cruise ship with life boats."

A twinge of annoyance passed over Kotkin's face before he launched into another flowing persuasion of how this should all work out. Pete found himself staring at Kotkin's hands again as the lawyer wove his argument in the air between them. He thought about the pack, wedged in the back of that cleft, and about promises. What was the debt owed a promise to someone who wasn't rational? He thought about promises he had made and been unable to keep in Vietnam. He realized Kotkin had finally drawn to a close and was looking at Pete with an expression of intense interest and encouragement, the look of a parent coaxing a small child into performing a stunt.

"Mr. Kotkin, I brought your boat back because it was the right thing to do. I have told you as clearly and unequivocally as I can that neither Annie nor I have anything that belongs to your client."

Kotkin started to launch into another flow of words about it all being just business, but Pete cut him off. "I'm sorry, but it is becoming obvious that you must be charging somebody by the hour for this. I need to get back to work."

The geniality dropped off Kotkin's face leaving beneath a look of frozen hostility. "Mr. McLaughlin, you are being very foolish. Mr. Galvan is an extremely successful businessman, and he always gets what he wants. If you are not willing to work out this problem with me in a way that is mutually beneficial for all parties, other gentlemen will be sent to resolve this problem. Men who do not bill on an hourly basis and who will not be interested in a solution that has any benefits for you."

"It must be a heavy responsibility to always get what you want, probably a burden in its own way. You'd have to be very careful what you wish for. It's not something most of us have to contend with. In this case, however, please give Mr. Galvan a message for me. I don't have anything of his. If he has suffered a property loss, I suggest he contact the Coast Guard and his insurance company."

"You are going to make Mr. Galvan very unhappy, which is not a smart thing to do."

"Mr. Kotkin, I've been a disappointment to many people whose opinions I actually cared about. I'm not concerned about disappointing Mr. Galvan. I've already asked you to leave. If you don't leave, I'm going to evict you and I'll probably rumple your suit and scuff your loafers in the process."

The lawyer slowly rose to his feet with an icy glare. "You

are a very foolish man Mr. McLaughlin," he said and stalked out of the office.

Annie was working afternoons, and Pete decided he had to talk with her about Kotkin and the pack. He stopped by the hospital, but she was with a patient. He sat with Randy for a while, making conversation with an unconscious man, and then headed home. Early in the evening, Annie called briefly to check in, but when midnight came and went without her arrival home, he began to worry. Annie was now the shift supervisor for the emergency room nurses, and it wasn't uncommon for her to have to work overtime. Normally, though, she would try to call. Pete told himself he was being silly, but he kept thinking about Kotkin's veiled threats.

At 1:00 a.m. he called the ER and got one of the admitting clerks at the front desk. When he said who he was and started to ask for Annie, the clerk interrupted him. "Hey, I'm glad you called. Annie asked me a while ago to give you a call, let you know she is going to be late. It's been so crazy here I haven't had a chance. Hold on a second."

Pete listened to the canned music playing over the telephone while he waited.

A lot of seconds later, the clerk was back on the phone. "Sorry to keep you holding so long. This place was quiet till about nine, and ever since then it's been nuts. We had a bad car accident come in just before shift ended. Kids. Annie's part of the team who's been working on them ever since. My guess, it'll be another hour before she's out of here."

He hung up feeling relieved she was OK and wondering about the morality of feeling relieved that the reason Annie wasn't home was because kids had been injured in car accident.

He went over and aimlessly poked the fire he had going and then went to the kitchen. He dug out a bottle of Laphroaig from the cupboard under the counter and poured himself a small shot. He added a touch of water and took the scotch into the living room to settle on the couch with a book.

Shift work was part of Annie's job, but neither of them liked it. He wasn't sure if he disliked afternoon or night shift most. When she was on afternoons, he tried to move his work at Reader's later so they could have time together in the mornings. On night shift, they saw more of each other, but he missed sleeping with her, waking up in the night and feeling the warmth of their bodies molded together, one turning or shifting and the other reconforming in sleep to a fit that was good for the soul.

When Annie got home, it was pushing three in the morning. Heck greeted her at the door, talking to her, shoving against her legs, and wagging the whole back half of his body. She knelt down and gave him a fierce hug, pressing her face into the short fur on the top of his head. Pete was on the coach, waking up. When she was on afternoons, he would never go to bed before she got home. She picked up his glass, went in to the kitchen and poured herself a substantially larger shot than Pete had. She didn't add any water.

"Tough night, huh?" Pete hugged her and she held on a long time before she started talking.

"We lost the girl. The boy may not make it either. They're operating now. Such a waste, such a damned waste." Annie was silent again for a long time, pressing her forehead into his shoulder while he slowly massaged her shoulders and neck. "Both sixteen, coming back from a party out at Echo Cove. He was going too fast, missed that last turn before the gravel turns into blacktop. Neither one was wearing a seat belt. The paramedics said the car went over the edge and rolled three times. She was thrown out, broke her neck. She was still alive when they brought her in and regained consciousness briefly before she died. He has massive internal injuries."

They moved back into the living room. Pete put more wood on the fire and poked it back to life. The lamps were off and the fire's reflection danced in the windows. Outside the fine rain was still falling and they could hear the dull wash of waves breaking on the rocks below the house. He held her there on the couch for a long time, both of them staring into the fire, before she began to speak again. "You wouldn't remember which one she was, but we've seen her, Pete. She was on the high school dance team, was an honor student. She was the tall girl with the glossy brunette ponytail and great smile. Seemed incredibly full of life and youth and good spirits."

Pete thought back, but in his memory they all had been full of life and youth and good spirits. He'd known a lot of death, but it wasn't something that happened to pretty high school girls.

"The boy was on the basketball team. Both sets of parents were there in the waiting room. Stunned; looked like they had been hit in the stomach with a baseball bat. They couldn't comprehend, wouldn't accept, what had happened. Pete, I was holding her hand when she lapsed out of consciousness the last time."

Annie was talking so quietly now Pete could barely hear her, long stretches between her sentences. "I don't know why I let some of them get to me. You work in a hospital; you have to deal with people dying. Most of the time I do OK with it. There are times you even know it's a blessed release. But sometimes, sometimes, God, sometimes it seems like such a waste.

"Howard was the resident on duty tonight. As a doctor, he's a great mechanic. If I ever suffer major trauma, I hope he's there to work on me, but when it comes to people's feelings, he's a total jerk. Resents the hell out of it when he loses one and tends to blame the patient, their family, my nurses, anyone else. After the girl died, I cleared out the room, brought the parents in to be with her. Family needs time to let go, to say goodbye, to begin to understand what's happened.

"Howard hates it when I do that. He regards any death as failure and wants the body, the evidence, gone as quickly as possible. He kept trying to get her moved down to the morgue. The family was just bewildered, still stunned, but knew something was going on. They were feeling guilty if you can imagine. They whispered to me. Should they leave? They didn't want to impose."

Annie lapsed into another long silence and began to weep quietly. Pete continued to hold her, rocking slightly, occasionally kissing her head. At last she pulled herself up with a slight shake, and stroked his face with her hand. "I'm OK, really, I don't know why I let this one get to me like this." She got up and went into the kitchen where she ran cold water and splashed her face. She dried her face and refilled the glass, this time with a smaller shot of Scotch.

She walked back into the living room and stood stretching in front of the fire. "I will probably be in trouble for it tomorrow, but finally I had to confront Howard about leaving them alone. He was OK after that." What she had actually done, the third time he tried to interrupt the parents, was ask if she could consult with him for a moment. In a carefully modulated whisper that no one else could hear, she told him they were all having a tough time with the girl's death, but if he didn't leave the girl's parents alone so they could grieve, or if he continued to give her nurses a hard time, she was going to make his life so fucking miserable he better start planning his transfer out of emergency medicine or to a different town right now. Howard almost stumbled away from her, angry retort forming, but when he looked into her eyes he thought better of it and turned away without another word.

Annie came back over to the couch and rejoined Pete. "I'd have been home sooner, but her folks stayed a long time, and when I got off, I wasn't sure I could make the drive. I went up to maternity. There were no births happening right then, everybody was asleep and the lights were turned down low. I just went up there and looked at the babies for a long time. Those little babies, those little lives that represent such a bundle of their parent's hopes and fears and ambitions. I don't know why it is, but when I let one get to me, I just go up there and look at the babies, all those little new lives. It scares me, but it seems to help."

The wind was picking up, and they could hear it in the trees, a low moan that bent and tossed the tops of the spruces and hemlocks and began to pull off the first of the alder leaves along the shore. It mixed with the growing boom of the waves breaking on the rocks. As Annie talked, with long silences between sentences, he wondered if Annie wanted him to hear more than she was saying when she talked about the babies. He rocked very slightly, still holding her, and as the pause after Annie's last sentence lengthened, he became aware that her breathing had evened out and she was sleeping. He held her for a long time, listening to the wind and waves outside and watching the fire slowly die.

Pete thought about kids and parents, car crashes and loss. He said a short and silent prayer, "Dear Lord, please let the kids be with you and please be with their parents." He was still a moment longer and asked God to also be with his parents and brother, and with the men he had killed.

It had been his junior year in college. They were going to play Ohio State in their annual grudge match. His parents and brother had left Friday night after his brother's high school game, spelling each other with the driving down from Michigan's Upper Peninsula to make his Saturday afternoon kickoff. The Ohio State quarterback was being talked about as a contender for the Heisman, and his dad and brother said they wanted to watch Pete sack him a few times. His brother would be coming to school with him next year, and Pete felt fairly sure his brother would start as a freshman.

Pete had had small daydreams about the McLaughlin brothers' future successes as bookend defensive ends. He and Eric had always been close, and he was inordinately proud of his younger brother. Pete was six five and two-seventy, but as a high school senior, Eric was already bigger, quicker, and would probably soon be stronger. More important to Pete, Eric worked hard with none of the arrogance or cheap reliance on size that's so easy for big men to develop.

His father and brother excitedly talked to him on the phone about the game, but Pete knew it was his mother who was the instigator of the trip. She knew that Sally, the first girl he'd ever really been serious about, had recently broken up with him and despite his telephone assurances to his mom that everything was fine, she was determined to see her boy.

He didn't see them before the game, but assumed they had been delayed and would be waiting outside the locker room afterward. He played an OK first half, no embarrassments, but no big plays, slightly distracted, wondering about his folks. He sneaked a few looks at the stands where they should be sitting, wary of a coach yelling at him to get his head in the game.

The team had just come into the locker room at half time, down by one touchdown, when an assistant coach called him into the hall. A young police officer was there. Sorry to have to tell him now, but they had just tracked him down through neighbors. It was in a sleet storm on I-75, just after they had crossed the Mackinac Straits in the middle of the night. A drunk with his lights off, driving the wrong way on the interstate, had hit his folks head on. His folks, his brother, the drunk, all were killed instantly. No suffering the policeman assured him. Pete later learned the drunk had four previous DUI's, didn't have a license, and had just left a bar on the outskirts of Cheboygan. His blood alcohol tested .32, a level where most people would be unconscious.

The coach wasn't going to put him back in for the second half, but he'd insisted. He never remembered much about it, just impressions of rage during each play and deadness in between and afterwards. They told him later he had sacked Ohio State's quarterback four times, the last time putting him out of the game with a concussion. The Buckeyes didn't score again and Michigan won twenty-four to ten. Several weeks later, he overheard that when he made the last sack, the defensive coach had turned to one of his assistants and said, "Holy shit! We should start killing a couple of parents before every game."

He drew back into himself; stopped going to classes, pretty much stopped everything except football and the necessary business of dealing with the aftermath of the deaths. He wasn't overtly feeling sorry for himself, rather he wasn't allowing himself to feel at all. Only during those seconds between the snap of the ball and whistle did he swing wide the door to an inner furnace of grief and rage.

Pete woke with a start from a dream he could only remember as confused and threatening and full of loss. The last of the embers were dying out, and he looked at Annie, around the darkened room, their home. He shifted and worked his other arm underneath Annie. Ever so carefully, trying not to wake her, he lifted her and carried her up to bed.

8

Annie woke at 10:30 the next morning, gradually becoming aware it was Pete's pillow, not Pete she was snuggled against. One of the bedroom windows was open a bit, and she listened to the waves lapping the shore below and the rain gurgling in the gutters. It made the bed seem even warmer. She tried pulling the pillow over her head, but slowly yielded to consciousness, her last dream just out of reach. She dimly remembered Pete carrying her upstairs last night and helping her undress. She didn't remember him leaving at all. The sleep of the dead, she thought to herself, and didn't like the thought.

On the bedside table was Pete's battered old Stanley thermos, a mug, and a note from Pete with several sprigs of small yellow wildflowers laid across it.

Annie,

Had to go to work – there's coffee in the thermos. It was after four when you fell asleep, and I didn't want to wake you. Hope you've slept in. Heck's been out, we had a short run. Call me when you're up.

Love you,

Pete

She poured herself a cup of coffee and stared out the window. The peaks of the Chilkats were intermittently visible across Lynn Canal through the shifting clouds. A flock of scoters were rafted together about fifty yards off the shore, riding over the swells, parts of the flock suddenly disappearing as they dove together, popping back up in a different place. She could hear the whistling of their wings as the flock continually rearranged itself, ducks in the back beating across the water in takeoffs and then plowing to landings on the other side of the flock. There were only about fifty ducks, but in the spring there would be rafts of hundreds out in front of the house. Heck came over to the big old four poster, and she said OK, patting the bed beside her. He hopped up and after circling a time or two dropped in a heap tight beside her, his head on her lap.

Annie watched the scoters and finished her first cup of coffee. She poured a second and called the hospital, asking for intensive care. The boy was still on the critical list, but they thought he might make it. She sat there for quite a while, thinking about the fragility of life and the kids' families last night, about the little babies in the maternity ward.

When she finished the second cup she dialed Readers' and got Jeremy. He said Pete had gone to the Post Office and the bank, but had said she might call and to let her know he'd be right back and would call her as soon as he returned. Said he needed to talk to her about the sailboat. She stretched and looked out the window. Despite the weather, she decided a run would help shake off the shadows of last night. The key to living in a rainy climate was to not let it restrict what you did. Usually the rain seemed much worse when you were inside than when you actually got out in it. She could maintain that attitude most of the year, but around October, the rain and increasing darkness would make her long to be on a beach in Aruba.

As she dressed for the run, Hector recognized the clothes and began to talk to her in approval, long rrruuu's and wuuuu's, and pawing her foot to hurry her up. By the time she was pulling on her running shoes, he was bouncing around.

For the sixth time, Pete listened to his own voice tell him, "This is the McLaughlin's. We can't get the phone right now, but – " Pete hung up before the beep. When he walked back in the store, Jeremy had told him Annie had called. He called back and left a message the first time, figuring Annie was probably in the shower, but knowing it might be a while before she noticed the blinking number on the message machine down in the kitchen, he called back every ten minutes, hanging up without leaving an additional message.

On the first two calls he had figured she was in the shower. By the third and fourth calls he thought perhaps she had decided on a long hot bath. He knew she tended to crank the music up when she was by herself, making it hard to hear the phone. With the rain, he didn't think she'd be out in the yard, and by the fifth call he decided that, rain or not, she must have gone for a run. He liked to run on the beach or through the woods, but she liked the road where she could stretch out and lose herself in the rhythm of her stride. He wondered whether she would run toward town or out the road, he could visualize both routes she might take, the road looping through the coastal forest and curving by the water. It was a beautiful, but isolated. Pete thought about Kotkin's veiled threats for the hundredth time.

He told himself he was being foolish, the threats hadn't been explicit and were probably a bluff anyway. Even if they weren't a bluff, there had been no specific threat against Annie. They probably didn't even know what she looked like. It was too soon to worry anyway. Kotkin could barely have had time to tell Galvan about his answer yet. Would he have called, or would he have flown back to deliver the news? The more he tried to reassure himself, the more concerned about Annie and the madder about Kotkin's threats he became. Yesterday he had only been irritated. Today he wanted to hurt Kotkin.

He thought of each of the normal places that Annie might turn around, depending on how far she was running. In his mind, he urged her to turn back after a short run, hoping it was still raining out the road, making it miserable to run. He knew Heck would be with her and would never let anyone hurt her, but he also knew how easy it is to shoot a dog. He tried to tell himself there were few people who could catch Annie if she had even a couple of steps on them and could cut into the woods. Pete could shamble along all day at slow jog or hike up into the alpine with a heavy pack without stopping, and he could beat Annie in a sprint, but when she really wanted to run, there was nothing he could do to keep up with her.

When they ran together, they would go along at Pete's pace for the first mile or two, and then Annie would say she was going to pick it up a bit and would catch him coming back in. The bounce in her stride would lengthen out, and despite his best efforts, she would steadily draw away from him. Once she drew out of sight, he would slow to a comfortable jog. As soon as he saw her coming back the other way, he would turn and run back the other way, pushing himself until she caught him, and they would jog back at Pete's pace again. Her stride made Pete think of watching deer in the woods, the spring in their legs floating them over windfalls in effortless leaps. He could become mesmerized running five feet behind her, watching the pulse of muscles under the Lycra and rhythm of the red-golden braid, as thick as her wrist, flipping from one shoulder to the other and back on each stride.

"Answer the phone, please pick up the phone," he thought as he listened to the first ring, and then the second, and then heard the answering machine cut in again before he hung up. He kept thinking about the places on the road with rock faces formed by road cuts on the uphill side and steep cliffs down to the water on the other, leaving nowhere to escape from a car. *"Turn around, come home and call me."* He tried to will his thoughts to her as he went through small tasks mechanically. He knew he wasn't being productive, and he grabbed the phone each time it rang.

Annie was running a little slower than normal today, the shadows of last night still with her. The mist swirled about, starting to soak through her ball cap, dripping down her neck and mixing with sweat to slide down her back and trickle down the back of her tights. She had been tempted to turn around at the first little waterfall. That would give her three miles, but she decided to hang in for a couple of more miles and then push herself a little coming back to see if she could warm up a bit.

Where the road went through the woods, the sides were thick with goat's beard, most of its white flowers gone now, the remaining feathery fronds hanging down with raindrops at their tips. Behind the goat's beard, the bright red berries of elderberries and devil's club glinted with water drops against the backdrop of spruce and hemlock. A fat marmot sat up at the edge of the road ahead of her and watched for a moment before scuttling back into the undergrowth. The road curved along the coast, the ocean sometimes washing the bottom of the cliffs fifty feet below, other times visible through trees. Benjamin Island was only about a half mile off the coast here, and in the spring when she ran by, she could hear the roars and grunts from the sea lions hauled out on the rocks.

Usually, even on a gray day like this, she could lose herself in the beauty of the run. That wasn't working today, so she began to visualize running her leg of the Klondike Relay. Almost a hundred ten-person relay teams raced from sea level in Skagway, up and over the 3,500 foot Chilkoot Pass. The 110-mile course roughly followed the route of the Klondike Gold Rush stampeders to Whitehorse in the Yukon Territory.

Annie hit her turnaround and started back, picking up the pace. She was running hard now, almost oblivious to the scenery or the occasional car that passed. She concentrated on turning it up another notch, keeping her stride long, trying to keep the push from her toes. The rain and wind had picked up, but she pictured coming down to the relay point, kicking to give her team the biggest possible lead.

When she rounded the last bend, she could see the entrance to their driveway less than a quarter of a mile out. Her breath was ragged now, but she pushed herself into her closing kick, running more upright, pumping her arms, trying to make every stride explosive. She envisioned Pete running ahead of her, yelling over his shoulder that she was slowing down, that she wasn't going to catch him this time. Fifty yards out, her body, her lungs and legs were screaming at her to quit, but she tried to put the pain in a little triangle in her mind, keep it there, isolated from what she was doing, willing the legs to pump faster and faster. Pete had told her about the triangle and she saw him now, breaking into his full sprint as he always did when she was almost up with him, pulling back out ahead of her for a few paces and holding it as long as he could, until he faded and she edged past.

She kicked the last couple of paces past the driveway and slowed to a shaky walk, sucking air in huge gulps. The memories of Pete trying to laugh and breathe at same time were with her as she walked fifty yards past the drive and back. Heck was marking his territory at the head of the drive and then, unfazed by the run, found a large stick in hopes she would throw it for him. Annie walked down the driveway to the garage with wobbly legs, and then down the stairs to the house. She didn't like to carry a key with her when she ran and always left the house unlocked. She'd almost locked herself out this morning, just noticing as she started to pull the door closed that unusually, Pete had locked the door when he left. She went inside and Heck trotted down to the beach to see what the tide had brought to his doggy kingdom.

Annie was thoroughly soaked. In the arctic entrance, she pulled off her shoes and put them on the boot dryer and hung her cap and jacket. She squished into the utility room, leaving wet footprints. Socks, tee shirt, tights, panties and running bra were peeled off to wait for the rest of a load. She pulled the hair band loose from her braid and shook her hair loose as she walked into the living room, punching on the CD player and cranking it up.

She went up the open stairs surrounded by k.d. lang's voice from *Absolute Torch and Twang* singing about luck in her eyes. As she climbed the stairs, Annie absentmindedly rubbed her breasts, grateful to have the running bra off. When she ran, it helped to bind them down as much as possible. When she finished running, she always wanted the bra off as soon as possible.

Annie turned the electric wall heater and vent fan on in the bathroom and adjusted the shower as hot as she could stand it. The wind continued to pulse down Lynn Canal, and a branch from one of the big spruces bumped the bathroom window in the big gusts. She stood there under the spray, her eyes closed, losing herself in the beat of hot water after the cold of the rain. Annie soaped herself, the slickness of soap on smooth skin feeling good. The washcloth down her thighs, over her bottom, between her legs, made her wish Pete was home. The slight roughness of the cloth over her breasts, across her nipples, made her think again of the babies in the maternity ward.

She and Pete had been dancing around the idea of having a family for over a year now. So far she had been the one more hesitant. She knew Pete loved children, but he also had hesitations he'd never explained to her. More and more she found herself thinking about babies, holding the children of friends when they were together, paying attention to babies she saw when they were out, stopping by the maternity ward on breaks. Before she came to Juneau, she had dated a police detective for a while. He once told her that the problem with being in law enforcement was that because most of the people you dealt with were crooks and lowlifes, you started thinking everyone was that way. She wondered if that was similar to the problems of being a nurse. You were far too aware of everything that could go wrong having a baby, raising a child. She wondered if it was really her childhood she was thinking about, knowing how many things can go wrong.

She stayed in the shower until the hot water began to fade. After she dried off, she toweled the steam off the full length mirror across the bathroom and looked at herself speculatively, over her shoulder checking out her bottom, facing the mirror with a slight intake of breath to improve posture, cupping each breast in her palms to check for sag. She thought she was attractive, but Pete thought she was beautiful. She liked that, but even more, she liked that it seemed to be only a small part of what he loved about her.

As she was drying her hair, she thought she heard the phone ring, but when she switched off the hair dryer it was silent except for the wind and k.d. lang belting her heart out about the scars of childhood in a small town.

Annie tried to call Readers' twice before she left for work, each time getting a busy signal. She drove in, taking Heck with her, so Pete could stop by and pick him up on his way home. She wondered what it was about the sailboat that Pete wanted to talk with her about. She had only seen it that once, lying on its side on the sand bar. She knew it was at the public float in Auke Bay, near where the Coast Guard cutter *Liberty* berthed.

In Norfolk, when she was thirteen, she belonged to a troop of Girl Scouts that were Sea Scouts. They did a lot of sailing in small boats, and she loved it. The woman who was the scoutmaster, Mrs. Morris, had raced on a lot of boats when she was young, back when that was unusual for a woman. She made all the girls in the troop feel they could accomplish anything. Annie remembered how guilty she used to feel when she wished Mrs. Morris was her mother. She never told her mother about any of the mother-daughter events the troop had, never trusting her to show up sober. They moved again when she was fourteen, and she hadn't sailed again until she worked in San Diego.

As she approached Auke Bay, she tried to see if the *Bon Temps* was still there, but it was too far and there were too many boats to be able to tell. The rain had broken and she had a little bit of time before she needed to be at work. She turned into the parking lot, and within a few minutes was walking out the main float. Pete had said the *Bon Temps* was near the Coast Guard cutter, but as she walked farther out, she realized the *Liberty* was gone. The mega-yachts that came through in the summer moored out on the floating outer breakwater. She and Pete used to joke about them, the paid crew in matching outfits, the boats on their rear decks bigger than the boats most people in Juneau owned. Only one of the big yachts was in today, and it sat silent, impenetrable behind smoked glass windows.

Annie slowed as she approached the *Bon Temps*, tied up by herself near the end of the breakwater. The boat's bow was toward her and Annie looked up at the rigging. She paused beside the boat, taking in the gleaming brightwork, trailing her hand along the toe rail. She thought about Mrs. Morris and the Sea Scouts. She thought about working in San Diego when the America's Cup had been held there, fun times with the moving parties that floated through the waterfront. As she was daydreaming, she was startled by a sound that seemed to come from within the boat. She walked toward the stern and saw the companionway door was open. Someone was onboard. "Hello, anybody home? Hello?" No one responded to her call at first, and she called again. She could partially see into the main cabin. It was a mess, cushions pulled out, cupboards hanging open, floor plates to the bilge pulled up. As she started to call a third time, a man peered out the companionway door. He looked incongruous on the boat, tan trench coat over a suit, straightening his carefully-knotted silk tie, smoothing his hair back. Looking up into the light, it took a second for his eyes to adjust. He gave a look of smug satisfaction. "Ms. McLaughlin! I'm delighted to see you. Very happy! Very, very, pleased! Please, come aboard."

9

When he heard the recording of his own voice answering again, Pete hung up and asked Jeremy if he would cover the store. He knew he was probably being silly; she'd probably just gone for a run and headed into work early. He knew what was probable, but it didn't ease the anxiety that metastasized from the loop of Kotkin's veiled threats playing in his head. From the turnoff of Hospital Drive, where he checked first, to the driveway of their house, it was a straight shot out the road. Pete was pushing the old truck at sixty-four in the fifty-five, watching for police and, even more intently, for Annie's car coming from the opposite direction. As he passed Auke Bay, he glanced out at the several hundred boats moored in the harbor, wishing the *Bon Temps* had not come into their lives.

He knew she could have stopped at a store or come in early to see a friend, but the anxiety grew as the houses thinned out, and then as the asphalt ended and he passed the "No Winter Maintenance" sign without seeing her car coming towards him. When he reached the turnoff into their house, he pulled the truck about fifteen yards down the driveway and stopped between two big spruces so the drive was blocked. He rummaged briefly among tools behind the seat, considered a pry bar, and then selected a large framing hammer before quietly shutting and locking the truck door, looking like a man who wanted to bang the hell out of a big nail.

He wasn't far enough down the drive to see the parking pad and garage and he circled quietly down through the woods until he had a clear view. No strange cars, he couldn't tell yet whether Annie's car was in the garage. He moved down to the garage and looked through the window; her car was gone. That was good, evidence that she'd probably just left early, and stopped somewhere on her way into work. His concern for her was morphing into a greater anger at Kotkin, unhappiness with himself for not telling her about the pack and Kotkin the first moment he'd had the chance, and annoyance with her, only slightly diminished by the fact he knew it wasn't really justified.

Pete crossed the parking pad and looked down the stairs at the house. Through one of the house windows, he could see the little cat dozing on the sill. The cat disappeared whenever a strange person came into the house and Pete thought seeing her in the sill was a good sign. He knew it was over-dramatic, but he wanted to make sure there were no signs of a struggle. Inside things looked normal. Annie's wet running clothes were in sink in the utility room, which confirmed that she had been running and had made it back OK. In the kitchen he pushed the message button on the phone and used the erase button to delete the first two messages, which were from him. The third message was from Jeremy, saying Annie had called and was at the hospital and Jeremy had emphasized to her that Pete really needed to talk to her.

The fourth message was from Annie. "Pete, this is Annie. What the hell is going on? I was early on the way into work and I stopped at Auke Bay to take a look at the *Bon Temps*. There was a guy on the boat named Kotkin. He knew me, knew our names, knew where we lived. He started talking about how glad he was to see me, that he'd meet with you at the Readers' yesterday, and how you were being very foolish and I should help you be reasonable. Pete, I had no idea what he was talking about, and I really didn't like it! Without him ever saying anything directly, he left me feeling threatened and slimy. I'm at work. Call me."

Pete jabbed the erase button again. He realized he still had the framing hammer in his other hand and was squeezing it like he wanted to crush the handle. He put the hammer down and took several deep breaths, looking out the window at the Chilkats across the channel. He called the E.R., but Annie was with a patient. The clerk said she could have Annie call as soon as she was free, but Pete said no, just tell her he got her message and called, but he was coming back in town and would stop by.

Driving back in the road, Kotkin's image roiled Pete's mind, the perfect suit and manicured nails, the subtly implied threats, the assumption that the weight of the wealth he represented would ensure that Mr. Galvan would always get what he wanted. The unctuous bastard! The fact that Kotkin was correct, at least to the extent that Pete knew where the pack was, only made him madder.

He was on his way in to see Annie at the Emergency Room, but without previous thought found himself turning down into the Auke Bay parking lot to see if Kotkin was still on the *Bon Temps*. The image in his mind, the need in his arms and hands, was to lift Kotkin by the front of his suit and shake him till his arms and legs jerked and flailed, his head rag-dolled, and his teeth snapped, while Pete carefully explained why he should never think of talking to Annie again. Don't do it, don't do it, don't do it, Pete. You have to think before you act this time. You can't have Kotkin go to police.

He parked and sat for a minute. If Kotkin was still on the boat, they were going to talk, but first he had to will himself back into the carefully guarded place where he lived, weighing every public action, every exposure. Just then, Kotkin came hurrying up the ramp, a pursed-lipped, slightly pained expression on his face.

Pete hesitated, his hand on the truck door, watching Kotkin turn to the porta-pots near the head of the ramp. Kotkin opened the door of the closest and took a step back with a disgusted look on his face. He went to the second, opened that door and then, with an even more pronounced look of distaste on his face, went back to the first and went inside.

Pete didn't consciously make the decision. He was sitting in his truck waiting for Kotkin to come out. He looked at the framing hammer, now lying on the passenger seat floor, and told himself "no", that could only make the situation worse. His gaze stopped on a large roll of gray duct tape, also on the truck floor. "The Alaska State Tape," Annie always called it. The next thing he knew, he was striding towards the porta-pot, striping off an arm's length of tape from the roll. He counted on the normal instinct of a person sitting inside with their pants down, to have their first concern be about someone opening the door. By the time Kotkin figured out his problem was getting out, Pete had a four or five wraps of tape around the outhouse. Kotkin was yelling, but it was raining hard again, and no one else was in the parking lot. Pete took a couple of more wraps for good measure. Kotkin was screaming now, he was going to find out who was doing this and sue them for every penny they're worth.

He knew he shouldn't, but the thought of Kotkin and his impeccable attire and money and scaring Annie infuriated him. He gave the porta-pot a hard push. It went over, splashing inside as the tank spilled out and the stench hit Pete like a wave. Kotkin was screaming now, "every penny you have in the world, criminal and civil remedies," but it sounded like he was gagging and vomiting between his threats. Pete was tempted to shove it back a few more feet and tumble it down the rip-rap into the shallow water. If he did, someone would probably find Kotkin and let him out before the tide came in and drowned him, but Pete knew he'd screwed up enough already. He left Kotkin screaming threats from inside the outhouse and drove away, the truck windows down to help clear the memory of the smell.

Pete studied Annie's face, looking for signs of a truce. When he had finally caught up with her at the hospital, it was another busy shift. She had stepped out between patients and he enveloped her in a bear hug, feeling foolish about his earlier imaginings, but immensely grateful she was OK. Annie, however, was not in a mood to be hugged. She was mad, determined to know what the hell was going on, what the guy on the boat had been talking about. They were already calling her back for another patient, so he promised he would be there at the end of shift, would tell her all about it when they could sit down and talk.

They were at Squire's Rest. The bar overlooked Auke Bay harbor and was the only one directly on their way home. There was a little Thai restaurant downstairs, and they occasionally came up here for a beer while waiting for a table. It was a light crowd on the rainy Thursday night, a couple of young guys playing pool, seven or eight guys and a couple of women talking quietly at the bar. She and Pete didn't go to bars very often, but this brought back memories of other cities where she had worked, sometimes stopping for a drink with a group of other nurses after work. As the state's capital, Juneau had a large population of state and federal workers. These folks, though, were young construction workers, fishermen, people who made a living with their hands, or so it seemed to Annie as she surveyed the jeans and work shirts and ball caps. Fewer pretensions or at least, she corrected herself, different ones.

They each got a beer, Corona for her, Alaskan Amber for him, and Pete took two bowls of pretzels from the bar. They went to a table away from everyone, down at the far end of the room, underneath the wall decorated with fishing net, large bronze propellers, and a mounted king crab.

Annie was hurt and mad that he hadn't told her about the pack the first day.

He was trying to explain. "When I was carrying Randy out, I promised him I wouldn't tell about the pack. I don't make many promises, but I've always kept them . . . all except the other time I carried someone out. I was wading then, too, but through a rice paddy instead of down a salmon stream. I promised we were going to be OK, that we'd called for air strikes and the helicopters were coming to get us out. He kept saying, 'Do you promise me, Pete? Do you promise?' and I promised him, but we didn't get out and nothing was OK or fine. Fact is, things were about as far from OK or fine as they can get. For better or worse, I made this promise to Randy, and I want to keep it if we can. I also don't want to be talking to the police about why we didn't tell them about the pack to begin with."

"Pete, you have a perfectly good explanation. We'll just tell them the truth."

"I can't go to the police about this."

"I can't believe Kotkin will be anxious to talk to the police," Annie said. "I doubt he even tells them about the porta-toilet, and if he does, he doesn't know who did it."

"I'm not worried about the outhouse, but I don't think it would be the right thing to go to the police on this. At a minimum, let's find out what's in the pack and then figure out where to go from there."

"When you decided to tape him in the outhouse, did you think it was a good idea, that it was going to help things?"

"No, I knew it was a bad idea, it was juvenile, but it was way better then the other things I was likely to do. When he came up the ramp at Auke Bay and went into the porta-pot, I was sitting in the truck and I thought of the scene in Jurassic Park where the Tyrannosaurus rex bites through the outhouse and eats the lawyer. Well, I was wishing a T-Rex would come along right then and chomp him and the porta-pot in one bite."

"They're an unreliable species. I've never had one show up when I needed it." There was a little twitch upwards at the corners of her lips. Hopefully, a sign of détente.

"Anyway, I'm sitting there waiting for him to come out, and thinking about him threatening you."

"I said it seemed like he was threatening us," she said. "He never came out and said things directly. He was scary, though, in a snaky sort of way. This guy I've never seen in my life looks up out of the boat and calls me by name, acts like we've known each other all our lives. I hated not knowing what he was talking about 'Ms. McLaughlin, I'm sure your husband has discussed with you our little talk yesterday. I'm afraid your husband is being a very foolish man, Ms. McLaughlin. I'm sure you can help your husband understand that everyone would be far better off, safer in this dangerous world, if he would simply be a reasonable person.' Says it all with this smug look on his face. Pete, I didn't have a clue what he was talking about, and I hated that."

"I'm sorry, I should have told you when you got home last night, but you just seemed wiped out by the kids' wreck. I wanted to talk with you as soon as you got up."

"It's OK. When I called and you were at the post office, I should have probably waited for you to call back before I went running. I wasn't going to admit to him that I didn't know what he was talking about, but I really didn't like it. We've never kept secrets from each other."

The mounted crab on the wall seemed to stare at Pete with its beady eyes. Pete stared back at it for a minute and didn't like the look it was giving him. He didn't respond, and they gazed out over the lights of Auke Bay.

"So, you realize being here, you're making the classic mistake of returning to the scene of the crime?"

"Yeah. I guess I'm never going to make a criminal mastermind."

"It was a shitty thing to do, Pete."

"Yeah, it was."

They talked a while longer, watching the harbor lights through the rain trickling down the window. Droplets of condensation trickled down their glasses, and the headlights of an occasional lonely car lit up the highway. Annie agreed to finding out what was in the pack and then deciding how to proceed. She was adamant, however, that she was going back with him to the cove.

He protested. He should get over and check on the pack as soon as possible, figure out what was going on. The bear might still be hanging around. Someone else might be looking for the pack. The weather was looking snotty, and the ride over would probably be rough.

None of it had made a dent. "Pete, the pack has been there for a while now. I have Monday and Tuesday off, and it can wait until then. If the bear is still around, or someone else is, it will be safer with two of us. Regardless, the cove is one of my favorite places. There ought to be more silvers in the stream by now, and last time I never got to make a cast."

They went back and forth about it until they left for the drive home. His one small victory was convincing her to wait in her car with the motor running while he went down the steps and checked the house. He told her he was probably being way over-cautious, but that it made sense to be aware and consider remote possibilities. He didn't tell her that he had not only insisted on meeting her at the end of her shift, but that he'd spent the evening in his truck sitting in the hospital parking lot where he could keep an eye on the emergency room.

The moon was still up, a small sickle in the sky when they left Monday morning. They ran down Lynn Canal and into Stephens Passage on flat water. The sky lightened in the long dawn of high latitudes and a light fog rose off the water. In front of them the sky over the mountains on Admiralty Island began to color in hues of rose and orange and red. The snow was early this year. In late August, the first light powdered sugar dusting had appeared on the mountain tops. The early miners called it termination dust. It was their signal to head out of the mountains, back to town for the winter. Rays of the sun began to shine through the gaps between the mountains, lighting up the peaks and giving the slight fog on the water a rose glow.

They anchored in the creek mouth and waded upstream together. The creek was higher now with the fall rains, colored by the runoff of tannin-stained water from the muskegs. The water flowed swiftly, smoothing out some of the riffles, forcing Pete and Annie to keep close to the creek's banks.

Silver salmon were working their way up the stream to spawn. Pacific salmon hatch in fresh water creeks and rivers, and then the smolt swim out to the ocean to live and grow. Skeletons and the decomposed bodies of pinks and chums from earlier runs were rotting in the creek, giving their nutrients back to the creek's food chain that would nourish the smolt when they emerged from their eggs in the gravel next spring.

The warmth and slant of the autumn sun lit up the greens and golds of the grass flats against the dark, somber green of the shadowed mountains. Before every turn in the stream, Pete would yell and whistle, giving warning to any bears. The day he found Hal and Randy, he hadn't been able to pick up a blood trail from the bear that killed Hal and mauled Randy or he would have felt obligated to try and track it down. He knew Fish and Wildlife Protection had come out the following day and hadn't been able to find the bear either, but he didn't want to chance surprising a bear nursing a gunshot wound and a grudge against people.

Once, when he had clapped and yelled, something bolted through the grass around the corner, causing each of them to tense, thumbs on the rifles' safeties, straining to see through the tall grass. Pete had brought the .375 again, and Annie a 30.06 Ruger 77 he had given her the past Christmas. Her gift had caused some chuckling and kidding among some of the other nurses, but up here, a wife or girlfriend getting a rifle as a present wasn't all that unusual. One of the nurses from pediatrics had heard about it and stopped by to chat knowledgeably about hunting.

"Pete, you remember how you've always told me that when we run into bears, we're supposed to stand side by side to look larger and cause the bear to retreat."

"Yeah."

"When we heard that sound, you stepped in front of me. I know you did it instinctively to protect me, but if you step in front, we can't stand side by side to discourage a charge, and if a bear does charge, there's no way I could get a clear shot."

"You're right on both counts. Probably old football instincts, protecting my quarterback."

"Nice try, but I thought you played defense."

"Both ways in high school. You doing OK?"

"I'm fine. Let's find out about the pack and then get back to the boat and get the rods. The fish I'm seeing still look nickel bright."

Pete agreed, and after another few moments of listening and watching, they proceeded up the creek. She had a Leupold 2x7 scope on her rifle, and she double-checked to make sure the power was adjusted all the way down to give her the widest field of view and quickest sight picture. Cranked down like that, she felt it was almost as quick as the peep sight Pete had on the .375. As they waded, her thumb felt the safety to ensure it was still on.

She had started hunting with him several years ago, at first just going along for the hike on early season alpine hunts and gradually becoming intrigued and seduced by the heightened sense of awareness, the magnification of perception and the senses that hunting demanded. She had come to like the sense of self-reliance and the rhythm of the seasons

– filling the freezer with fish in the summer and venison in the fall, feasting on Dungeness and king crab, ducks and geese as snowline began to inch down the mountains, and ptarmigans with spruce tip jelly as the spring sun began to melt the same snow.

There was bear sign as they continued up the creek, scat and partially eaten salmon. None of the tracks appeared as large as the ones on the sand bar where Hal's body had been, but he knew that his memory could be exaggerating.

They rounded the last bend to the pool along the base of the rock wall. The rains had deepened the pool, and they couldn't quite see the bottom through the stained waters. On the small sand bar, half of a salmon, freshly bitten through, lay in the sand amidst bear tracks. These tracks were easily as big as he remembered.

10

"You think it's the same bear?"

"I don't know, his tracks seem as big. I couldn't do this with any of the other tracks we've seen."

Annie looked down at Pete's feet. He wore size fourteen hip boots, and was standing with his right foot completely inside the bear's track. "That salmon hasn't been dead very long, has it?" she said.

"I think if the bear wanted trouble he'd still be here. Let's just be careful, get the pack and get out of here. Looks like the rains have this pool too deep for us to wade across. We'll have to go back down a ways to cross and then work our way up the other side."

They held hands for mutual balance as they crossed at the tail of the pool, the current tugging at their knees, the pressure of the water pushing the hip boots in against their legs. On the far side they scrambled along the ledge at the base of the rock wall, occasionally having to swing out around or fight their way through bushes or clumps of small alders.

Pete looked at the pool of water flowing in front of them. He hoped that if a bear came up the opposite side of the creek, the expanse of water might make the bear perceive them as less of a threat. He hoped, but he'd seen bears cross bigger creeks in seconds, their huge bounds exploding the water around them.

"Hold my rifle and I'll get in there and get the pack," he said.

"Let me get it. I can squeeze back into the cleft easier than you. Besides, you're a faster shot than I am and have the heavier rifle." It made sense, and they did it that way. The entry to the cleft was easy, but then the rock walls narrowed. An overhang had kept most of the rain out. Bits of cloth still littered the floor of the crevice. What seemed to be dried blood darkened the rock.

Annie had to turn sideways and press herself back between the rock walls to reach the pack. Randy's frantic efforts to escape the bear's reach had jammed it in tightly. She couldn't turn enough to use both hands and had to tug and twist it to get it to budge. The pack finally came loose, almost overbalancing her.

The pack was heavy. Pete opened the top compartment and pulled out a blue gym bag. He unzipped it and they both stared for a moment before she gave a low whistle. "You ever seen more cash?"

"Only in the movies." It hadn't been this much, but the last time he had seen cash in a gym bag, it was lying on a dusty California road. The scene replayed in his mind, and he ceased to see the pack before him until Annie gave him a nudge.

"You OK?"

"Yeah, sorry, I'm fine. Just thinking," he said.

"Seemed like the sight of all this cash had you mesmerized."

He joked back with her, giving himself a small almost invisible shake, which she noticed anyway and looked at him oddly. Pete unzipped the lower main portion of the pack. It was stuffed with one-gallon Ziploc bags. Inside every bag was what appeared to be a vacuum-sealed pouch filled with white powder.

"I guess that answers the question of where all the money came from. It's hard to tell through the plastic but this looks like it sparkles, so I'm guessing cocaine. I saw heroin in Vietnam, but I can't tell for sure without opening a bag, which I don't think is a good idea."

"Is there anything else in there?"

He had rummaged through the rest of the pack and found a pistol in an outside pocket. It was a Glock Model 22, in 40 S&W. It was loaded, and there were two spare fifteen-round magazines. Pete pressed the magazine latch and ejected the magazine. He cleared the action, catching the round from the chamber in his cupped palm. He stuffed the drugs and money back into the pack, but put the empty pistol and the magazines in his pocket.

"What was that song, *Send Lawyers, Guns, and Money*?"

"Warren Zevon. At least we know what it is that Kotkin wanted back so badly. Pete, promises or not, we have to call the Troopers and turn this over."

He felt trapped. He knew what Annie was proposing was right, but he'd meant what he told her about his promise. More importantly, he didn't want to risk inadvertently bringing his past crashing down on them. He was worried that if he told her, he might lose her as well. Pete tried to deflect the question about calling the Troopers, tried to convince her that for now it made sense to put the pack back in the crevice and wait. He told her that Hal was dead and that surely what the bear had done to Randy was punishment enough. His reasons for not going to the police sounded hollow, even to him.

In the end, they put the pack back in the crevice and the decision about what to do with it, up in the air. Annie agreed, not because he convinced her, but because he resorted to asking her to do it on trust, that it was important to him, to both of them.

They were at the right side of the flats now, upstream from the mound where they had camped the night before they found the *Bon Temps*. Generations before, the stream bend had undercut and toppled an ancient Sitka spruce, shifting the flow and gouging out a wide deep pool. Nothing was left of the giant spruce now but the heartwood. Three smaller spruces grew out of the nurse log, their roots anchoring it in place, repaying the scores of years it nurtured them. On normal tides, this pool was at the upper edge of tidal influence. During the biggest fall and spring tides, 21-footers, Pete had seen the entire grass flat flooded, just small hummocks and islands of grass sticking out. Each piece of dry land would be crawling with voles and field mice, flooded from their burrows. Marsh hawks would glide over the flats eating until they could barely flap back into the sky.

To fish this pool well required long, difficult casts. Timing and rhythm are more important than strength in fly casting and Annie had a natural sense for it. Pete had taught her to cast and always enjoyed watching her. She wasn't yet quite as accurate, but she could cast as far or farther than he could. She was putting a little something extra on her casts now, the line rolling out behind her in a long tight loop and then hissing forward as she double-hauled to accelerate it. After a few false casts, she would shoot the coils she had looped in front of her, sometimes so hard she bounced the fly off the log at the head of the pool.

The sun shifted out from behind a cloud far above him, and all the colors of the scene seemed to jump out at him; the greenish gold of the grass and yellow of the alder and willows, the deep, deep green of the spruce and hemlock, the long brown glide of the pool. Half-seen shapes of coho shadowed the bottom of the pool, awaiting something in their genes to click and tell them it was time to continue their journey up the stream to spawn and die. The reds and golds of Annie's thick braid against the dark purple of her fly vest seemed to absorb and radiate the sun's colors.

He ached inside watching her. He wanted to engrave every detail, every nuance of color and shape and form in his mind so he would have them forever, no matter what happened. He called out her name tentatively, but she didn't answer, instead firing another cast, the loop so tight and level, the timing and the backcast so perfect he knew a video of it could sell a million fly rods.

He was just about to call to her again, tell her fish can tell when you're angry and won't bite, when a coho struck, a shattering tumble of fish and air and water and then silence. The rod quivered upright, loops of line hanging in the guides, the leader waving slightly in the breeze, hookless where the tippet had parted.

"Darn! I hit him too hard on the strike. I know better than that. You going to fish? They're in here."

"I will in a few minutes. I'm just enjoying watching you for now."

Annie waded out on the bank by him and tied on another Showgirl, a creation of pink and purple marabou. She was silent as she concentrated on threading the eye of the hook, then she turned the same focus on him, trying to see into his head, to figure out what was happening there. "Darn you, Pete, I'm not mad about what we do or don't do with the pack. I'm hurt though, and mad, too, because it's clear there's something you're not telling me, something about why you don't want to call the Troopers. It's beyond your promise to Randy. I know you well enough to be pretty sure it's not about wanting to keep the money. Besides, you were acting funny about this way before we knew what was in the pack." She tightened the cinch knot to the new Showgirl and clipped off the tag end of the leader. She checked the sharpness of the hook on her thumbnail and, satisfied, hooked it on the rod's handle.

He hugged her. "Hang in there with me just a little longer on this one. I know it seems I'm not making a lot of sense. We know a little better what we're dealing with now. Nobody's going to find the pack. Don't be mad and please don't be hurt, just give me just a little more time." Fly boxes, forceps, fly float and leader sink, and all the other stuff that gets jammed in fly vests were lumpy between them as she grudgingly hugged him back.

She had agreed, but it had been the coho, more than anything he had said, that lifted her mood. As the tide changed, the fish suddenly went on the bite, and the silver salmon tailwalking across the pool or surging away, melting the line off their reels, demanded all of their attention. When the bite ended, as suddenly and mysteriously as it began, they had six coho, all shining silver, some so fresh from the salt that sea lice still hung on their flanks.

He was grateful for the reprieve, but wading through the stream and walking back to the skiff through the yellowing high grass, rifle in hand, the memories of carrying Randy kept coming back and mutating to other memories of broken bodies in tall grass and flooded fields.

He'd stopped going to classes after his folks and brother were killed, and when the notice from the draft board showed up, he appeared when and where directed, though he'd hummed a few bars of *Alice's Restaurant* to himself while he took his physical. In the army he went where he was sent, did what he was told and spoke only when spoken to. He went through basic with no unusual events, other than scaring a few people in the hand-to-hand combat training, and shortly after wound up with an infantry platoon upcountry in Vietnam.

Afterward, he used to wonder whether there was such a thing as a good war, and if so, what made the difference. He came back alive, though it wasn't something he had cared about much at the time. Because he wasn't overly concerned with living, but not trying to die, he did what they asked and sometimes did more. He was able to keep a few of his platoon alive and unable to prevent the death of many others. They gave him some medals, which meant nothing to him at the time, and tried to promote him, which he steadfastly refused.

His platoon sergeant had noticed he was very good in the woods, quiet despite his size, and put him on point, and then on long range patrol. He spent most of his time by himself, easing through the forest, trying to be sure he saw before he was seen, trying not to lead his platoon into harm's way unaware. He killed men over there. Sometimes during the impersonality and insanity of firefights. Other times in the jungle by himself, intimately, feeling the life struggle out of bodies, his hand over mouths, smothering sound as blood ran down his forearms.

He was surprised how little he felt about the deaths. He had been brought up in the church and had always taken the commandments seriously. He had tried to shut himself off from all feelings after his family's death. He wondered how little you could feel before you were no longer alive and if that was the same as being dead.

Pete had always been self-conscious about his size. In football he never took satisfaction in beating smaller opponents. In wrestling he preferred to wrestle above his weight in the unlimited class. There was never a doubt that the small men he killed were trying to kill him, but he began to think of himself as a serial child murderer.

He went on leave a few times, but R&R was neither. He had never liked crowds. In the packed streets, huge among the throngs, he felt like he had the mark of Cain branded on his forehead, constantly fighting an edge of panic he never felt in the field. Back in the jungle, solitary in the blackest night, he would see himself from a distance, tears seeping silently down his face as he waited motionless beside a trail before materializing as a nightmare apparition, seen only too late as a shadow and the faintest glint of blade.

The wind had shifted around to the north and began to kick up a bit on their run back. He focused on the waves, constantly steering, picking the smoothest route over the waves, throttling up and back to maintain the fastest speed possible without banging. He loved driving the boat in such conditions and tried to let the wind wash away the old bad memories. He didn't consciously think about what to do, but by the time he steered into the tiny cove in front of their house and picked up the mooring buoy, he knew that for better or worse, he had to tell Annie about California and why he couldn't go to the Troopers.

11

The salmon came off the grill perfectly, but Pete was distracted throughout dinner, trying to form in his mind what he needed to tell her, wondering how it would affect her, how she would feel about him afterward. There was a bit of chill in the air, so he made a fire in the fireplace and they ate inside. He found himself looking around the living room, noticing how it had changed since Annie had come into his life, changed in ways he liked. The room had lost its austere look. It was comfortable now, lived in, the kind of place that friends liked spending time, watching the late sunset of a long summer day or settling deep into the couches in front of the fire on a winter's night. The friends were almost all through Annie. Even when it was people they had met in connection with him, Annie was the one who reached out and took the extra steps necessary to change acquaintances you met and liked into friends with whom you shared portions of your life. She was the one who had brought home the little cat she found abandoned by the roadside when she was out for a run.

The claymore still hung above the mantel, the big sword's blade gleaming dully with reflected firelight. He found himself looking at the art on the walls, fitted in between the bookcases. Mostly prints and a few small originals they had bought together; Juneau and Alaska artists like Kristi Allen, Ann Miletich, Gary Smith, Mark Vinsel and Rie Muñoz. In large part because of the tourism, Juneau supported a strong local arts community, out of proportion for a town its size. Pete and Annie had developed a small tradition together of buying one modest piece each year during the Christmas gallery walk.

Annie had surprised him with an artist's proof of Byron Birdsall's called *Southeast Sunset* on his birthday several years ago. He loved it and had been overwhelmed with the gift, but more at her divining so accurately what a special present it would be. He had asked her afterwards how she even knew how much he liked it, and she reminded him that when they first saw it, he told her how much it reminded him of the view from their house. She had kissed him lightly and told him, "We pay close attention to each other. It's one of the reasons we do so well together."

She was paying close attention to him now, as they were clearing away the dishes, focused on him, but waiting until he was ready to talk. He rummaged under the kitchen cupboards, and found the bottle of Courvoisier. He poured a small amount in two glasses and put them in the microwave for 15 seconds, just enough to warm the brandy and bring it to the point where you inhaled it as much as drank it.

"Whoa! This is special. You planning an explanation or a seduction?" Annie was smiling at him, reaching out to cup the side of his neck in her palm.

"It's an explanation." He tried to grin back at her. "If

you're still interested afterwards, I'll be happy to try the seduction."

They settled in on the couch. He looked into her eyes and wondered how she would be looking at him afterward.

"I've told you that I had a tough time when I lost my family and I compounded it by making some very bad decisions?" He tried to explain it to her. That for twenty years he had a charmed life. Along with his size and athletic skill and the smarts to do well in school, he'd been blessed with a great family that grounded him in faith and values.

"I was consumed with football and spent a lot of time working very, very hard at it, but I never saw football as an end in itself. Business or politics, I'm not sure where the path was leading, but I was filled with all the zeal and passion of youth. I wanted to change the world, to make it a better place. After the accident, I felt like I had this tremendous rage inside of me. In football, it was socially sanctioned for me to swing open the door to that rage as long as it clanged shut when the whistle blew. None of those other kids, and Lord we were all kids, no matter how big and tough, none of them had anything to do with my family's death. But every play, I would hit whoever was in front of me like I was going to make them personally pay for my death of my folks and my brother.

"I wasn't playing for the game anymore, I was trying to hurt people. Did you know that on fourth and goal, if you meet a 230-pound fullback head-on at the line of scrimmage, a fullback that by all accounts is not only a very good football player, but also a heck of a nice guy, and you lift him up and try to drive him down right through the turf so hard that you break his shoulder blade and ribs and end his season, over a 100,000 people will stand and roar and chant your name?

"When my family was killed, I began to make some very

bad decisions. We didn't have extended family, but there were a lot of people who tried to help me. There were friends, some of my professors, a couple of the coaches, an old girlfriend, the minister from our church at home. I've talked to you about my dad being a sheriff. I grew up with some of the deputies in dad's department as unofficial uncles. They had taught me to shoot, taught me bunches of things. I shut them all out, wouldn't talk to anybody. Coach finally figured out I had totally stopped going to classes, and if I flunked out, I couldn't play the following year. He got a counselor from the university to come around and talk to me.

"You've seen Star Trek reruns, Counselor Troy? First time I saw that show, it was slightly spooky how much she reminded me of that woman back at school, Susan something, I can't remember her last name. She took me on as sort of a personal project, kept trying to get me to talk with her, but I shut her out as well. Annie, when I was a kid we never had much money, but our life was good. We've talked a fair bit about your life, your dad leaving and your mom's drinking and her death. You overcame all of that, worked your way through school and got your master's. You're somebody who makes people happy to be around you." Pete had to stop a moment; he had a lump in his throat, which he tried to conceal.

"In football I used to pride myself on never showing the effect of a hit, no matter how much it hurt. In fact, I usually didn't play as well, until I'd taken a good hit. In life, I took one really hard hit and I quit. I quit on everything for a while.

"You're a nurse. You spend your days caring, comforting, literally saving people's lives. I know how completely dedicated you are to it, how fiercely you feel about it. Annie, there was a period where I was the opposite, what I was doing was the antithesis of everything you stand for."

"That was war, Pete. You told me once that you killed people over there. I hate that, but they were trying to kill you."

"Yeah, there was no doubt that we were trying to kill each other and both sides were being way too successful. There were a lot of questions about why we were trying to kill each other, but not that we were. Unfortunately, I also never had any doubt that they also had mothers and brothers and fathers and all the rest. Hell, over there that was about all they had.

"My great-grandfather brought the claymore that's over the mantel with him from Scotland. It was about all he had when he arrived. It is supposed to have been in the family for generations before him, used to defend the honor and property of the clan. I brought it back from Michigan with some of my folks' stuff. Over there, in the jungle at night, I could hear it. It used to slide from its scabbard with a silvery, exultant whisper. It always whispered 'Death'.

"I went to my sergeant once and told him I thought I was going crazy. He said, 'Well, sure you are son, that's what makes you so good at this'. Told me to get some sleep cause they needed me back out there that night.

"When I got out, there was no one lining up across from me on a line of scrimmage, there was no one trying to kill me in a jungle. I spent a lot of time lying on the beach where the biggest threat was sunburn. But Annie, I could still hear that sword whispering to me. I didn't always deal with it well.

"I've told you I made some bad decisions. The worst one was after I got back . . ." Pete's words ground to a halt as he remembered it all, tried to think how to explain what he'd never talked about to anyone.

He had just returned from Vietnam, bewildered to be alive, never expecting to come back. He and Dale were the only two members of their original platoon to survive. During his two year hitch, he had come to know Dale better than he wished. They were mustered out together, but he never expected to see him again. Dale would show up at his door, though, and Pete would feel obligated.

Dale had been full of himself that evening, excited, jittering. "This is the big one Pete! The big one!" Dale insisted they go out for a beer so he could so he could tell him about it. Dale drove them to a strip club a couple of miles away. It was early evening, and he remembered walking in from the still bright sunlight to the dim smoky air and blasting rock music, eyes taking a moment to adjust to see the sparse crowd and bored dancers. Leather or lace were the dancers' major fashion statements. Dale led the way to a table on the far side of the stage and ordered a couple of Budweisers. Each stripper danced to three songs, wearing her skimpy outfit for the first, shedding her top for the second, and in the third, when the dancers were down to high heels or boots, offering gynecological views to the customers who placed dollar bills on the edge of the raised stage.

Normally Dale would have pitched his latest scheme plus a half dozen side angles on the way over. This one was clearly different. Dale was working him, trying to buy him another beer, reminding him of all they had been through together, telling him this was going to be the big one, but not getting around to what "it" was or what he wanted from Pete. When it wasn't their turn to dance on the stage, the strippers strolled through the crowd trying to sell lap dances. A tall, slim young woman with improbably large breasts stopped by their table, trailing her hand across Pete's shoulders.

"Dale, is this your big friend you told me all about?"

"Pete this is Tiffany. She's already had several major auditions. She's going to be a star. Tiffany this is Pete."

"Pete," she whispered in his ear, "I really like <u>big</u> men." Her breasts brushed the back of his head and the smell of her cheap perfume was overpowering. "I've been really looking forward to meeting you. You're such a good friend of Dale's, maybe you'd like a free lap dance?"

"Tiffany, thanks, but I – "

"Pete, Pete, you and Tiffany need to get to know each other," Dale said.

"Pete," Tiffany said, "Maybe a little later I could get out of here. We could go party and have a really good time, no charge."

While she talked, Tiffany, if that was her name, was standing very close behind him, her breasts touching the back of his head, her fingernails languidly tracing patterns down across his shoulders and chest.

Pete could still remember the swirl of emotions. He was embarrassed, aroused, but more than anything, amused with the effort that Dale was spending on the sales pitch. Whatever made Dale go to this much trouble must be really dumb.

Pete took Tiffany's hand in his and lightly kissed its back. He told her she was exceedingly lovely, but he and Dale needed to talk and she was much too distracting for him to think clearly. He told Dale he would wait for him in the parking lot. He remembered looking back at the stage as he walked out. A lithe young woman who could actually dance was lost in the beat of *Hey Joe*. Her eyes were closed, dancing with almost no one paying attention. He stepped outside and the harsh rays of the setting L.A. sun hit him in the eyes, the acrid smell of the smog replacing the cigarette smoke of the bar.

Pete had been quiet for a while, thinking about it when Annie prompted him, "Pete?"

He decided that Tiffany and the size of her breasts probably weren't a helpful part of his explanation. "It turned out it was dumb, dangerous and illegal, all three. Dale had a buy set up for the following day for van load of marijuana. He was supposed to meet two guys in the Angeles National Forest, up in the mountains behind L.A. where they grew the stuff. He was bringing the cash and they were going to meet him up there and turn over the grass. They had insisted Dale come alone, but he was worried they might rip him off. He wanted me there hiding in the weeds, no pun intended. If things started to go bad, I was supposed to stop them."

Pete explained how he had told Dale no, there was no way he was going to be part of it. They went round and round about it. Dale had already arranged a sale for the grass at a very large profit. He had borrowed the money to buy it from a loan shark. When he took the money, the amount he had to pay back instantly became far larger than the amount he received, the interest mounting rapidly.

"Pete, these aren't people you can change your mind on. I got to get that grass and sell it now or it's my ass that's grass. I got to do this. I just need you to watch my back. Pete, Pete, just like the old days, you'll make sure I stay alive. Nobody better Pete. You gotta help me. Pete, you kept us alive. I just need you one more time."

Pete could remember standing there in the parking lot, the asphalt hot beneath their feet, exhaust fumes drifting over from the highway. The guitar came muffled through the club's thin walls and he could hear parts of the song as it asked where Joe was going with the gun in his hand. Where he was going to run?

He didn't know why he finally agreed. In contrast to Dale, he knew how dumb it was, it was against everything his folks had stood for. His father had once told him that roughly ninety percent of the criminals he dealt with as sheriff had made very bad decisions while drunk or on drugs. Pete was sober and knew how wrong this was, and he let Dale talk him into it anyway. He made it clear he didn't want any part of the money. He was going to watch Dale's back this last time for whatever they might owe each other for two years of mutual survival, and then he didn't want to see Dale again. Dale was so pleased he was going to do it without taking a cut of the deal that Pete's injunction to stay away in the future didn't faze him.

The sale was scheduled for noon the next day, at the end of an obscure spur road up a canyon. It was before sunrise, the smog turning red and pink and orange with the first hints of the sun rising behind the San Gabriels. The road wound up and around, the vegetation changing with the elevation to oak, sycamore and laurel before dipping back down into the canyon and rock, yucca spikes and stunted brush. Asphalt gave way to gravel, which gave way to dirt. They bounced through another rut, and the 7-11 coffee slopped in Dale's lap.

"Fuck, that's hot! I still don't see why the fuck we need to be out here at the butt-crack of dawn."

"Dale, we've been through this. We're going to go up and look at where you're supposed to meet. You're going to drop me off and then you're going to go away. You're going to stay far away until it's time to come back, and when you do, you're going to do exactly what I've told you. If not, I'm out. Turn around now and take me back."

"Hey, Pete, it's all cool. It's just early. We're almost there."

The road snaked along the canyon's edge until it

abruptly ran out of room, dead-ending in a slightly wider spot before a jumble of rocks, the canyon's bare slope rising above them on one side and falling away on the other.

Pete looked over the scene, mentally assessing potential hiding places and fields of fire. Before Dale left, Pete gave him careful directions about where he should try to park and where he should stand when he returned. Dale wanted to know where he was going to be, but Pete told him not to worry about it, if he didn't know, he wouldn't have to worry about not staring at the spot.

"Pete, man, this is going to work out great. We'll watch each others' backs just like in Nam. This is going to be cool. Tiffany liked you, man, not just cause I was paying her to. We're going to party tonight. Pete, this is going to be so cool."

Dale drove off, the sound of the van slowly fading, leaving Pete with silence and his misgivings. He couldn't remember a time Dale had ever watched his back or why he felt obligated to him. He had never been able to figure it out, but knew when this was over, he was not staying around for any celebrations, despite Tiffany's charms.

The jumbled rocks at the end of the road were the obvious hiding place, too obvious, and a parked vehicle could block the view. The red-tan clay of the barren uphill slope was studded with granite outcroppings, boulders, and sparse brush. It didn't look like a cat could hide on it, and no one would give it a second glance. He selected a boulder with a clump of chaparral beside it. He climbed up, careful not to kick the scree loose or make tracks. Last night, he and Dale had gone to a surplus store. He used the entrenching tool they'd purchased to scrape a shallow depression to form a reclining seat in the slope between the boulder and the bushes. He put most of the dirt into burlap bags and carried the dirt down and scattered it over the lower edge of the road where it blended in.

Pete climbed back up to the depression. He tried out the seat and then got back up and scraped a rest for his feet. A couple of times while he was working, he thought he heard an engine, but each time, when he stopped and listened intently, the sound faded away. He knew comfort made a difference and he took his time picking out the small rocks. When the dirt was as smooth as he could get it, he settled in, lying back with little wiggles until the fit was right. He placed the entrenching tool beside his legs and put the burlap bags over his legs and lap and chest. He had saved some of the dirt and scattered a light layer of dirt and rock over the bags. He was wearing khaki pants, a long-sleeved khaki work shirt, brown jersey work gloves and a tan ball cap. He rubbed dirt on his face and draped another torn burlap bag around his head and across his face like an Arab's burnoose. He had two burlap bags left, and he slit their bottoms open.

Dale had gotten the shotgun for him, a Remington 870, a twelve gauge pump, the barrel cut off a quarter inch above the legal limit, no choke. Last night he had taken it apart, carefully cleaning and oiling and checking every part. He checked it again and then fed four rounds of double-ought buck into the magazine. He made sure the safety was off, but didn't jack a shell into the chamber. If things started to go wrong, the ka-chunk of the pump racking a shell into the chamber had an ability to command attention far beyond anything he could call out. He had another eleven shells, six more of double-ought and five slugs which he divided among his front pockets.

He held the shotgun by its pistol grip and slid both bags over the shotgun, his left hand fitting between the bags to grip the fore-end. He settled back to wait. Four and a half hours until the sale was scheduled. It felt like he was in plain view, but he knew as long as he didn't move, they could stare right at him and not see him.

He lay there trying to empty his mind, not to think or feel, but to absorb everything, every sight, every sound, every smell. An hour and a half later, the sun, already high in the sky, cleared the canyon wall behind him. Almost immediately he could feel the ground and rock begin to heat in its unblinking glare. He listened to the sound of the creek, down in the bottom of the canyon, its trickle just at the edge of audible hearing. Another half hour and insects established a low hum in the background. He watched jets scribe contrails across the high, hard blue and watched a buzzard float by. He tried soaring with the buzzard for a while, floating on the thermals, looking down on the canyon, patient, watching everything.

The San Gabriels were created by the San Andreas fault, and he had read that the upsurge continued to push the range north at the rate of two inches a year. He tried to feel the rush of the earth's spin under the sun and the slow northward creep of the mountains underneath him. He didn't look at his watch. He just waited and tried not to think.

When he had been there for four hours, a coyote trotted up the road, sniffing, pouncing on a grasshopper, then sniffing some old trash someone had thrown out long ago. The coyote stopped near the rock rubble at the end of the road, vaguely disturbed, its ears cocked up, nose twitching. It looked up at the slope, looked right at him, but couldn't identify what was bothering it. It began to sniff at the base of the rubble, looking for a mouse or another grasshopper. Suddenly its attention was fixed down the road, ears quivering. It listened for a moment and then with a quick hop, vanished. Pete listened intently, but it was almost another full minute before he could make out the faint sound of an engine grinding its way up the slope at the base of the canyon.

12

"The way it was supposed to work," Pete told Annie, "I was going to hide there just to make sure nothing got out of control. The guys Dale was meeting had insisted on him being by himself, so he wanted me hidden. If they started giving him a hard time though, if it was looking like they were going to rip him off, I was going to rack a shell into the shotgun to get their attention. Then Dale was going to tell them they were covered. 'Covered,' sounds hokey doesn't it, like something out of the Westerns I watched as a kid. I was actually more concerned about Dale getting cocky with me hiding there, about him trying to rip them off. Before he dropped me off, I swore to him that if he did, I would shoot him in the knees and leave him there. I thought we had talked through all the different scenarios, agreed on what would happen depending on how it developed. I was wrong. None of it went that way."

The engine sound the coyote had heard gradually turned itself into an old white Ford panel truck, bumping along the road slowly, its driver and passenger looking intently out the windows. At the end of the road, the driver stopped and turned the truck around. They got out. The driver was a tall, skinny, white guy, greasy lank hair falling down past rounded shoulders. His partner was Chicano, much shorter, broad shoulders and chest, broader in the belly, looking like a hard medicine ball. Massive arms bulged the sleeves of his white T-shirt and jailhouse tattoos decorated his knuckles and forearms. They looked behind the rock pile at the end of the road, over the edge, down into the canyon. They scanned the top of the slope where there was a fringe of thicker brush, but didn't waste more than a glance on the barren slope right in front of them.

Pete could see them clearly, could hear the white guy flick a cigarette butt over the edge and the rasp of the match as he lit another, but they weren't saying anything. When they finished looking around, their total conversation consisted of, "Gonna be fuckin' hot again," and, "Yeah, half an hour," and, "Let's do it." They got in the truck and drove back down the road. Pete watched the dust plume and listened to the engine noise retreat. He wiggled his toes and flexed the muscles in his legs so he would be able to move quickly. Within the burlap sack, his finger checked the safety again to make sure it was off, the small bolt at the back of the trigger guard pushed all the way to the left. The buzzard still floated in the sky, higher now, a speck, the sun beating almost straight down.

More engine sounds, another dust plume coming up the road. Dale's van stopping and turning around, parking where Pete had told him. So far so good. Dale got out and looked around. After a few minutes of looking around, Dale went over to the rock pile and tried a stage whisper, "Pete?" When there was no answer he tried again, slightly louder, "Pete, where are you?" Looking down at him from the slope, Pete didn't make a sound, but remembered anew why he had always tried to stay away from Dale in the field. He was saved from further whispered interrogations by the sound of the panel truck returning. Pete figured they had only gone back a couple of miles to where the canyon branched and waited for Dale to pass before following him in.

The truck stopped about fifteen yards shy of Dale's van, blocking the road. Dale had retreated back to his van and stood by the driver's door as the pair climbed out of their truck. Pete could still hear them, sometimes still did hear them in his sleep.

"Hey, man, you got the money?"

"I got the money. You got the grass?"

"We got the grass. You show us the money. We show you the grass. We count the money, it's all there, we'll pull the vans beside each other, help you transfer the stuff."

Dale reached in his van and pulled out a blue gym bag stuffed with the money. He walked halfway toward the truck and put the bag down. As Dale bent over to unzip it, Pete, from his vantage point, could see the lump in the back of his shirt. He knew it was the .45 Dale had taken from the body of their Lieutenant when they were down to the last rounds in the weapons of the dead platoon members, trying to hold out until the helicopters arrived. He had smuggled it back to the states. Dale couldn't hit anything with a rifle, much less a pistol, and Pete had warned him a number of times that it was going to get him in trouble. The Chicano had put on a loose dungaree work shirt over his T-shirt and the white guy's shirt was now unbuttoned and untucked, revealing a hollow chest tattooed with a small broken heart. Pete figured they both were concealing pistols as well.

Dale unzipped the bag and lifted it up to show them the money inside. "It's all there, man."

The Chicano looked in, "Looks good to me, what you think, Jim?"

The white guy grinned, showing bad teeth, and said, "It's definitely a deal."

The sound of gunfire began almost before he finished speaking, the sharp barks of their pistols shooting Dale, then the deeper boom of Pete's shotgun. He could still feel it, rising up out of the hillside, dirt and burlap bags falling from him and the shotgun as he rose, jacking the first shell into the chamber, the ka-chunk that was supposed to have been a warning if needed. Even as he rose he was swinging the muzzle, the sunlight glinting off the blue-black of the barrel, the buck and blast of the twelve gauge simultaneous with the swing onto the Chicano's chest. Pumping the next shell in while he continued the swing onto the white guy. Pete centered the muzzle on the small broken heart tattoo, and squeezed off the second shot just as the guy was looking into Pete's eyes with astonishment and rage, bringing his pistol over to shoot at Pete. Without pausing, he swung back and shot the Chicano again, and then the fourth shot back for the white guy.

He ducked down behind the partial shelter of the boulder, reloading, feeding slugs in this time in case there was someone in the truck. He rolled out on the other side of the boulder quickly enough that the sounds of the gunfire were echoing back and forth in the canyon, and a few bills were floating down to the road in the still air. The shots rang in his ears, but everything else was quiet, the echoes fading out, the smell of the gunpowder hanging in the air, bills settling lightly in the dust of the road or sticking in the blood that now soaked the dirt. He kept the shotgun trained on the bodies for a long minute, then climbed and slid down to the road.

He made sure there was no one else in their truck and then went over to the bodies. They were dead, all of them, flesh torn, limbs akimbo. The tall white guy was still wearing the angry, astonished look, eyes still wide. Dale had thrown the duffel bag up in front of himself in a vain attempt to deflect their bullets, but had been hit several times in the chest and at least twice in the face.

Pete squatted down beside Dale, the earth feeling unstable beneath him. He thought he had left all this behind him, half a world away. He brushed Dale's hair up out of his eyes in a vain attempt at something and waved away a fly that had suddenly appeared.

"Annie, there was no warning, no 'give us the money.' There was no period of things sliding out of control with a chance to intercede. As soon as they knew the money was there, they started shooting. I've just made a lot of excuses, but the real bottom line is, there was no excuse. I failed to save the life of a friend, or at least what passed for a friend in those days, and I murdered two men.

"It's not like in the movies where the bad guys can't hit anything, the good guys never miss, and most importantly, there aren't any consequences as the body count piles up. In real life, to kill another human being is an act of evil, not something you make a clever wisecrack about. When they started shooting, I didn't think at all. I just rose up shooting. I've thought about it ever since.

"What I did back in that canyon and what, just a short time before, I got medals for, were essentially the same, but the difference is more than one of sanction. It's necessary, not hypocritical, for society to differentiate, to say, 'This is combat and we'll give you a medal,' and 'This is murder and we'll imprison or execute you.' Without those distinctions, society breaks down. Killing kills a portion of everyone involved, those that get buried and those that walk away, and what makes it worse is that it makes it easier to do again."

Pete was looking at Annie as he talked, searching for any of the signs and feedback that were normally part of their conversations. She had a closed, guarded look on her face and was pressed back into the arm cushions, as far away as she could get and still be on the same couch. He felt he was floundering helplessly, drowning five feet off the end of the dock because he couldn't find the words to encompass all the thoughts that had raged in his head over the years.

"The worst part is that if I somehow found myself in the same situation, I'd probably do the same thing. I know if you were threatened, I wouldn't hesitate. The basic mistake I made was letting Dale go, not convincing him how wrong it was. If he had gone on his own and they shot him, I would feel equally guilty. In a way, what I did was worse, because I understood how dumb it was. Dale was always clever, but never had any sense, particularly any sense of right and wrong."

"Pete," she spoke slowly, forming the words carefully, "as you said, you've had years to think about this. I need to go slowly here. You talked about the world shifting beneath your feet. That's what's happening to me right now."

He paused, waiting, hoping she would continue, but she didn't. He told her the rest, just touching the highlights, but remembering every moment. The temperature was in the mid-eighties and climbing, but he could feel a too-familiar coldness falling over him as he moved. He pulled the .45 from under Dale's shirt and checked it. It had a round in the chamber and was cocked and locked. He shoved it in the back of his own waistband and then shucked the shotgun shells he'd reloaded back out of the 870. He left the shotgun empty, pump back and action open. He had been careful about fingerprints when he'd cleaned and checked the gun the previous night and he still had on the brown cloth work gloves. He took Dale's hands and put fingerprints on the barrel, receiver, and stock, and on the shotgun shells. He placed the shotgun so it lay in Dale's right hand and tried to wrap the resisting fingers around the grip, placed Dale's index finger through the trigger guard. He put the unfired shotgun shells in Dale's pants pockets. He left one lying on the ground as if Dale had dropped it while starting to reload.

He went back up to the slope and picked up each of the spent shells that had ejected from shotgun. He scraped loose dirt back into the depression and tried to smooth out the edges to make it less noticeable. He picked up the entrenching tool and the burlap sacks and came back down the slope, using the sacks to brush out his tracks. As he came down the slope, he looked for the wads that cushion the buckshot from the burning gunpowder in a shotgun shell. Down on the road he found three of them where they had slowed in the air and fallen to earth behind the shot string. He looked for a few more minutes, but was unable to find the fourth. He thought that it might have gone over the edge of the slope on the far side and hoped he wasn't missing the obvious. He tossed down the four empty shells where they would have ejected if Dale had been shooting the shotgun and he dropped the wads in line from Dale to the dealers. If anyone spent much time on shot angles they would know something was wrong and might find the depression where he had waited, but he hoped the police might not spend too much time on what appeared to be a drug deal gone bad with both sides shooting each other.

He looked again in the panel truck the dealers had driven. There was no marijuana in the truck, there had never been any intent other than murder and robbery. He shook the dirt out of the burlap bags and put them and the entrenching tool in the back of the dealer's truck. He took a quick look in Dale's van, making sure there was nothing in it that might lead to him and wiped off the passenger door handle, dashboard, seat adjustment and other surfaces he might have touched.

Pete left the scattered money, twenties, fifties, and hundreds, lying in the dirt. He walked down the road, sticking to the edge to minimize footprints, prepared to slip down over the edge of the slope if he heard a car coming. When he reached the branch canyon, he climbed up the steep slope. It was a scramble, but it put him up near the paved road on the north side of the canyon and saved him a dozen miles of walking. Here on top of the canyon, the terrain was not as steep and the vegetation thicker. He paralleled the road, staying back in the laurel, sycamore and oak so he wouldn't be seen by passing motorists. He looked back and could see the buzzard that he had watched as a solitary speck high in the sky. It was now lower and had been joined by others, floating in lazy circles, waiting, waiting, as he had waited this morning.

Pete moved down through the woods at a slow jog, avoiding dry branches and heavy brush, moving quietly from long practice. He came to a parking pull-off where a trail led up from the parking area toward a view from a rocky bluff. A battered two-tone green VW bus was parked there. He crossed the trail, concerned about being seen.

He was edging back into the brush when he heard a light, thready snore. He crept toward the snore, coming out on a small bluff, where a couple slept on a blanket. Most of their clothes and an empty Lancer's bottle were in a jumbled pile by the blanket. He could smell the lingering sweet, harsh odor of marijuana smoke. Pete quietly felt through the clothes and removed the VW key. He also took the man's driver's license from his wallet, leaving the three dollars and a condom that remained.

The VW bus sputtered to life, an eight-track tape blasting *Stairway to Heaven.* Pete turned down the music and headed down the highway, back toward his motel. He adjusted the mirror, and the face looking back at him gave him a start. He'd forgotten the dirt he'd smeared on his face when he camouflaged himself that morning. Rivulets of sweat streaked the dirt down his face like war paint and somewhere during his run, a branch had scratched across his left cheekbone, adding blood drips down that side.

He scrubbed his face with the tail of his shirt while driving, traveling most of the way against the start of rush hour traffic. He drove to a public parking area at the beach about a half-mile from his motel and parked the VW bus. For the second time that day, he wiped down a vehicle for fingerprints. With a small mental apology to its owner, he left the bus with the windows rolled down and the key in the ignition. In this neighborhood, it would be stolen again within the hour.

He walked through the crowds, gradually working his way back to his motel. He showered, changed and packed. He guessed that the VW had been worth maybe $400 on the outside. He copied the owner's name and address from his driver's license on to an envelope. He retrieved his cash from its hiding place behind the fridge and put the license and five one-hundred dollar bills in it.

In Norwalk, he stopped at a post office box to mail the letter and at a service station to fill his truck and get a map. Just before he got on I-5 headed north, he stopped at a McDonald's. He hadn't eaten since before dawn that morning and he got four quarter-pounders with cheese, a chocolate milkshake and a large coffee to go.

He used the pay phone to call the San Bernardino Police Department on the southeastern edge of the Angeles National Forest. It was in the opposite direction, and he knew it wasn't the right jurisdiction for where he left the bodies. The sun was just starting to set, and if the bodies hadn't been found yet, he wanted a little more bureaucratic shuffling to delay the police arriving at the scene until after dark when it would be more difficult to prevent police tire and footprints from mixing with any he had left.

He dialed the number, and in a higher-pitched voice, striving for a different speech pattern and inflection, he told the dispatcher that he and his girlfriend had spent the day up in the Angeles and they had gotten turned around when they were driving out. He told her they had accidentally got on a dead end road, and at the end of the road there were three dead men, two trucks and guns and a lot of money in the road. The dispatcher interrupted to ask his name and address, but he told her wait, let him give the directions first. As he placed the receiver back on the hook, he could hear the dispatcher's voice asking again for his name and address.

Pro football tryouts were way too high profile now. Pete tried to focus on events since the shooting, in large part to try and block out the scenes that were running themselves over and over in his mind. He could think of many ways for the police to connect him to Dale, and he didn't feel clever about anything he had done.

That morning, as he waited, he had tried to feel the earth's spin and the mountains' movement underneath him. Now the earth felt unstable, treacherous, beneath his feet. The shooting had lasted maybe five seconds, but he knew a fault line had shifted and nothing would ever be the same.

13

"Annie, I made a lot of mistakes, with Dale and the dealers being the worst. Mistakes is too small a word. There are things I wish I could undo, but when I look back, I know I wouldn't do one thing different if it meant I didn't end up here with you."

They were both still sitting at opposite ends of the couch. She'd never seen Pete clearly miserable before. Different emotions warred within her. In the emergency room, she regularly dealt with the results of the pain and injury humans inflict on each other. She had often expressed to Pete the depth of her contempt for the assailants. When she learned that he had killed people in Vietnam, she had a difficult time with it, but didn't say anything to him. She had been twelve when the war ended, and their age difference combined with the geographical distance made Vietnam seem distant, historical. Now she was hearing that this man, who she loved to the core of her being, was in Alaska because he had shot two men in Los Angeles and might still be wanted for it.

There was a tightness in her throat that made talking

difficult. He looked at her, not saying anything, but with questions in his eyes that she didn't know the answers to, didn't trust herself to try and respond. After a little while, she told him she needed to go to bed, that she needed some time to come to grips with what he had told her. She got up and, with a small kiss on his head, left him sitting on the couch while she went up the stairs. She heard the door to the deck open and close. She knew he would be out there, staring into the dark at things only he could see.

Hector had followed her upstairs, pushing against her, demanding her attention. He could tell there was something wrong and with dog wisdom was offering the only way he knew to make things better. She gave in and spent some time sitting on the floor, hugging him, scratching his chest and behind his ears. She pressed her face into the smooth, soft fur on the top of his head and whispered nonsense in his ears. Heck had been right, it did make her feel better. She went to bed with the dog curled in the doorway of the bedroom, on guard against whatever made her so sad.

A light mist was falling, and out on the deck the air was cold and clean washed. The light breeze blowing on Pete's face felt good, the air so pure it should be able to wash away sins. The moon above the clouds gave just enough light to pick up the white of small waves breaking out in Lynn Canal. The light from the upstairs windows above cast down three rectangles of illumination on the foliage and rocks. After a bit, two of the rectangles of light disappeared, and then a shadow passed through the third. He knew it was Annie turning off the hall and bathroom lights, and then crossing between the windows and the bedside lamp to her side of the bed. Some time later, when she cut off the bedside light, its sudden absence hurt his heart.

The wind was picking up a bit, scattering the clouds, and it smelled like snow. He said a small prayer, the substance of which he had repeated many times. It was mainly a prayer of thanks, mainly thanks for Annie. There was special emphasis tonight to his normal request that the Lord watch over her and protect her. He asked God to be with them and, as always, asked that those who had died, his family and Annie's, Helen and the rest of her boat's crew, all the dead members of his platoon, and those that he had killed, be with God.

The chill eventually forced Pete inside. The day before he had made brownies, and he got several and poured a large glass of milk. In the bookshelves tucked under the stairs there was a shelf of tattered Louis L'Amour paperbacks, remnants of his days scrounging for books in far-flung fishing ports. He had three other books currently going, but tonight he needed solid craftsmanship and no moral ambiguity - milk, brownies and Louis L'Amour.

Sleep finally began to come in the early morning hours, just as he was finishing the book. The little cat had been sleeping on his chest while he read, and now she followed him up the stairs. She jumped up on the bathroom counter, contemplated him as he brushed his teeth, and then with a quick bound, jumped on his shoulders. She sat there, swishing her tail around his neck, pleased with herself. Pete remembered a couple of weeks ago she had done the same thing when Annie was in the bathroom as well, both of them getting ready for bed. He had joked that if weren't for her, he would have ended up a strange, lonely man living way out the road with a cat on his shoulders. She responded that he was a strange man with a cat on his shoulders and he said, "Yes, but I'm no longer lonely."

He slipped out of his clothes and slid into bed with Annie. Normally, whenever he got in bed, she would wake just enough to snuggle in tight. Tonight she lay sleeping on the far side of the bed and, in her sleep, pulled away when he lightly kissed her. Pete lay on his side of the bed, sleep having retreated again. For the first time since Annie had come to his bed, he felt alone.

Annie was confused. She knew it had been years since she'd worked in San Diego, but she was there again. After a few moments, she recognized the night, and this time she knew what was going to happen. She tried desperately not to be part of this, to climb back to reality, but she was swept along, not remembering, but rather reliving the night. She was working as the triage nurse in the emergency room. She recognized the little girl with tonsillitis, the homeless man with the abscessed sores on his legs, the gang member with stab wounds. She watched herself meeting the ambulance with the business man who had the heart attack at the convention.

It was a Friday night, a little busier than normal, but she blamed it on the full moon that hung over San Diego that night. She'd read studies that said the phases of the moon had no effect on people's behavior, but she'd never met a cop or nurse who believed it. Tonight, though, was different. Tonight, she knew what was coming. She tried again to reassert reality, but it was no use. The radio crackled to life and told them of the bus carrying a college pep band, on its way back from a basketball game, hit by the tractor trailer. The accident was less than a mile from them, and a flood of the most serious cases would be coming through the door in a matter of minutes. They immediately started the established crisis procedures, calling in additional doctors and nurses, clearing out as many of the non-critical patients as possible, laying out supplies.

Calls were still being made as the paramedics rolled

the first of the injuries through the door. This time, she knew in advance that all the nearby hospitals were also busy, that the broken bodies were going to come in the door faster than they could possibly keep up. She was reliving each moment as she took the information from the paramedics, made the quick assessments, started aid, but was also outside herself, watching, knowing what was coming. She was doing a good job, but already feeling the horror that would mount as the injured, the crushed and the torn, the dead and the dying continued to come through the door. She never had any doubt that at its most basic, triage was ordinary mortals making decisions about who could hang on for a while, who was going to die regardless, and who, with immediate medical attention, might be saved; decisions that would have been far more comfortable left to God.

College and grad school had not been that many years ago for her, but the difference in years seemed enormous. These were just kids who were dying. She had made it through the night with the horror growing and growing inside her, not letting it bubble out, because she knew if she didn't do her job well, more might die. They finished in the early hours of dawn, exhausted and numb. She tried to focus on the many who they'd saved, and that kept her together as she finished off the paperwork, checked out, and changed in the nurses' locker room. By then most of the others were gone, the new shift already on duty, and she was alone. She kept herself together while she changed, but made the mistake of sitting down on a metal folding chair in the corner. That's when it all came out, all the horror and grief and doubt about the decisions she had made. Suddenly she no longer had the strength to keep herself in the chair. She slid down into a huddle on the floor. She could see herself, curled in a fetal position on the polished linoleum, sobbing uncontrollably. This was the first time during the dream that the knowledge of what was going to happen was comforting.

Mrs. Garcia walked into the locker room and stopped, looking at her. Mrs. Garcia was the supervising nurse for the emergency room, a tall, spare black woman in her fifties with such personal presence and professional competence that even the most senior doctors treated her with deference. Annie had never heard anyone call her anything other than Mrs. Garcia, had never heard her raise her voice, but knew that any nurse in the department would rather have the Chief Administrator scream at them than have Mrs. Garcia take them aside, and in quiet and measured tones, discuss a mistake or failing.

She could hear those calm and measured tones now, careful English with just a hint of a Central American accent. She could feel the cool hands as they handed her a tissue, wiped her tears. Many times she had watched with admiration as Mrs. Garcia had worked with patients, watched as calm and strength seemed to flow into them in a process that seemed to be a bit closer to sorcery than medicine. Annie seemed to feel the cool flowing into herself now. She pulled herself upright to sit on the floor, leaning back against the lockers.

Mrs. Garcia was talking to her, talking about what it took to be a good nurse, telling her that she did a very good job last night under very difficult circumstances. They had talked about the melding of care and medicine, about the responsibility of a job where some of the decisions were literally life and death. She could still hear Mrs. Garcia talking to her.

"Annie, we owe the dead and dying and their families our respect and sympathy, but more important is what we owe the living, those we can save. You're worrying that you made decisions that let people die. What you did is make decisions that helped people live. You're going to be a very good nurse, but you have to be able to make those decisions and be at peace with yourself."

"Mrs. Garcia, he's alive and they're dead. I think I can save him, but he killed them. He told me about it. I feel like I was part of killing them now, and I'm not sure I really know who he is."

"Do you know he loves you?"

"I've never had any doubt about that."

"And are you sure you love him?"

"I'm sure about that. I'm scared, though. Pete's the kindest, gentlest men I've ever met. It's who he is. I knew he was in Vietnam, but when he got back, he killed those two men in the canyon, the drug dealers. And now we're involved in something with drugs again, and it seems like we are on the edge of violence. We sat on the couch, and he told me if he thought I was threatened, he wouldn't hesitate to do it again. This isn't what I do, you and I, we help heal people, we help repair the violence. We don't cause it or participate in it."

Mrs. Garcia was quiet for a long time, looking inside herself, and when she spoke her voice was slightly different, the accent thickening as she spoke. "I grew up in a little village way back in the jungle in Nicaragua. I used to be sure about who caused the violence there, but that was a long time ago, and I'm not as sure anymore. But I participated in that violence, and when I finally left there as a young woman, it was because I would have been killed if I'd stayed. I do what I do now, in part, to atone for what I did back there."

Annie didn't know what to say. Mrs. Garcia was starting to look like she wanted to go, vanishing for moments, but when Annie focused on the polished floor, she found she could will her back.

"I need you to stay here with me. I don't know what to do."

Mrs. Garcia reached out and held Annie's face in her hands. "Child, life is a confusion, death is a confusion, and love, ah, love is the grandest confusion of all. You respect the dead, but you save the man who's alive and who needs you. He's a good man worth saving. I gotta go now. I'm glad to see you turned out so fine. I knew you could."

Annie tried to keep her there, tried to focus and bring her back, but Mrs. Garcia was gone. She left a feeling of cool and calmness in Annie though, and the feeling stayed as the nurses' locker room slowly faded away and she realized she was in their bed, tight at the very edge of her side. The clouds had partially cleared, and the moon was shining in the window on her face. She lay there for a few moments, half awake, trying to bring the dream and Mrs. Garcia back. There were high clouds racing across the night sky, and the moonlight in the room dimmed and brightened. The San Diego emergency room began to mix with memories from her childhood, baby-sitting and reading bedtime stories. The phrase "In the great, green room" seemed to fill her mind. Pete was sleeping on his side of the bed, turned away from her. She rolled over and snuggled into him, her leg thrown over his leg, her body melded to the curve of his back, her arm thrown over his arm, her face tucked into his neck. In his sleep, Pete wiggled backwards slightly for a better fit, a sense of happiness and rightness entering his sleep as he became just conscious enough to enjoy the feel of her, the hug of the leg and arm, the weight of breasts on his back, and the feeling that a much greater weight had just been lifted from him. In the morning he would have the faintest of memories of Annie murmuring in her sleep, "Mrs. Garcia," and "Goodnight moon."

14

Consciousness slowly invaded, and the first two things he was aware of were the warmth of Annie sleeping next to him and a profound feeling of relief, peace and gratefulness. His shoulder was cramped, but he was willing to lie there forever, held by her, cradled in commitment. He didn't know how she would feel when she woke up, but the weight of carrying his secret felt lifted.

He felt the little cat bound up onto the bed and the pressure of her footsteps. He could feel her stare, but refused to open his eyes. When staring didn't work, she tried a firm bat to his nose. He squinched his eyes tighter, but couldn't stop his smile. Satisfied he was in there, the little cat began to scrape her head across the stubble on his chin. Pete knew it was a lost cause, but tried to feign sleep a little longer. He felt another slight pressure on the edge of the bed and knowing what it would be, opened his eyes into Heck's stare. Attracted by the activity, Heck was standing there, pressing his head on the bed, staring into Pete's eyes with a message that said, get up and let me out.

Pete tried whispering to him to go lie down, but knew it was futile. He gave up and tried to slide out from under Annie's arm and out of bed without waking her. He tucked his pillow where he had been, but she roused enough to whisper, "Coffee," as she pulled the covers around her more tightly.

When he brought the coffee back from the kitchen, he found that Annie's embrace in the night had not been just an unconscious reflex. In the gathering light of dawn that suffused the room, their lovemaking had a mutual fierceness and tenderness of reaffirmation and possession.

Pete replaced their coffee, which had grown cold, and they talked about what to do. Not only his mood, but the skies were clearing this morning. As they talked, the northern dawn yielded to a blue, blue sky, the pink slowly fading out of the small clouds above the Chilkats.

They didn't decide what to do, in fact they reversed positions. Pete suggested they go to the Troopers about the pack, that all these years of hiding he'd probably been reacting to his own guilt, and that there was no reason to think the police had not accepted the shooting as Dale and the dealers shooting each other. Annie, new to the revelation of why her husband so rigorously obeyed all traffic laws, shied away from photo-snapping tourists, and refused to go through Customs to cross the Canadian border, was now unwilling to start any course that might somehow lead back to California and take him away from her.

Pete had to be at Readers' to open, and they agreed she would meet him for dinner. He drove in, feeling unreasonably happy despite the lack of resolution. KTOO, the local public radio station, had a good rock show on, and he had the volume turned up as he thought about the pack and Kotkin and their situation. There were little wisps of fog still lying over Auke Bay when he passed it. The *Bon Temps* was out there, but he couldn't pick out its mast through the thicket of power trolling poles, antennas and other masts.

The road curved in past Auke Lake. The lily pads all gone yellow now, a few float planes pulled up among them. The reflection of the Mendenhall Glacier and the snowy mountains behind it floated in the still water. In the Mendenhall Valley, Egan Drive turned into a divided four lane and continued along the edge of Gastineau Channel toward town. The high tide was lapping at the edge of the road, but six hours later there would be a mile of sand and mud between the mainland and Douglas Island.

He arrived at Readers' a half hour before time to open. He was still preoccupied with what to do about the pack, but he stopped to clear his head for a moment before he walked up to the front door. Whenever he had been gone from the store for over a day, he tried to stop to look at it fresh, as if he were a customer walking in for the first time. The window display looked good, but there were some cigarette butts on the sidewalk in front and he made a mental note to sweep. There was a bulletin board for announcements of community events just inside the door and he was pleased to see Jeremy had already purged it of the past weekend's events.

The store was a little larger than he needed, so when he had first bought it, he had spent many evenings building more shelves so he could display as many titles as possible face out. He had found several old drift logs that were riddled with marine worm holes and had cut them into silvered, worm-holed shelving.

Pete moved through the sections, straightening books, reshelving books that had gotten out of order. He turned on the lamps by the chairs. He had gone to garage sales and bought used lamps and comfortable chairs and small couches and scattered them throughout the store to make it an inviting place for people to spend time. Several book groups met there over lunch or in the early evening. He knew of two married couples who had first met while browsing at Readers' on their lunch hours.

There was a cork board on the end of each shelf. He encouraged customers to write book recommendations or comments on three by five cards, and he tacked them up along with reviews from the *Washington Post Book World*, the *New York Times Review of Books* and the *Wall Street Journal*. Title Wave, a bookstore in Anchorage, had a section of shelves where each employee of the store put twenty or thirty books they particularly liked and he'd done the same. He worked to develop a feeling of belonging among his customers, and the store was slowly making money, doing a little better each year.

Throughout the day, Pete tried to focus on the store. The lunch rush was over and he was up in the office when the phone rang. Jean got the call down at the front counter, and a few moments later, her voice came over the intercom, "It's Annie."

"What did you do to Jean this time?" Annie asked.

"Hi, hello, and I love you, too. And I didn't do anything to her, why?"

"I believe her words were, 'Your husband is up in the office trying to understand how to put a book order together.' Anytime she refers to you as my husband, instead of Pete, I know you've transgressed."

Pete chuckled, "You know what the back of her car looks like."

"I know what the bumper stickers look like. There are too many of them to actually see the back of the car."

"Yeah, this morning she came in mad because under 'Save the Whales' someone had written 'Collect the Whole Set' and under 'Free Tibet' had written, "with one purchased at regular price.' I made the mistake of laughing when she told me."

Annie laughed lightly, and the sound made him feel good.

"You still coming in for dinner this evening? I haven't had lunch yet, but I already have visions of enchiladas dancing in my head," he said.

"Your idea of romance, 'Mexican food, a glass of beer, and thou.' I'll come in a little early so Jean and I can commiserate about what an insensitive brute I'm married to. Maybe she'll forgive you by tomorrow. "

They chatted for a little while longer before hanging up. The pack and what had happened in the canyons of Los Angeles were still very much there for both of them, but now it was something to be dealt with, rather than a hidden land mine, awaiting a misstep to wreak devastation in their lives.

The promise of the morning's weather held through the afternoon and tourists off the cruise ships kept the business steady. He wondered if he should delay shifting away from the tourist-oriented displays. Cruise ships now came well into September, but the bad weather that was typical then tended to keep the tourists huddled in the T-shirt shops on lower Franklin near the docks.

With the tourists and the normal lunch crowd, it was pushing three o'clock before the customers slacked a bit. Jean had had her lunch and seemed to have defrosted slightly. He promised her that he would be right back, and ducked out the door. The Triangle Bar was a quick half block down the street, and Doreen, the bartender, greeted him as he came in the door. "Hey, Pete, haven't seen you in a few days. Four?"

"Nah, Annie's coming in for dinner, how 'bout three today?"

He wandered back to nod at the guys playing pinochle at the table in the back corner. The players seemed to change, but he had never been in the bar when the game wasn't going, the old men absorbed in the cards and their quiet conversation. There were several regulars sitting at the bar, beers or shots in front of them, watching three different shows on TVs over the bar, with the sound muted on all of them.

Not many tourists wandered into the Triangle, but today an older fellow sat there, a mixed drink in front of him, looking as though he had found refuge while his wife visited the gift shops up and down the street. He swiveled to look at Pete appraisingly when he had heard Doreen ask about four. Now he slowly grinned and lifted his glass in a mock toast as he watched her ladle chili onto the three hot dogs. "Hi there, big fellow. I thought you were ready for some serious drinking when I heard you order."

"Just a late lunch." Pete tried to be polite as he paid and thanked Doreen. He never liked anyone, except Annie, calling him, "big fellow," but knew the man meant no harm. He finished two of the chili-dogs as he walked back to the store. The sun was warm on his face, and he had a sense of contentment, a feeling that things were starting to slide back into their normal place.

He was hungry again long before Annie came in, but now they were seated in El Sombrero. Liz came out to chat.

Back when Pete was living almost as a hermit, when he forced himself to start going out where he had to talk with people, El Sombrero had been the restaurant where he came most often. Liz and Fritz's parents had owned it then, and they and the rest of the kids had been the waiters, waitresses and assistant cooks.

It had been like eating with family who served great Mexican food and didn't object that he read at the table. He knew it was silly, but the first time he ever took Annie there, he felt a little like he was taking her home for a meal with the folks. He had been embarrassed, but foolishly pleased, when Liz and Fritz both surreptitiously flashed him big grins and thumbs up from the kitchen.

Music was playing in the background at the restaurant. Just after they had started on the enchiladas, it switched to the guitars of the Gypsy Kings. Pete grinned at Annie and waggled his eyebrows. "I could clear the table?"

She smiled back at him, "I'm pretty sure there are health department regulations against that."

They were both thinking back to early August. She and Pete had been in the kitchen cleaning up after dinner. It was a stormy evening and they had a fire in the fireplace. Van Morrison was on the CD player singing *Have I Told You Lately?* Pete hugged her, softly kissing her neck and ears. They wound up slow dancing around the kitchen, just them and the music and the storm outside.

Their CD player had switched to the Gypsy Kings and they had progressed from slow dancing to desperate haste. Using the kitchen table and the living room floor on the way, they wound up on the couch as the last song of the album played. Afterward, they lay together, watching the fire, listening to the music and the storm outside, chuckling about where did that come from and feeling the world was a very good place.

They were still joking with each other when Annie's beeper went off. When the hospital paged her, it was rarely good news. Pete watched carefully as Annie borrowed the phone at the cashier's stand. It wasn't her ER face, preparing herself as she went in to help deal with an emergency, and it wasn't the look of annoyance he would have expected if they were calling to see if she could cover for someone who'd called in sick. She was on the phone for some time, mainly listening, occasionally asking a question. When she hung up the phone, she just looked very, very sad as she stood there for a moment.

"Randy died," she told him as she slipped back into the booth. "I'd asked the nurses on his floor to call me if he had any change. I kept expecting to get a call saying he was conscious."

Pete held her hands, not saying anything, just giving her time. "The nurses asked me to tell you how sorry they were," she said. "You know, they'd always wondered if his coma was real. Every time you visited him, his vital signs would be better for a while.

"This evening, a man who sounds a lot like Kotkin, came in to visit him. He was in there by himself when Beth at the nurses' station noticed on the monitors that all of Randy's signs were starting to depress. She went to the room and found Randy, still unconscious and the man leaning over him, whispering right into his face. She said the man had the most malicious look she'd ever seen on a person. She told him to leave immediately, but Randy's signs just kept going down and within the hour he died. The doctors did the full Code Blue, crash cart procedures, but none of it worked. It has them all slightly spooked, it seems to them that he just decided to die and there was nothing they could do to stop it."

"What happened to Kotkin?"

"He left when Beth told him to. They don't know anything about him, except to get in to see Randy, he had told them he was an attorney representing Randy's mother. Since she went back to Los Angeles she's had an attorney calling every day to check on his condition. It has Fred, the administrator, totally frazzled, this lawyer calling every day. When they called Mrs. Dionne to notify her, she hadn't sent her attorney. There's no sign that Kotkin, if that's who it was, did anything other than talk to Randy, but Fred is paranoid about Mrs. Dionne suing, and they don't know who the man really is."

"You didn't tell her who Kotkin is?"

"No. I figured we ought to think about that first."

15

Toni Price was singing her heart out on the store's stereo about how money couldn't buy love or a good man's touch, conveying pain and passion in her dark voice. Pete was hunched over his desk working on a display. It was a quiet morning, Jeremy working the counter, only a few customers in the store. Annie would be working the afternoon shift at the hospital and Pete had left Hector home with her.

She was just starting to sing about how if teardrops were diamonds from the African mine when the music suddenly stopped and after a moment, Enya's soothing tones came on the stereo. Jeremy's reproachful voice came over the intercom, "Pete, I've told you and told you about music suitable for the store. We just had a woman who was looking at books in the Interpersonal Relationships section, and in the middle of that song she put her face in her hands, started sobbing and rushed out of the store."

He had inherited the name, "Interpersonal Relationships" for the section when he took over the store. He had intended to change it, but it was one of the many small battles where he had decided it was wiser to yield to Jean and Jeremy for now.

"It was probably the section's name made her cry," Pete said. "Next time she comes in, put on the same CD, back it up a few cuts and play *Hurtback* for her. Then show her the books on guns."

He could tell Jeremy didn't think he was funny. He was probably right. Enya's soothing chant continued. The problem was, he didn't want to be soothed.

It had been four days since Randy's death, and he and Annie had made no progress toward any decisions. They phoned all the hotels in town and asked for Kotkin, but it appeared he'd left town again. The *Bon Temps* was still in Auke Bay. Pete learned that while Kotkin was here, he had arranged for moorage and someone to watch the boat until it could be delivered down south. This late in the year, they would be hard pressed to find a delivery captain willing to face autumn's storms.

Pete and Annie talked about dozens of different courses of action. Giving the drugs back wasn't an alternative either of them could accept, but every other alternative seemed to create its own set of problems and dangers. It had become like a sore tooth he couldn't leave alone. Doing nothing seemed like the best course of action at the moment, but doing nothing left him in a dark mood, grouchy about things out of his control.

He tried to focus on the task at hand. He was putting together a display of young adult books. It was part of his annual fall replacement of tourist-oriented Alaskana displays with fresh ones aimed at local readers and customers. Katherine Patterson, one of his favorite young adult authors, had won another Newberry Medal and he had obtained an oversized replica of the medal from the ALSC to use as the display centerpiece. He marked a line on colored poster board to back the medal display. We was using a heavy old yard-stick he had found in the building's attic. It was printed with advertising from a turn-of-the-century hardware store that used to be in the building.

"You Pete McLoglin?" Pete started slightly; he hadn't heard the man climb the stairs.

"McLaughlin, Mac-Lauf-lin. May I help you?"

The man walked in, shut the door behind him, and stared disdainfully around the office. He didn't look like the average customer or tourist who wandered into the shop. Pete looked at him curiously. He was in his early thirties, big, about six-four with a bodybuilder's physique bulging under tight white jeans and a yellow cashmere sweater. The sweater's V-neck revealed an expanse of tanned hairless chest and a heavy gold chain. He had almost shoulder length blond hair, which he brushed straight back. Pete thought he looked like someone from the cover of a romance paperback except for the sneer and something not quite right about his eyes.

There was no answer as the man continued to inspect and dismiss the contents of the office, the books stacked in every corner, the boxes, the aging computer on a battered wooden desk, Heck's couch. His inspection came to rest on Pete. Pete was still sitting at the desk. It was chilly in the office and he was wearing an old cardigan sweater over a canvas shirt. The half-frame glasses he wore for close work perched on his nose. Pete tried again, "Do you need help finding a book?"

"A book? What do I look like?"

It was an interesting question, but Pete thought the man probably wouldn't like his answer.

"You found a sailboat, you took something off of it, and I came to get it."

So this was one of the men Kotkin had told him he would not enjoy having visit him. In some ways it was a relief to have all his amorphous worry made tangible here in front of him.

"Please listen to me carefully. I told this to Mr. Kotkin and I want to tell it to you. I don't have anything that belongs to you or Mr. Galvan. I turned the boat and everything on it over to the Coast Guard. "

"No, you fat old fuck, that's been checked. If you didn't have it, you would've gone to the police about us by now. You've got it, and I want it."

Old? Fat? Pete smiled to himself. He wants it, maybe he'll get it, maybe I'll sit on him. "I should warn you, I grew up reading tough guy detective fiction, all of Dashiell Hammett and Raymond Chandler and all of John McDonald's Travis McGee series. I just finished the latest Robert Parker. For that matter, not only have I read all Parker's Spenser novels, I've read all of Richard Starke's Parker novels, and all of T. Jefferson Parker's crime novels, though I have to concede his protagonists probably are outside the classic tough guy genre."

"What the fuck are you talking about?" The man was bobbing on the balls of his feet now, looking confused and angry, whatever was wrong with his eyes more evident.

Pete tried again, "Seriously, I don't have anything from the boat, and if I found something illegal, I'd call the police. You need to go back to your Mr. Galvan and tell him he's mistaken."

"Fatman, Mr. Galvan doesn't make mistakes, and I'm not here to play with you. He told me I could use my complete discretion. You could get hurt. This dump could burn. You know what might happen that I would really enjoy?"

"You might find a new flavor of steroids that doesn't make you constipated and impotent?"

"Listen, you fat fuck, I was out at the hospital yesterday watching your wife. Good-looking cunt. Can't understand what she sees in you."

"Please listen to me carefully, you're about to make a mistake."

"I already told you, we don't make mistakes. Mr. Galvan has this kid that can find out anything on the internet. He researched both of you, went back over ten years. Saw your wife had a little problem keeping her credit cards current before she moved here. You must not amount to much, kid said he'd almost never seen less about someone." Pete was briefly grateful his football days were pre-Internet.

"I like what they found on your wife, though, all these stories and photos about her winning those races. You wanna see my favorite?"

It was a striking photo and Pete recognized it as soon as the man unfolded it and held it up. One of the local paper's photographers was known for his penchant for photographing attractive female athletes for the sports page. The clipping was from last year, the two-mile race that was part of the Fourth of July festivities. Annie had won the women's division, beating two other runners to the tape by inches. It was a hot day, she like most of the women runners, was wearing only brief shorts and a running bra. It was a color photo taken right at the finish line with Annie in full stride, her head and both arms back, her hair gleaming more red than normal in the sun, her chest thrust forward to break the tape.

"You know fatman, I really like the picture, we all did. The part I really like was the part in the article where they're talking to this other woman she beat. The woman says 'If you can't get in front of Annie before the last quarter mile, it's awfully tough to beat her. She just doesn't seem to feel pain when she's in her finishing kick.' That part got me hard, reminded me of a young lady I had to do some business with once. She thought she was tough, but, oh, she felt pain during her finishing kick, she surely did."

"You've made a mistake," Pete's voice sounded quiet and dead, and far away.

"Miss-stake? Miss-stake? I don't think so. I think she needs some beef steak." The man grabbed his crotch with both hands, doing a poor Michael Jackson imitation.

"Tell you what, fatman, because I feel sorry for her, married to a fuck like you, I'll give her some of my special beef steak, give her some pleasure with the pain, before I – "

Pete swung the yardstick as hard as he could, trying to decapitate him, wishing the yardstick were the claymore that hung above the mantel at home. The man was quick and got his chin down in time to partially deflect the blow, but holding his crotch, he wasn't able to get his hands up in time to completely block it. He gasped for air, but threw a looping right, which Pete took on his left arm and shoulder. It was a hard blow that rocked him a little as he stepped in and with the side of his right fist, came down as hard as he could on the man's right collarbone, swinging through, feeling the bone crack. Pete followed with a short left hook to the man's middle that bent him over. He grabbed the long blond hair and, holding the man's head down, brought his knee up into his chest, four, five times.

The man's legs were buckling, but he tried to grab Pete's leg. Pete let go of the hair and drove his elbow down as hard as he could over the kidney, knocking the man to the floor. He rolled over as he hit and Pete dropped on him with all his weight on one knee landing on the man's chest. Pete grabbed the long hair again, stretching his head back. The yardstick had broken off into a jagged stub and Pete pressed the point into the man's throat hard enough that the sharper splinters broke the skin.

For almost a minute they stayed frozen there, Pete breathing hard and trembling with fury. Finally he got control of himself enough to whisper, "I really want to kill you, but I might not. Are you listening to me very carefully? Just nod."

The man nodded his head a quarter inch. "I tried to tell you were making a mistake, but you wouldn't listen. Do you know how stupid that is? Nod." The man nodded, a very small, careful nod.

"I still want to kill you. I want to put your body in that box over there, and tomorrow I'll say I'm going fishing and run over to Chatham Strait where there are places the water is six thousand feet deep. Tie you to cinderblocks. The water is so cold, you won't bloat and try to float back up. The crabs and sand fleas will eat out your eyes first. It'll only take maybe a week for them to strip your whole body down to bones. Do you think I should do that?"

The man shook his head side to side very carefully.

"I'm going to explain your mistake to you so you don't ever make it again. If I let you live, it's only so you can explain the mistake to your friends, so they don't ever make the same mistake. Do you understand?" Pete's voice was still a bare whisper, trembling with fury.

A nod.

"The mistake was, you threatened my wife. I used to be a nice person, and then I wasn't for a long time, but I've been happy lately. Ever since I met her, I've been working hard on becoming a nice person again. She saved my life, not my body, but my soul. You know anything about souls?"

The man was frozen, trying to figure out the right answer with the jagged stub pressed into his throat by a crazy person.

"She's the only reason I haven't killed you already. She's what keeps me alive. If you ever do anything to her, I wouldn't have any reason to care about living, and I would have every reason to make sure that you and your friends all die. Do you understand me?"

A careful nod.

"And if I ever think you might do something to her, if I ever even think you might be thinking about doing something to her, I'm going to find you and kill you. Do you understand?"

Another nod.

Pete had to stop, to keep himself under control, his arm was trembling from the warring muscles trying to hold back from shoving the jagged stub through the man's neck. Pete took several deep breaths, eased the pressure on the broken yardstick, and let go of the man's hair. With his free hand, he fished through man's pockets and found a wad of cash and a large Spyderco knife with a serrated blade and a thumbhole in the blade so you could flip it open with one hand. He pulled out his wallet and found one of the electronic cards that serve as hotel room keys. A California driver's license and credit cards identified the man as Vincent R. Strellhi. "Vincent, huh? What do they call you? Vince? Vinney? Never mind. Your license says you're from Los Angeles. These credit cards have enough room on them for a plane ticket home?"

"I already got a ticket." It came out as a croaky whisper, sounding like something was broken in his voice box.

"Doesn't matter Vince. We're changing your flight plans. I happen to know there is an Alaska Airlines jet that leaves for Seattle in about an hour. One advantage to all these tourists, lots of flights in and out. We are going to call and buy a ticket right now. We're using your credit card, so I'll book you first class. You can self-medicate with the free booze. You and I are going to take a cab to the airport, which you're also going to pay for. You're going to get on the plane, fly home, and never come back. I'll check out of your hotel for you after you're gone. You're going to tell your friends that I don't have anything of theirs. This is important. I do not have anything of theirs. Tell your Mr. Galvan that you used this discretion you talked about to thoroughly investigate, and I do not have anything of his.

"Vince, do you understand that the only reason I'm letting you live is so you can deliver this message? If I ever see you again, no matter where we are, I'm going to kill you on the spot because you thought about taking my wife away from me. Vince, do we understand each other?"

"I can't go back like that. Galvan will have me killed."

Pete was still trembling with fury. "Then you have a serious problem, cause if you don't go, I'm going kill you right now. And if you don't deliver my message properly I'm going to find a way to tell Galvan that I gave you the pack and you must have double-crossed him. We understand each other?"

"Yeah."

Pete grabbed him by his waistband and by his hair, and with care not to show any effort, he lifted Vince off the floor and set him on his feet.

"Vince?"

"Yeah?"

"Right about now it would be natural to be thinking, son-of-a-bitch sucker punched me. Hadn't landed that first lucky swing with the yardstick, I'd have hurt him. If that's what you're thinking Vince, it would be a serious mistake."

"Fuck, you broke something inside me, and my collarbone's broken. I need to go to the hospital."

"You want to stop off in Seattle, have a hospital patch you up before you fly down to L.A., that's your business. Right now we're going to get you a reservation. Sit in that chair while I call."

Pete called Alaska Airlines and identified himself as Vincent Strellhi. Using Vince's MasterCard, he bought a first class ticket, one-way to L.A.

He called down on the intercom and asked Jeremy if he could watch the store for a while, to call Jean if it got busy and he needed help. Before they started down the office stairs, he reached out and tapped Vince lightly on the broken collarbone. Vince cursed and doubled over in pain. "Vince, we need to hurry out to the airport to make sure you don't miss the plane. I gave you a little tap 'cause I want you have a tiny sample of how much it's going to hurt if I hit you there again. I don't want you to even look cross-eyed before you get on the plane and leave. We clear about what you're going to do if I don't kill you?"

16

"**This is the final boarding call** for Flight 76, Alaska Airlines nonstop service for Seattle. All passengers should be on board." The last of the passengers were hugging family members before heading down the ramp.

"Sounds like it's time for you to get on board, Vince." Pete had Vince's boarding pass, and they were sitting together in the far corner of the departure lounge. Though they didn't look like each other, they were both much bigger than anyone else there. Pete hoped anyone who wondered might decide they must be related, perhaps a brother seeing off his sibling, who wasn't looking too good.

"Shit, I can't fly, I . . ." Vince's words trailed off as he saw something in Pete's eyes and knew he wanted to be far away from this crazy man as soon as possible. Vince's clutched his right arm tightly across his body. He had an angry welt on his neck. It was a cool day, but he had a sheen of sweat.

"You don't have to flap your arms. You can just sit there

in first class and drink heavily. Vince, this is very important for all our sakes. You listening to me?"

Vince nodded warily.

"Make sure your friends know that I don't have anything that belongs to them, and if they ever even think about doing anything to Annie it would be the worst mistake they ever made. I still want to kill you for what you said about Annie, so don't screw this up."

Pete watched as Vince boarded and the jet shut its doors. He figured his time of greatest immediate risk was now, while Vince was out of his control and before the plane left. He had told Vince that if he asked the stewardess to call the police, they would see whether the police believed a local business owner or a hired thug up from L.A., but he hadn't felt confident in his bluff. He kept having visions of interviews with police leading to a follow-up visit; Mr. McLaughlin, it seems that the Los Angeles Police Department has been wanting to talk to you about a shooting for a long time now.

He watched the yellow tug tractor back the plane away from the gate and wished he could see through the skin of the plane. The old Eskimo painted on the tail of Alaska Airline's jets smiled inscrutably, offering no clues.

When the jet finally lifted off the runway, he felt a small portion of the tension drain away. During the cab ride back into town, he wondered what Vince would tell Galvan, whether there was really any chance of this just going away.

He was used to making this drive almost every day, but riding as a passenger, he had the luxury of gazing out the window. It was a low tide and he watched the sunlight shafting through the clouds to illuminate patches of the sand and marsh grass as they drove alongside Gastineau Channel. For millions of years the Mendenhall Glacier, just back of town, had been grinding bits of the mountains into glacial till to flow down the river and gradually fill in the channel with the Mendenhall Flats. Boats still crossed the bar on high tides, but on a minus tide you could walk across to Douglas Island in a pair of rubber boots. Red and green channel markers sat stranded by the low tide on the sand on either side of what looked like a small shallow creek. The clouds shifted again and the autumn sunlight came through, slanting in under the dark clouds and making the channel markers and the sand around them glow against the shadowed background.

To welcome the tourists, the city put the flags from the fifty states on top of the streetlight poles along this section of Egan Drive coming into town. The wind was building, snapping the flags when Pete got out of the cab in front of the Westmark. The key card didn't have a room number on it and as Pete rode up the elevator, he wondered if Vince had been truthful about his room number. Gray herringbone carpet, green herringbone wallpaper, green doors with brass knobs and locks. Pete slid the card into the lock of 602 and there was a soft click as the door unlocked. Pete wondered if this was technically a burglary. He guessed it was.

The room had already been made up, but Pete hung the 'Do Not Disturb' sign. The room was far nicer than those he'd stayed in scattered through Alaska's fishing ports, a king-size bed, prints on the walls, an exercycle in one corner. The windows across the far wall had a view looking out over the cruise ships in the harbor and across the channel at Mount Jumbo on Douglas Island.

He stood there for a moment, trying to absorb what he could of Vince. He was neater than Pete would have guessed. The clothes were hung in the closet all aligned the same way, pants and shirts grouped together with two inches between each garment. Toilet articles were aligned precisely on the bathroom counter, a variety of body building supplements arranged by size of bottle on the back of the toilet. On the bedside table, there were several muscle magazines, one about professional wrestling, and a *Hustler*. A laptop computer was on the desk by the window.

Pete took the hotel's plastic laundry bag and scooped in Vince's toilet articles, supplements, magazines and other personal items. From the drawers, he threw in the socks and underwear, little bikini things that looked very uncomfortable. There was a suitcase and a locked computer bag on the closet shelf. Pete put the laundry bag and clothes from the closet in the suitcase. He fooled with the small combination lock on the computer bag for a few minutes, wondering why the bag was locked with the computer sitting out on the table, and then stuffed the computer and its bag into the suitcase as well.

He checked the rest of the drawers, under the mattress, and under the bed, satisfied that he had everything. He took a hand towel from the bath and meticulously wiped every surface he might have touched. He rode down the elevator, wondering what he was going to say if the desk clerk questioned him while he walked out with Vince's bag.

He made it through the lobby without challenge and walked several blocks to his truck, relieved that he didn't run into anyone he knew. He drove to Harris Harbor, where there was a convenient Dumpster and threw away the laundry bag with Vince's toilet articles, supplements, underwear and magazines. He put the computer case and the laptop under the truck seat, and then drove to the Salvation Army, where he put the suitcase of clothes into the donation bin.

He wanted to see what was on the laptop and open the lock on the computer case, but he had been gone so long he was going to have to deal with too many questions from Jeremy as it was, and if Jeremy had called Jean in, she would be worse. He left the computer and its case under the truck seat and returned to the store to try and concentrate on the half-finished display he'd left on the desk.

Five hours later, he locked up the store and headed home for the day. He had called Annie at the hospital, but had decided to wait until she came home to tell her about his visitor. When he got home, he went in the garage and clipped the lock off the computer case with a pair of bolt cutters. Inside was the return portion of Vince's ticket and a wallet with another driver's license and credit cards. The name was Brian Vitter, but the face on the driver's license was Vince's. There was $570 in cash and another fully loaded pistol. This one was a Model 19, the compact version of Glock's 9mm.

Pete walked down the steps to the house, got a beer from the fridge and sat on the deck for a while. The sun was setting over the Chilkats, and he watched the purples and oranges fade from the early snow on their tops, watched the reflections in Lynn Canal grow dim. No inspiration came, and he decided a second beer wouldn't be helpful to the process.

He retrieved Vince's laptop and turned it on. After a few moments of clicks and whirring, the Windows 3.0 emblem flickered on to the screen. The photo that Vince had imported for desktop wallpaper sprang at Pete before the icons and folders started to appear and pop into place around the edges of the screen.

The desktop photo was of an impossibly busty woman in thigh-high leather boots and open black leather jacket. She wore a cap styled like an SS officer's and dangled a riding crop from one hand. She stood cocked forward, arms crossed on one knee, her high heeled foot digging into the breasts of a young nude woman, lying supine on the floor. The most arresting thing in the photo was the look on the woman's face, sneering a challenge directly into the camera, a look of carnal knowledge, and cruelty and contempt.

Pete felt himself physically drawing back from the screen. He tried to focus on the icons and folders that had popped up. There were the standard Windows icons, but the folder that fixed his attention was labeled, "AnnieMcL". He opened the folder and saw about a dozen JPEG icons with abbreviated labels he couldn't decipher. He clicked on the first one and waited while another photo filled the screen. The photo was of a bound young woman screaming while a nude man in a black hood attacked her with a whip.

With growing fury and loathing Pete methodically clicked through each of the photos in the AnnieMcL folder. It wasn't until the third or fourth that he realized it. The victims in most photos were different, but each had reddish-gold hair and bore at least some resemblance to Annie. He continued to click through the photos and a murderous rage and feeling of contamination joined the loathing.

The photos got steadily worse. Most of them appeared to be posed shots with cooperating porn models, who probably sat around and smoked cigarettes during the breaks, but he didn't see how the last several could have been faked. Most of the people were nude or wore bizarre costumes, but these pictures were about torture and brutalization, not sex.

He used the Internet every day for the business, but perhaps like life, he had ignored the sewers that ran under it. These photos were beyond anything he had ever thought about being out there. He wondered how long it had taken

Vince, wading through the excrement, to find these victims who all looked like Annie. Pete gave a brief wish for the young ladies whose lives had led them to such distress.

Pete closed the computer, the desktop photo now looking benign in comparison, and closed his eyes, trying to cleanse the images from his mind. He was furious with himself that he had let Vince go, and he thought back over the whole encounter. Suddenly, he realized what he had done. He let out such a cry of primal rage that Heck, who had been sleeping at the far edge of the deck jumped up snarling, looking for the unseen enemy.

Pete smashed the laptop on the deck railing so hard he broke the two-by-four cap rail and cracked and bent the computer case. He threw the laptop backhanded, like a Frisbee, out over the water and it skipped once, twice, three times before sinking beneath the dark waters, gently rocking side to side as it settled to the bottom.

Annie yawned and stretched as she drove home. It had been one of those rare shifts when everything went smoothly. They had a good crew, who worked together well. The cases had been steady, but never overwhelming. A woman in her eighties had fallen and her husband brought her in with a knee injury. She was in obvious pain, but had been so gracious she managed to convey that the knee injury was a privilege that enabled her to meet Annie. Annie thought about growing old with Pete and hoped they would do it with as much grace and obvious love as the couple had.

She'd called home about nine, but Pete hadn't answered; she figured he was out working on something in the yard or garage. She thought about calling again before she left the hospital. He liked her to, but she didn't want to wake him if he had fallen asleep on the couch. Better to surprise him by coming home on time.

She passed Auke Bay, then Lena Loop and Tee Harbor. Houses were few and far between out here, but the moon added light to the road as it curved in and out of the forest along the coast. The commute was sometimes brutal in winter, but their home gave her such a sense of peace and contentment that she never regretted the drive. She stretched again and massaged her neck with one hand.

The local radio stations began to fade out, one by one, but scanning the dial she happened on a station from somewhere down in British Columbia that was taking an errant bounce off the ionosphere. It had a blues program on, and she listened to black voices from the fields of Mississippi and Texas and from smoky bars in Chicago as she drove along the ocean's edge in Alaska.

Freddie King was singing *Ain't No Sunshine When She's Gone*, as she came to the drive, "*. . . and when she's gone, she's always gone too long.*" She smiled to herself, she knew that Pete actually felt that way, without ever being over possessive about it. In all the time they'd been together, she had never walked into a room without seeing his eyes light up. From up on the driveway the house appeared dark. Maybe Pete had actually gone to bed. She had a quick vision of coming into the house quietly, slipping off her clothes, and sliding under the covers to wake him.

She liked the idea, but as she came farther down the driveway, things seemed out of place. Even if Pete had gone to bed he would have left some lights on for her. If the power were out as sometimes happened, he would have lit the oil lamps. She cut off the radio and headlights, driving down the rest of the driveway by the moonlight filtering through the trees and reflecting off the water.

She stopped outside the garage, not wanting to cause the noise and light of the electric door opener. She got out and listened for a moment, not hearing anything other than waves lapping the rocks of the cove. She paused again at the top of the stairs that led down to the house, but was unable to see anything out of place other than the house's darkness. She'd always thought it dumb when you saw someone in a spooky movie call out, but Annie found the urge to call for Pete and Hector almost irresistible.

She walked down the stairs to the house, pausing several times to listen. To the left of the front door, underneath the porch roof, were chunks of firewood and a camp ax for splitting kindling. She pulled the ax free from the log round and grasped it both hands. She was scared and felt foolish and mad about being scared. There was a push on the back of her thighs and she gasped, whirling, ax at the ready. It was Hector and something was clearly wrong. Instead of his normal exuberant greeting, he pressed against her, looking as close as a dog could look to worried.

She bent down, giving Heck a hug and whispering to him, asking him where Pete was and what was happening. She felt better with Heck there. She knew he would give his life for hers in an instant, but she wanted to know where Pete was. Annie was just starting to open the front door when she heard what sounded like labored breathing and a grunting sound that seemed like it was coming from down in the cove.

17

Annie eased around the outside of the house to the front, listening hard, trying to decipher all the familiar shapes that suddenly looked strange in the darkness. She had gone through the yard and down to the cove hundreds of times in the dark. She'd never been afraid, even during the spring when a young black bear kept hanging around the house.

She stopped suddenly. There was a large dark shape at the head of the little path that led down to the cove. It was big, almost the size of a couple of cars. It was something that had never been there before and she stared at it in the darkness, trying to make sense of it. Up high, winds were moving scattered clouds across the moon. She gripped the ax tightly and wondered if she should go in the house and get a shotgun or her rifle from the gun cabinet. Whatever the shape was, it wasn't moving, and Heck wasn't growling at it, which offered her some small comfort.

Annie took several steps closer and tried looking at the shape out of the sides of her eyes where her night vision was better. The clouds were over the moon, and she waited for it to come out again so she could see better. Just then, she could hear something coming up the path from the beach. She could make out a big distorted shape, moving painfully, one step at a time, coming into view as it climbed up the path. At the top, just before the last tall step over a small rock ledge, the shape paused, and she could hear tortured breathing.

The cloud slid on by the moon and she saw the shape was Pete. He was carrying a boulder larger than any rock she ever conceived a person could pick up, the weight of it on his thighs while he hugged it into his stomach and chest. He was still in the pants and shoes he'd worn to the store, but his shirt was off, and his arms bulged out of the sleeveless undershirt, every fiber and tendon in his arms and neck visible. The temperature was in the high 30s, but he glistened with sweat. He gave sort of a low growl and came up over the last tall step with the rock and then, with a few waddling steps over to the dark pile, dropped the rock.

The moon came clear of the cloud, and she could see that the large dark shape she'd first seen was the pile of rocks which Pete, over the years, had collected at the bottom of the cliff from clearing a path up the beach for their skiff. She'd helped him use pry bars to roll some of the big ones up the beach. He insisted he was going bring them up to the yard someday to build a retaining wall. He'd explained how he was going to get them up the cliff, drawing a sketch of a ramp with a come-along at the top.

"What are you doing? Pete, what on earth are you doing?" Annie's fear and adrenaline was suddenly converted to anger.

Pete looked up at her slowly, like he was hearing her from a great distance. He was breathing in great gulps of air and didn't seem to be able to talk, but the ferocity and wildness in his eyes made her take a step back.

Once, when driving out West, she had been the first car to come on an accident where a stallion had escaped from his field and ran across the highway, so spooked that he had run into the side of a new Ford pickup. The pickup was wrecked, the young couple inside cut and bruised, but it was the stallion she remembered. He had broken both of his front legs and lacerated his chest. He would lie still for a moment, but then thrash terribly trying to get up, bone sticking out of his leg.

Pete looked like that horse now, his eyes wild, every muscle and tendon bulging. The moonlight glistened on shiny patches on the boulder and she realized it was blood from his hands and stomach, cut and worn raw by the rocks.

"Pete, Pete. Pete, it's me Annie. What's happening? Are you OK?" She reached out and touched his arm and felt his flesh give a small, almost electric jump. She continued to talk softly to him, touching his other arm and then stroking his cheeks, her speech turning to whispered comforting sounds as she took him in her arms, holding him, breathing his rank scent, feeling the rigidity seep out of his body.

"Annie, are you OK?"

"I'm fine, Pete. I had a good night. What's going on here?"

"The pile of rocks I always said I was going to bring up for you and make the retaining walls so you could have a flower garden? I brought them up for you?"

For no reason she could make sense of, Annie felt tears forming in her eyes. "Pete, I see you brought the rocks up, but what's going on?"

"I screwed up. I screwed up big time." There was a long pause as he seemed to look all around, orienting himself, pulling himself back from wherever he had been. "I've probably put you in danger."

She made him shower first, and told him to wait until she finished cleaning and bandaging, before he told her. It was still steamy and she had him turn a bit so she could get better light while she scrubbed the ground-in rock fragments out of his abrasions. He didn't make any sound, just stood there with his eyes still looking wild and miserable. She told him she wanted to fully focus, but mainly she wanted to give him more time to settle.

The Highway Patrolman had shot the horse. She'd been working on a cut on the young woman's face, closing it with butterfly bandages from the first aid kit she carried in her car. The horse was whinnying, almost a scream. She looked up to see the young Patrolman, younger even than she, approaching the horse with his revolver out.

The horse was kicking out, trying to get up, and the Patrolman didn't want to get too close. His first shot didn't kill the horse, but sent it into convulsive shudders. The awful screaming went up, climbed further up the scale into a sound she didn't know a horse could make. She could remember the metallic smell of blood and the smell of the gunpowder and the sudden silence as his second shot killed the horse. She had been blindly furious at the Patrolman. She knew if the horse had been a person, it could have been saved. She was gathering herself to yell at him when he tottered over to the side of the road and threw up in the tall grass growing in the ditch. Pete's abrasions or cuts were minor, but as she finished her bandaging, the irrational thought that filled her mind was that she wasn't going to let anyone shoot him.

They talked there in the bathroom, Pete, looking huge, sitting on the edge of the tub in a white towel and white gauze bandages. She sat on the closed toilet seat as he told her about Vince's visit to the bookstore. He told her about Vince coming in, making threats about if he didn't give him the pack. She asked what type of threats, and he told her they had been indirect, somebody could get hurt, the store could burn. She asked if he had told the man they didn't have the pack, and he said yeah, he had told him several times they didn't have anything off the sailboat. She asked if the man had believed him and Pete told her no, he didn't think he had.

Annie asked him what had happened then and he said Vince had made a threat that Annie could get hurt and he had lost his temper and hit the man a couple of times. Annie asked him if Vince had hurt him and Pete said no, he had just hit him and then took him to the airport and told him to fly home and tell Galvan they didn't have the pack.

"You hit him a couple of times, and he flew home to tell them we don't have the pack?"

"I think, like a lot of bullies, he wasn't used to being hit himself. When someone gets hit, it's usually the surprise and insult as much as the actual hurt that has an effect."

"I'll try to remember that," she said. "It sounds like we have to figure out what to do, but you didn't screw up, you didn't do anything to endanger me."

"I did Annie. I screwed up in a bunch of ways. I told him if he didn't go back and tell them we didn't have anything of theirs, I would find a way to get word to Galvan that I had given him the pack and he had taken off with it."

"That doesn't sound so bad."

"I was so mad I wasn't thinking carefully. Up until then he had been talking about 'something that belongs to us', but no one had mentioned a pack specifically until I said I'd tell Galvan he took off with it."

They both sat there in silence for a long time. Annie finally broke the silence. "So they know we at least know about the pack, and they think we have it."

"Yeah."

After another period of silence, Pete spoke again. "Annie, that was the worst, but I also screwed up in another way." He told her about Vince talking about the kid who did research for Galvan on the Internet. He didn't tell her about the photo of her crossing the finishing line, but he told her about Vince's crack about her credit report and that they knew she was a runner, had found those articles on line. He told her about getting Vince's gear from the hotel and finding the laptop and the locked computer case.

"Where is it? It may have email or who knows what else on it that could help us."

"That's the second way I screwed up. I had the same thought you did, so I brought it home. I had just started looking at it when I realized what I had said about the pack. I lost my temper again. I hit the computer on the deck rail and then threw it out in the cove. Made a heck of a Frisbee, but it's in about twenty feet of water now and I have to fix the railing."

"In all the years we've been together, I've never even seen you get mad, much less lose your temper."

"I lost it twice today. It was dumb. I knew it before it hit the water, but it was too late."

"I really hate it that they could go in and snoop around like that, look at our credit reports. Sort of makes me feel like they've been here poking around our house. Did he know where I worked?"

"Yeah." Pete thought again about the downloaded photos that resembled her. He had told her Vince had threatened to hurt her, and she was taking it seriously. He didn't like holding anything back but couldn't see any benefit in telling her about the photos.

"Pete, you said they didn't find anything on you. There must have been a lot of articles from when you were playing football and wrestling and even more when your family was killed."

"Yeah, there was a bunch of stuff. My mom kept scrapbooks on both my brother and me. She was really proud. After they died, there was a whole bunch of stuff in the papers, but I never looked at any of it. There was a *Sports Illustrated* article toward the end of the season, but I wouldn't talk to the reporter and never read the article. Anyway, that was all a long time ago, and I guess none of that old stuff has been archived onto the net. I suppose it wouldn't make any difference, but I'm glad they don't know. It's none of their business." He was quiet for a long time and then spoke again so softly she had trouble hearing him.

"After they died, when I cleared out the house, I got rid of everything she had saved about me. I burned it cause I didn't want it lying around the dump or the garbage men seeing it and feeling sorry for me. Truth was, I was feeling sorry enough for myself. I saved my brother's scrapbook though. It's in some of those boxes up in the attic. Maybe sometime you might like to see it."

She got up and came over, hugging him fiercely, holding his head to her chest. "I'd like to see it very much." They held each other a long time, each thinking private thoughts about all the fates of life that you can't control, no matter what.

A few small, puffy clouds drifted over Lynn Canal in the morning, and the slightest of breezes caused tiny wavelets. A flock of Barrow's Goldeneyes and buffleheads bobbed off the point, occasionally diving for their breakfast. Last night didn't seem real in the warmth of the morning sun.

It didn't seem real, but Annie was standing in the yard staring at the pile of stones, mute witness to the fact that at least some of last night had been very real. The larger boulders were heaped in a haphazard pile, smaller ones, the size of basketballs, were scattered around the pile where Pete had thrown them.

Last night she had asked him why he had moved the rocks. He had said he knew it didn't make any sense, but when he threw the laptop, before it even hit the water, he knew what a mistake he had made. He'd rushed down to the water's edge with some vague idea of trying to retrieve it, to see if someone could save some information from the hard disk. He wound up standing at the water's edge, knowing there was no way to get it back without diving, and he'd broken it almost in half hitting it on the porch rail anyway.

As he walked back up the beach, he was thinking so intently that he wasn't looking where he was going. He stumbled on one of the smaller boulders that had rolled off the pile at the bottom of the cliff. Still caught in his anger, he picked it up and hurled it up into the yard. It hit something up there, bounced, and rolled back down, falling over the ten-foot cliff with a bounce halfway down that ricocheted off and nearly hit him. He grabbed it and threw it harder with similar results, the stone coming even closer to hitting him this time. The third throw, slightly to the right, stayed up, and he picked up the next rock off the pile and threw it up as well.

He started throwing the smaller rocks and somehow that evolved into bringing up all the rocks so he could make the retaining wall for the garden she'd wanted. He said, even while he was doing it, he knew it had made no sense. There was the thought that if something happened to him, she could take care of the rest of the house, but she wouldn't be able to bring the stones up the cliff.

Annie had slowly coaxed him into the bedroom. It was the only time in their marriage that Pete was slow to respond, but she told him to lie there and let her take care of things, and it had wound up tender and fierce at the same time. Normally, she fell asleep with her head on his shoulder while he read. Last night he had fallen asleep almost immediately afterwards. She lay awake a long time, thinking about Pete and life.

Annie was sitting on one of the sun-warmed boulders now, watching an eagle ride the thermals high above Lynn Canal. The sun glinted off tiny bits of mica in the boulder, and with her hand, she felt the rough texture of the granite interlaced with the smooth of thin veins of quartz. There were several brown streaks on the gray and white of the stone, which she realized were streaks of Pete's dried blood. She was thinking about making love with him. Over the years, many of the memories blended together, times that were slow and tender or raw and urgent, sleepy and languid, or over the edge of sexual tension, but for all of them, the term "making love" was truly accurate. Last night had been lovemaking as therapy, mental and physical.

She realized she was smiling to herself. It wasn't therapy the hospital would approve of, nor that she had any interest in offering to anyone else, but there was no doubt it was strong medicine.

18

The crack of each shot was loud, the recoil sending a jolt down the bones of her forearms, the smell of gunpowder strong.

"What you're trying for now is two quick shots in the center of mass," Pete said. "Just think about it like shooting a halibut before we bring it in the boat."

Halibut look like huge flounders, and are notoriously hard to land and kill. She didn't believe the stories about giant halibut killing fishermen who brought them into the boat before they were dead, but she had treated a fisherman in the ER with an ankle broken by a thrashing halibut.

"When I shoot a halibut, they're about two feet away."

"Yeah, but here you don't have to hit a peanut-sized brain. The target's not flopping around and splashing, and you don't have to worry about hitting the fishing line or the harpoon line, or especially my hand or the boat. This is about fifteen feet, but the target is much bigger. It's easier."

They had left a desolate Hector shut in the house and walked along the deer trail just inside the edge of the woods.

It was easier walking than down on the rocky beach, and the trees partially sheltered them from the fine mist in the air. At the edge of their property, there was a break in the rocky shoreline where a ravine ran down to the water. Behind the brush line at the beach, under the shelter of the high canopy of giant Sitka spruces and western hemlocks, the slopes of the ravine formed a small, natural amphitheatre thickly carpeted with needles.

They could see patches of Lynn Canal through the beach fringe, but the wind didn't reach in here, and even the sound of the waves was muffled. No one lived near enough to hear the shooting, and boat and car traffic was sparse. They had started out shooting the Ruger Single Six, a stainless steel .22 revolver they used on halibut. Pete set out a half dozen tin cans at the base of the slope. They had done this a number of times in the past, and she was a good shot, cocking the hammer back and squeezing off each shot, jumping the cans around.

Then they switched to the 9mm Glock that had been in Vince's briefcase. Pete told her to take her time, and get used to the different gun. The Glock was a semi-automatic instead of a single action revolver, and the 9 mm ammo more powerful than the .22 she was used to. After she adjusted to the Glock's two-stage trigger pull, she shot well, hitting the cans at their base to hop them into the air and hitting them again as soon as they dropped.

Pete picked up the cans and the brass of the ejected shells. He replaced the cans with three roughly man-shaped pieces of cardboard. He'd drawn a circle about a foot in diameter on the chest of each one. Using his .45, Pete shot each of the targets, showing her what he wanted her to do. Three times now, she had raised the gun, centered the front post of the sight on the first target, and lowered the pistol without pulling the trigger.

The third time she lowered the gun, she shook her head. "It's very different, and I don't mean the difference between the Glock and the Ruger. I don't have any problem shooting a halibut we're going to eat, and we've plinked at cans plenty of times before. That's fun, but you're asking me to practice shooting people. I'm a nurse. I help heal people. When I worked in the San Diego ER, I can't count how many gunshot victims I worked on. I don't know if I can do this."

"Annie, I'm desperately sorry I got us into this. I want to do everything I can to avoid trouble. I should've told the Troopers about the pack the first day, before we knew what was in it. It was dumb to make a promise to someone who wasn't even coherent, without knowing any of the consequences. I just..." Pete trailed off staring at the ground for a few moments before he started again.

"After Vietnam, I didn't make promises to anybody, not even to myself, for a long, long time. In fact, the next promise I made was the one that's important to me above all others; to love, and honor and cherish..." Pete trailed off again and Annie was aware that he'd realized if he kept reciting the marriage vow it was going to end with "... till death do us part." Pete was quiet again, and then said, "That's the one I'm going to keep no matter what."

Annie was shaking her head slowly, unwilling to accept their situation. Pete gently took the wrist of her arm still holding the Glock and pointed it out to the side. He hugged her and she hugged him back, a strange one-armed hug with a black and ugly pistol pointing downrange.

"I love you, Pete. I hate this situation, though. All we want is to be left alone to live our life together. We helped someone, and it's turned into this. Helping him was the right thing, and I hope we would do the same thing tomorrow, but I don't know if I can do this. I can shoot your cardboard, but I don't think I could shoot a person."

"At this stage, if I thought it would put you out of danger, I would tell them where the pack is," he said. "But we know who they are and we know about the drugs. Even if we told them now, I don't know if they would leave it at that."

"You didn't get us into this, and we can't give the pack to them. I talked about all the gunshot wounds I worked on. Well, a lot of those gunshots were caused by drugs, as were a lot of stabbings, and beat up women and abused children, and just plain overdoses. We can't give it back to them, and we are not going to the police. How about if I started carrying a can of bear spray?"

"Tomorrow, when I go into town, I'll buy you the biggest can of bear spray I can find. Just don't go dabbing any behind your ears."

She tried to grin back at him, appreciating his attempt to lighten the situation. Bear spray is a highly concentrated cayenne-pepper spray for repelling charging bears. The past summer a story had made the rounds about a young fellow who had come up to Alaska determined to "experience true wilderness and solitude". He had hired a floatplane to drop him on a small island south of Juneau. The pilot left him and a huge pile of high-tech camping gear on the beach with arrangements to return in two weeks to pick him up. As the plane spiraled up, gaining altitude after takeoff, the pilot looked down for a last check on his passenger. He saw the man writhing on the ground, looking like he was having a seizure. The pilot relanded and ran up the beach to the man who was on his knees sobbing and clawing at his face.

"I can't stand it, I can't stand it. How do you do it?" the man sobbed.

"What're you talking about?" the pilot asked, noticing his eyes were also starting to water.

"The bear repellent. I just sprayed on a little before I went up into the woods."

Pete didn't want to lose the slight easing of tension. "For now just shoot the cardboard. You're a good shot already, but if you aren't comfortable with this pistol, it's dangerous to you as well. You need to practice until you can devote all your conscious thought to the decision to fire or not, without having to worry about how the pistol works. We'll get the bear spray, but if the other person has a gun, as all these guys seem to, it's not much use."

"We just have to figure out a way to talk with this Galvan, make him understand."

"I talked with Kotkin, that lawyer they sent up. It didn't seem to do much good."

She was the one smiling at him now. "You duct-taped him into a porta-potty and turned it over with him inside."

"Yeah, well, I talked with him beforehand. I talked with Vince, too. I just had to get his attention first."

Pete had taken the Glock back and unloaded it while they talked. He was holding it now, its action locked open. "I really do believe it's way better to talk. The problem is that both sides have to be willing to talk, and there has to be reasonable ground in the middle. Sometimes one side is simply wrong or evil. These folks aren't going to agree to take back half the drugs and only sell them to adults who pledge not to use to excess or engage in antisocial acts.

"Gandhi, Nelson Mandela, Martin Luther King, were all remarkable men," he said. "They were successful, though, not just because of the righteousness of their causes, or their remarkable qualities, but also because they were dealing with larger societies that ultimately cared more about morality, image and playing by the rules than maintaining the status quo. I know I'm preaching, but if any of them had been in Nazi Germany, or in Uganda or the Balkans or most of the Middle East, they'd be in unmarked graves."

"Pete, I don't disagree with you, but even to save my life, I don't know if I can shoot someone. I don't want you to either. I'm still having a hard time dealing with what happened back in California. It happened, though, and we can't change it. This is about both of us now. We have to find a better way."

Pete paused before he responded. "You remember I told you once about my coach getting a counselor to try and talk to me when I stopped going to classes? When I got my draft notice, she talked me into going to see some folks about conscientious objector status.

"They talked about being a pacifist and asked me a bunch of questions. They asked me if someone was threatening my life, what I would do. They were real happy when I said I probably wouldn't defend myself.

"Then they asked me if I could be willing to renounce violence in all its forms, even self-defense to protect my family. They weren't being insensitive. They just didn't know my folks had been killed. I didn't think it was any of their business, so I hadn't told them.

"I said that if I could save my family, I would kill whoever I had to, in whatever way I could, and I would do it without hesitation. They all sort of drew back in this horrified silence. It was pretty clear to all of us that I wasn't conscientious objector material, so I got up and left.

"Unfortunately, I know better than most, the consequences of killing someone. You live with it the rest of your life. No one 'gets away with it'. Neither of us wants to shoot anyone. But, I believe every one of us has a moral responsibility to stand up to evil, we can't depend on government to do that for us. I'm much less certain about a lot of things than when I was young, but I'm pretty sure about that."

Annie told him that at the slightest hint of trouble she would call the police, and for now, she was going to shoot the cardboard. She put the ear protectors and safety glasses back on, reloaded the Glock, and took several deep breaths. She stepped back up to the line they had been shooting from and brought the gun up, left foot forward, right hand holding the pistol, pushing forward, left hand cupping the right, pulling back, head tilted over to sight along the top of the pistol, both eyes open like shooting a shotgun. She concentrated on focusing on the front sight, with the rear sight and the target slightly blurry.

When Pete had shot, it had sounded like one rolling explosion of Morse code; dot-dot, dot-dot, dot-dot, dash, dash, dash. She tried to do as he had shown her, not hurrying, a smooth swing up centering the front sight in the middle of the target. Squeezing the trigger once and then again as her left hand pulled the pistol down against the recoil, a smooth swing to the next target for two more quick shots, and then a swing on to the third target for the next double tap as he called it. She was slower, but she did pretty well.

Pete went to the targets and used a Sharpie to mark through each of the bullet holes so they would be able to tell which hits were new. Pete's double taps were all centered in the middle of the circle, right next to each other like two fingers tapped on a breastbone. The holes from her shots weren't as close, but they all hit the targets with only one flyer outside of the center rings.

Neither of them mentioned the three additional shots Pete had fired. At the top edge of each target, where a person's forehead would be, there was neat hole where Pete had swung back across the row of targets with a final shot for each.

Annie touched the bullet holes, each a tidy geometric circle in the paper, the target healed with strokes of the marker, to be shot again. She thought of all the young bodies she had seen wheeled into emergency rooms, not getting up to dust themselves off after a director had yelled cut, but rather leaking blood and other body fluids, pieces of flesh and bits of bone missing, families screaming or sobbing or just sitting stunned into incomprehension. She stopped to gaze out through the trees at a patch of Lynn Canal. A fishing boat, visible as a white speck against the far shore, was making its way down from Haines.

"See that boat out there?" she asked. "I find myself thinking about the sailboat we found. I think about our going down and getting on it and just sailing away over the horizon where nobody knows who we are, where this problem doesn't exist."

Pete joined her looking out across the water for a moment. "That boat is the first sign of any other people we've seen today, and they're way too far to hear our shots. I've always loved living way out here, even when the drive is at its worst in the winter. Now I'm having lots of second thoughts about being so isolated. We've been shooting now for over half an hour. There's no one to hear, no neighbor to help you or call the police if something happened. You mentioned calling the police at the first sign of trouble, but even in a big city, police mainly react to crime, not prevent it. If you had the opportunity to call, there's almost no way they could respond in less than half an hour under ideal circumstances, and it would take me at least 45 minutes to get home from Readers' if I sped the whole way."

The mist had thickened and was starting to sift in under the spruces and hemlocks, wetting their faces. Annie put a fresh magazine back into the pistol, index finger along the front to guide it in, slamming it home with the heel of her hand like Pete had shown her. She lifted the pistol, centered the front sight on the first target and started to take up the slack in the trigger. As she did, a stronger gust of wind slammed in from Lynn Canal. The wind brought a sudden moaning sound from the branches overhead and swirled the targets away through the trees.

19

The two-pound monofilament was thinner than a spider's web. Pete carefully strung it through the devil's club, stretching it tight from point to point before tying it to the switch. Most of the big leaves had turned bright yellow by now, the red berries making them look pretty until you touched one. He was wearing Carhartt coveralls, leather gloves and a ball cap, but already had thorns in a cheek and ear. Heck was snuffling through the woods, making sure all the red squirrels stayed up in the trees where they belonged. Over the years Pete had thinned the understory on most of the property, making it easy to walk through, but he was now grateful for the past paranoia that had made him keep and encourage dense tangles of devil's club, wild Sitka rose and alder thickets along the property edges.

He had tried to talk Annie into taking leave from work and visiting out-of-state friends until this was resolved. She flatly refused; they couldn't afford it, they weren't sure there was really a problem, the friends she was most likely to visit were in California where Galvan was from, a host of small invented reasons that repeatedly came back to the bottom line. She wasn't going to leave him in this situation any more than he would leave her.

In the end, Annie won. He told her it had been easier getting Vince on the plane. She told him that was because she was a lot tougher than Vince, and he figured she was probably right. Pete had to settle for Annie's promise that she was taking the danger seriously and wouldn't give him too hard a time about taking extra precautions.

They figured that she was relatively safe at work. There were always people around the emergency room, and police were there often with accident or assault victims. From working in the ER, Annie knew most of the cops. Other nurses had joked to Pete about the cops and paramedics hanging around the ER longer when she was on shift. He didn't blame them. Annie looked good even in green scrubs and she had an easy way that made both men and women enjoy being around her. At Pete's suggestion, she told one of the sergeants that some creep was making anonymous calls to her, and now the cops were stopping by a little more often, paying attention to anyone sitting in cars in the parking lot.

Both Pete and Annie were trying to make their non-work activities more random, but there was no way for them to alter their route to work. Annie promised to lock her car while she was driving, and after long discussion, she agreed to start carrying the 9mm.

Their greatest vulnerability was at home. Pete got down on his hands and knees to thread the monofilament through a particularly thick section of alders. If they killed Annie or him, it wouldn't help them find the pack. He supposed that was good news. If Galvan sent another crew up, trying to kidnap one or both of them, or invading their home and taking them prisoner would be their most logical move.

Pete paused to suck on his wrist where a devil's club stalk had slipped between his glove and the sleeve of the coveralls. His mind was in the same endless spin cycle of whether he could arrange to give the pack to the Troopers without attracting a spotlight of scrutiny. Could he just tell Galvan's people where the pack was? Annie insisted not, and he knew she was right. And even if he did, would Annie and he then spend the next years looking over their shoulders for an "accident" so they could never say anything about Galvan.

Every time he thought about the possibility of anyone harming Annie, he heard an answer in his head. It was the sound he used to hear when he was by himself in the jungle at night, the silvery sibilant sound of the claymore that hung above the mantel, the great two-handed sword whispering, "Death," as it slid from its scabbard. Fly to L.A., find Galvan and anyone else who might ever be a threat to Annie and kill them all.

Heck interrupted him with a sharp poke of his front paw and a questioning, "Woof?" Pete realized he had been still a long time. He began threading the line again. He was trying to get it high enough to avoid constant false alarms from Hector or the deer and bear that crossed the property, but not too high to miss a person trying to work their way through the tangle. At each corner of the property, the monofilament connected to an electrical switch wired back to a doorbell he installed in the house as an alarm. He had rigged an infrared eye about twenty-five feet down the drive and wired it in as well.

He wondered if they came, how patient they would be. Pete had learned from small, silent men of infinite patience who were trying to kill him. Pete knew if he were working for

Galvan, he would wait until he was at the bookstore and then catch Annie as she came out to go to work. He expected the next men Galvan sent to be better, but he doubted they would have the patience to spend hours waiting in the rain for the right moment. He finished threading the line to the final switch and double-checked the switch and wiring. The big question was what happened when and if the alarm bell sounded.

What was the demarcation between paranoia and preparedness? When he found Hal's body and then Randy, he had to fight not to fall back over an edge into a past he thought he had left far behind. It had been the thought of Annie that had anchored him, kept him in the here and now where life was good. Now though, the thought of someone harming her was driving him toward a rage he could feel growing in the basement of his soul. He knew he would do whatever it took to protect Annie, but he also knew Annie was right, if he simply went down and killed Galvan and his friends, he would lose her and also lose the self that he had worked so hard to regain.

Pete went into the enclosed porch that served as an arctic entrance for their house. He took the .45 out of the coverall pocket and rested it on top of the freezer they kept out there. He pulled off his gloves and boots and zipped out of the overalls, hanging them and the ball cap on a peg. He picked up the .45, brushing away some small bits of twig and leaf that gotten into the pocket with it. He wondered if it was stupid to still have it. He didn't believe there was any record that connected it to Dale, but assumed its serial number could be traced back to Vietnam, possibly to his platoon.

The checkering on grips was worn now. Over the years, he'd added a speed safety and longer match trigger, beveled the magazine well, polished the feed ramp and filed down the ejection port, fitted better sights and replaced the barrel bushing. He had changed it, but it was still very much the pistol Dale had taken from the lieutenant's body on a small hummock on a different side of the world, and that he had taken from Dale's body in the canyon. Among the stuff he had brought back from Michigan when the house was nearing completion were his grandfather's old carpenter tools. When he used them, there was a feeling of substance and continuity. In a way, the .45 was like that, for better or worse it had survived along with him.

Pete went inside the house and switched on the radio. He started rummaging in the refrigerator to find something to eat. It was Saturday afternoon and "Thistle and Shamrock" was on. Fiona Richie was playing modern Celtic music on KTOO. He built a couple of sandwiches; ham and swiss, lettuce, tomato, and dill pickle, mayonnaise and hot mustard, and poured a large glass of milk.

He was sitting at the kitchen counter now and found himself staring at the claymore that hung above the mantel. Fiona was playing Silly Wizard. He listened to them rip through *Donald McGillavry* and *O'Neill's Cavalry March*. He walked over and cranked up the volume, listening to the swell of the pipes and beat of the drum, the soar of the fiddle and power of the accordion and could understand why the English had outlawed the pipes as weapons of war.

He reached up above the hearth and took down the claymore. The double-edged battle swords had developed in the Scottish Highlands in the 1400s. According to family lore, this sword, over five feet long, had been in the family for hundreds of years, passed down from father to son.

Pete's great-grandfather had come to America in the late 1800s during the tail end of second great wave of Scottish immigration that had spread Scots through America, Australia and New Zealand. He arrived at Ellis Island with a change of clothes and the great sword wrapped in a blanket. A Customs official promptly confiscated the sword saying such a weapon must be turned in to the police. His great-grandfather must have seen the gleam of avarice in the custom officer's eye, however. After the ferry brought him over from Ellis Island, he waited at the docks for the men who worked on Ellis Island to head home at the end of the day. He saw the Customs officer come off the boat struggling to look nonchalant as he carried the long, heavy bundle. He followed him, trying to be as inconspicuous as a man of his size could be. When they reached a quiet residential street, his great-grandfather came up from behind, and grabbed the man by the back of his belt. With one hand he lifted him up on his toes while taking the sword with his other.

In his thick, almost indecipherable highland brogue he said, "My little man, that's much too big a bundle for you to be carrying now. Let me help you, and if you'd like to linger I'd be most honored to show you how it works."

The Customs officer looked at his grim smile and fled up the street. Pete's great-grandfather, thinking it prudent to move on quickly, took a sight on the setting sun and started walking west in great ground-eating strides.

Pete held the great sword in his hands, listening to the swirl and power of the music. He knew it was foolish to ascribe karma to a tool, whether it be the .45, one of his grandfather's wooden block planes or the claymore. There was no denying, though, what he felt through the hilt. He just wondered how much of it was his own craziness.

He rehung the sword. As he rinsed the plate and glass and put them in the dishwasher, the set slowed down with *The Queen of Argyll*, a song about a woman of wondrous beauty. He was thinking about Annie. He was going to stop by and see her at the hospital and then go to the store and work on paperwork until her shift was over and he could follow her home. She had a rare Sunday off tomorrow, and he figured if he pushed on the bookwork this afternoon, he could take most of the day off to be with her. The song ended, and he turned off the radio as he headed up to take a quick shower.

Another song had come into his head, an old Scottish song his mother used to sing to him. As he climbed the stairs he was singing softly:

> *Oh Froggy went a-courtin', he did ride,*
> *Uh-huh, Uh-huh,*
> *With sword and pistol, by his side,*
> *He's going to make Miss Mouse his bride*

He tried to remember more of the lyrics, but had to hum the rest. He was still crazy, he decided, but it was OK.

20

Annie lay still, thinking she would fall back asleep. The bed was warm and Pete's body felt good next to hers. She listened to his slow regular breathing and to Hector's faint snore from the low armchair across the room.

In the summer, the long days made the black-out curtains important, but now they were losing five minutes of daylight each day, and it was dark enough to sleep with the curtains open. She could just make out the Chilkats across Lynn Canal under the slowly lightening sky. Only the bottom half of the mountains were visible, a petticoat of descending snowline peeping out under the skirt of clouds. She slipped out from under Pete's arm. He stirred, and she kissed him gently and told him to keep sleeping. Out of the bed she looked at him. He slept less than she did; it was rare to be able to watch him like this. The covers half off, she thought he looked like one of the big rocks, half-covered by beach sand, too big even for him to move.

When she came back upstairs with two mugs of coffee,

he opened first one eye and then the other and watched her come across the room. She'd pulled on an oversized sweatshirt she had commandeered from him, and he eyed her long, bare legs.

"I heard a song yesterday on Thistle and Shamrock that reminded me of you."

"Good morning to you, too. I brought you coffee."

He took the coffee and quoted to her,

> *"The swan was in her movement, and the morning in her smile.*
>
> *And all the roses in the garden, they bow and ask her pardon,*
>
> *for not one could match the beauty of the Queen of all Argyll."*

"You're sweet when you're half asleep. Take your coffee and scoot over. It's chilly out here."

Afterwards, long afterwards, he'd gone for more coffee and they were still in bed. Outside the mist had thickened into a steady rain that blew in under the eaves to streak the windows. The clouds had lowered and they could barely see past the waves breaking on the point of the cove.

She reached under the covers, and with her nails, traced a long, slow line up his thigh and stomach and chest.

"Yes?"

"I just wanted to get your attention. What are you so deep in thought about?"

"You have regained my full and undivided attention. Mostly I was just lying here feeling good."

"Yeah, I feel pretty darn good myself. You were lost in thought, in your staring at the horizon mode. I can tell these things, you know. And when I ask you, you usually deflect the conversation."

"So how's that new doc in the ER working out? Ouch!"

"We have ways to make you talk."

She snuggled in a little tighter, and he smiled. "I was thinking how, in life, sometimes there are great big obvious things that you know in advance will change your life. Big road signs across the highway, flashing arrows, left three lanes, I-one life, right four lanes somewhere very different, last exit for many miles. Other times you can look back and things that seemed so important to you at the time had almost no real effect. You think you've set off on a very different direction. It turns out you've just wandered around on a detour for a while and it's led you right back to the path you were on before."

"Wherever you go, there you are? Pete, I didn't realize the impact their talking about building the Auke Rec bypass was having on you." With her head on his shoulder, he couldn't see her face, but he could hear the gentle smile in her voice.

"Hey, listen respectfully or I'll start reciting Robert Frost. *Two roads diverged in a yellow wood . . .* You made the mistake of asking. The sneaky ones, though, are the little things you don't even notice at the time. Where decision and chance combine to ambush you and make a huge difference you never saw coming.

"Yesterday, I was thinking about my great-grandfather. There were the big things, the industrial revolution, that led to the Clearances and waves of Scottish immigration, or the little things, the Customs officer stealing his sword and him stealing it back so he had to flee west as soon as he came to the states."

"Pete, we go to Robbie Burns night every year. It wasn't the Clearances that caused Scottish immigration."

"Huh?" It was a half yawn, half question.

"They were fleeing the food. The purpose of Robbie Burns night is for people of Scottish descent to get together once a year, eat a traditional Scottish meal, where boiled rutabagas are the best part, and say 'Thank God they left.'"

"I can see my unified field analysis of choice, chance, consequence, and horizons is not getting a lot of respect," he said. "I have to admit, though, there're a reason there're Mexican and Chinese and Thai restaurants and no Scottish restaurants."

"Maybe I'm joking 'cause it makes me a little nervous. I do want to hear the rest. It's so seldom that you say what you're thinking. Sometimes when you're staring off at the horizon, it makes me nervous that you aren't happy with the way things are."

"I feel incredibly blessed with the way things are. I believe that a lot of life is about choices. Every choice has a consequence, and cumulatively, those consequences tend to determine the horizons of our lives. But there are also times that grace intercedes and saves us in spite of ourselves. Meeting you saved me. Earlier, we could see all the way across to the Chilkats. Now fog's moved in, the visible universe is about a hundred yards. No matter how near or far my horizons, the center of my universe is being here with you. There are a lot of things in my life I wish had been different, but together they all worked out so that I am here with you, and there is nothing I would change, if it changed that."

"As I said before, you're very sweet when you're sleepy."

"And satiated. Never underestimate the healing power of love."

"So, do you always think such deep thoughts afterwards?"

"Sometimes I think about the meaning of life, other times I think about quantum physics. I'm also starting to think about the eight-pack of canned chili I bought at Costco last week and wondering how three or four chili dogs would be for breakfast. Ouch! OK, if you don't want to talk about chili dogs for breakfast, what are you thinking about?"

Annie traced another long slow line with her nails. "I'm thinking that this is a rare morning where neither of us has to be somewhere, and perhaps we should stay in bed a while longer?"

Pete smiled and extended his arms and legs in a huge languorous stretch. "See, great minds think alike. The meaning of life through quantum physics."

Annie was in the bedroom making the bed, and she could hear Pete singing in the shower, *"Amazing Grace, how sweet the sound, that saved a wretch like me."* She smiled and shook her head. He was flat on almost every note and had no notion of the proper key, but this morning, after what he'd said about interceding grace, she found it endearing. *". . . I once was lost, but now I'm found."* She was smoothing out the last wrinkles in the spread when the alarm bell gave its muted ding.

Annie glanced out the back window, but couldn't see anyone. She went into the bathroom where Pete was still singing. He was in the shower, rinsing shampoo out of his hair and she reached in and touched his shoulder, knowing it was irrational, but feeling she needed to be quiet.

His eyes closed against the soap, Pete smiled as he felt her touch, but when the touch turned to a firm grip and small shake he realized something was wrong. Wiping the soap and water out of his eyes, he nodded as she told him the bell had gone off. The alarm beam was far enough down the drive that a car using the drive to turn around wouldn't set it off. Perhaps a half dozen times a year, a car, usually full of teenagers, would ignore the "No Trespassing" sign and come down the drive looking for a place to drink and party, but that was almost always in the summer. He knew from Annie's face that she was not expecting anyone. He took a couple of swipes with the towel on the way to the bedroom and was grateful he'd never lost the habit of leaving a set of clothes out, ready to pull on.

Pete reached under the edge of his side of the bed and picked up the .45, checking to be sure a round was chambered. He thumbed the hammer back and put on the safety. He took two more loaded .45 magazines from the gun cabinet and grabbed the Browning Auto-5 that had been his father's shotgun. He fed in four rounds of magnum buckshot, worked the action to put a shell in the chamber, and then fed one more. He pulled on his old Filson Cruiser from the closet, the green wool was quiet and would blend into the woods. He filled each side pocket with a handful of 12 gauge shells, buckshot in the right, slugs in the left. The whole process took less than three minutes.

"Annie, take the phone with – " Pete turned to her to suggest she hide, but stopped. Annie had taken her deer rifle from the gun cabinet and was loading it.

"I know all the things I've said about not using violence to solve this," she said. "That doesn't mean we don't defend ourselves. I'm going to be up in the attic window where I can see the drive and the woods in the back. You go."

Pete looked at the set of her jaw and unflinching gaze and knew it was no use arguing. Hector had immediately picked up that something was wrong, but then watched with growing excitement as Pete took the shotgun from the gun cabinet and put shells in his pockets. Pete told him to stay with Annie, and then, as he tried to follow, gruffly told him to stay again. Heck was crushed, not quite believing that Pete was going out with the shotgun and leaving him. Pete paused and called Hector's name softly, holding up his hand palm flat in a stay signal. "Heck, you stay here. You take care of Annie, don't let anything happen to her."

Pete checked through the downstairs windows and then went out the back door to the deck, locking the door behind him. Heck turned and went to find Annie. Pete had told him to take care of her, and besides, she had had a gun as well. It didn't seem likely, but maybe she was going to take him out to get some ducks.

Below most of the deck was a steep drop down the cliff to the beach, but at the back corner, away from the steps and front door, it was only five or six feet down to the yard. Pete swung his legs over the rail and lowered himself until he touched ground. He thought he heard a car, but couldn't be sure. He went under the deck to the other side of the house where he could peer out and have a better view, but saw nothing. They stored the kayaks, paddles and miscellaneous gear from the skiff under the deck and he noticed the spare gas tanks. He couldn't do anything about it right now, but he kicked himself for not moving them and other flammables somewhere inaccessible, away from the house.

He watched for a moment longer, then cut back under the deck and in a quick silent sprint, ran to the shelter of a big spruce surrounded by rhododendrons and blueberry bushes. He was totally still for a moment, listening intensely, but all he could hear was the drip of the rain, the lapping of the water below on the rocks and the soft sighing of the wind in the trees. He moved again, tree by tree by tree. After the first quick sprint, he forced himself to move at a deer-stalking pace, a long wait to look and listen and smell between each slow careful step. He worked his way up to the far front corner of the lot. From here he had a view down the slope through the big trees, across most of the land, down to the house and the lower part of the driveway. The canopy of the woods partly sheltered him from the rain. He waited for fifteen minutes, moving nothing except for his eyes, as he examined every thing he could see, making sure that every stump was really a stump, each shadow, really a shadow. A few small birds flitted in the bushes and a squirrel worked on a pine cone, squeaking occasionally, the bits of cone slowly drifting down from a high branch to join other bits in a small heap at the base of a neighboring tree.

When Pete was sure there was no one on the portion of the land he could see, he began to work his way toward the head of the drive, along the inside of the brushy fringe that bordered the road. He continued to wait and inspect the slightly altered view each step offered. From time to time, he could see the road through the tangle of brush, and he watched for a car or for men walking. The monofilament trip line along the right and front borders of the property appeared to be unbroken.

When he could see the top of the drive, there were no cars or people in sight, but he waited, watching and listening. The rain had eased up, but, just at the edge of audibility, he could hear it hitting the road. It was different from the sound of rain falling on the water down by the beach, or dripping through the canopy of trees in the middle of the property. There used to be sounds in the jungle, and later in the woods, that were always just beyond hearing. It used to sound like children crying, too far away to be heard. He wondered if this didn't happen anymore because his hearing was worse or because his mental state was better. Maybe it was just how the wind happened to be blowing in the trees. There were no sounds out of place. There were no smells of smoke or cologne or sweat or exhaust, nothing but the clean smell of rain-washed woods with a bit of sea smell in the background.

He'd been trying to keep every sense open to what he was seeing, hearing and smelling, to not let thinking get in the way of his perceptions. Now he began to wonder if it had been a deer or bear or even a falling branch that had set off the alarm. Fifteen feet from the drive, if you knew where to push certain branches aside and how to duck under the trip wire, there was a twisting path through the devil's club and alder and Sitka rose. Rather than walking up the drive, where a potential watcher might expect him to emerge, he eased through the brush until he could look up and down the highway without revealing himself. Again nothing, just small pools of water in the ruts, dimpling with the misting rain.

Stepping out on the highway, Pete walked to the mouth of the drive. Many things had changed about the house since he married Annie, but he still kept the first part of the driveway purposely uninviting. Brush and tree branches crowded the rutted single lane dirt track with nothing to catch the eye other than the battered "No Trespassing" sign. Visible in the wet, packed dirt were two sets of tire tracks, apparently from the same car. He followed the tracks down the drive, ducking under the infrared beam. The tracks continued down past the turn, to where a person driving a car could see the house. It appeared the driver had pulled down this far, stopped, and then backed out and left.

Pete examined the ground to try and tell if anyone had gotten out of the car or how long it had stayed there, but on the gravel there was no way to tell. He crossed the drive and continued to the property line on the far side, double-checking that the trip line on that side had not been broken. He came up behind the garage and checked it carefully. Nothing seemed amiss. He wanted to get back to Annie, tell her everything was OK, but he told himself to be patient and be sure. He retreated back to the shelter of another big spruce where he could watch the land and the water. He was fairly sure that no one was there, but he forced himself to wait and be still, to absorb the sounds, to be aware of any flicker of movement in his peripheral vision, or if the shifting fog might reveal a boat waiting offshore.

He glanced at his watch again. He'd promised himself he would be still for twenty minutes. He was good at estimating time and was surprised to find only twelve minutes had passed. He knew anger causes foolish mistakes, but with each slow drip from the trees, with each lap of the waves on the rocky beach below, sounds that normally lulled and soothed him, he found his anger growing. A short time ago, he had been in bed with his wife, holding her after making love and telling her how happy she made him, and now he was crouched under a tree in the rain with a gun. He was fighting phantoms, phantoms that might harm his wife and other phantoms of hate and fear and death from two decades ago that came sliding back, eager to join his life again. He waited beyond the point when he was sure there was no one there, waited until he had his emotions under control before he went back to the house and Annie.

21

"And if you did that we would be no better than them! You can't do it."

"I'm not going to let our lives be ruled by fear, wondering when the shoe will drop."

"The saying is 'the other shoe,' and we don't know that there has even been a first shoe. Right now all we know is that they sent a man up here – "

Pete interrupted her, "Two men, don't forget Kotkin, the lawyer."

"OK, two. They've lost a sailboat and a pack of money and drugs, had two men die from a bear attack. The only thing that has actually happened to us is, you had to tell me about what happened down in California. I wish that that had never happened to you, but it did and I'm glad I know."

"Annie, they threatened you – "

"They threatened both of us, and don't you dare think that losing you would somehow mean less to me than losing me would mean to you. But the only thing they have actually done to us so far is make us argue with each other and go creeping around with guns when a car pulls in our driveway. I'm not going to live like that."

"Then it makes sense for me to fly down there and resolve it."

"Pete, what the heck does 'resolve it' mean? Are you going to go down there and ask them to promise to leave us alone?" Annie bored ahead in his uncomfortable silence. "Do we have any way of knowing whether that might not just refocus them on something they've decided to write off? Pete, you know if you go down there, they might kill you, or you might wind up killing them. You've lived your life up here in partial hiding over what happened last time you were in California. You're the one who told me there's been too much death in your life. It's our life now and it's not some Greek tragedy where every couple of decades you're condemned to go to California and kill people."

Pete stared out the window, wishing he could see through the fog, could foresee what waited for them out on the horizon. Annie was right. It could have been just folks out on a Sunday morning drive, wondering what was down the driveway and backing back out when they got far enough to see the garage and the roof of the house.

He would love to believe that Annie was right, that if they simply left it alone, the whole situation would go away. She hadn't met Vince, though, hadn't seen the sick gleam in the wrestler wanna-be's eyes as he held Annie's picture, hadn't seen the catalog of horrors on his computer. He knew Annie was right about his going to California, but he also knew how vulnerable they were.

She was in the kitchen now, making a big breakfast, scrambled eggs with cheese, smoked salmon and chives mixed in, thick slabs of toast with homemade rhubarb jam, more coffee, a declaration of normalcy. He came up from behind and hugged her, holding on until she freed herself to serve the plates. While they ate, they talked about the store and the ER, about how soon the rain was going to shift to snow, by some unspoken agreement, about nothing but day-to-day events, with no mention of the loaded 12 gauge leaning in the corner.

"Annie, you know what this reminds me of? Do you remember me telling you about that piece I heard on NPR about a man from New York visiting his grandfather's village in Africa? Part of the story was about how people there greet each other? It was considered the height of rudeness to discuss anything substantive until each person had inquired about every member of the other's family and all of their possessions."

"I do remember, and the part that you liked was that unless the relative had died, the required answer to every inquiry was that they were fine. Those were the only two conditions, dead and fine. You said it would cut out a lot of whining in this world."

"I still think that, but I also think we have properly greeted and inquired, and we now need to talk about what we're going to do."

"What I'm going to do is put a load of wash on and then take Hector for a run. Afterwards, I'm going to drive in to town. Stephanie up in Med-Surg is having a baby. Helen's giving a baby shower, and I promised her I would stop by and help her plan it. Afterwards, I was thinking of going to Annie Kaill's to look for a present. Is Kaill's still open on Sundays now that the tour ships are done for the season?"

"Yeah, I think it is."

"After that, since I'll be downtown, I thought I'd come by the store?"

"That'd be good."

"Right now, what I hope you'll do is the dishes." She was smiling as she said it, as she reached across the table to take both his hands. He knew she was using the same qualities she used in the ER to calm and soothe frightened patients, but that knowledge made it no less effective.

"Pete, I promise to be careful, but we don't know if there really is any problem. We need to pay attention to our own lives, not the spectre of things that may not exist. I'm doing OK. How are you?"

A story he hadn't thought about in decades, one his mother used to tell about him, suddenly flashed through his mind. They had been at a picnic when he was three or four. He was playing on the grass near his mother when a big dog, taller than he was then, came over stiff legged and bristling and began to sniff him. He had the vaguest memory of rescue, of her striding over to swoop him up with a laugh. The story she would later tell people was that as she approached she could hear Pete talking to the dog, repeating in his small, earnest voice, "Doing fine, thank you, doing fine."

They compromised. Annie and Heck went on their run, and Pete followed in the pickup. She protested, insisting she would be fine and that she wanted to run to forget about all this, which she couldn't do if he was following along. He told her to think of it like the Klondike relay where the other runners and support team followed each runner in a van. As he drove along, he felt both silly and fiercely protective. She looked back several times in the first mile. Each time he waved, trying to look like it was perfectly normal and happy to be following his wife as she ran, .45 in his coat pocket, shotgun across the seat. After the first mile, she lengthened her stride and didn't look back again. He could tell she was pushing for that edge she talked to him about, the edge where endorphins were just keeping the pain at bay - where her mind blanked and she didn't think about anything, but when she finished, the day's problems seemed to have resolved themselves.

This far out the road, there was almost no traffic on a rainy October Sunday, but he kept trying to see around the next corner at the same time he kept an eye on the rear view mirror so no one came up unexpectedly. Annie was wearing Lycra running tights, a running jacket and ball cap, the thick red-gold of her hair in a braid. Pete knew that before Annie, if he had driven past a beautiful woman like this, it would have left a slightly hollow ache and a wish that there was some way to meet, to just say hello.

He reminded himself that he was supposed to be watching out for her, not watching her. He glanced back down the road behind them in the mirror and smiled, trying to formulate the joke he would tell her about being distracted from the rear view by the rear view.

As they'd agreed, Annie took advantage of his following in the truck to run as far as she wanted, without doubling back. She sprinted the last quarter mile hard, and under other circumstances it would have been a beautiful thing to watch. What it kept reminding Pete of now, what he hadn't told her, were Vince's comments about finishing kicks. Annie crossed her imaginary finish line and slowed to a walk, cooling down and getting her breath. Heck, happier with this pace that gave him time to explore, promptly began to lift his leg on bushes and search for a proper stick to entice her to throw.

She stopped walking at the pull-off above Sunshine Cove. It didn't look much like its name today, the fog and steady mist making it hard to even see the islands at the mouth of the cove. Pete gave her a towel and bottle of water he had brought in the truck and watched the smooth glisten and movement of her throat as she tilted back and chugged half the bottle. Annie was always a little unfocused when she first stopped running, and they stood for a while in the mist, not talking yet, each thinking their own thoughts, letting her breath and heart slowly slide back toward normal. She would take short walks around the pull-off and then return to stand beside him and drink more water. Eventually she used the towel while he used another old one to clean off Hector before he got in the truck.

They drove back toward the house, defroster blasting and not quite keeping up with the steam coming off wet dog and woman. Heck was up on the seat beside the passenger window thinking that life was pretty fine, first a run and now a ride with Pete and Annie. Annie sat in the middle and Pete could feel the heat from her radiating into him where shoulder, arm and thigh touched. He reached forward, wiping the fog from the windshield, trying to see around the next corner.

He drove past their driveway for a mile or so, making sure there weren't any cars parked down the road. When they returned to the drive, he checked the twigs he had positioned in the drive to see if they had been crushed or disturbed. He tried to convince Annie to wait in the truck with the doors locked and motor running while he and Heck checked the house, but she was adamant that she wasn't going to start living like this just because a Sunday driver had turned around in their driveway.

From mid-September until the start of the Christmas season, Pete closed the store on Sundays. It was the day he caught up on all the office work. Pete tried to talk Annie into coming in to Readers' with him; that they should stay together for the day. She made it clear she had things to do at the house, errands to run, and a baby shower to help plan. He suggested he stay with her for the day, but she gently insisted he get going. She did agree to him staying until she had showered, dried her hair and dressed, and that she would keep Hector with her for the day.

She peeled out of her running gear and Pete stood in the bathroom doorway, talking with her as she showered, watching her outline through the steamy shower glass. What did they need from the grocery? What should she get as a shower present for Stephanie? Maybe they should rent a movie to watch tonight; all the little items that make up life.

They continued talking as Annie toweled off. She was comfortable in her skin, nonchalant about nudity around him, but never totally unaware of the effect. Rather than shout over the hair dryer, they paused their conversation while she dried her hair and he just watched her. She had an extension cord on the hair dryer, and she strode around the room, drying her hair while pulling the day's clothes from closet and dresser. He watched the long legs, the flex of the muscles in her bottom, the lift of breasts, the amazing play of light in her hair.

He left reluctantly after a kiss and a long hug. When he didn't get to go with Pete, Hector was crestfallen for almost a minute. Then Annie gave him a dog biscuit, and he decided the world was a pretty good place after all. He curled up on the rug in front of the deck door to keep an eye on the seagulls that swirled by on the wind.

When she left the house, the rain had eased off into a mist that didn't seem to fall, but simply filled the air, driven by the wind in a hundred directions at once. Heck bounded up the stairs ahead of her, eager to make sure that this time, he didn't get left behind. Annie topped the stairs and was halfway across the gravel parking pad to the garage when Hector started barking, and she looked up to see a maroon car that looked like a rental Taurus coming down the drive. There were three men inside, and she could tell they were equally surprised to see her up there at the parking pad. The man in the passenger seat pointed at her and yelled something, and the driver, who had been creeping down the drive, accelerated, spurting gravel from beneath the tires. For a split-second she thought of running back down the stairs and locking herself in the house, but the car was almost on her with the men jumping out. She called frantically to Heck and sprinted into the woods.

The man who had been in the back seat was very quick, and for the first ten or twenty yards, he gained. Heck ran beside her, barking ferociously, not sure of what was happening, but knowing it wasn't good. The man's hand brushed the back of her jacket and Heck launched; he and the man going down in a snarling, screaming ball. Annie glanced over her shoulder, and as she did, tripped on a root. The driver, a big Hispanic guy, had a pistol and was trying to get a clear shot at Heck without getting too close. The man from the passenger seat ran straight past, intent on her. She had gone down hard, banging a knee and jamming her left wrist, but she rolled and came up running again. Her knee was hurting, but she could still run, and she focused on where she was going, hurdling over logs, ducking under branches. The knee and the hard run this morning slowed her. She didn't look back again, but could hear from his footsteps the man was gaining slightly. Every time he had to duck under a branch or bust through bushes he grunted obscenities at her. There was a shot, and suddenly Heck's snarling was gone.

"You bastards, you bastards, you bastards!" is what filled her mind and the pain from her knee was gone, replaced with a white hot anger.

"You next, bitch!" the man behind her yelled. He was very close, but she could hear the raggedness of his breath in his yell.

She had gone from being terrified to furious. Just ahead was the edge of their property, marked by the thickets of devil's club. "OK, asshole, let's see what you're made of," she thought and deliberately cut straight through it. She put her forearms up to protect her face, but could feel the thorns ripping at her sleeves and pant legs. The thorns slowed her, but every needled stalk and branch she pushed through, sprung back to hit her pursuer. He was screaming curses at her, and when a large branch at face level whipped back past her, she could hear the smack on flesh and his scream. She heard him stop running and then felt as well as heard the blast of a shot as bark exploded on the tree next to her. She instinctively dodged right and left as more shots ripped through the brush around her, each stride putting her farther away from the man as he continued to yell obscenities and fire the pistol. She risked a quick glance over her shoulder and could no longer see him, but knew he could probably still hear her in the thick underbrush.

She began to work her way downhill until she hit the game trail just inside the tree-line at the top of the small cliffs along the beach. On the trail, she lengthened her stride and was able to make better time without making as much noise.

A half-mile farther on, the road and beach dipped close to each other, and she cut up to the road. She crouched in the bushes beside the road, looking and listening. Satisfied there was no one coming, she sprinted across the road and cut uphill until she was well above it, then began circling back towards the house. She was limping, trying to be quiet and watching in the woods ahead of her. Her knee throbbed and wrist ached from the fall, and she could begin to feel the chill of her wet clothes, but she tried to shove those things back and concentrate on getting back to check on Hector and warn Pete. The road and beach looped out where she had run like the curved side of a capital D, so by cutting straight back across she was able to get back above the house more quickly. When she could see down to the road and the entrance to the drive, she stopped and crouched for a minute trying to tell if they were still there. She couldn't see anything, but as the wind twisted and eddied, she thought she heard a snatch of someone talking.

Annie crouched there straining to see or hear anything. There were no neighbors. If a car drove by she could flag it down. Up here people did stop for others in trouble, but this time of year it could easily be several hours before someone drove by, and then it might be someone who would insist on calling the police. She didn't want to, but decided she had to see if they were still there. Her car was in the garage. If they were searching the house, she might be able to get Hector, get him into her car and get away before they noticed. The 9 mm was locked in her car, but if she could get the car and be gone, that wouldn't be an issue.

She listened again and ran across the road, cutting into the same small break in the briars below the driveway entrance that Pete had used that morning. She crept through the brush until she could see a glimpse of maroon sheetmetal.

She could hear angry voices, but couldn't make out what they were saying. They were in front of the garage so there was no hope of getting to her car, but if she could circle behind them, behind the garage, she could get to Heck, check on him, and overhear what they were saying.

The drizzle had made the woods quiet underfoot, but every sound seemed magnified to Annie. With each step closer, it seemed the slight crunch of the gravel underfoot as she crossed the driveway, the whisper of blueberry bushes against her pants, the sound of her pulse pounding in her ears must be so loud they couldn't help hearing. Her body heat from the run was draining away, and she was wet from sweat and the rain. Trying to be so careful where she placed her feet made her knee throb even more. She stopped, closed her eyes, took several deep breaths. She tried to focus on everything Pete had told her when they had gone hunting together about moving quietly in the woods and thinking about him helped.

Annie made it to the back of the garage. She could hear the men clearly now. One man, he had to be the one Heck had jumped, moaned a steady stream of obscenities. He interrupted his cursing to demand that the other man go down to the house. "Mother fucking dog! Get Richie so we can get the fuck outta here. I gotta get to a doctor!"

"Shut the fuck up, tú maricón. He's so pissed off about the thorns in his face and you fucking up and not catching her, he'll probably shoot you just to put us all out of the misery of listening to you."

"I didn't fuck up! It was that fucking dog. If you had – "

Their bickering was interrupted by a shout from the house below. She could hear one man leaving, clomping heavily down the stairs to the house. The other returned to his soft singsong of obscenities.

Annie peeped around the back corner of the garage where she could see Hector's still body. The man in front of the garage was still cursing softly. She thought she could reach Heck without coming into his view. Step by careful step, she moved toward her dog.

22

Pete liked spending Sunday afternoons in the closed store by himself, after the last cruise ship left for the winter. Usually it was a time without distractions when he could catch up on the week's business. The peace and comfort he normally drew from the shelves, from the quiet of the store, wasn't there today. He decided a walk might clear his head or at least shed some of the nervous energy that seemed to be preventing him from finishing any one task.

The rain had slowed to a light mist, but the temperature was in the high thirties, the wind still building, swirling among the buildings, slamming up the street in sudden gusts. Readers' was just a half block up North Franklin, above the main tourist loop of downtown, but that extra half block, slanting suddenly uphill, deterred a significant percentage of the folks off the ships even on the nicest days of summer.

The rain-slick streets were empty. Without the tourists, fall was the leanest time of year for his store, for all merchants downtown, but it had become his favorite time; Juneau belonged to the residents again.

He headed for the Armadillo, walking down South Franklin, deciding that a plate of steak fajitas would be a good half-way break for the walk. Juneau was founded as a mining town in the late 1800s, and South Franklin had been born as a narrow band of bars and brothels shoved up tight against the foot of the mountains by Gastineau Channel. Downtown was cleaner and more attractive now than when he first came to Juneau. Now flower boxes and brass informational plaques and new antique streetlights adorned the street. Art galleries and gift shops had replaced the hardware stores, groceries, clothing stores and an old fish processing plant. The new shops were brightly painted and clean, but particularly as you walked south, closer to the cruise ship docks, the windows of the stores were boarded over as soon as the last cruise ship left. You could buy stunning art, all kinds of jewelry or more types of T-shirts than could be imagined, but you couldn't buy a bag of nails, a gallon of milk or a halibut jacket downtown anymore.

He was thinking about this as he walked down the street. He passed the "world famous" Red Dog Saloon. In the display window were souvenir coffee mugs, T-shirts and thong panties embroidered with the Red Dog emblem. The original Red Dog had been up the street, packed every night with a rowdy mix of fishermen, loggers, government workers and young folks heady with the excitement of making it to Alaska. He wasn't sure that anyone from Juneau ever went in the new Red Dog, but it did a booming business selling packaged Alaskana to the tourists. He couldn't condemn it; he'd thought about moving farther down South Franklin Street himself, nearer the cruise ship docks. Financially, he knew it would make sense. The increased tourist business in the summer would more than make up for the loss in local business, but it would change the character of Readers'. The reason he enjoyed the store, enjoyed working among the shelves, was because of the good books that filled them. He already considered tourists in his summer ordering, but if he had to make his book buying decisions based exclusively on what the folks off the ships wanted to take home as souvenirs, he was pretty sure that he wouldn't enjoy the bookstore anymore.

The Armadillo was the farthest south of any of the stores or restaurants still open this time of year, a survivor from before the cruise ships, when this had been the cheap end of town. By the time Pete reached it, the wind and mist had blown some of his restlessness away. The fajitas also helped and by the time he had walked back up the hill to Readers', he'd almost decided that his past was making him paranoid.

The phone was ringing as Pete unlocked the door. He picked it up just in time to hear someone hang up and the line click to dial tone. He hit star 69 on the phone, but didn't recognize the number. He used the reverse directory in the middle of the phone book to look it up. It said Tom Millman, and after a moment's puzzlement, he realized Millman was Helen's last name, the friend who Annie was going to see about a baby shower. He figured it was Annie calling from Helen's house and punched in the number to call her.

"Hi, this is Pete McLaughlin, Annie's husband. I just got a call from this number and thought perhaps she was there."

"Oh, hi, Pete. This is Helen. Actually I called. I thought Annie was going to stop by earlier. I need to go out and wasn't sure if I should keep waiting. I thought she might be there with you at the store."

"You haven't heard from Annie today?"

"No, see that's why I was calling you. She was supposed to stop by earlier – "

Pete cut her off before she could repeat it all again. "Helen, let me call home and see if she's there. I knew she was going to run some errands today, but I thought she was going to stop by your house first."

"Yes, she was going to stop by here earlier," Helen repeated for the third time, "but, the reason I called you is I called out at your house and I got a recording that said the line was temporarily out of service. I know that happens to you more often, living way out there. I don't know how you do it. Seems like it would be an awful drive in the winter. I was telling Tom . . . Pete are you still there?

"Yes, I'm here. I'll check on Annie."

"Oh, good. For a moment it was so quiet I thought it was another phone problem, and we'd been disconnected. Anyway, I was telling Tom – "

"Helen, I have to go now. If Annie does stop by, would you please ask her to call the store and leave a message where she is going to be? Ask her not to go home until we've talked."

"Pete, are things OK? You sound real quiet."

"Things are fine. I have to go now, but I appreciate you calling." He stared at the phone for a moment after he hung up and then, taking a deep breath, punched in the home number. As Helen had told him, the recording cut in on the second ring to tell him the line was temporarily out of service. He put the phone receiver gently back on its cradle and wrote a short note:

Annie –

Helen called looking for you. Our telephone is out of service and I have gone home to check. If you come here and get this, please leave me a note

*and go to the hospital and wait for me there – It's
a public place. Please humor me on this for now.*

I love you,

Pete

He had the .45 in a hip holster under his jacket, and on
the walk back from the Armadillo the weight of it had begun
to feel silly. He took it out now and popped the magazine. He
clicked off the safety, and with his left thumb hooked forward
in the trigger guard, squeezed with his forefinger on the
bushing under the barrel to ease the slide back a quarter inch
till he could see the gleam of the brass in the chamber. He let
go, the recoil spring closing the slide with a sharp snap, and
he thumbed the safety back up. Cocked and locked, he put the
.45 back in the holster. He stood very still for a moment, said
a quick silent prayer, and then cut out the lights and went to
find Annie.

Heck was lying still, blood soaking his fur and the moss and
hemlock needles beneath him. When Annie got to him, the
return of raw anger swept away the cold, the pain from her
knee, and concern about men coming back up the stairs. She
thought again of the pistol locked in her car. She wasn't sure
she was glad or sorry she didn't have the pistol with her, but
she knew if she did, she would walk around the garage and
start shooting.

One of Heck's ears was flopped back, and she knelt
beside him and smoothed it out. She kissed him on top of
his head, talking to him in her mind. As she did, she felt the
faintest twinge. Lifting up, she saw his nose twitch almost
imperceptibly, sniffing for rabbits in his dream she would
have called it under happier circumstances. Slowly an eyelid
rolled up, and after a moment his eye seemed to focus on her.

Heck didn't move or make any sound, but his nose wrinkled and upper lip curled up baring his teeth in what looked like a snarl, but she knew was his "I'm really happy to see you" smile. Annie found her eyes filling with tears, and for a moment she pressed her face into his neck, whispering soft endearments and telling him he was going to be OK. Heck gave one very small thump of his tail and then lay completely still as if the wag had taken all his resources.

Annie drew a fierce, deep breath and rubbed her eyes with the heels of her hands. She tried desperately to summon her Emergency Room resolve and detachment. She felt through Heck's thick undercoat, pushing the hair back to look, and was able to find entry and exit wounds, high on his back, behind the shoulder. She put an ear to his chest and listened, trying to shut out all other sound. His heartbeat was too fast and irregular, but still seemed strong. It was hard to tell, but his lungs didn't sound like they were filling with blood and there was no whistling noise that would be caused by a sucking chest wound.

"Shhh, shhh, you're my very, very good dog. Yes, yes, yes, you're going to be OK," Annie was whispering in his ear. She reached underneath him and tried to lift him, but he weighed almost as much as she did, and all she could do is raise him a bit, which caused a low groan and the eyelid to roll open again with a pleading look from Hector. "Hush, hush, now. You hang on here. I'm going to get some help and you're going to be OK."

Annie started to edge back around the garage, but froze as she heard one of the men coming up the stairs from the house. "Fuck, can you imagine living way the fuck out here? Who the hell would want to walk up this many stairs every time you left your house?" It was the man with the Mexican accent and he was panting slightly.

"Where the hell is Richie? I need to get to a fucking doctor."

"He's down there in the bathroom trying to pick thorns out of his face. You're going to love this. He sent me up to find an ax or something and cut off the dog's head. He's going to leave it in their bed."

"That psycho watched the Godfather too many times. Galvan told us just to snatch the bitch and not leave traces. Now Richie's tried to shoot the fucking bitch, and he wants us to cut off the fucking dog's head?"

"Oh yeah, well why don't you hump your ass down all those steps and tell Richie that? You remember what happened when Marshall told him he was psycho?" There was a long moment of silence as they seemed to reflect.

"Chollo, do you want to be there when Galvan finds out that we missed the bitch and left a mess?"

"Richie's here and Galvan's not."

"I hope you chop that fucking dog to pieces, but I need to get to a doctor. Get in the garage and get something to do it with and then let's get the fuck out of here. She may have gotten somewhere to call the cops."

Annie desperately tried to lift Hector again, but he was just too big. She got down on her stomach and began to wiggle under him. Heck reopened an eye and looked at her, but she pleadingly told him to hush, to stay quiet. When Annie got her back under him, she rose up on her hands and knees and began to crawl. Any moment she expected the men to walk around the corner, but as she tried to crawl faster, Heck would slip and she kept having to stop to get him repositioned.

She could hear the men discovering the garage was locked and then kicking the door. She looked behind her and saw drag marks from her knees that even these idiots couldn't miss, so she turned and began to crawl backwards, brushing out the marks with her hands. As she crawled, she could feel the warmth of Heck's blood soaking through her jacket and top. She heard glass breaking in the small door to the garage and then she could hear the men inside.

Attached to the far side of the garage there was a low shed-roofed enclosure where they kept the garbage cans to keep them away from bears, and kept the recycling. Annie crawled toward it, listening to the men in the garage. It seemed an obvious place for them to look, but there was nowhere else she had a chance of reaching in time. She had taken out a bag of trash that morning before her run, and she knew two out of the three cans were empty. She swung open the doors, wincing as a hinge squeaked.

She could hear the men rummaging in the garage and then one of them giving a small cry of triumph. "All right! Look at these babies! He wants that dog's head, I'm going to do it right. Hell I may cut down their house."

She couldn't figure out what the man was talking about. Then, from in front of the garage, she heard the cough of a chainsaw trying to start. There were two chainsaws in the garage, a big Husqvarna logger's model that Pete had used building the house and a smaller Stihl they used for firewood. Annie slid Heck from her back and pulled one of the rubber trash cans down on its side, desperately hurrying. She whispered apologies to Heck and slid him into the can as gently as she could and righted the can. She took a bag of trash from another can and put it on top of him. Satisfied the bag hid him, she replaced the top loosely so it wouldn't block off Heck's air.

She could hear the repeated coughs of the chainsaw engine as they pulled the starter cord. It sounded like they were trying to start the big one and she hoped so. Pete always emptied its tank when he finished with it.

She was planning to retreat back into the woods after hiding Heck, but just then she heard the smaller chainsaw start, sputter for a moment, and quit. She crept to the front corner of the garage and listened as they argued with each other and tried to restart the chainsaw. Kneeling down to be low where they were unlikely to be looking, she peered around the corner.

Their car was right in front of her. The man Heck had mauled was leaning on the rear fender. If she tried to run back up toward the road there was no way he could miss seeing her. She could hear the other man and the repeated coughs of the saw as he tried to restart it, but she had to lean her head a bit farther out to see where he was. She felt totally exposed, realizing that at any moment the man at the car might forget his dog bites and look up at her.

She forced herself to lean a bit farther out, just in time to see the man who had shot Heck kick the chainsaw and then curse as he rubbed his toe. He walked to pick up the saw where it had landed beyond the far front corner of the garage. She realized he was now in a position where she couldn't run back down towards the beach trail without being seen by one of them. Worse, if he looked, he would realize Heck was gone.

Even with her leg stiffened from the fall, she believed with a little head start she could still outrun them. Whichever way she went now, though, they would see her as soon as she made a break and they might simply start shooting. The chainsaw caught again for a moment, and she bunched to run, already feeling the bullets in her back, willing herself to keep running no matter what.

The saw died again and Annie looked desperately around for alternatives. She went back to the trash shed and opened doors, trying to avoid the squeaking hinge. She was worried about Heck making noise from his can, but there was no sound and she didn't know if that was good or bad. Annie got into the other empty can and pulled the doors to the shed closed as well as she could from the inside. It was awkward and a bad fit and despite the fact they had always put their trash in plastic bags, it smelled. She was pulling another bag of trash on top of herself when she heard Chollo shout, "The fucking dog's gone!"

She lay curled in the garbage can, the trash bag covering her, listening to them search and argue. She could only make out portions of the conversation, but was amazed and repulsed by the relentless, unimaginative obscenity of it. Then the tone and cadence of the conversation changed and she realized that the one they called Richie had come up from the house.

She heard the men pass by the outside of the shed several times. Even with her efforts to brush out her tracks, she knew Pete would take one glance at the ground and know where she was. She tried to tell herself that these jerks were city boys.

She was cold, fighting claustrophobia, and her banged knee was throbbing. The muscles in her legs were cramping from the contorted position and the thorns from the devil's club stung. All of that went away as she heard Richie yelling, "I don't care! You find me that fucking cunt. She did this. She came back and got that dog. I'm gonna make her scream till she can't scream no more. Look in the garage again, look under her car, look in that shed, you find her!"

She heard the door to the trash shed open and recognized the voice of the man Heck had attacked, muttering to himself. She heard him lift the lid off the can next to hers. When she had climbed into the can, she had grabbed the top of a soup can from the recycle bin as the only potential weapon she could find. Annie focused on smoothing her breathing, telling herself she would have the element of surprise if he lifted the bag, and to slash for his eyes before he could react. She took a breath and held it as she felt him lift the lid off her can.

23

"They were idiots. They couldn't figure out the big saw didn't have gas in it, and when they gave up on it and started trying to start the smaller saw, they didn't know about using the choke. They were idiots and bastards, and they shot Hector." Annie's voice dissolved into tears and Pete hugged her again, kissing the top of her head. They rocked slightly and Pete said a silent prayer of thanks that the man who looked in the garbage can hadn't bothered to lift the bag of trash Annie had pulled in on top of herself.

They were in the waiting room of the old barn that had been converted into the vets' office. The building was very quiet; no one else was there except the two veterinarians who had come in on the late Sunday afternoon and were in the back operating on Heck. Pete held Annie, his cheek on the top of her head.

By the windows, there was a bulletin board where owners tacked up cute photos of their pets; dogs in birthday hats or sunglasses, dogs and cats curled up together. There weren't any cute pictures of a Chesapeake mauling a gunman. Normally he liked to look at the board, check out the new pictures that had been put up since Heck's or the cat's last visit. Today, though, he was staring past it, out the window, watching each car that passed, his mind filled with a constant metallic whisper.

He had been heading out to the house, driving way too fast, when he passed Annie, also driving way too fast, heading in. He flashed his lights, been pretty sure she had seen him, but she hadn't slowed down. He had to wait a moment for oncoming traffic before making an illegal U-turn. She was out of sight by the time he headed back in her direction with the accelerator floored. If she hadn't had to wait for oncoming traffic before making the left turn at the Fred Meyer intersection, he would have missed her and sped back into town. He caught up with her in the vets' parking lot. She was at the back of the Subaru wagon, checking Heck's breathing and pulse.

Annie said the vets would be there in a moment. She'd stopped at the Auke Bay ferry terminal, which was the first place with a pay phone on the way in and called the veterinarians' answering service. Pete hugged Annie, asking her if she was OK, asking what had happened. Annie gave a little "not now" shake of her head, shifting her eyes past him to Austin, the vet, who just pulled up beside them.

Pete turned down Austin's offer to help carry Heck and carefully lifted him from the car, giving him a kiss on the soft fur on his head, whispering to him that he was going to be OK, but despairing at the inertness of his form. They followed Austin into the office, back into the operating room. Annie walked beside Pete, stroking the dog's head and murmuring to him. The vet asked Annie what had happened and before answering, she gave Pete a long look that contained grief and fury and love.

Seconds stretched before Pete started to speak, to tell everything, but Annie interrupted him. "I don't know. I was down in the house getting ready to leave and thought I heard a shot. When I came up the stairs, I called Heck to go with me, and when I looked around for him, I found him like this behind the garage. Some stupid, malicious bastard or some idiot who thinks he's a hunter, but can't tell the difference between a deer and a big, brown dog."

"Any neighbors that might dislike your dog enough to shoot him? We have that happen once in a rare while."

"No, we don't have anyone that lives close to us, and the folks who might visit all know Heck and like him." Linda, the other vet, came in and Austin suggested that this was going to take a while, to go home and they would call, but Pete and Annie both shook their heads simultaneously, saying they would wait.

Annie crossed to the receptionist's desk for Kleenex. She came back, and after two false starts, told Pete the story in a voice so quiet he could still hear the ticks of the wall clock. Pete listened, trying not to interrupt with questions, his fury at the men growing. When she reached the part about sneaking back to check on Heck, Pete interrupted, "Annie, what were you thinking! I love Hector, too, but you'd gotten away and you went back and almost got yourself killed!"

"You would have gone back, too! He was still alive, and they were going to cut off his head!"

"You didn't know either of those things until after you were back!"

"And if I hadn't gone back, I wouldn't have found out! Don't be snapping at me for doing something you would have done, too. What would you have done, Pete? Answer me honestly, what would you have done?"

There was a long silence, and Annie asked again, "Pete, what would you have done?"

He was quiet, staring at the floor now, and then answering in a quiet voice, "I'd have killed them all and then checked on Hector."

"Well, pardon me if I don't think that killing a bunch of people is the best answer. I don't know if I know you anymore. I don't know if I've ever known you!"

Annie was glaring at him, her lips compressed, the tears she had been holding back suddenly welling in her eyes.

Pete enveloped her in a hug. "I'm sorry, I'm sorry. It's just the thought of losing you scares me like nothing ever has." Annie tried to push him away, but he hugged her tighter. So softly she could barely hear he whispered, "Ann am fianais Dhé 's na tha seo de fhianaisean tha mise a' gealltainnwas a bhith 'nam fhear pòsda dìleas gràdhach agus tairis dhuitsa, gus an dèan Dia leis a' bhàs ar dealachadh."

"What's that? Are you speaking in tongues now?"

"It's Gaelic, or at least it's supposed to be. My pronunciation is probably pretty rusty. It means, 'In the presence of God and before these witnesses I promise to be a loving, faithful and loyal husband to you, until God shall separate us by death.' It's from an old needlepoint that was in my folks' house. It's one of the things I brought back when I went to Michigan and closed out the storage unit. It's in a box up in the attic now."

Pete could see the needlepoint, the phrase interwoven with the same phrase for the wife, a border of thistles around the whole thing. It had been a wedding present to his folks, but it was old, from Scotland, his mother's side of the family. The needlepoint on the wall and the claymore hanging over the mantle were the only things in his house that he knew came over from Scotland with family members. When he was a kid, he had been fascinated with them and made his mother teach him how to say it and a few other Gaelic phrases. It had been true for both his parents.

They were quiet for a time, and then Pete said, "It's been so long not knowing that I've allowed habit and reflex to cause me to be stupid about not going to the Troopers. Ever since the canyon, I've lived my life in camouflage, hidden in plain sight. No sudden movements to attract attention, nothing to make me stand out from the crowd. Speeding back here to catch up with you was one of the few times I've driven over the speed limit because I never wanted to risk a traffic stop.

"A couple of months ago you were working afternoons, and I was working late at Readers'. I'd walked down to the Triangle to get some chili dogs to take back to the store for dinner. You know how they have three TVs above the bar there? One of the shows was *America's Most Wanted*. I'd read about it but never seen it before. The host was talking to the camera. You couldn't hear what he was saying, but I was almost convinced that before Doreen could finish ladling the chili on the dogs, he would flash my picture on the screen, and all the old guys playing pinochle at the table in the back would suddenly look up and shout, 'It's him! Call the cops!' "

He was glad to see he got a small smile out of Annie. She reached forward and touched his cheek, looking at him for a moment and then, gently holding his head with both hands, kissed him on his forehead. "You're always going to be my most wanted. But I think the chance of you getting fifteen minutes of fame on television is pretty slim."

"I know. It's become so ingrained that I think it's just habit, not reality. Going to the police isn't going to lead back to what happened in that canyon. It's been the combination of concern about that and also the promise I made to that kid when I carried him out not to tell about the pack, not to let his mother find out about the drugs or him and Hal."

"You made those promises under duress, but it doesn't matter, we're not going to say anything because I'm not going to take a chance of it leading back to that canyon."

"By not going to the Troopers, I've put you at risk, and violated the promises I care most about, the promises I made to you, the promises I made to myself, the day we got married."

They held on to each other, not talking, thinking; listening to the tick of the wall clock and the occasional car passing in the rain outside. They stared at the door leading out of the waiting room to the back of the vet's, and each, without knowing what the other was doing, said a short, silent prayer for Heck.

"Maybe we tell Galvan where the pack is. That's what they want. I could get ahold of Kotkin, the lawyer that was here, and tell him we found the pack."

"Yeah, Pete. I'm sure he would have warm feelings for you after you trapped him in the outhouse and turned it over." Pete was encouraged to see the slight upturn of the corners of her mouth again. "There are two big problems with giving the pack back to them. The first is we know their names. I've seen Richie and Chollo and the other one, and most important, we know Jonathon Galvan is who they're all working for. You were the one who said earlier they might not be content with just getting the pack back, that once they do, they might want to be sure we can never tell anyone about them."

"I've been thinking about that," he said. "We could use the device you read about. We could write out the details as clearly as possible in a letter to the Troopers, seal it in another envelope to be opened if anything happens to us and give it to a lawyer. We would tell them what we've done when we give them the pack."

"That might work, though from what you've told me, I have the impression that they're so arrogant they think they're immune. Even if it would work, you know what's wrong with it. You know we can't give the pack back?"

"Yeah, I do."

"I'm sorry. I'm not a fan of how we've done our 'War on Drugs', but folks who talk about drugs being a victimless crime have never held a crack baby or a child who will never have a chance at a decent life because his parents are addicts, or never tried to comfort parents, folks who thought the world was a decent place and have just learned that their child, who they cared about more than anything in the world is dead from an overdose. I'm sorry, I'm preaching to you, and I know you know this." Annie smiled sadly, putting her hand on his face. "We're smart people, and we're going to figure this out. We need something, a solution that destroys the cocaine, makes Galvan and his thugs leave us alone, doesn't cause the police to become interested in us, and punishes these bastards for what they've done to Heck."

"I can go to California and take care of all those things."

"No. I said it before, but just then I left out the most important thing. When you talk about going down there and taking care of things, what you're talking about is a bunch of people dying. And when you say it, your voice gets very quiet and dead. You go down there like that and all we do is lose. We lose if they kill you, I couldn't live with that. We lose if you kill them and the police figure it out. And we lose if you kill them and the police don't figure it out, because I'm not sure we would ever unlock wherever it is you lock away your feelings. Look at yourself, Pete. Just talking about going down there, you stopped holding me, you get this very quiet, flat voice and you're absolutely still, like you're waiting for something to come near enough to strike.

"If I'd had a gun when that bastard shot Hector or was chasing me, I'd have shot him," she said. "But not now, not after the heat of the moment. I couldn't live with myself. I'm not sure I could live with you if you went down there to kill people. You've spent decades drawn into yourself, because you shot the guys who shot Dale. If you go down there and kill them, I think no matter what happens, it goes badly for us."

Pete was still for a long, long time. They listened to the clock, the rain, listened to see if they could hear anything from the back that would hint about what was happening with Hector. When he finally spoke it was still with the quiet voice, but he reached over to hold her hand. "You're the person who saved me, who brought me back to life, but Heck's my dog who started me back. If it hadn't been for him, I would have never spoken to you. I don't mean just that he was tied up so I needed to ask you about untying him. I mean he had caused enough change in me that I was able to speak to you. They've shot my dog and tried to shoot and kidnap my wife. One way or another, I am going to even it out and end it."

"We can do that, Pete. When we first came out here to the waiting room, I thought any minute Austin or Linda would come through the door and say, 'I'm sorry, we did everything we could,' but the longer we sit here, the more hopeful I am that Heck's going to be OK. But even if he's not, even if they aren't able to save him, I need you to promise me we're not going to solve this by killing people."

He was quiet again for a long time. "Promises are what got me into to all this, but I promise you I'll do every thing I can to avoid it."

"No, I want a real promise. I'm not asking you to stand by if one of our lives is in jeopardy. I wouldn't either. I have some ideas about what we might do, but I want a real promise, OK?"

"OK, you have my promise. We'll figure out a way to solve it." Pete was quiet again for a long pause. "One more exception I need to be clear about, though. I think they've already killed my dog. They shot at you. If they do anything to you, if they harm you or try to again, I'm going to kill them all."

"Shhh, Austin and Linda are really good. If anybody can help Heck, they can. I hate those bastards for what they did to Hector, what they were going to do. But we're going to be OK, nothing's going to happen to us." They were both quiet for a time again, holding hands tightly. Annie had just started to tell Pete her idea when they heard steps coming from the back, and Austin opened the door to the waiting room.

24

Annie hadn't cried until Austin and Linda came out from the surgery to give them the news, but now there were tears of joy running down her face. Pete swept her off the floor in a hug so tight, she had to tap his arm to be put down so she could breathe. The bullet had punched a hole through the top of Heck's right scapula and hit the top of the C-7 and T-1 vertebrae. The trauma had bruised the nerves of the brachial plexus and caused a partial paralysis that the docs assured them should be temporary. Austin explained that while the injuries were serious, given time, Heck was going to be OK.

Hector was still unconscious from the anesthesia, but they let Pete and Annie go back and see him. Pete felt tears in his eyes, seeing him lying there, partially shaved and bandaged, the anesthesia causing his tongue to loll out of his mouth in a way that made it clear he wasn't just sleeping. Annie discussed the clinical details of Heck's injury and prognosis with Austin and Linda, but Pete just concentrated on the regular rise and fall of Hector's chest and the vet's promise that he was going to make it. He stroked his head and whispered to him.

Pete wanted to take Annie to a friend's afterwards, to have her stay there while he went looking for the men. Annie wanted to go home and check on the cat.

"Little cat disappears anytime we have company," he said. "They wouldn't have even seen her, much less get near enough to do anything."

"But, Pete –"

"We need to find them now. Now's when we have the best chance."

Annie reluctantly agreed, but was insistent that they stay together. She pointed out that by himself he would have only her descriptions of the men and their car. Pete had been watching carefully out the vet clinic's window, aware that the men might be hunting for them as well, and the vet's was a logical place for them to look. In the entryway, out of sight of the vets, he drew the .45 and held it in the pocket of his Filson. Outside, it was getting dark. The rain was still misting down, the road gleaming under the vet's yard light. He made sure he didn't see anyone at the houses across the road and then took a quick walk around the building and checked in the back seat of Annie's Subaru. He unlocked his truck, moving the shotgun from behind the seat to the floor in the front before going back to get Annie.

He followed her to the nearby Fred Meyer, so she could park her car in a less conspicuous place. Pete noticed with satisfaction that there were at least three other green Subaru wagons already in the parking lot and hoped the guys hadn't noticed Annie's license plate number. Annie used the pay phone at Fred's to call the hospital's emergency room and Urgent

Care. She talked to nurses she knew, told a heavily altered version of the story and determined that no one had come in for treatment of dog bites. She was quiet as they walked back to the truck. When they reached it, Annie paused, her hand on the door handle. "Pete, I just lied to two women who are my friends. I really didn't like doing that. I have a feeling that we'll wind up doing other things I don't like before this is over."

He nodded, sad because he knew she was right, but glad that she realized it. Annie had to move the shotgun out of the way to get in the truck, but only said, "Let's find them."

They first checked all the hotels in the valley and then headed into town. They scanned the parking lot of the Breakwater, the first hotel in towards town from the vet's. Annie spoke again. "I meant what I've been saying to you, we're only trying to find where they are staying right now, to find out more about them."

He reached out, touching her cheek. "You said you have an idea. Let's hear it."

"OK, I haven't thought this all the way through, but here's the basic idea. We find out where these guys are staying. We take the skiff back over to the cove and get the pack with all the money and drugs, cocaine whatever it is, and we plant it in their car, in the trunk or something where they don't notice it. Then we watch for them to get into the car and we make an anonymous call to the police. They all get caught with cocaine and probably with their guns. Galvan, down in Los Angeles, knows that the police have all his cocaine and money and he leaves us alone. It could work."

Pete hesitated and then spoke carefully, cautious of offending her, "Seems mighty complicated. In mysteries and movies, the plots need to be complicated to keep folks interested, but in real life I think the more complicated the scheme, the less chance of it working. You know that saying I like, 'In theory, there's no difference between theory and practice. In practice there often is'?"

"I know there are a lot of details to figure out, maybe there's a better way to deal with this, but we can figure something out. You're the one who told me most criminals get caught because they're dumb. We're certainly a lot smarter than this bunch of cowards and cretins. They couldn't even figure out how to start a chainsaw."

Pete still wasn't sure how that related to anything, but if focusing on their incompetence with a chainsaw helped her deal with being chased and shot at and Heck being shot, he was grateful.

"You know, Annie, even if it all worked and the police got the guys and the cocaine, it doesn't guarantee that Galvan will leave us alone."

"Life doesn't give guarantees, I know that. Let's talk about this, though, and either figure out how to make it work or figure out a better idea. It seems to me there are two main questions. The first is strategy; would it work and end the situation? The second is tactics; if we think it would work, how do we do it?"

"I admit I don't have any better ideas that you would find acceptable. Let's kick this around a bit," he said. They talked as he drove through the parking lots of the Driftwood and the Prospector and headed downtown toward the Westmark, the Baranof and the Bergmann looking for the Taurus. Juneau had many bed and breakfasts, but they agreed that they should check the hotels first. These guys seemed like they would prefer anonymity over frilled quilts and homemade muffins in the morning.

"If we could plant the drugs and money and the police get them," he said, "it would end Galvan trying to get the pack from us and would keep these guys in jail. That amount of cocaine and gun charges would put them away for a long time. Up here it would be a much bigger deal than in a big city."

"They'll know we were the ones who planted the pack. My main concern is that they tell the police about us and start them poking around in your past."

"I've been thinking about that a lot, and I don't think they will," he said. "If they tell the police about us, they put themselves at risk of additional charges of attempted kidnapping and attempted murder. There have to be bullets in the ground where they shot Heck and in the tree where they shot at you. That would verify your story. If the police start questioning us, we tell them the truth about everything, except knowing about the pack. We tell them that they had threatened to kill us if we went to the police.

"I think I've always known I've probably been in a two-decade purgatory of my own making. With all the money left lying in the dirt, I think and hope the cops believed that Dale and those guys shot each other. Even if they had doubts, there was nothing I am aware of to tie it back to me. There were no witnesses, and I don't believe there was any physical evidence."

The mist had thickened into rain and the wind was picking up steadily, beginning to shake the trees and street signs. The marine forecast predicted a big low coming onshore from the Gulf of Alaska, bringing gale-force winds and mixed rain and snow to most of the Inside Passage. The snow had already been piling up in the mountains, and it looked like they were going to get some at sea level now.

Pete drove the truck from the parking lot behind the Baranof, down the steep alley to Seward Street, across from Readers'. They'd checked the parking lots and streets around every downtown hotel without success.

"What do you think?" he asked, "Back out by the airport, make sure they haven't turned in the car, then recheck the valley hotels?"

Annie nodded "If that doesn't work, let's find a phone book and start checking all the B&B's, I guess. It doesn't seem as likely, but what's your Sherlock Holmes quote, 'When you have eliminated the impossible, whatever remains, however improbable, must be the truth.'"

"I usually say that when I can't find my reading glasses."

"Same principle. These bastards are here somewhere, we'll find them."

The long twilight had yielded to a black night. They were driving back out Egan now, the wind buffeting the truck. They had to wait at the stoplight at the Hospital Drive intersection. The wind shaking the street lights caused the intersection to seem to vibrate. Twin Lakes were on their right now, and a high tide had brought Gastineau Channel crashing up to the riprap along the left. Spray joined the rain hitting the truck.

They were approaching the Lemon Creek intersection when a car passed them in the left lane. "Pete, that looks like the car! It only had one person in it, but it was a maroon Taurus, and I saw a portion of the license plate that looked right."

Pete settled in to follow about a quarter mile back. He sped up a bit as the tail lights ahead disappeared over the rise at Sunny Point and slowed when he could see them again. The turn signals for the Taurus came on as they neared the airport access road, and Pete slowed again to widen the gap before turning toward the airport.

"Do you think he's leaving or picking someone up?"

Annie thought for a moment and then shook her head. "Unless they've changed the Alaska Airlines schedule, it's too late to be picking someone up from the afternoon flight and it'd be mighty early to be checking in for the evening flight. Maybe turning in the rental car? "

"That might make sense, especially if they're worried about you having seen it. I don't know if they know this truck or not, but if we follow him all the way into the airport, there isn't going to be much other traffic, and even in this weather it's going to be hard for him to miss us."

"Slow down to give him some more room," she said. "If you pull into the Coastal Helicopters lot up here, we'll be able to see the terminal door nearest the rental counters and the cab stand."

Pete cut his lights as they pulled into the parking lot, adjacent to the main terminal. He backed into a space beside the building where they could see. He turned off the engine and the rain seemed to drum even louder on the truck roof.

The driver of the Taurus pulled into the rental lot. The Juneau airport was too small for in-lot rental car check-in, and they watched as he left the car and sprinted through the rain for the terminal.

They sat in silence for a while, listening to the rain, watching through the water sheeting down the windshield. Pete cracked his window so the inside wouldn't fog up. Sitting here in the truck, it seemed wrong not to have Heck with him, lying partially in his lap, snoring gently. His mind drifted to other times of watching and waiting - in the jungle, with bugs chewing on him, in California, the hot sun beating down as he sorted out the faint sounds in the canyon. He thought of happier times waiting and watching, sitting in big timber with a soft snow filtering down, watching deer trails on the benches below him, eating homemade fruitcake that a friend of Annie's gave them every Thanksgiving and drinking coffee out of his battered old Stanley thermos. He looked at Annie's profile as she watched the terminal.

His eyes had grown misty, but he blamed the water on the windshield when it took him a second to spot the man coming out of the terminal. The man stood underneath the awning in front of the terminal lighting a cigarette. He was in his late twenties, about six-three, slim, wearing some type of designer jeans and a hip-length black leather jacket. There was something about the clothes and haircut, and just about the guy, that instantly caused Pete to catalog him from a big city. The man finished the cigarette and went back inside where they could see him waiting just inside the door.

Annie took a small pair of binoculars from the glove compartment and stared intently at the man. She watched as a black Audi Quattro pulled up in front of the airport doors. The man came back out, lit another cigarette, and started to get in the car. He hesitated for a moment as the driver seemed to be protesting something. Through the binoculars, she could see the man flick his cigarette at the driver. He laughed as the driver frantically scrambled out of the car on the other side, pawing the cigarette out of his clothes. The passenger settled into his seat and lit another cigarette. As the driver got back into the car, she could see the passenger blow a cloud of smoke into the driver's face and say something that caused the driver to immediately go silent and pull away from the curb.

"It's the bastard they were calling Richie. I'm going to remember that sneer for a long time." She handed the binoculars to Pete so he could look as the car swung out by them and headed back toward downtown.

Pete watched through the binoculars as the Audi passed them. "Annie, the guy driving, I've seen him around town. He does something around the capitol, a lobbyist, I think. I remember him coming into the store last winter and standing around in a black cashmere coat looking bored, while a very expensive-looking young woman bought a card."

Annie raised an eyebrow. "Good thing he had the young woman with him so you remember, huh? So what was it that made her look very expensive?"

"No, honestly. I just remember because it was so strange that a person would stand in a book store, obviously waiting and bored, and not look at books. It just seemed weird."

"OK, so they have a local connection. We know he's not a poster boy for Reading is Fundamental, he does something around the capitol, has expensive tastes in clothes, cars and women, doesn't like people smoking in his car, and somehow that young man riding with him scares him enough to let cigarettes be flipped at his face. Let's follow and see what else we can find out."

Pete started the truck, but waited until the Audi taillights were almost out of sight before pulling onto the road and turning on his own lights. The wind shook the truck, and he turned the wipers on high as they pulled onto Egan, following the black Audi back toward town.

25

"Can you still see their taillights?" she asked.

"Just barely. I don't want them slowing down in this rain and us getting too close to them."

Pete and Annie stared through the windshield as the wipers beat off the rain, tying to keep the twin red dots in sight. They were on the channel side of the highway now as they drove in past Lemon Creek, and the spray from the channel mixed with the rain, making visibility worse. Pete sped up a bit to keep the Audi in sight. They passed the hospital and the hatchery, and he let the gap close up a bit as the Audi slowed down coming into town.

"If I hang back too much here I'll lose them when they turn, but this is where it gets chancier on their noticing us," he said.

"I think we're lucky the driver is too worried about his passenger to spend time watching his rear-view mirror. Pete, slow down, they're turning by the high school!"

The driver of the Audi had obligingly put on his turn

signal well before he moved over into the left turn lane. Pete slowed to let the Audi make the turn without his coming up behind it. He had to wait for several cars from the opposite direction to pass before he could turn. When he did, the Audi was no longer in sight. He made a guess and headed up Highland toward the more expensive houses. They drove up the steep hill cautiously. If they had stopped up here, he didn't want to come upon them inadvertently while they were getting out of the car.

He reached the top of Highland, without seeing the car, but made a guess and turned uphill again. They were probably five hundred feet higher than town here, but even the small increase in elevation caused the rain to change to a mixture of rain and wet snow. The houses perched up here among the big spruces were some of the nicest in town, their location trading the risk of avalanches thundering down the flanks of Mount Juneau for stunning views of town and the mountains of Douglas Island. He rounded a curve and saw a house up a steep driveway with the motion lights on above the garage door. Pete pulled to the side of the street and cut off the truck lights.

"Do you think it's them?"

"I don't know," he said. "In this wind, a branch or something could have made that light go on, or it may just be a light someone has turned on. This street dead ends, so if they did come up this way, I don't know where else they could've gone."

"Let's sit here a few minutes. If it's really a motion light, it should go off soon."

Pete turned the truck off, and they sat there, silent, each deep in their own thoughts. They watched the house and driveway, the wind buffeting the truck and swaying the trees and shrubbery. Pete turned on the wipers occasionally to clear the rain and snow so they could see.

"Pete?"

"Yeah?"

"You're starting to hurt my hand."

They were holding hands and Pete realized that he had been thinking about these men shooting at her and unconsciously had been squeezing tighter and tighter. "Sorry." He gave her hand a kiss. "The light has gone off. I want to go up. If I can look in the windows, I may be able to see if this is where they're staying."

"It looks like Cashmere Coat is some kind of local connection for them, but what on earth could they have to do with the legislature?"

"I don't know. They had to be taking the coke somewhere, but I admit this doesn't fit my preconceptions. I want to go up."

"What if they're keeping watch, or some neighbor sees you and calls the police?"

"We need to know what we're dealing with. The wind and rain are in our favor. Not many folks are going to be strolling around the neighborhood tonight. I'll be careful."

"I want us to stick together."

"Two of us up there peering in windows would double the possibility of our being seen, and with your knee, I don't want to take any chance of you needing to run again. Why don't you take the truck down to the Breakwater parking lot at the bottom of the hill? I'll look, and then I'll walk down. "

"I think my knee's just bruised, but I'll admit it would make creeping through the bushes tough. If we can't go together, though, I can wait right here. I'll turn the truck around so we can make a quick getaway." Annie punched him in the arm. "Don't give me that look. I could be a good getaway driver."

"I think you would put Dale Earnhardt to shame. I just never thought of you and 'getaway driver' in the same sentence. Seriously, it wouldn't be good to have the truck here in case they come out. We have to assume they know what I drive and could spot it. Nothing's going to happen, but if someone is after me, I'm heading straight up the mountain. None of these folks are ever going to catch me in the woods."

Annie didn't answer, she just stared back at him. She didn't like it, but understood the logic. He tried again, "While I'm doing this, why don't you drive over to Foodland and buy a couple of cold packs to put on your knee? Go next door to Super Drug and get an Ace bandage or a slip-on knee brace? After that I'll meet you in the Breakwater parking lot."

"If you think I'm going shopping while you sneak up on the bad guys, you're more nuts than I've always known you were. Just to put all the other arguments to rest, I still have Heck's blood dried all across my back. I'd attract a good bit of attention shopping in Foodland. I'm the medical person here, and my knee will be OK for a while." Her smile was gone, and he could see she was dead serious now. "I'll take the truck down to the Breakwater and wait in the parking lot there, but I don't like it. You're not down there in half an hour, I'm coming back with the shotgun."

"I'll be there. Just give me a little leeway in case anything interesting is going on inside." Pete grinned at her. "I don't want to be looking in a window and have you come in the door shooting up the place." Pete leaned over and gave her a kiss and started to get out the door.

She stopped him holding out a leather leash of Heck's that had been lying on the truck floor. "Take this. If you run into someone on the street, you can say you were out walking your dog, that he took off and you're looking for him."

Pete took the leash and got out of the truck, pulling his cap down and turning his collar up against the rain. He waited until Annie left and then walked up the street toward the steep drive, trying to look like a man whose dog had run away.

He crept up the drive, watching for a light beam or other sensor, ready to disappear into the thick rhododendrons that crowded the drive on either side. Pine cones from the spruce and hemlocks, needles, twigs and small branches littered the street and driveway and the wind tossed the rhododendrons. At the top, the driveway leveled off into a parking area in front of a three-car garage. The house was cedar over a half story of stone, and from the street, it hadn't been obvious how big or fancy it was. The double front doors, to the left of the garage, were eight feet high and carved in Alaska totemic designs. The handles were bronze castings of salmon. Light came out of mullioned windows to the left of the door. The slate roof and copper gutters converged in multiple gables. He edged back into the bushes and waited for a moment, checking for any motion, looking for lights or video cameras under the eaves. From his vantage point he couldn't count the gables, and somewhere in the back of his mind he wondered if anyone inside had ever read Hawthorne. He felt foolish about looking for alarms or cameras; this was Juneau where most folks didn't even lock their houses, but until a little while ago, he wouldn't have believed that there were people here who would shoot his dog and try to kidnap his wife.

The garage was dark, but through a window, he could see the Audi and the outline of another car. He eased his way past other darkened windows until he came to the kitchen. Through the kitchen window, he could see into the living room where there were several people. In the front of the house, the slope of the yard made the windows too high to see in, but he figured he could circle around to the far side and be uphill enough to have a good view in the side windows.

The wind whipped the rain and snow down his neck. In the midst of the litter falling from the trees, a larger limb came crashing down. He froze, waiting to see if the noise would attract anyone to look out the window. It would be ironic if, after all his concern about the men, he was brained by a falling branch. At the edge of the yard, he picked his way through a tangle of brush and then, feeling very exposed, stepped onto the grass of the side yard.

Avoiding the light cast through the windows, Pete moved closer one step at a time, until he was just outside the window. He could see clearly now, but if one of the people inside looked directly at the window they would see him. There were five of them inside and Pete watched, trying to sort out the gestures and body language. Occasionally he could read their lips or hear snatches of what they were saying. He recognized the lobbyist who had accompanied the expensive looking young woman into Readers' and who had picked up Richie at the airport. A different woman, about the same age as the lobbyist, looking very unhappy and even more expensive, sat across from him.

The other three guys were all in their late twenties or early thirties. Pete recognized Richie from the airport. He had high cheekbones, very pale blue eyes, and a peroxide blonde buzz cut. The previous year a Russian ballet troupe had visited Juneau and Annie had convinced him to go. Richie's long ropey body and the way he moved reminded Pete of the lead male dancer who did amazing lifts and leaps.

Pete figured the guy with his hand and arm bandaged heavily and administering his own anesthetic by drinking steadily from a bottle of Maker's Mark, had to be the one Heck had attacked. The third guy was Hispanic and had to be Chollo, who Annie said shot Heck. He was wearing very baggy jeans and looked like he'd lifted a lot of weights.

Chollo was drinking beer steadily; when he would finish one he would crush the can in his hand and give it a little toss at the woman. If she didn't hop up to get him a new beer, he would yell at her and sweep his arm towards the kitchen. She was glaring at him, but if looks could kill, the glares she was giving her husband would have vaporized him.

She had to walk past Chollo to get to the kitchen and as she did, he grabbed her bottom and Pete could see him making some comment with a tremendous leer. She wheeled and slapped him so hard her handprint was visible on his face. For a second, it looked like all hell was going to break loose. Chollo was swelling up, savoring the outrage. He rose up off the couch with his fist going back for a haymaker that would have killed or maimed her. Her husband started coming up out of his chair as well, but it was obvious he knew persuasive arguments were going to be useless and he didn't know how to do anything else. As Chollo swung back, Pete pulled the .45, centered the sights on his chest and was taking up slack on the trigger when Richie stepped between Chollo and the woman.

Richie snapped a command at Chollo that stopped him mid-swing and at the same time, put a hand on Cashmere's bald head and shoved him back down in his chair. He had been standing behind the husband's chair, but suddenly, without any sense of hurry, he was around the chair and in front of Chollo. They were yelling, and Pete was able to hear bits and pieces and partly read their lips.

Pete eased the pressure on the trigger, but kept the .45 up, sights centered between Richie's shoulder blades. Chollo had turned almost purple with rage and was shouting at Richie. Richie was up very close to him, invading his space, a small smile on his face. Pete could tell that Chollo was yelling that no one slapped him, that he was going to hurt the bitch, when Richie gave him a small slap with his right hand. Chollo went silent, looking like his effort to contain his fury was going to make his veins pop, but also looking down at the knife that had materialized in Richie's left hand and was now tracing a slow pattern back and forth across Chollo's stomach.

Richie hooked the knife under Chollo's belt and with a quick twist, cut it. Chollo was suddenly standing there, looking ridiculous in a pair of oversized patterned boxers, baggy jeans around his ankles. With the knife now tracing its lazy patterns lower across Chollo's abdomen, Richie leaned even closer and appeared to be whispering in Chollo's ear. As he did, he reached through the fly of Chollo's boxers and began to fondle him, whispering and fondling and watching Chollo's rage mingle with stark fear.

Pete couldn't hear what they were saying anymore, but could see Richie was asking Chollo questions, pausing as Chollo shook his head yes or no, beads of sweat breaking out on his forehead and dark stains spreading under his arms. After the last question, Richie smiled and started to squeeze Chollo's testicles, increasing the pressure and dipping slightly as Chollo sagged, the knife sliding up to rest against Chollo's neck.

As Chollo's knees hit the floor, Richie let loose and carefully wiped Chollo's sweat off his knife, first one side of the blade on Chollo's right shoulder and then the other side across his left, murmuring something, looking as though he were knighting him.

When Richie first slapped Chollo, the wife had a look of vindication and hate, but that look drained into terror as she watched. She moved over to her husband and they held hands like if either let loose, they would slide into the abyss. Richie walked over to her, the knife dangling loose in his hand.

He gave a contemptuous look at the husband and moved very close to the wife, taking her hand and holding it, almost as if they were going to step on a ballroom floor together. He gave it a small kiss. With his left hand he had flipped the knife closed and slipped it into his back pocket. A strand of her hair had fallen loose and Richie gently tucked it behind her ear. He stroked her cheek with the back of his fingers, staring intently into her eyes. He turned his hand over and wiped Chollo's sweat on her cheeks and her lips.

Still looking into her eyes, he very slowly slid his hand across her cheek, down her neck, down across the silk blouse and the swell and tip of her breast. By the time his hand traced down her stomach, she stood rigid, but had squeezed her eyes tightly shut and was trembling violently. Richie leaned even closer and began whispering in her ear as his hand continued its slow journey downward, down across the waistband of her skirt, down, ever more slowly, down to the inside of her thigh, and slowly down to the hem of her skirt where he hooked his forefinger under the hem and lifted slightly.

As Richie lifted the skirt, he turned and talked to her husband. Richie was grinning widely now, his face flushed, obviously enjoying himself and excited. He had partly turned and though Pete couldn't hear, he could decipher some of the words from reading his lips. He could make out "any good?" and "share some" and "too old" and "any daughters around?"

The husband sat slumped in his chair, an important man, suddenly impotent in a situation where he had neither the skills nor courage to cope. Pete wondered about the mental calculus that had gotten the man into this situation and if he had ever considered how out of his depth he was when he entered into whatever arrangement he had with these folks.

Richie ran a quick hand up under her skirt, up the inside of her thigh, lifting her up on her toes for a moment. Pete could see him say something in a changed tone and point to the kitchen. The wife opened her eyes and gave both her husband and Richie a look of loathing and despair and after a small shudder, turned to go to the kitchen. Richie slapped her on the ass as she went, exactly where Chollo had, and laughed loud enough for Pete to hear through the window.

The wife went into the kitchen and got a beer for Chollo. He had struggled to his feet and was attempting to pull up his baggy jeans. Richie had to speak sharply to him to make him take the beer. Richie rubbed the husband's head again, laughing like they were sharing a joke, and leaned over and planted a large wet kiss on top of the bald pate.

Outside the window, Pete slowly lowered and holstered his pistol. He looked at his watch and reluctantly, moved away from the window and crept back into the woods. Five careful minutes later he was back on the street, walking rapidly downhill, trying to look like a man looking for a dog, but looking far more like someone ready to use the leash as a garrote.

26

"I didn't drag you to the ballet." Annie said. "Afterward you said you liked it. And that guy was striking. Richie is scary looking."

"I didn't like being in the crowd, but the rest of the ballet was interesting. Right now Richie has a very nasty rash across his forehead and left cheek that looked like someone beat him in the face with devil's club."

"Good! When those branches snapped back and got him, he screamed. I was hoping they got him in his eyes. I put my arms up in front of my face as I ran through the thicket, but I'm going to be picking thorns out for a few days myself."

"When we get home, we'll do some work with tweezers on any that are above the skin. Soon as the rest fester for a day or two, we can squeeze them out."

"So, do you have a better idea?"

"Let's do some more thinking. As you said, we have new information that changes the equation and we can't get back to the cove until this gale blows through anyway."

Annie started to answer and then paused as the wind made a keening sound where Pete had his window rolled down an inch. They were sitting in the truck in the Foodland parking lot. The headlights were off, but he had the truck engine on to run the heater and defroster. Annie had her foot propped up on the dashboard. She folded the two bags of frozen peas in a dish towel and used a roll of four-inch gauze to wrap the improvised cold pack onto her knee. Pete struggled through the childproof seal on a bottle of ibuprofen, and she washed four of them down with the mocha he had brought her to warm her up.

Even down here, just above sea level, the rain was thickening, mixing with snow, and starting to stick. Pete occasionally flicked on the wipers so they could see out. He guessed that out the road at their house, where it was usually a bit colder, this was already real snow.

"OK, I have my knee wrapped, and I want to go home and check on the cat and the house. We can try to figure this out on the way to pick up my car."

"You car will be fine where it is at Fred Meyer's. We can pick it up tomorrow. I don't think there's any chance of those guys going out again tonight, but we're staying together."

They were both silent for a while as they drove out of town, and then Annie started again. "All of this because Hal and Randy ran aground in the storm, and then ran into the bear."

"Event cascade."

"What?"

"Event cascade," Pete said. "It's a term I read in connection with plane crashes. Most crashes are not the result of a single disastrous event, but the culmination of many small things gone wrong. It's always made a lot of sense to me in life as well."

"Professor Herdman, Shakespeare's tragedies, *Richard the Third.*"

"My turn. What?"

"You know. The Battle of Boswell, where Henry defeats Richard III. Richard loses his horse and cries out, 'A horse! A horse! My kingdom for a horse.'"

"Ah, 'For want of a nail . . .' etc. Yeah, there were probably a dozen things that they did wrong to manage to run aground. Then when they decide they have to get the drugs off the boat before the Coast Guard or someone shows up, they run into the bear. I can easily think of a half dozen things they did wrong with the bear, but regardless of how it happened, it doesn't appear that they're going to quit, and we won't win a war of attrition with them."

"Pete, I've been thinking about Cashmere Coat and his wife. It would be easiest to find out about them for starters. In particular, I'm thinking about what Richie did to her and how you said she looked at Richie and her husband."

"And?"

"Right now she must desperately want these guys out of her life. We want them out of our life. If we could convince her that we can get rid of these guys without involving her or her husband, she would have very strong incentive to help us, to give us information."

They kicked it back and forth until they reached agreement and had a rough plan. They passed the intersection where you turned to go to the vet's and both fell silent. Pete glanced over again and could see Annie's silhouette, her head bent forward and hands clasped in front of her. Pete kept his eyes on the road, but said his own silent prayer for Heck and asked forgiveness for his rage.

It was all snow by the time they reached the valley and drove out toward Auke Bay. When they passed the harbor where the *Bon Temps* was still moored, Pete spoke again. "I've been thinking about the boat in connection to all of this."

"What about it?"

"I spent some time at the store checking ads in the back of *Sail* and *Cruising World,* and that boat's worth at least a half million. Kotkin mentioned the same thing the Coast Guard told me when I brought it in, that I could file a salvage claim on the boat. I did some research. Our claim would be "pure" salvage, which means we didn't have a contract with the owner limiting the amount. The main determinant of the value of a claim is the value of the property saved."

"Didn't you tell him we weren't interested in filing a claim?"

"I wasn't. Getting the boat off the sand bar was the right thing to do. I don't think they've ever believed that we wouldn't file a claim, though. A guy like Galvan is used to taking maximum advantage and tends to think that's the way the rest of the world is, unless they're suckers. It's like liars think everyone else lies."

"So what are you thinking?"

"We've had two problems with going to the Troopers about all of this. The first was I didn't want them looking into my past. The second problem was what we would tell the police about why these folks were after us. 'We don't know, Officer; these mean men just started flying up from California,' would guarantee that the Troopers would start looking at us very closely. But the truth, 'Officer, we have a large pack full of drugs and money that belongs to them, but really, our intentions were good," would be much worse. I'm thinking that if we filed a salvage claim, it could provide a plausible reason of why these guys are after us."

"Pete, I'm still serious about not going to the Troopers. It's a chance I'm not willing to take."

"We're going to limit our risks, but this is something the Troopers or the Juneau police may become aware of without our contacting them. If so, we want to be able to give them a reason these guys are after us. A salvage claim would provide that. It's not one Galvan's guys would dispute. 'No, we didn't care about the salvage claim. We just want our drugs back.' If it gives us any financial leverage on Galvan, that's good as well."

"Is it too late to file a claim? It's been three months."

"No, I checked that while I was reading. The Salvage Act of 1912. A claim can be filed for up to two years."

The snow continued to thicken and Pete shifted into four-wheel drive. They lived five miles past where the State stopped its winter maintenance, but even before that, the plowing tended to be sketchy. As they neared their house, they were both quiet, thinking about what had happened earlier that day and what they might find.

There weren't any tire tracks in the snow on the driveway and they knew where the guys were, but even so Pete convinced Annie to take the shotgun and wait outside the door. He went into the house and did a quick room-to-room search. He was less concerned about anyone being there than what he might find.

"I'm amazed; I thought they would've torn the place up."

"When I was behind the garage, one of the guys was saying that they were supposed to grab me and not leave traces. He was complaining about Richie wanting to cut off Heck's head. Have you seen any sign of the little cat?'

"No, but if he'd done anything to her, it sounds like he would have left her prominently displayed. You know how she disappears when company comes. She's here. She'll come out when she's ready."

"I want to find her." Annie was insistent, but Pete was equally insistent that she get out of her wet clothes. While she took a hot shower and changed, he searched the house and called the cat without success. He shook fresh cat food in her bowl to lure her out, but even after Annie joined him in the search they had no luck. Pete finally convinced her there wasn't anything else they could do and the cat would appear when they quit looking for her. He made them supper so Annie could stay off her knee, but it didn't do any good. She went around the house, changing the sheets, scrubbing the baths, and generally trying to disinfect the house from the memory of Richie's presence. After dinner, she told Pete there was one more thing she wanted.

"What was that Gaelic phrase that you told me at the vets? The one from your mother's needle point?"

"*Ann am fianais Dhé 's na tha seo de fhianaisean tha mise a' gealltainnwas a bhith 'nam fhear pòsda dìleas gràdhach agus tairis dhuitsa, gus an dèan Dia leis a' bhàs ar dealachadh* – In the presence of God and before these witnesses I promise to be a loving, faithful and loyal husband to you, until God shall separate us by death."

"Yeah, I want you to go up to the attic and bring that down. I want to hang it in our bedroom. Tonight."

He did, and at her insistence also brought down his brother's scrapbook. After supper they had a glass of wine in front of the fire and debated the wisdom of approaching the wife and the mechanics of planting the drugs on Richie and his friends.

The last thing before going to bed, he listened to the marine weather – a gale throughout northern Southeast, blowing snow, heavy freezing spray, eight to ten foot waves for most of the Inside Passage including Lynn Canal and Stephens Passage. He went out on the deck. Lynn Canal was invisible in the swirling snow and dark, but he could hear the crash of waves below on the rocks. It would be a while before anyone could get to the cove to get the pack.

Pete went back inside and made a final circuit of the house, checking the locks and the alarm box for the trip wires and trying to call the cat again. He joined Annie in bed, silently vowing that if they had done something to the cat, he was going to add that to the price he was going to make them pay.

He slept lightly that night, waking up several times to listen to the wind and waves and catalog the miscellaneous creaks and bumps of the house in a storm. It was pushing four when he awoke again and became aware of the furry warmth of the little cat curled into the crook of his neck. Annie snuggled her back into him. He kissed her and she murmured something in her sleep. Pete lay there for a long time before he fell back asleep.

27

"What'd they say?"

Annie hung up the phone from talking to the vet. "He's doing OK. I talked to Linda. He lost a lot of blood, but she's given him a transfusion and says he's just going to need time."

"Where do they get the blood? Could I donate?"

"No, sweetie, you two are already way too much alike and we don't want him picking up any more bad habits." Annie smiled at him, joking to diminish their concern about Hector. "Actually, Linda says she uses her Malamute as a donor in emergency cases like this. Turns out dogs have thirteen blood types. Makes humans seem simple. Her dog is A negative and tests positive for only DEA 4. That means he can function as a universal donor. She's concerned about whether the amount they were able to give him the first time was enough. She says dogs sensitize very easily through transfusion or pregnancy so she wants to avoid a second transfusion if possible. She's watching him closely for hemolytic reaction."

"So what does all that mean?"

"It means those bastards almost killed him, but Linda and Austin are very good veterinarians and with a little luck, he's going to be OK."

"Can we stop in to see him?

"She said he was still sedated and suggested we wait, but after some discussion, she agreed we could."

They talked softly to Hector's inert form and Annie gave him a kiss on the top of his head. They retrieved Annie's car from Fred Meyer, dropped it at the employee lot at the hospital, and then drove downtown together. At the city building they went to the assessor's office and looked up the property files for the house in the Highlands. The owners were Donald and Renee Barrington. Pete remembered reading about him in the papers from time to time, always with references to his being one of Alaska's most influential lobbyists.

They went up Main Street to the Alaska Public Offices Commission. The building where APOC was located probably had some official name, but neither Pete nor Annie had ever heard it called anything but "the spam can" because of its unfortunate architectural resemblance.

At APOC they looked at Barrington's client list which included an insurance association, several local governments, a phone company, a cruise line, an Alaska Native corporation, an association of radiologists and the local theater company in Juneau. The only one that looked like a possible connection was a company called Carter Corrections. It was based in Los Angeles and ran private prisons around the country. The news had followed its controversial push in the legislature to build several private prisons in Alaska.

"There ought to be a way to figure out if Galvan has some connection to Carter Corrections," Pete said, "but I'm not sure of how to do it without calling attention to ourselves."

"Barrington representing Treadwell Theater makes me wonder. There isn't any other client on his list paying less than $40,000 a year. Treadwell is listed at $1,000 a year which sure doesn't seem to fit with the rest."

"I'd suggest he's a theater buff, but that doesn't match his behavior when he came into the store. He was waiting there, bored, and didn't even pick up a book."

"No, I think I know what the Treadwell connection is," Annie said. "Ever since we saw Renee Barrington's name on the property file, it's been tugging at me, but now I've got it. A couple of months ago, I was listening to "Juneau Afternoon" on KTOO. They had a couple folks from Treadwell Theater talking about the upcoming season. I'm almost sure that one of them was Renee Barrington. I think she runs fundraising for them. Treadwell's been very successful, but they're heavily dependent on government grants. That could explain why they would need a high-powered lobbyist and why he's willing to do it at such a reduced rate. It also tells us where we can find her."

Annie called Treadwell Theater and talked to Renee. Using a false name, Annie told her that her mother had recently died leaving her as the executor of her estate with instructions that half of it be distributed to arts and culture organizations in Juneau. Annie said she'd heard her on the radio and been impressed. They arranged to meet for coffee at the Douglas Café at 1:30 that afternoon.

Douglas had grown up around the Treadwell gold mine and for a period in the early 1900s had been the largest community in Alaska. In 1917, a cave-in right at the high tide line had flooded the seventeen levels of the mine underneath the channel and started the end of the community. Old photographs on the walls of the café and ruins in the regrown forest south of town were all that recalled its glory. Douglas continued as a small residential community that was officially part of Juneau, but fiercely retained its separate identity.

Pete and Annie arrived twenty minutes early. They parked across the street and up the block. Through the blowing snow, they had a good view of the restaurant and, several doors farther down the block, the theater. Pete walked down to the block, checking each car in case Richie had someone watching her. He went into the café and bought a brownie. While they were bagging it up he went back to the men's room and checked for anyone waiting in there. He paid for the brownie and returned to the car by the opposite side of the street, double checking the cars.

About 1:35 Renee came out of the door of Treadwell and headed for the café, walking cautiously as the wind buffeted her on the icy sidewalk.

"That's her," Pete said. "They were pretty empty when I checked. If you sit back by the left windows, I may be able to see you." As Annie got out of the truck, he spoke again, "Annie, you're a really nice person, but you are going to need to put intense pressure on her. Think about Richie shooting at you."

"I'm thinking about them shooting Hector. I'll do OK."

Renee hadn't been seated yet, and Annie was able to steer her to a back table where their conversation couldn't easily be overheard and she could see the truck through the window. They made introductions, Annie giving the false name again and the woman responding with, "Please call me Renee." As they subtly inspected each other, Annie thought about what Pete had said about Randy's mother wearing clothes that cost more than all the clothes he owned. Barrington's lobbying contracts listed at APOC added to up to about a half million a year, so she had to figure Renee's job was more about something to do than a second income.

They chatted about winter coming early and with a vengeance this year and Treadwell's fall season. The waiter came and took their order. Annie ordered coffee, and Renee started to, but then hesitated and changed to a glass of white wine. The waiter knew her and seemed to be used to the order, confirming that she wanted the Toasted Head, not the house chardonnay. They continued to make small talk, Renee talking about the theater and their plans to expand using a grant they hoped to get from the National Endowment for the Arts, about the importance of local match. Renee had just started to express condolences about Annie's mother when their order arrived. She interrupted herself to take a needy drink and close her eyes for a moment as the wine hit. When she put down her glass and looked up to see Annie looking at her she blushed slightly. "It's a little early, but I'm dealing with a few things right now."

"I can understand. It can't be a picnic having Richie and his friends as house guests."

It took a second for Renee to process what Annie had said, and as she did, the blush drained from her face until she looked blanched. "I don't know what you're talking about. Who are you?" Her voice was an intense whisper, and she looked over her shoulder as if worried someone might overhear.

"I have bad news and good news for you. The bad news is that my mother died a long time ago, she didn't leave any estate, and I'm not here to give Treadwell money. The good news is that I want to help you. I want to get Richie and Chollo and all of them completely out of your life and do it without affecting you or your husband.

"I don't know what you're talking about!"

"Renee, I understand that in addition to being Treadwell's fundraiser, you've appeared in several plays. Right now, though, your acting's terrible. I want to help you."

"No, I don't know what you're talking about! I have to go now."

She started to stand, but Annie put her hand on her forearm, restraining her. "Renee, you can't enjoy having Richie and Chollo slapping your bottom, having Richie wipe the sweat from Chollo's testicles on your lips and fondle your breasts, or having him lift you up on your toes by your crotch. We can make them go away, but I need a little help from you."

As Annie had talked, Renee slumped, scrubbing her lips and lower face with her hand. She looked down, almost uncomprehending for a moment at the lipstick smeared across her palm and then wiped her hand and mouth with her napkin. When she first saw her, Annie had guessed that Renee was five to ten years older than she, but now revised her estimate upward by at least five years.

"How do you know ...? How do you . . .? You're FBI? You have our house bugged? I knew it would come to this . . ." Renee stammered into silence.

"I'm not FBI or any other form of law enforcement. I don't want to involve the law or cause you or your husband problems. I just want a little bit of help to get a problem out of your life."

"If you're not FBI, who are you? It's not just them. It won't do any good. There's nothing you can do."

"I'm not interested in talking to the law about this. I just need a little information, and then we are going to take care of it. I don't want to involve you or your husband, but if you don't help, we'll have to."

"If you aren't the law, you must be who they're talking about. They weren't saying much in front of me, but when they came back yesterday with Nick chewed up by a dog and Richie's face full of devil's club thorns, they were cursing and swearing that they were going to get that bitch. They used a lot of worse names, too. Is that you?"

Annie smiled a small grim smile, "Yeah, I guess that would be me."

"Then I think like you, but I also think you should be changing your identity and getting on a plane out of here to somewhere far away. What'd you do, cross them on some drug deal? There's way more to this than you can know."

"I know about Galvan. We're going to get him out of your life."

Renee took a deep shuddery breath and pulled her shoulders back, sitting up a little straighter. She was silent for a long minute and then picked up and drained her wine glass. She used her empty glass to signal the waiter for another and while she was waiting, took a lipstick and small mirror from her purse to repair the damage with a shaky hand. When the second glass arrived, she had another long swallow before she spoke again with a strange mixture of bitterness, surrender and hope. "That bald, ballless bastard! I told him what he was getting us into, and he just kept talking about the money. Now we have a bunch of psychopaths staying in our house, and he just sits there, scared to death, while Richie runs his hands over me like he's judging a dog show! I'm terrified in my own house."

"We can help you, Renee."

"I don't want Don caught up in this. When Richie rubs him on his bald head and calls him old man, I'm furious with him for taking it, but scared to death that Don will try to do something and Richie will kill him. They're evil-scary, and you can tell Richie likes hurting people."

"You need to tell me. How did it start?"

Their talk lasted through a third glass of wine. They met Galvan the year after her husband started representing Carter Corrections. He had gone down to La Jolla for a corporate retreat, and she went with him. They all stayed at the La Valencia. Galvan was on Carter's board of directors and, according to her husband, was a major stock holder. She disliked him from the first over-intimate hug he gave her when they met, through his smug assumptions and patronizations of Don, to the fact that the young woman with the amazing figure who came with him to the meeting was clearly not a wife or girlfriend.

"I didn't mind what she was; I minded how he treated her. It was always 'Honey, get us some more martinis. Honey, call Jack's La Jolla and get us reservations for eight. Make sure it's the corner table with the great view. If they give you any crap about being full, make sure they know it's for me and to bump someone.' She was very polished, all the latest fashions, but her clothes were always just a bit too suggestive. If Galvan was talking to you and she was with him, he would run his hand across her bottom, or up her leg or a little too low across the top of her chest. He'd smile and look into your eyes while he did it. He never introduced her and I never learned whether her name was actually Honey or Galvan just couldn't be bothered to remember what it was."

While the husbands were in business meetings, the wives spent their time sitting around the pool, shopping or at the spa. Talking with the wives didn't seem to be in Honey's job description, but she spent long hours at the pool in a floss bikini, interspersing sunbathing on a chaise with swimming laps in a precise Australian crawl, punctuated with flip turns at each end that spoke of competitive swimming somewhere in her background. The wives' favorite conversation topics seemed to be possessions, Honey and Galvan (they told Renee that the hooker Galvan had brought last year was much more obvious), and the potential expansion into Alaska. Talk of Carter being successful in Alaska always centered on the effect on share prices and bonuses and circled back to more possessions.

Renee enjoyed the hotel and La Jolla, but had resented the assumption that Alaskans were a bunch of rubes, ready to give Carter Corrections an open tap to the state treasury without asking any questions. It particularly bothered her that her husband was doing his best to foster that impression. It would be a tough sell, he told them, but he was the one who could do it. Just pay him a little more, and with his connections and a little wining and dining, he would take care of it. He even joked about a couple of legislators who were fond of powder up their noses and could be potential clients of Carter Corrections after they helped get the bill passed.

Renee paused and stared into the wine glass a long time and then said it was funny, when Alaskans were busy screwing each other, when her husband was working the legislators to gain some advantage for one of his Alaskan clients, it never bothered her.

"I was born in Ketchikan. My dad was a logger and we grew up in logging camps on Prince of Wales Island. Strange as it sounds, that's where I got interested in theater. My mother used to subscribe to movie magazines and when they arrived, usually a month late, I would read every word. I used to organize little plays with the other kids in the camp, until they got big enough to realize it wasn't cool. Prince of Wales is just over two hundred miles south of here, but a long, long journey to where I am now. What's funny is that a lot of what those women in La Jolla were all about, is what I've been climbing toward most of my life. I have it now, a beautiful house, a fancy condo in Palm Springs, and so much goddamn crap you wouldn't believe it. When these folks who have even more crap started talking about Alaska that way, though, all of sudden I was that little girl in a logging camp, a chip on my shoulder, determined to claw my way past anyone who tried to stop me . . ."

After another long pause, Renee continued. All the guys had gone golfing together. Galvan and her husband were in the same foursome and shared a golf cart. When her husband returned he'd had too much to drink and was flying high. Galvan wanted a much more aggressive lobbying campaign, and they had agreed on a huge bonus when the bill was signed into law. Renee knew contingency bonuses were illegal under APOC, but her husband had brushed off her questions, telling her that there were a few things she might have to get used to, and she should be happy about it. She later learned that he and Galvan had discussed which legislators might be responsive to inducements beyond the normal campaign contributions, vote trading and wining and dining. Months later she learned that he and Galvan were using cash, girls, drugs and blackmail to try to put together enough votes to pass the bill. As far as she knew, Don had never used such tactics before. He started receiving cash and small amounts of coke from Galvan to pass on to the several legislators they jokingly referred to as "our future clients." Then Galvan informed him he would sometimes be receiving larger amounts of drugs, not connected to the private prison bill or legislature, but to pass on to others. Her husband protested, but quickly learned that he no longer had the option of refusing. Don wound up picking up packages at the post office and meeting dealers at assigned times and places to distribute them. Both of them felt trapped, but her husband insisted there was no way out, just hang in there. Galvan had promised that when the legislation passed, they'd be finished.

"Did the rest of Carter Corrections know about this?" Annie asked.

"I think they worked hard at not knowing. I definitely don't think they knew about the drugs that weren't connected to the lobbying, and probably not about the details of the rest. There was a generalized knowledge that, after Don and Galvan had talked on the golf course, Don was pushing much harder. I used to help him think up ways to describe his expenses. No one at Carter ever questioned them. Don was supposed to report to a vice-president for government relations, but he talked to Galvan a lot more. Galvan was relentless in his pressure and wanted to be sure he knew in advance how critical committee votes were going to go."

At Galvan's instructions, Don even arranged for a crucial committee to vote the bill down, and then two days later, reconsider and pass the bill out. Galvan manipulated a large short sell of Carter stock before the first committee vote and had then sold long before the reconsideration. Don was worried about the SEC and insider trading, but Galvan kept telling him not to worry, that it was through so many layers of dummy corporations there was no way to track it. They wound up laughing on the phone about that, talking about how it was like printing money. Renee didn't know how much Galvan made, but he sent Don fifty thousand dollars in cash.

Renee said that the main Senate bill and a companion House bill had both advanced pretty well at first, but had run into determined opposition toward the end of last spring. It was turning out that most of the Alaska legislators were honest and were increasingly uneasy about what they suspected regarding the bill and some of their colleagues. It was driving Galvan and Don nuts. Now, if the bills didn't pass next year, they would be dead and the process would have to start all over again.

Several dull booms followed by a muffled roar interrupted them. Last night's snow had been the first real accumulation at sea level, but the snow had been building up on the mountains for over a month. The highway department used a surplus howitzer for avalanche control. In high avalanche conditions, they fired across the channel at the snow packs high on Mount Roberts to trigger small preemptive avalanches and prevent the snow from building up into a big avalanche that would roar down and close off Thane Road. Annie looked out the window and saw that the snow had stopped and the wind was tearing a ragged hole in the clouds to let weak sunshine come in through the window.

As she talked, Renee was tilting her right hand slightly back and forth watching the scattered reflections thrown on the wall from a large diamond and sapphire ring she wore.

"It's a beautiful ring," Annie said.

"It is, isn't it? Don bought it for me when Galvan sent the fifty thousand. He's bought me lots and lots of things. He buys his girlfriend lots of things too, but he doesn't know I know about her. You remember what I was saying about Honey, the woman Galvan brought to the La Jolla meeting? Well, I know what my grandmother would say about this ring, and all the other things Don has bought me, and about me these days."

After another long pause, and more wine, Renee talked more, about how Galvan's pressure to line up the votes before the session had become more and more relentless and about Don receiving instructions about meeting a sailboat that was going to be carrying cash and a much larger delivery of drugs to pass on and cash for bribes. Renee had urged Don to go to the police and tell them, but he had insisted that they were in too deep, that she didn't understand what Galvan would do. Something had gone wrong; the sailboat and drugs never arrived. Don told her she should know as little as possible; that he was trying to know as little as possible. She did know that some attorney from L.A. had come up and Don had met with him, but other than that, Don had been focused on flying around, meeting with legislators in their home districts on the private prisons bill or concerns of his other clients. Then suddenly, this pack of psychopaths had arrived and taken up residence in her home.

They talked some more, making arrangements for Annie to call her at work to get status reports, making sure she understood the information Annie needed. When they finally finished, Renee said to go ahead; she was going to stay and have one more glass of wine. Annie felt compelled to ask about her driving, but Renee promised that she would get a taxi.

The sun had gone behind the mountains, casting Douglas in late afternoon shadow. Annie left Renee at the table with her fresh glass, still tilting her hand back and forth, trying to recapture the glitter and reflections.

28

"Do you think we can trust her?" Pete asked.

"I don't know for sure, but I think so. I'm sure she won't tell Richie or his crew. She's traumatized by what he did to her and is staying as far away from them as possible. The question is whether she tells her husband and if so, what he does. Right now she's pretty furious with him, not just about the drugs, but about the girlfriend, about Richie and Chollo, about the whole mess he has gotten them into. They've been together a long time, though, so who knows for sure."

"You're supposed to call her tomorrow?"

"Tomorrow morning at ten, at the theatre. She gave me her direct number. You know, the strange thing is I wound up liking her and feeling sorry for her. With all their problems, I felt most sorry for her when she talked about him having a girlfriend, about her knowing, but not saying anything."

"Not a problem you will ever have."

"Nor you." Annie smiled at him, "You also realize that

if you ever strayed, I would instantly renounce all these high-minded things I've been saying about nonviolence."

"I do and am held in your thrall through a proper combination of love and fear."

Annie reached up and caressed his neck, "Good. Let's make sure to keep it that way."

They were on the way home in the truck. Her adrenaline had pumped the whole time she was talking to Renee and now she felt drained by the events of the past two days. Annie leaned on Pete's shoulder and let her eyes slide closed, just for a moment.

She awoke with a start and a moment of disorientation. It was dark now and Pete was gone. The truck was pulled over beside the road, engine idling, thick snow coming down in the headlights. She sat up with urgency, looking for him. She reached for the door handle just as he straightened up from where he had been stooped by the right front wheel. He saw her through the windshield and waved before bending back down to the wheel. She watched until he stood back up, slapping snow off his coat and ball cap before getting back in the truck.

"Hey, how's sleeping beauty?" Pete kissed her before re-buckling his seat belt.

"It was scary for a second, I woke up and didn't know where I was, then I didn't know where you were."

"Sorry, I was hoping not to wake you, but I had to stop and put on the chains. This snow is deep enough that even in four-wheel I was having problems. It's on top of the ice from the last few days of freeze and thaw, which doesn't help."

Pete got the truck in gear and pulled back onto the road. Annie stared out at the snow.

Pete asked, "Now that you've slept on it, however briefly, what do you think? With everything we now know from Renee, do you think our plan still makes sense?"

"I can't think of anything better. Renee told me that last night when we spotted Richie taking the rental car back to the airport, he was planning on turning it in and getting another. I guess they knew I had seen the car and Renee said Nick, the fellow Heck chewed up, had bled on the rear seat. When Richie got there, it turned out that all the other cars were rented, which is why Barrington had to come get him. They were going to get another today. She agreed to get me a description of the new rental and the license plate number when we talk tomorrow."

Even in four-wheel drive with chains, Pete had to slow to twenty in the swirling snow. He tried the high-beams, but the snow was so thick that the reflection back from the big flakes made visibility worse. "I'll check the marine weather when we get home. I know there's a big low moving inland from the gulf. There's supposed to be gale conditions over all the inland passages in northern Southeast for the next several days. I'll have to wait for a little break in the weather before I can get over and get the pack."

"I want to go with you to the get the pack."

"You go back on dayshift tomorrow, and with this weather, I want to make the run in daylight. It should be a quick run over and back in the skiff. I'll trailer to Auke Bay and launch from there to minimize the distance. Right now the hospital is one of the few places I feel comfortable about you being safe. I'll drop you off and be back by the time you get off."

Pete slowed the truck as a blast of wind blew snow off the spruce and hemlocks lining the road and brought the visibility to several feet. He switched the wipers to high and slowly sped back up as the gust abated. "Man, this sure seems like a lot of snow for November!"

"Helen grew up here, and she says it's one of the earliest winters she can remember. What about Readers'? You've been taking more time off than usual."

"I've talked with Jean and Jeremy. They can cover, no problem. No tourists, no legislature and before the Christmas rush. I think they are both glad to be getting the extra hours. Getting the pack will only involve missing one day."

Occasionally headlights would appear out of the dark and snow, and they slowed as they passed a car or truck heading into town. By the time they reached 20-mile, there were no more cars, and the road was a smooth swath of unbroken white. Pete drove slowly in the center of the road, judging his position by the trees that appeared and disappeared in the cone of the truck's headlights.

Their house had always seemed snug to her during big snows or storms. Her mother's phrase about a safe harbor had often come to her mind. Tonight the house seemed empty without Heck. She turned on lights, and Pete made a fire. The wind tossed the trees, the waves broke black on the rocks below, the muffled boom and moan coming through the walls. Tonight, the house felt isolated.

Before they went to bed, Pete called the weather. He listened to the recording tell him, *"Tonight - Heavy Snow. Very windy. Blizzard warning in effect tonight through noon AST Friday... Snow developing this evening and continuing through the night. Up to 24 inches of accumulation through noon tomorrow. Northwest wind increasing to 30 to 40 mph. Gusts to 55 mph in exposed areas and near downtown Juneau and Douglas. Visibility reduced to less than 1 mile. Areas of blowing snow reducing visibility to near zero at times. Chance of snow 100 percent.*

Travel is discouraged unless it is an absolute emergency.
Extended forecast - Snow...continued heavy accumulation. Very windy."

Pete set his alarm for five the next morning to have time to plow the drive and make the slow drive in to take Annie to the hospital. Annie's Subaru had all-wheel drive and was great on slick streets, but didn't have the ground clearance to handle the deep snow where the State hadn't plowed.

He was in the office at Readers', catching up with the mail and paying bills, when Annie called. She'd called Renee and received her first report. Yesterday, the bastards, as she and Renee referred to them, had rented another car, a tan Toyota Camry. The all-wheel drives were all taken and Richie was pissed. Renee laughed about them getting stuck at the turn off Highland Drive, sliding into a snow bank and having to dig it out. They had slid back down the hill to a parking space and then had to slop back up the hill in their California shoes. By the time they reached the house, they were cursing this godforsaken place, the job that brought them to Juneau, and wanting to know who in their right mind would live here.

"Pete, if their rental is parked down the street, it would make it easier to get the coke in the car."

"It will if I can get out and bring the pack back while the snow keeps them parked down there. If I can get in the car, I'm pretty sure that Camry's have a space under the trunk floor where the spare tire is stored. If so I could remove it and put the drugs there. They wouldn't see it if they threw luggage in the trunk. If not, I – "

"We."

"OK, we, but we'll talk about it."

"The other thing Renee said was that they seemed

to be settling in to wait for something. Richie was grousing about having to wait around in the snow and Nick called the cable company, pretended he was her husband, and signed them up for all the porn channels. She was really mad." Annie was chuckling a bit on the phone, but Pete was remembering Vince's computer with all the photos of women being hurt.

"They may be waiting for a break in the snow or until they can get a big four-wheel drive with chains to get out to our house," Pete said.

"I always wanted DOT to extend winter maintenance five more miles to reach us, but right now I'm glad they haven't."

"If this is what we are going to do, I'll be happier once I have the pack."

"Let's hope the wind dies before the snow stops."

The temperature hovered just below freezing for the next three days, and neither the wind nor the snow stopped. The big snowplows, graders, and dump trucks rumbled around the clock, striking sparks off the road, but the wind-driven snow writhed across the road after them, recovering the surface with twisting eddies of white that gave the roads an untrustworthy, semi-animate appearance. The sounds of plows and back-up beepers were a constant background noise and berms of heavy wet snow grew along the sides and in the middle of the roads. Wind whirled the snow off the rooftops and under the overhangs covering the sidewalks. Ravens huddled on the bare branches of the mountain ashes, puffed up like black feather dusters. Only a few hardy souls came to the store and when Pete went out for lunch the streets were almost empty, the occasional lonely pedestrian with collar up, hat pulled down, bent into the wind.

Pickup trucks with snowplows and yellow flashing lights were everywhere and snow blowers hurled plumes of white into the headlights of passing cars. On the radio, "Problem Corner" was crowded by people wanting someone to shovel their roofs or plow their drives. It was dark now when Pete dropped Annie at the hospital every morning and picked her up each afternoon. The weather also brought out a sense of camaraderie, and multiple times Pete joined with others to give a stuck car a push out of the snow. Pete kept track of the rental Camry at the bottom of Highland Dr. that had turned into a large snowdrift with only the antenna sticking out.

The drive in and out the road was becoming increasingly difficult, but the difficulty in reaching the house made it seem a safer retreat. Pete hoped that wasn't an illusion. Annie called Renee each day. The first two days Renee had nothing new to report other than to complain that the bastards were still camped out in her house, smoking, drinking, watching daytime soaps and dirty movies, and complaining about the weather. She said, given the weather, the only reason she was going to work was to get away from them.

On the third day when Annie called, Renee had information.

"Galvan's coming!"

"When?"

"Whenever the snow breaks and planes can land. He started out on the Carter Corrections jet, but it had a mechanical. They had to put down in Portland. He flew Horizon up to Seattle and then got on the next Alaska Airlines flight which turned out to be the milk run, one of those freight/passenger combis with no first class. I have the impression it's been a long time since he had to fly anything other than a private jet or first class. I only found out about him coming because he called for Richie. I answered the phone and talked to him for a few minutes. Not talking, really. Mainly I just listened to him complain about Alaskan weather, which he seems to believe is happening to personally inconvenience him. He ranted about how he doesn't have time for this, we're all a bunch of incompetent imbeciles, Richie, Chollo and Nick included, and he can't believe he has to come up just to take care of a simple problem. The planes keep over-heading Juneau, so he's been doing the Southeast shuffle for two days now. He's been to Ketchikan, Wrangell, Sitka, Yakutat and Cordova. He spent night before last in Yakutat. "

Annie was laughing "That must have been a particular thrill for him."

"Yeah, he had a number of highly politically incorrect comments, and the rest of it was mainly obscene."

"You should have told him that if he goes through Sitka he should be sure to have some pie at the airport restaurant."

Renee had joined her in laughing now "I told him that they had particularly good pie. Turned out he was calling from Sitka. He told me he has now been through Sitka three times. That he has had their fucking pie twice over the past two days and it isn't that good. He said I was about the ninth person to tell him to eat pie in Sitka and he was going to gut the next fucking person who told him to eat fucking pie in Sitka."

They both chuckled for a minute and their laughter had almost subsided when Annie said, "Well it is very good pie," and they started over again.

When they finished, there was a silence. Then Renee said, "We're laughing, but for me it's because I'm scared to death. I'm not safe in my own home and don't know what else to do."

"Renee, we're almost there. We are going to get these people out of your life. I just need for you to keep giving me the best information you can. If the weather clears and planes start getting in, I'll call more often to see if Galvan got in and what's happening."

"I'll let you know, but I'm highly skeptical that anything is going to work. When I'm home now, I mainly stay locked in my bedroom. Don has a pistol. He doesn't know it, but I got it out and I'm keeping it with me. If they ever try to break in my bedroom, I'll shoot them, I swear I will."

"Have you ever shot the pistol?"

"No, but I'm an Alaska girl. My dad taught me to shoot a rifle when I was in high school. I'm going to defend myself."

"You hang in there. We're almost there. You said you and Don have a condo in Palm Springs?"

"Yeah, we would normally be there now if this weren't happening."

"Do you keep clothes down there? Could you convince Don to leave with you and go there on very short notice?"

"We do, we keep clothes there so we can travel back and forth with just an overnight bag. I don't know if Don would just pick up and go without knowing why, though. He hates what this has turned into, but he's still clinging to how much money we're going to make off this. We don't need any more money. There isn't any amount of money that's worth this, but that's something I don't know if he will ever realize."

The snow stopped and the wind shifted to the east and slacked during the night. When Annie called Renee the next morning, Renee said that Galvan had called at six-thirty. Richie and the rest were still asleep, and Don answered. Galvan was even madder than before. He'd spent the night in Sitka and had caught the shuttle from the hotel to the airport at four-thirty that morning to try and get on the plane on standby. The Alaska Airlines staff failed to be impressed with how important he was and took the standbys in the order they had signed up. He missed it by two people and was now stuck in Sitka until the evening jet about seven. He told Don to take Richie out today and buy good snow gear for all of them, and Don was going to take them to the Foggy Mountain Shop and Nugget Outfitters that afternoon. Renee said she and Don hadn't been talking much lately. She hadn't told him about the part of her conversation with Galvan the previous day about pie. She said they were just finishing the call when Don made the mistake of suggesting that as long as Galvan was stuck in the Sitka airport, the airport restaurant there was known for its pie and he should –

Pete and Annie were in the truck, parked in the Coastal Helicopters lot again that evening, watching the airport. The lights of Flight 67 materialized in the high clouds over the Chilkat Mountains and gradually formed into a jet. The jet came down, side-slipping in the wind and bounced once on the icy runway before the pilot deployed the deflectors and raced the engines to brake the plane. The plane was turning at the far end of the runway, when Richie pulled Don's Audi into short-term parking and jogged to the terminal. The flight was packed and they watched a stream of passengers come out of the airport before spotting Richie emerge with another man.

"Is that him? Crossing the traffic lanes between the terminal and the parking lots? What does he look like? It's too far for me to be able to see any detail."

Annie was watching through the binoculars and said, "I'm assuming it's Galvan. I don't think Richie would be carrying anyone else's bag for them. He's very tan, in his mid to late thirties, and looks fit in a tennis court kind of way." She handed the binoculars to him and said, "Here, you need to take a look to fully appreciate the effect."

Pete was confused for a moment, but got the binoculars focused and started chuckling. Galvan was wearing a red puffy down parka with a fur ruff. "Byrd, Peary, Amundsen and Shackleton, all the polar explorers would have all been jealous of that coat. Do you think he sent an assistant to buy that in L.A. and they didn't know the difference between Southeast and the North Slope?"

Pete and Annie pulled out behind the Audi and followed it back on to Egan and downtown. They kept just close enough to see the Audi's taillights. They were still joking about the parka, but Annie thought of Renee's comment about laughing because you're scared to death. She told herself that wasn't the case with her and Pete. They were going to do something, and there was no reason to be scared.

That evening, after they had cleaned up after dinner, Pete poured them each a glass of wine, and they sat in the living room in front of the fire.

"Annie, I checked the marine weather again. There's supposed to be some sea fog tomorrow, but the winds are predicted to continue to lighten, and I shouldn't have any problems getting to the cove and back. We'll do the plant tomorrow night."

"What do you think the odds are that they try to do something tonight or tomorrow, before we get a chance to plant the pack?"

"I'm worried about that. The snow's still too deep for them to get out here in the cars they have now, but I've double checked the alarms and trip wires just in case. If they can find one, they could rent a big pickup with chains. If I were them, and the snow doesn't melt significantly in the next couple of days so they can drive out here, I'd use a boat. Have one person stay with the boat, drop off the rest up or down the beach a little way. Galvan owns the *Bon Temps* so we have to assume he knows something about boats."

"That coat he was wearing looked like he was ready to go out and rent a sled and dog team. Maybe sign up for the Iditarod."

Pete was glad they were still joking. "If we hear anyone outside yelling, 'Mush' or, 'On King!' we should go on alert." He paused for a moment and then continued, "I'd like to wait to hear what Renee has to say before I go tomorrow, but if I wait, I won't make it back before dark. I'm wondering whether Galvan is going to try to talk to us first. Either way, we need to avoid or stall them past tomorrow night."

They both were quiet for a while thinking, listening to the crackle and pop of the fire. She held up her wine glass and watched the flames through the red of the wine. When Pete spoke, it seemed as though he had been reading her mind. "I worry about them burning the house, but they can't be sure the pack isn't hidden in here and they'd burn it up accidentally. Getting you seems to still be their most likely approach. I'd feel a lot better if they couldn't know where you were, if you tell Helen that we had a fight and you need to hide out with her for a couple of days until Heck is home and we're through this."

"Pete, we've talked about this and talked about this. I'm not hiding anymore. I'm not hiding in garbage cans; I'm not hiding with friends. We have a plan on how we're going to deal with this, and until it's finished I'll be at the hospital or with you."

"OK. I feel relatively safe about you at the hospital, but especially with Galvan here, promise me you'll be extra cautious."

"Both of us."

"Both of us."

29

Overnight the clouds cleared and the temperature dropped. The cold air flowing down over the warmer ocean was forming the thick sea fog that had been predicted. Pete pulled the tarp off the skiff and hooked the trailer to the pickup. The fog filled the darkness, shrouding the garage and muffling small sounds. On the road in to town, the truck and trailer bounced in the deep ruts and the trailer axle dragged in the snow between the tire tracks. When Pete and Annie reached Auke Bay, they turned down into the harbor lot. There were just a few parked trucks and empty boat trailers of deer hunters. They unhooked the trailer, leaving it above the launch ramps. The parking lot lights cast fuzzy haloes in the fog, and Pete could barely see past the end of the launch ramp to the boats docked in the harbor beyond.

Pete drove Annie into the Emergency Room and dropped her at the doors after a long hug and mutual promises to be careful. Before leaving the hospital, he drove through the parking lot, checking for any of the cars they knew and looking in every car for anyone who might be watching the ER. Satisfied that for the moment Annie was as safe as she could be, he left the hospital and headed back to Auke Bay, stopping at the Breeze-In for a large coffee and an egg salad sandwich to go.

At Auke Bay, Pete hooked the trailer back up. Last night he loaded a day pack and this morning he'd added lunch and a thermos of coffee. Now he took out a flashlight, handheld VHF radio, marine chart and small GPS and put them on the skiff's console. The .375 H&H was in a padded waterproof case, and he laid it across the seat. With this snow, bears should be denned up for the winter, but it wasn't uncommon to cross the tracks of a bear who didn't understand that. He pulled on a pair of thick neoprene chest waders and a Mustang float coat, and then backed the truck and trailer down the ramp to launch the skiff.

Auke Bay was a deep wedge cut into the mountains of the mainland coast. A collection of islands, scattered across the mouth, guarded the opening. The launch ramps were at the apex, with the harbor filling in the point behind a floating breakwater. He stood behind the center console, idling through the no-wake zone. The big Yamaha outboard emitted a low burble. He clicked on the skiff's running lights, but the glow in the fog from the red and green bow lights made it harder to see and he turned them back off. The fog made it difficult to differentiate between the dock lights and their reflections in the water. Boats in their slips emerged from the fog, many with winter covers of Visqueen or canvas, others recently shoveled, and a few sitting low in the water from snow on their decks. The live-aboards had congregated in as close as possible to the dock ramps. Here and there, Pete could glimpse someone stirring inside their boats. During the summer, the harbor was a constant commotion of whale-watching boats, private fishermen and charter boats hustling in and out with loads of tourists eager to catch salmon and halibut. All floated silently now. Heat lamps cast red glows through some portholes. The water in the harbor was black beyond black and absolutely still except for the faint ripples spreading from his wake.

Last night, when he heard the prediction for sea fog, he had punched in the coordinates for a set of waypoints into the GPS, laying out the route from the end of the Auke Bay breakwater to the cove in a series of legs. He clicked the GPS into its holder on top of the center console and turned it on. He had the rheostat for the skiff's compass light and fathometer turned all the way down and now he adjusted the backlighting on the GPS screen to its lowest level as well to protect his night vision. He was approaching the outer breakwater when he thought he saw a light near where the *Bon Temps* was moored. Curious, he swung the skiff down the last fairway between the inside of the floating breakwater and the docks. The skiff idled along, Pete steering with a knee as he zipped up his coat and pulled on his cap and gloves. In the dark and fog, he was almost beside the sailboat before he realized the light was coming from inside the *Bon Temps* and someone was coming up the companionway into the cockpit.

Pete turned the skiff away from the boat in a tight U-turn, coming close to the big charter boats berthed between the fingers of the dock on the other side of the fairway. He shut the engine off, hoping to silently glide away into the fog and dark before he was noticed. The person coming up the *Bon Temps'* companionway turned towards the breakwater, away from Pete. Pete couldn't see his face, but the red Arctic down parka and fur ruff were unmistakable. The tight turn had almost killed the skiff's momentum. Pete willed it to keep coasting away before Galvan turned around, but just at the edge of visibility, the skiff drifted to a stop.

The big Yamaha was a quiet motor, but clearly audible when Pete started it and shifted into forward. Galvan turned at the sound, peering out into the fog. All he could see was the stern of a skiff idling away, its indistinct shape and the back of a man dissolving into the dark. Pete nudged the throttle forward a hair and didn't turn to look until he reached the end of the breakwater. The fog remained thick and the *Bon Temps* had receded from visibility. He swung wide to the middle of the harbor entrance to minimize being illuminated in the red flashes from the light on the end of the breakwater or the back-lit by green flashes from the marker light on the other side. He was out of the harbor and the no-wake zone now, but Pete hesitated before hitting the throttle. Instead he circled quietly back outside the breakwater until he was roughly abreast of the *Bon Temps*, about fifty yards off, invisible to anyone in the harbor. He cut the engine off and drifted in the dark.

He should have thought that Galvan would want to check on his boat. It was one of the first things Pete would have done under the circumstances. Galvan was up earlier than Pete would have guessed. Maybe he hadn't adjusted from Pacific Time yet. He hadn't seen anyone else with Galvan. While Galvan wouldn't need someone with him to check on his boat, he seemed like a person who liked to have an entourage to emphasize his importance. On the other hand, not having Richie and the gang with him was probably a good sign. A sailboat like the *Bon Temps* wouldn't be the best choice to come to the house, but if they were planning on using it, they would have all been there.

He had told Annie that the scheme to plant the drugs was overly complex, that simple solutions were usually the most effective. He could bring his skiff in where the floating breakwater attached to the main dock, intercept Galvan as he walked back to the main dock. A punch to the solar plexus to knock the air out of him so he couldn't yell. The water temperature was in the thirties. Water that cold causes an involuntary gasp reflex, usually accompanied by the inhalation of several quarts of water. Pete looked at the impenetrable blackness of the water. It was almost a hundred feet deep here. If Galvan simply disappeared would that end it, or would the rest of the crew try to get the pack for themselves?

He hadn't seen anyone else out on the docks. It would be a long time, if ever, before the body was found and there would be no way to tell that Galvan hadn't slipped when getting on or off his boat. The skiff drifted in the dark and fog in its own little universe. Pete thought about Vince's threats about Annie, about Richie shooting at Annie, and Chollo shooting Heck. He thought about his promise to Annie. He thought about Annie and his parents and about souls and promises and if there was a heaven. He wished he was sure about any of it. After a few minutes he zipped the float coat's collar high and cinched the hood down over his cap so only a narrow strip of face around his eyes showed. He restarted the outboard and nosed the boat back around until it was facing the GPS waypoint for the end of the first leg out of Auke Bay. He shoved the throttle down. The skiff jumped up on plane, flying through the fog, leaving the howl of the big motor echoing back over the harbor.

Passing out of Auke Bay between Coghlan and Indian Islands, Pete slowed slightly, shading to the right of his waypoint until he could pick up the muffled green flash of the Indian Island light. A half-mile farther west, the GPS shifted to its second waypoint off Outer Point, and he accelerated again, banking the skiff in a smooth turn to head south. The sky began to lighten above, but the fog was still thick. He was staring ahead intently trying to see into the fog for floating logs or other boats. He came out of the lee of Douglas Island and began to pick up a long, slow swell coming up Stephens Passage. Pete realized he had been gripping the steering wheel like it was Galvan's neck. He took long deep breaths of the cold air and rolled his head to relax his shoulders. There was an anxiety to get back, to be with Annie and protect the house, but being out on the water was always therapeutic. Gradually the rhythmic rise and fall of the skiff under his feet began to relax him. It was going to be like he had told Annie, a quick over-and-back, no muss or fuss, and an excuse to be out in the boat in the winter. He would have felt differently if it hadn't been dark and foggy. He would have seen Richie, Chollo and Nick standing in the cockpit of a big Bayliner charter boat, across the fairway from the breakwater, silently watching him turn away from the *Bon Temps*.

It was about two hours before high tide when Pete reached the cove. It was daylight now, but in the fog, he had to follow the shoreline carefully before he found the right creek mouth. He worked the skiff into the creek and waded ashore. He tied a line to the roots of a big spruce the stream had partially undercut. The winter flow in the creek was running low so he changed into his hunting boots, stuffing the float coat inside the waders and leaving them on the stream bank. He shouldered into his daypack and removed the .375 from its case. The magazine was already loaded and he took a round from his pocket, chambering it and pushing down slightly on the top round in the magazine so the bolt slid over it as it closed.

The ice crunched underfoot as he walked up the edge of the creek. He didn't mind the noise. In case there were any insomniac bears out wandering around, it was good to provide warning. In the summer the grass had been chest high, but now it was beaten down and the snow a smooth blanket over the flats. The left bank of the creek steepened into the small cliff, and he passed the sandbar where the bear had killed Hal. It was covered with snow and pancake ice, and it all looked different in the fog. He worked his way upstream along the slippery rocks at the creek's edge. The creek had gouged a pool about fifty feet long at the base of the cliff where the crevice was. Where the water slowed, the creek was frozen over. Snow covered the ice, and at the sides, it was difficult to tell where the ledge ended and the ice over the creek began. He kept close to the cliff. The water level was low under the ice, but he didn't want to chance breaking through and possibly going over his boot tops.

In the crevice, the overhang had kept the worst of the snow out, but the walls were icy. He shrugged his daypack off, put it on the ledge and rested his rifle on it. He had told Annie to shove the pack back as far out of sight as she could and he regretted it now. He was much larger than she was, and it was tight for him to get back to the pack. He turned sideways, wiggling his body as far back in the narrowing cleft as he could and reaching out. He could just touch it with his fingers, enough to grip the fabric with his thumb and fingertips, but not enough to get a good grip or reach a strap. He wiggled back out and took off his gloves, shoving them into a pocket. He wedged himself back into the crevice, stretching until it felt as though his joints were disconnecting. The ice on the walls seemed to have frozen the pack in place and he couldn't get in as far as he needed to get a good grip. He thought of Randy desperately squeezing into the crevice, trying to get out of the reach of the bear's raking claws, realizing the terrible mistake of shoving the pack in first. Pete was so much bigger it wouldn't have made any difference; he couldn't get in the opening as far as Randy or Annie.

This wasn't working. He decided he would hike back down the creek and get the emergency paddle from the boat. The paddle had a telescoping aluminum shaft and a boat hook on the end of the handle that he could use to snag the pack and pull it out. If it was frozen too solidly to the crevice walls to pull out with the boat hook, he would make a small fire in the bottom of the crevice to thaw it loose. He was chilled from the run over in the skiff and the thought of having lunch and coffee from the thermos while warming himself over the fire was appealing.

When Pete shifted to begin backing out, he realized his chest and shoulders were stuck. His first response was minor irritation. He shoved harder, but his chest was farther in the crevice than his legs, and he couldn't get an angle to help shove himself back. Pete's right arm was extended into the crevice and he searched for something to push on. He used his fingertips to shove on the side of the pack, but couldn't get any purchase. He strained harder to pull back out, but had no leverage. He had never been claustrophobic, but found himself breathing quickly now as he strained to jerk his body loose. He stopped and forced himself to breathe slowly, to be calm and analyze the situation. Alaska, its weather, seas, mountains and animals regularly killed people with total indifference, but he told himself he was wasn't going to let anything this stupid take him away from Annie. He tried to look out over his left shoulder, but the crevice was narrower towards the top, and the rock caught his head as he tried to turn. He heard a low growling noise as he forced his head around. Panting replaced the growling and he realized it was him. His head had twisted inside the cap and it was askew, partially over one eye. Blood dripped down in the other eye from where he had scraped his forehead, but he could see out of the crevice now. That was better. It helped him to think more clearly. With his left arm, he stretched to reach the mouth of the crevice to catch the edge, but it also was just beyond his fingertips.

There was a small crack below his waist level, halfway to the entrance. It looked like he should be able to get his fingers in and pull. He tried, but the angle was wrong, pulling him down instead of out and there was ice in the crack. He realized he would have to melt the ice to get a better grip. He placed his bare hand over the crack and held it there until the burning and stinging of the cold was replaced by numbness. He tried to rewarm his hand by blowing on it and holding it against his neck. When feeling returned he put his hand back on the ice. It was slowly melting, but his hand was going numb more quickly each time between rewarmings. He constructed a triangle in his mind and focused the cold, the cramp in his muscles, and the stinging of his forehead into the triangle, isolating the pain, concentrating on other things. He thought about Annie and making this into a funny story to tell her.

His head was pressed against the rock and he listened to the mountain to see if it had anything to say about his plight. He could imagine hearing the slow cycle of eons, of spruce trees hundreds of years old, of salmon returning century after century, of brown bears' trails worn deep in the hillsides from countless generations of bears stepping in the same spots, of the snow piled deep on the mountain peaks. He listened to see if it had any wisdom about his getting out of this, but decided if he heard anything, it was a deep rumble of a chuckle about the folly of humans. His leg was cramping, and his fingertips now left red streaks each time his grip slipped.

He paused, letting his hand recover for a last attempt before trying something else. He realized he was unconsciously taking a deep breath each time just before he pulled, as you would if lifting a heavy weight. This time he took a number of deep breaths and then exhaled as totally as he could, trying to decrease the size of his chest as much as possible. At the same time he picked up his feet, letting all his weight pull down towards the slight widening of the crevice while he tried to get a grip in the crack and pull outward. He didn't make any progress towards the entrance, but moved about a half inch downward. He rewarmed his hand and repeated the process, this time rewarded with an inch of downward of movement.

He realized he was growling again as he tried to pull out. The third try, he not only made another inch down, but a definite half inch out. By the sixth attempt, he made enough progress that he could brace his elbow on the opposite side of the crevice to help force his fingers into the crack. With a deep growl he dropped and pulled again. It felt like he had strained all the tendons and ligaments in his arm. The rock was still tight to his chest and back, but he was no longer stuck and his legs were back under him.

Pete stood still for a moment breathing deeply. As he regathered his strength he closed his eyes and prayed. He gave thanks for meeting Annie and her rescuing his life. He gave thanks that he would be able to return to her and asked the Lord to take care of Annie. He was saying Amen, about to open his eyes, get out of the crevice, and to go down to the boat for the boathook when he was startled by an amused voice.

"Dr. McLaughlin, I presume."

Pete's eyes snapped open, and he squinted out to the opening of the crevice. There was a very tan man standing there, mid-height, wearing a red down parka with a wolf ruff around the hood. He grinned as if he and Pete were laughing together at a private joke. Just behind the man and slightly to the side, stood Richie. Richie held a rifle pointing directly at Pete's chest. To his side, peering over their shoulders was Nick, holding Pete's rifle. Neither Richie nor Nick seemed amused.

"Mr. McLaughlin, whatever are you doing you in there? When we followed your tracks to this hole in the rocks and heard all the growling, I told Richie that perhaps we were wrong. That we had followed you all this way on our assumption your trip had something to do with my property, but really you were cheating on the lovely Annie and had sneaked over here for an assignation with a bear."

Pete stared back, his face showing as much emotion as the rock and ice.

"Richie, I can see our Mr. McLaughlin is the strong silent type, or perhaps he is just reticent about discussing his love life with strangers. Mr. McLaughlin, let me introduce myself. My name is Jonathon Galvan."

30

"Mr. McLaughlin, if all that growling is not you having a romantic encounter in your cave with a bear, why don't you come out and tell us what you are doing in there?"

Pete eyed Galvan and Richie. They were both standing on the narrow ledge in front of the crevice where Pete had left his pack and rifle. Nick had stepped back out of sight and Pete assumed Chollo was there as well. Under the circumstances, he couldn't see any immediate advantage in coming out of the crevice on their terms.

"I'm stuck."

Galvan looked at Pete's bloody fingertips and forehead and the bloody streaks on the wall. It seemed to amuse him hugely.

"I'm curious about why you've gotten yourself stuck in there, but perhaps we should use this opportunity to have a conversation. Pete, may I call you Pete?"

Pete continued staring back, but didn't respond.

"Pete, I suppose I should thank you for saving my boat,

but since then, you have caused me a great deal of annoyance. You seem to have hurt Vince and seriously scared him, and I'm assuming it was you that turned over the outdoor toilet with one of my attorneys in it."

"Pull me out, and we can discuss it."

"No, I think this is a fine place for you to be while we talk. Then we will decide whether it makes sense to get you out. You know that outhouse event traumatized Kotkin. He included the cost of a ridiculously expensive suit on his expenses. Custom shirt, handmade shoes."

"We have a Costco in town. Perhaps you could take something back for him to wear."

Galvan smiled bleakly at the thought. "No, that wouldn't work, but I think you should reimburse me for the considerable amount of money and trouble you've cost me. You should compensate me for three repugnant days stuffed in a middle seat between fat men and women with crying babies, flying around trying to get into this hellhole. I particularly think you should tell me where my property is right now."

Pete knew it was probably a bad idea, but he couldn't resist. "When you went through Sitka, did you get to try the pie? The airport restaurant there has very good pie."

Galvan's pose of amused condescension disappeared. "Fuck you! Fuck you and fuck this bunch of lackwit incompetents who couldn't fix this without me! 'We can't get out to their house, Mr. Galvan, the snow's too deep.' 'Then rent a boat!' 'We don't know how to run a boat, Mr. Galvan.' And they're supposed to be good. Fuck all of this! And especially fuck the pie!"

Pete watched Richie during Galvan's outburst. He didn't look happy about being called a lackwit incompetent, but hadn't let the rifle's aim stray from the middle of Pete's chest.

It was a bolt action, but Pete couldn't tell the caliber or make. Looking down the barrel, most rifles look distressingly similar. He could tell that the scope was a Zeiss, which probably meant that the rifle was also top end. He hadn't seen Galvan bring a rifle case off the plane, so he figured they had borrowed it from Barrington. The only part that was relevant was that the scope looked too powerful for quick shots.

"Seems like none of your guys are very good on boats," Pete said. "There was a storm that night, but I still couldn't figure how Hal and Randy managed to sail the *Bon Temps* onto that sandbar."

"Fucked by love."

"Pardon me?"

"Fucked by love. Hal was bringing the boat up for me so I could take legislators and clients out on it next summer. That would make it deductible, and a boat's a good place to have private discussions. As long as the boat was coming up, it made sense to use the opportunity to deliver a larger amount of property up here than was feasible through more usual methods. I had a good crew for him, but Hal had fallen in love with that little fairy, Randy. Kept whining to me to let him just take Randy. The delivery was going to be their honeymoon, and he wouldn't charge me. I knew it was a mistake, but Hal was so useful to me in many areas, I let him talk me into it."

"Did you know Randy actually hit the bear trying to get it off Hal? Seemed a pretty brave thing to do."

"Until he met that little fairy, I never even knew Hal liked men better then women. I just knew he liked to hurt people and was very, very good at it. I wouldn't have to be here if Hal were still here. You would've been begging to return my property if Hal were here."

"The bear wasn't impressed."

"I'm tired of this. Here's what's going to happen now. You're going to tell me where the pack is. If you don't, Richie is going to shoot you in your knee. If you need further inducement, he will then come in there and begin to carve on you until you are forthcoming. If you die before you tell us, we'll leave your corpse here, stuck in that cold hole in the rock forever. We'll then go have a similar session with your lovely wife. Similar, but more enjoyable for my employees."

"Annie doesn't know anything about this. I've never told her."

"That is a risk I'm not prepared to take. I'm going to ask you one time now, and then Richie will shoot you. Where is my property?"

Pete wondered if Galvan had unintentionally left off, "unless you tell me where it is," after "then Richie will shoot you," or if he was simply being accurate.

"Half of it's in the crevice behind me. I was trying to get it to bring to you. The other half is hidden farther up the creek. I can't properly describe it to you, but I can show you where."

"Thank you. Thank you at last. While it's been obvious since we found you, I wanted to watch as you were forced to tell me, perhaps watch you beg a bit. You've been curiously unsatisfying in that regard. I also think you're trying to game me with the story of half being hidden farther up the creek."

"Without a paddle," Pete said.

"Richie, get him out of there. If you can't pull him out, carve him out. If he's lying to us, we're going to find out how long he thinks he's a funny man."

Richie handed the rifle to Galvan and edged back into the crevice. When he reached out towards Pete, Pete grabbed his wrist. Richie instinctively tried to pull away, but Pete had turned slightly, wedging himself in. Richie tried to jerk his hand loose, but Pete squeezed down on his wrist, watching Richie's eyes widen as he felt the bones in his arm compress. Richie was yelling at Pete to let him go, Pete was yelling to pull him out, purposely adding to the confusion. Galvan was in the entrance of the crevice yelling questions about what was going on and trying to see past Richie.

Richie was struggling to break loose from Pete and yelling to the others to pull him out. Richie had edged into the crevice, right side first and couldn't turn to draw his knife. He kneed Pete in his thigh and hip and without room to turn, hit, or cut Pete, tried to bite him in the shoulder. The knee strikes hurt, but Pete's wool coat and layers of pile underneath protected him from the bites.

Galvan shoved Chollo and Nick toward the crevice and Nick edged in, grabbed Richie's belt and began to pull. When that didn't work, Chollo, who was just inside the mouth of the crevice where it was a little wider, grabbed Nick's waist and tried to drag them out.

Galvan was screaming at all of them, yelling he couldn't believe what a bunch of lame-ass incompetents they were, just pull the fat fuck out of there. With the three of them pulling, it was difficult for Pete to hold on to Richie's wrist and keep himself wedged.

Pete could catch glimpses of Galvan over their heads and he yelled for Galvan to pull too. Richie screamed as Pete ground his hand into the rock, and Nick and Chollo were yelling at each other as they tried to brace themselves on the icy rocks and pull. Galvan put down the rifle and began to pull on Chollo. He was hollering, shouting at them to pull Pete out so he could get the pack and then they were going to hurt him.

Pete began to shout, "One, two, three, pull! One, two, three, pull! One, two, three, pull!"

To his surprise, they actually began to coordinate their pulls on his count. On the third count, as they all pulled, he untwisted his body to free himself and shoved forward as hard as he could. He roared as he pushed, visualizing bull-rushing the quarterback on the day he heard his folks had been killed, getting lower than the offensive tackle and shoving him back so hard and fast that he was thrown backwards into his quarterback. With the momentum of their suddenly-released pull and Pete's push, all of them popped out of the crevice. Galvan and Chollo both stumbled back across the ledge, floundering into the deep snow over the ice. There was a cracking sound as it gave way beneath their weight. Nick fell, and Pete and Richie trampled him as they struggled.

Richie pulled his knife and flipped it open, stabbing at Pete. Pete managed to grab Richie's arm, stopping the knife as the tip penetrated his coat. He had Richie's arm just below the elbow and had poor leverage as Richie struggled to shove the knife farther in. He hung on to Richie's arm and used his opposite forearm to smash him in the head.

The concession of a rifle's muzzle blast, fired from feet away, almost deafened Pete. He wheeled to see Nick working the bolt to chamber another round. Pete shoved Richie back into Nick and sprinted up the creek bank into the fog, skidding and almost falling several times as he tried to get to the end of the pool and cliff.

The rifle boomed again and he felt something tug at his jacket simultaneously with hearing an angry whine in the air. He was close to reaching the end of the cliff when a sharper rattle of pistol shots cracked out, blasting snow and rock off the cliff down on him. Someone opened up with a long series of shots from another pistol. The cliff was much smaller here, about four feet above the ledge. Through the fog in front of him, Pete could see a small gnarled hemlock growing at the top of the rock. He reached it and grabbed the trunk, desperately pulling himself up. As he got his body up over the edge, there was a blow across the back of his left shoulder and his left arm would no longer hold the tree. It was hard to keep a grip in the snow, and he scrambled to keep from sliding back over the edge. His bloody fingers left red streaks in the snow. He glanced back through the fog and could only see indistinct figures and muzzle flashes from the pistols. He struggled to his feet and headed up into the woods. Under the big trees, there was less snow, and he made better time. Like every hunted animal in the mountains, he headed straight uphill.

He hoped that Galvan would want to get the pack first. It might give him time to circle back to his skiff and escape. They had to have come ashore in an inflatable or dingy. Perhaps he could disable it or tow it away, stranding them here. He made about a hundred yards upslope into the big timber when that hope was dashed by sounds of them following him up over the edge of the small cliff. He looked back, but couldn't see them through the fog. He listened. It sounded like all four of them, but he couldn't be sure. Muffled instructions and curses floated up through the fog. The nylon of their new snow gear was noisy when it rubbed against the snow and brush. Pete's wool coat and pants weren't as high-tech efficient as their outfits, but were quiet in the woods.

His left arm was numb, and the ache from his left shoulder pounded through his back. He wondered how badly he'd been hit. He felt over his shoulder with his fingers, feeling through the jagged tear in his jacket to a gash about six inches long. He clenched his teeth as he felt inside the gash, but almost sank to his knees with the pain. He couldn't feel bone and told himself that was good. He was still walking, so his spine hadn't been hit, but he couldn't make his arm work. He unbuttoned his jacket halfway to act as a sling and put his arm in it.

He focused on moving steadily uphill. Just don't stop. There is no way these bastards are going to catch me in the woods, keep moving, get high enough to circle back down to the skiff. The pain from his shoulder began to merge with the ache in his leg and hip where Richie had kneed him. He thought of what Galvan had said, ". . . a similar session with your lovely wife. Similar, but more enjoyable for my employees." He used the rage to shove back the pain, to keep himself moving up the mountainside.

At last he had to stop, bent over to his knees, heaving for breath. When he could hear over his pounding heart, he listened and couldn't hear them. He looked back down the hillside at his tracks. Normally he could have lost them easily in the woods and fog, but in the snow, he was leaving tracks that required no skill to follow. To make it even easier, scarlet drops flagged the white of the snow along his tracks. He took time to pull on his gloves and adjust his cap down over his skinned forehead. That would slow the blood from his fingers and forehead, but the back of his jacket was saturated and slowly dripping from the hem. He listened a moment more and thought he could hear the rustling of their clothes. There was a soft womp of a tree dumping its load of snow and curses from whoever had been under it, followed by a "Shut up!" from someone else to the right.

Pete winced a smile, and began to move uphill again. He began to angle left to try to circle up and back toward the skiff. It sounded like they had spread out below him with one following his tracks and the others to the right and left. Unwounded he would have felt confident of his ability to stay ahead of them up the mountain. Now he was finding it more and more difficult to maintain his pace.

If he had been able to grab a rifle when he bolted from the crevice or if he'd brought the .45. Yeah, and if a bullfrog had wings, he told himself. As he climbed, he tried to stay in the old growth where the overstory caught most of the snow. He wondered how long before they figured out that if they just went back down and took his skiff, the chances of his survival were slim.

He was about a thousand feet up now, and realized that the fog was brighter, that he could look up and see the tops of the mountains and the sun shining through. The day was warming and a breeze was rearranging tendrils of fog above him. He didn't want to climb out of the fog, so when he hit a small bench in the slope, he began to sidehill sharply to his left, to head back for the skiff. Up ahead, through the trees, it looked even brighter. With the fog, he was almost at the edge of the old avalanche path before he realized what it was.

Pete weighed his options. He would have to cross the slide chute to get back to the skiff, but the fog prevented him from seeing how wide it was or how far up or down the mountain it extended. Old avalanches had wiped away the trees and the fog seemed to be thinning. There would be no cover as he crossed. Options were getting worse by the moment. He strained to listen, but the world was silent.

He started out across the chute. The snow had frozen into a thick slab on top that didn't break through if he was careful. He had taken four cautious steps out on the clean snow when the breeze cleared a rent in the fog. Suddenly, fifty yards below, he could see Richie slowly climbing up through the timber beside the slide chute. His pistol was in his hand and he was peering into the woods.

31

Pete crouched. Fifty yards was long for a pistol shot. How good was Richie? Someone had been lucky or good enough to hit Pete once. No second chances. He slowly turned to edge back to the side of the chute where the trees and brush would provide cover. Becoming aware of a presence, Richie looked up. He yelled and fired a series of shots. Richie hadn't allowed for the steepness of the slope and the shots puffed snow six feet above Pete's head. Pete lunged back into the trees at the edge of the chute. The rest of them were yelling back to Richie and to each other now. He could hear Nick above him to the right, Galvan closer at about his same elevation and Chollo below. He realized they had him flanked, trapped in a lopsided V that was moving up the mountain with him in the middle. Richie was the bottom of the V, the slide chute was its left side and the other three formed the V's right side.

Pete scrambled straight up, paralleling the chute, climbing as fast as he could, determined to escape out of the open top of the V before they could swing it closed. He gained several hundred more feet in elevation and was climbing through the last of the fog. Up here, the sun was bright, and he could see across Stephens Passage to the mountains of Douglas Island and all the way up to the Chilkats. It was beautiful, but more important was what he could see. The slide chute was over a hundred yards wide here. Above him, it necked down slightly where it went through a large gully in a series of cliffs and then widened into a bowl above timberline, reaching out of sight toward the mountain's summit. There was no way to climb above the cliffs and if he tried to cross the chute, even if he got far enough across to make it a difficult pistol shot, he would be a sitting duck for a rifle. So far they had missed because he hadn't given them a clear shot and he'd been lucky. He needed to climb fast enough to escape out of the top of the V and curl around them before they reached the cliffs.

The snow depth increased with the gain in elevation. He was climbing straight up and with each step, plunged knee, thigh or sometimes waist deep. His thighs burned and he was gasping. His leg ached. Feeling had come back to his left arm, and searing pain jolted down it as he lunged and floundered in the snow.

With one arm tied behind my back. I can beat these bastards with one arm tied behind my back. It was becoming increasingly hard to use the rage to hold back exhaustion. He told himself that they were city boys, that they had to be feeling it worse. He knew, however, that he was in the worst area of the mountain for moving swiftly. Out in the chute, the wind had packed the snow into a slab hard enough to walk on. Deeper in the woods, where Galvan, Chollo, and Nick were, the overstory of the timber had caught much of the snow. Richie was coming straight up behind him through the deep snow, but had the benefit of the trail Pete was breaking.

He heard more shouts and realized they were closing in on him. He was not going to make it out of the V before they reached the cliffs. He stopped again, gasping, lungs burning, leg muscles trembling. He looked out across the polished snow in the chute to his left. If they caught him exposed out there, there was no way they could miss. He turned back down the hill, angling into the timber. If he could slip through between Richie and Chollo, maybe he could outdistance them down the slope and reach the skiff.

After his first ten yards into the woods, he slowed down, watching and listening, sight lines becoming visible and disappearing as he moved. Except for patches where the fall of a tree had created a break in the canopy, there was little undergrowth here in the big old growth. It helped him to move quietly, but made him more exposed. Uphill and deeper in the woods a branch snapped, the sound distinct in the silence. Pete froze beside a tree trunk. After a moment, glimpses of Galvan's red parka were visible through the trees. They were too close. Pete began to move again quietly, angling more downhill.

The rasp of a nylon coat on a branch. Chollo stepped from behind a tree about forty yards down the slope. He was carrying the scoped rifle that Richie had earlier. He used the scope to scan the woods above him. Pete froze, knowing that motion attracted the eye more quickly than anything else. The wool of his green Filson coat and gray pants were coated with snow and made him a fair match for the tree trunks. The rifle barrel swung slowly past Pete, then jerked back with recognition. Pete broke and ran. A shot and then another crashed behind him. He couldn't tell where the shots hit, but he swerved and bounded as he ran, knowing it would be hard for Chollo to find him in the scope. He ran away from Chollo, heading back downhill to see if he could burst past Richie, but

Chollo was yelling to Nick now, hollering that Pete was heading toward him. Pete saw Nick seconds before Nick saw him and fired a string of shots, the high pitched cracks echoing off the mountains. He seemed to be a bad shot, relying on luck and a high capacity magazine, but Pete could hear the angry hornet sound of some of the bullets passing in the air near him as he ran.

Pete dodged back uphill, herded back towards the edge of the old slide chute. He had been sprinting through the snow after his long climb and had to stop behind a tree, gasping for breath again. They were all yelling back and forth now. Richie was below him, and it sounded as though Nick had closed the top of the V and was now coming straight down at him. It was obvious that they understood how easy a target he would be if they could drive him out of the woods onto the packed snow. What Pete was feeling now was not fear, but murderous rage. He said a brief prayer asking the Lord to take care of Annie. He then reached under his jacket and pulled his knife from its belt pouch. It was a Kershaw folding hunter and he opened it carefully to avoid the click as it locked open. If someone was going to find his body in the woods, he wanted them to find Galvan's body underneath.

He caught another glimpse of Galvan's red parka through the trees, much closer now. There was a fallen tree with its root wad sticking up between them. It might hide him from Galvan until he was close enough, if Galvan didn't change course as he approached, if he didn't see Pete's tracks in the snow first, and if one of the others didn't move in enough to see Pete from the rear and shoot him in the back. The odds were slim except in comparison with his other alternatives.

Pete began to creep forward, trying to keep the root wad between him and Galvan. He could hear Richie and Chollo below him, but couldn't see them. A porcupine was in the top of a small spruce in front of him, eating bark from the trunk. The porcupine moved to climb higher and the tree sighed and dumped a small load of snow. Almost instantly the boom of his .375 H&H shook the woods from below. There was no way he could reach the root wad and Galvan without coming into Chollo's field of fire.

Pete was fighting against a berserker rage that made him want to rush Galvan no matter what. He forced himself to stop and take deep breaths. Rushing Galvan would do no good if he was killed halfway there. He had always felt at home in the woods. The idea of running out of them, of being exposed on the blank snow of the chute made his shoulder blades tighten, but he couldn't see any path through the woods that wouldn't get him shot.

He took several more deep breaths and a long look around to be sure he wasn't running straight into a field of fire. He launched, sprinting straight back towards the avalanche chute as hard as he could. The woods erupted with shouts, and there were several pistol shots behind him. As he neared the edge of the woods, the deeper snow and breakable crust slowed him, but he plowed straight on. They were less than thirty yards behind him now, but they were still in the woods which denied them a clear shot.

As Pete came out of the woods into the chute, he was still breaking through the crust and against all instincts he had to slow down and climb up on top of the packed slab snow instead of trying to force his way through. On top of the slab he made better time, but the slope made it hard to keep his footing. He fell and plunged the knife into the snow, using it like an ice axe to arrest his slide. He scrambled up and began to run across again, as fast as he could without falling. Behind him he could hear Galvan shouting instructions to the others.

Pete dodged right and left to make a harder target. More shots cracked out and he fell again. He tumbled down the slope and landed on his back, head down, accelerating rapidly. He struggled to flip over as the small bumps and hummocks in the snow bounced him like a rag doll. Above him Galvan was shouting to get him. Pete caught fragmented flashes of them coming out toward the middle of the chute where they could get a clear shot. The slope steepened below him, and he slid out of control. Somewhere below him, this chute ended in big old growth trees with trunks three and four feet in diameter. Hitting one or going over a cliff raced through his head.

He was able to stab the knife into the snow. The speed of his slide almost ripped the knife from his hand, but he managed to hold on and it braked him just enough that he was able to twist around and have his feet slide down the slope first. Shots echoed off the mountain above him and kicked up snow around him as he slid. Pete was a difficult target to hit, sliding rapidly down away from the shooters. They could see where their shots were hitting in the snow though, which would help them correct.

Pete tried to remember what he'd read about mountaineers glissading down snow slopes. He settled for digging his knife and elbow into the snow, trying to steer his slide toward the far side of the chute. It gave him a small measure of control and he was sliding now in a shallow angle toward the woods on the far side. He began to hope that he could slow enough to get to the other side.

Galvan, Richie, Chollo and Nick had stopped just shy of the middle of the chute and were all firing now; Richie kicking his heels back into the snow so he could sit and fire more accurately. As he did, there was a deep *whumph*, and the snow settled slightly around them. Like the spreading ripples from a rock thrown into a river, the ripple of collapsing snow radiated out from them. The ripple hit their tracks where they had broken through the crust at the edge of the chute. A crack in the snow opened. Galvan stood transfixed, watching the crack shoot up along the edge of the slide path, through the gully in the cliffs above, up out of sight, into the bowl above timberline. The mountain seemed to give a small sigh. Rivulets of snow along the edge of the crack began to break loose and slide down over the surface of the slab. The sigh changed to a deep groan from the mountain above them as millions of tons of snow in the bowl suddenly detached and yielded to gravity. The avalanche exploded through the gully above them, a white wall of swirling powder churning with refrigerator-sized blocks of snow slab.

Chollo and Nick both tried to sprint back toward the side of the chute. Richie tried to race down the slope, away from the avalanche. He fell and came sliding down the slope after Pete. Galvan knew he should run, but his legs wouldn't work. In the seconds it took to reach them, his mind was filled with desperate shards of thoughts. This couldn't be real. It wasn't fair, all his wealth and power, there had to be a deal he could make. Galvan heard a high-pitched screaming sound, and just as the avalanche swallowed him, realized it was him.

Pete was sliding down the chute, down into the fog, slightly angling toward the chute's far edge. He felt, more than heard, the mountain give its low groan and then a sound like distant thunder. The shots above him stopped, and there were cries of panic. He looked back uphill to see a growing wall of white blink Galvan, Nick and Chollo out of existence. Richie was sliding down the chute after him, the avalanche above roaring down twice as fast.

There was no way Pete could outpace the avalanche straight down its path. He desperately dug in his right elbow and increased the pressure on the knife to make his slide angle more sharply towards the edge. He glanced back again. Richie was gone, as if he had never existed. The front edge of the avalanche was closer now, its roar deafening. He was going to make it out of the chute into the edge of the woods before it caught him, but this avalanche was larger than previous ones that had made the chute. It was spreading as it fell, the eddy line of moving snow well into the woods on either side, snapping off smaller trees near the edge and tumbling them end over end in the maelstrom of snow.

As Pete slid into the edge of the woods, he reached the softer snow and plowed to a stop. He churned to his feet and staggered away from the chute, the avalanche hitting him seconds later. His mouth and nose filled with powder snow. He was hurled down the slope, arms and legs akimbo as he smashed through the brush and saplings. He tried anything he could do to keep himself on the surface and keep moving into the woods. One moment he was on top and could breathe and glimpse where he was, the next he was somersaulted upside down or backwards and was struggling to breathe or know which way was up. He crawled, clawed, ran, staggered and swam in the descending torrent of white. He alternately slammed into unseen objects or was hit by blocks of snow and trees churning with him.

Several times, when Pete popped to the surface, he saw a huge old growth spruce below. Every part of his body was bruised. He had hit several smaller trees upslope and was fairly sure he had broken ribs. Hitting the big tree seemed like sure death. He was being swept straight at the tree despite his efforts to swim and crawl toward the side. He went under again, choking on powder, being pummeled by unseen objects. The snow popped him to the surface with the tree dead ahead. The snow was parting around it like white water around a boulder, the hydraulics of the rushing snow throwing up a pillow where it hit the tree. Pete slammed into the pillow and bounced around the tree. He hit the stub of a broken branch and it held for a moment before breaking. The snow shoved him around the back of the tree into an eddy on the downhill side. He grabbed at another branch, and it held long enough for him to stop being swept downhill. The snow in the eddy was more air than snow, and he fell down to the bottom of the trunk.

The avalanche continued to roar past. The spruce was probably four feet in diameter, but he could feel it shiver as blocks of snow slab and other trees hit it and the weight of snow on the uphill side continued to build. He had fallen into a small concavity at the base of the downhill side of the trunk. As long as the tree held, it was protecting him from the downhill rush of the snow, but fine powder was steadily sifting in around him, rapidly filling in the hollow and making it hard to breathe. He tried to stamp it down with his feet, to shove it out down the hill, to keep his arms and legs free and maintain a breathing space. It was probably less than two minutes, but seemed to be forever before it stopped. Minutes and seconds of bone-vibrating roar and then silence. Impossible and insane motion, and then stillness. A kaleidoscope of flashed images, and then whiteness.

The snow had closed above him. His head was braced against the tree trunk and the curve of the tree trunk formed a small hollow that gave him breathing space and allowed him to move one arm. The snow had filled in above his waist. He tried, but was unable to move his legs. He tried to shove back against the tree to create more space, but the snow was unyielding. The friction of the snow flakes rubbing against each other in an avalanche heats the molecules slightly and causes them to fuse together as soon as they stop, creating a hard frozen solid. The world was a dim white. The snow closed above his head filtered the light and made it hard to see. He listened, but the world was silent, the snow absorbing all sound. His leg ached. He thought of Annie.

Epilogue

The world was a dim white. The snow filtered the light and made it hard to see. He listened, but the world was silent, the snow absorbing all sound. He leaned against the tree trunk and shifted slightly to ease the ache in his leg. The climb up the slope and then being still for so long made it ache. As always, it made him think of Annie. He remembered the first time he had seen her, outside the Emergency Room door, the first night he held her as they watched the moon over Lynn Canal and the Chilkats.

He thought of all they had been through together, the life they had built. He thought of her smile and laugh, the line of her throat, the glisten of her hair, the way she smelled, the swell of breast and line of leg. He thought of how her simple touch made him happy. He thought of being with her under warm covers on cold nights, of talking with her over coffee in the morning. He thought about being there with her in the hospital when –

"Pop?"

The whisper interrupted his reverie. There was no wind, and the snow continued to fall heavily, big flakes sifting straight down through the trees. The world had turned a dim white and it was hard to see down the slope through the open timber. He often heard deer before he saw them, but now the snow muffled all sound.

"Pop?"

"Yeah?"

"My toes are about to freeze off."

"Mine too. I think the deer have all bedded down until this snow slacks off anyway. Let's work our way back down to the boat. If we don't cross any fresh tracks, we'll head home early and surprise your mom."

Pete looked at his son. At 15, Erik was already as tall as Pete and still growing. He looked amazingly like Pete's brother at that age, but his ready smile and the calm intellect in his eyes were from his mother.

They worked their way back down to saltwater and headed home. The big skiff ran through the snow, down over the big, slow swells rolling up Stephens Passage. They stood side-by-side behind the center console, knees flexing with each wave. Erik had loved to drive the skiff from the time he learned, sitting on Pete's lap, his hands under Pete's on the wheel and throttle. Erik ran a smooth course, angling slightly as they ran up and down the swells, without letting them stray from their compass heading. The rush of the wind and motor's roar made conversation difficult, and they were comfortably silent, lost in their own thoughts.

Pete found himself thinking of the boat ride back to Annie the night of the avalanche. He had been so battered, he hadn't been able to stand and wasn't sure he was going to be able to run the skiff home through the dark. He could remember the pressure of the snow and the dim bluish-white light that had filtered down through. After being stuck in the crevice, chased up the mountain, sliding down the chute, and being caught in the avalanche, there was strange sense of peace in the silence and dim light. He had rested for a moment and then slowly, bit by bit, tried moving. He had braced outward against the tree trunk as hard as he could when the snow was settling around him, and he had about a foot of room between his torso and the tree trunk. His right arm was free in that space, and miraculously, he had held on to his knife.

Pete used the knife to dig a hole upward past his right ear toward the dim light. The snow from the hole fell down as he dug, slowly filling the cavity between him and the tree. He realized that if he didn't reach the surface before the excavated snow filled the airspace to his mouth and nose, he wasn't going to make it. To minimize the amount of snow he was bringing down, he tried to make the upwards tunnel just big enough for his arm. From time to time he would bring his arm back down and tamp down the excavated snow to give himself more breathing room.

The snow inside was up to his collarbones when he felt the triumph of his hand breaking through the top crust. When Pete remembered the hour after his hand broke through, he always focused on images he hadn't seen; his hand with the knife breaking through the snow like Excalibur being thrust up from the lake; his hand digging away at the edges of the hole and trying to throw the snow out of the hole like a marmot flinging dirt from its burrow. He focused on those images because he didn't like remembering the constant sift of snow down the hole that kept threatening to bury his face and smother him. He savored the memory of uncovering his head enough to lift up his face. The fog had gone and the sun was sliding down behind distant mountains, but for the moment, it illuminated and warmed him, and he seemed to breathe in air and sun and life itself.

He was battered, exhausted, and in mild shock and had to rest frequently during the hours it took to dig himself the rest of the way out. He fought against falling asleep, afraid he would never wake up. His reserves were drained, and he had had to rest again before he could kick free from the last of the snow and climb out of the hole. It was night by then, but a full moon flooded the snow with light. He didn't remember much about coming out of the woods except falling and getting up over and over again and Annie in front of him like a steady beacon, beckoning him home to her.

He had made it to the skiff and let the last of the outgoing tide float him down the creek before he gathered his strength enough to start the outboard. In the dark, he almost bumped into the Bayliner they had followed him over in. It was anchored in about fifteen feet of water off the creek mouth. Pete thought for a moment and then painfully pulled the boat's anchor and put it in the skiff. He towed it out toward the middle of Stephens and dropped the anchor where it wouldn't come close to catching bottom. Maybe someone would find it drifting and get it back to whomever they had chartered it from. It would look like the Bayliner had pulled anchor, but it shouldn't lead anyone back to the cove.

Pete nudged the throttle up to the slowest speed that would keep the skiff on plane. Stars speckled the sky and the moon laid out a broad path on the water in front of him. Somehow in his memory, the stars from that night had become intermingled with the embers floating up in an evening sky when he and Annie had returned the following spring and burned the pack and the drugs.

He had followed the moon home, drifting in and out of consciousness. It was after midnight when he made Auke Bay. He sloppily tied the skiff to the dock between the two launch ramps and staggered to the pay phone outside the Harbormaster's Office. Annie reached Auke Bay in record time, not believing for a moment his reassurances on the phone that really, everything was fine, he just needed her to help him trailer the boat, there was no need to rush, he was just going to lie down in the boat and take a little nap until she got there.

Pete looked over at his son. Erik loved driving the big skiff fast, and his smile and the light in his eyes were so much his mom's it made Pete swallow. He thought about starting out with all of life before you, of all the opportunities and hazards. That night, when he had staggered free from being buried, he looked up the mountain where the avalanche had roared down. All obstructions had been swept away and the avalanche path stretched up the mountain toward the peaks and stars above him. The snow above him gleamed smooth, a clean slate illuminated by moonlight.

Author's notes and Acknowledgements

Clean Slate is a work of fiction, and Pete and Annie and almost all the characters (certainly all the bad guys) are creatures of imagination. That said, I've tried to be sure the descriptions of Alaska are genuine. The topography is accurate, the weather realistic, and all the businesses mentioned in the book are real. If you visit Juneau (and you should), stop and have a great Mexican meal at El Sombrero. I would like to start my acknowledgements by thanking the many, many people who I encountered in my thirty years of knocking around Alaska's wild places, and who, sometimes knowingly, sometimes not, furnished nuggets of information or personality that I wove into *Slate*.

Writing and publishing a novel requires many people to make leaps of faith, and I am deeply grateful to all those who helped me along the long path to publishing *Clean Slate*. In particular, I want to thank Flip Todd, Carmen Maldonado, and the whole crew at Todd Communications. Without their outstanding work, you wouldn't be reading this right now. Thanks as well to the folks at the Philip G. Spitzer Literary Agency; Philip Spitzer, Lukas Ortiz, and Lucas Hunt (now of Hunt Auctioneers). Their thoughts and suggestions made *Slate* a better book. In the book, Pete owns a bookstore, and it is mentioned how Susan and Deb, who then co-owned Hearthside Books down the street, could have viewed him as the competition, but instead provided ongoing encouragement and wisdom. Hearthside Books, is real and Susan Hickey was an early reader of the manuscript. Thanks to her for her encouragement, support, and advice. Jim Howe, author of *Red Crew*, read *Slate* more recently and provided encouragement and support at a critical time when I was close to dropping the project.

If one can thank a state, I want to thank Alaska. Its mountains and oceans, its weather and people, and flora and fauna are all part of *Slate*. It's unforgiving, but I want to thank it for leaving me alive a few times when it could have gone the other way. Hopefully the lessons I learned are part of this book.

Lastly, but most importantly, I want to thank all my family. Much of what I bring to writing is from them. My wife, Barbara Campbell, has been my editor extraordinaire, sounding board, and literary patron. We lived Alaska together, every step of the way.

BLUEWATER PRESS

PROUDLY PRESENTS

NORTH COAST

by

M<u>c</u>Kie Campbell

Available from BlueWater Press
March 2021

Turn the page for Chapter 1 of
North Coast . . .

1

The brash ice and bergy bits had almost closed around her, the path to clear water growing steadily thinner. Miles to the east, the air over the Stikine Icefield was growing heavier as it cooled, settling into crevices, filling depressions on the ice and flowing to the next low spot. Except for the movement of a few small mists, the gathering wind was invisible as more air was pulled down from the sky and slid across the theoretical line that divided Canada and Alaska, down the slopes of the ice that funneled out between the mountains, accelerating as the floes came together to tumble down the Dawes Glacier to tidewater.

Grace had broken camp early and paddled as close as she dared to the glacier's face, taking pictures of harbor seals, something about the misty light bringing out the blue of the ice. The face of the Dawes was over two hundred and fifty feet high, over thirty stories tall. Chunks occasionally calved off, the sound like thunder rolling across the water to her, the following swell lifting her kayak and causing the ice to hiss and growl around her. She could feel the wind starting to build, cold even now in late June. It was starting to shift the ice and grind it together. The granite walls on either side plunged into the water, and she knew the first decent campsite was a fifteen mile paddle. Reluctantly, she decided it was time to start the long trip home, twenty miles back down Endicott Arm and another forty-five north to Juneau.

As she was leaving, she saw another kayaker on the far side of arm, also paddling away from the glacier. Their courses slowly converged until she could see it was a young man, the first person she had seen in two days. He paddled closer and waved his paddle at her. He had long blonde hair and a thick German accent. The wind was blowing hard now, snatching away parts of the conversation as they shouted back and forth between the boats, "Did you see . . .? Amazing! Schön! Mother seal and two pups . . . Like a building calving off and crashing down into the water . . . Wunderbar!" He was heading toward the same campsite, and they agreed to paddle together.

The wind was at their backs, helping them on their way. They paddled hard up the backs of each wave, holding up their paddles as they crested to catch the wind and surf down the front, hooting and hollering with exhilaration. About five miles from the glacier, a large, white yacht passed them, coming up the far side of the arm. Endicott was over a mile wide here, and Grace didn't pay the yacht any attention other than being glad she'd left the glacier before it came. The man was a fast paddler, and she pushed herself, keeping pace. Even with the favorable winds and the tide helping, it was a long paddle, but they made the campsite sooner than expected.

"So, Kurt, how long have you been out paddling?"

"Since 30 May. I start in Ketchikan, stop. How do you say . . . reprovision? I reprovision in Petersburg. I'm going to Juneau, reprovision there and then go to Glacier Bay. Maybe down outside of Chichagof and Baranof Islands, depending on weather. It's incredible, ya?"

"It is incredible. You get any pictures of the big bergs calving off the glacier this morning?"

Above the tiny beach, the inward curve of the rock walls provided a break from the wind, and they fired up Grace's camp stove in the shelter of a huge drift log that had lodged here, half out of the water. They continued to talk while they boiled water for tea and shared freeze-dried beef Stroganoff. Kurt snapped a picture of Grace as she knelt beside the stove. Grace thought that Kurt was probably several years younger than she. His English was heavily accented, but fine for them to communicate. He kept gesturing around saying, "Can you believe? It is so beautiful!" The campsite was not really big enough for two tents, and Grace wanted to avoid any conversations about "Why don't we just share a tent?" She said that since they'd made such good time, she was going to push on the extra five miles to the mouth of Ford's Terror.

"There's a campsite above the mouth of the entrance that I used on the way in. It has a view over a little tide flat and the channel. When I stayed there the first time, I counted seventeen waterfalls, and there were snowcapped mountains all around," she said.

Kurt had also figured out there was really only room for one tent. "You're sure? This is nice campsite. Long paddle already."

She was sure, and Kurt said the next site sounded like a great place, and if it was OK with her, he would paddle along with her. He seemed like a nice guy, and after several days by herself, Grace was enjoying the company. She told him he was welcome to come, emphasizing that the next site had room for both of their tents.

They did the dishes at the edge of the water and repacked their gear, then headed out. The wind was still blowing hard. The waves here had been building down the fifteen miles of fetch from the head of Endicott Arm and were much bigger. Grace and Kurt alternately lost sight of each other as they slid down into the troughs. Grace was glad they weren't paddling into it and told herself it was only another five miles.

They paddled along the southern shore of the arm, where the waves seemed a bit less steep. Just before they turned to angle across the channel toward the entrance to Ford's Terror, they saw a sow bear and two large cubs on a little ledge above the water. Grace and Kurt both watched for a while, bracing with their paddles as the waves swept under them and back-paddling to hold position in the wind. Grace debated taking her camera out of its waterproof case, but decided that she would probably get it doused with salt water.

After a few minutes, Grace motioned to Kurt to stay and watch if he wanted. Even with favorable winds and tide, twenty miles was a long day in a kayak. It was starting to get dark, and she was ready to get to the campsite. He wanted to watch the bears longer, so motioning back and forth, they agreed she'd go on and he'd catch up with her. When Grace was almost across the channel, she stopped for a minute to rest and look back. Kurt had finished watching the bears by then and was paddling across as well. He was about a third of the way across the mile-wide arm. Up the arm, the big yacht they'd seen earlier was coming back down, toward Kurt. It was still distant, but seemed on a course that would take it uncomfortably close. Grace knew the height of the waves made it hard to see his kayak, and it was past sunset, the clouds hurrying the twilight.

She fumbled in the pocket of her paddling jacket and pulled a small pair of binoculars out of a Ziploc bag. The telescopic effect of the binoculars compressed the distance and increased the impression that the yacht was bearing down on Kurt. When Grace rode up on top of a swell, she could see him and the yacht. Then she'd go down in a trough and couldn't see anything. The waves made it difficult to brace with the paddle and look through the binocs at the same time. When she and Kurt were both on wave tops at the same time, she waved to him, trying to attract his attention and get him to look back over his shoulder. Kurt saw her and seemed to think she had changed her mind and was waiting for him. He waved back to her enthusiastically. Grace pointed to the yacht, trying to get him to look, but they were out of synch on the waves, just able to catch glimpses of each other.

She didn't know whether it was her frantic pointings or the sound of the yacht's motor that caused Kurt to turn and look, but when the next wave crest rode her up, she could see Kurt waving his paddle in the air so the yacht's driver would see him.

Through the binoculars, she couldn't see anyone on the bridge; it looked like it was on autopilot. Kurt was much closer to the yacht, and he must have seen the same thing, because Grace could see him suddenly turn the kayak and dig in, paddling as hard as he could back toward the southern shore. Just then, through the yacht's windshield, Grace could see a figure walk into the bridge with a cup of coffee or a drink in his hand. Unable to do anything, she watched the person standing there looking around, not seeing Kurt as he frantically tried to paddle out of the way. Grace's kayak slid down into a trough, and she lost sight until the next wave lifted her, just in time to watch the man see Kurt and lunge for the wheel, the yacht lurching in a violent turn.

It looked like Kurt might have been hit by the side of the boat or just flipped by its huge wake. The yacht slowed and about a hundred yards farther, stopped and came about, jogging in place against the waves.

It was difficult for her to see through the water-spotted lenses of the binoculars, and the sudden salt of tears mingled with the spray hitting her face. She couldn't spot Kurt at first, but then as a wave lifted her up, she saw the bottom of his kayak floating upside down and thought she saw a flash of color near it from his yellow paddling jacket and red life vest.

The yacht worked its way back up beside the kayak and several men came out on the back deck, peering down into the water.

"Pull him out you bastards! Get him out of the water!" Grace's shouts were snatched away by the wind and she knew there wasn't a chance of the men hearing her. She started to paddle back towards them. She hadn't made it more than three or four strokes when the men went back into the cabin, and the yacht suddenly throttled back up, leaving the scene, heading out Endicott Arm.

She hesitated for a moment, not believing they were just going to go off and leave Kurt and then continued paddling back towards him, fighting the wind and waves. If they were going to leave him, she wanted to get to him as fast as possible, to get him to shore somehow. As she topped a wave, a man walked out on the yacht's back deck and, by chance, looked straight at her. He stared for a moment before disappearing back into the cabin. The yacht throttled back and lay among the waves for a moment before turning and accelerating straight at her.

Grace turned and fled back toward the entrance to Ford's Terror, paddling harder than she ever had. When she looked back, she could see the yacht at full throttle, smashing through the waves, explosions of spray sometimes obscuring it from sight as it bore down on her.

She made for the entrance of Ford's Terror, praying for the growing darkness to hide her, trying to reach the part of the entrance channel where it suddenly shallowed and they wouldn't be able to follow. At the crest of each wave, she glanced back over her shoulder. The yacht was rapidly closing when they throttled back and stopped. The skipper must have been watching his fathometer and knew about the large boulders and rock peaks that hid under the water's surface as the channel narrowed. Grace felt a rush of relief, immediately canceled when she saw they were using the yacht's crane to launch its tender.

The water was more protected here, and she paddled hard, helped by the start of the incoming tide. Up ahead she could see more and more rocks sticking up through the water's surface. She considered beaching the kayak and climbing up into the woods, but thought they would be able to catch her even more easily.

They had the RIB launched now, a rigid-hull inflatable boat. A spotlight swept back and forth and then fixed on her. She glanced over her shoulder again, but the light blinded her as the boat sped toward her. She could hear the approach of its big outboard as she dug in with her paddle, trying to reach the rocks. She thought they were going to run her down and tensed for the collision, but at the last moment, the driver slowed the boat to create maximum wake as he wrenched the RIB in a sharp turn just before they would have collided. The wake almost capsized her, and she realized that's what they were trying to do.

The wake rolled her until her shoulder touched the water, but she used a high brace stroke to right herself as the men circled back for another run. This time the wake hit her, and the inflatable tube of the RIB bumped her kayak with a hard jolt, knocking her upside-down. As she went over, she grabbed a deep breath and fought the momentary burst of panic as her head went beneath the black water. Anger kicked in, and she used the paddle to lever herself up in an Eskimo roll.

Just as she came up, their wake hit again, and she went back over, this time without being able to get a full breath. She tried to roll back up, knowing that as soon as she did, they would hit her again with the wake. It was dark now, too dark to see underwater. Something brushed her cap and then caught her braid, tugging. Breath running out, panic threatened to burst within her. Her shoulder and arm brushed something hard, and she realized that is was the top of a boulder. The tide and the boat's wake were continuing to push her into the entrance's neck.

Hanging upside down in the water, Grace pulled loose the spray-skirt that had kept her in the kayak. She shoved herself down, out of the capsized kayak, and somersaulted under the water, her life jacket buoying her back up. She surfaced with her head in the air pocket under the overturned kayak so they couldn't see her. It was almost July, but the water farther up the arm was clogged with glacial ice. The neck, wrist, and waist seals of her paddling jacket kept most of the water from her torso, but it was still so cold it was hard to breathe. She tried to steady her breathing, and then ducked back under water as the beam of the spotlight swept toward her and found the overturned kayak.

Looking up from just below the surface, Grace could see the spotlight glowing through the translucent fiberglass of the kayak's hull. The light moved on, looking for her, and she came back up with her head under the kayak again. Her feet, hanging down, brushed the bottom. Underwater, she'd lost her orientation on which way was into the channel, but she assumed it was away from the spotlight. She tried to assist the drift of the capsized kayak in the current with subtle pushes from her feet on the bottom. She could feel the bottom starting to slope up, and her legs hit rocks. She bent her knees so she wouldn't come out of the water. One end of the kayak banged into a rock, and it slowly pivoted as it was swept farther into the channel. The current was accelerating as the channel shallowed. The kayak scraped along another rock.

Grace ducked out from under the kayak so she could see where she was. By now it was dark enough that she didn't think they could see her unless the spotlight hit her. She could hear the men talking to each other.

"Damir, see if you can wade over there and check."

"Fuck. Cold water, and you know I don't swim. She doesn't come back up. She's drown for sure by now. Both of them capsize and drown. It happens up here. End of problem."

"It's shallow, just wade over there and check the kayak. I want to see her body."

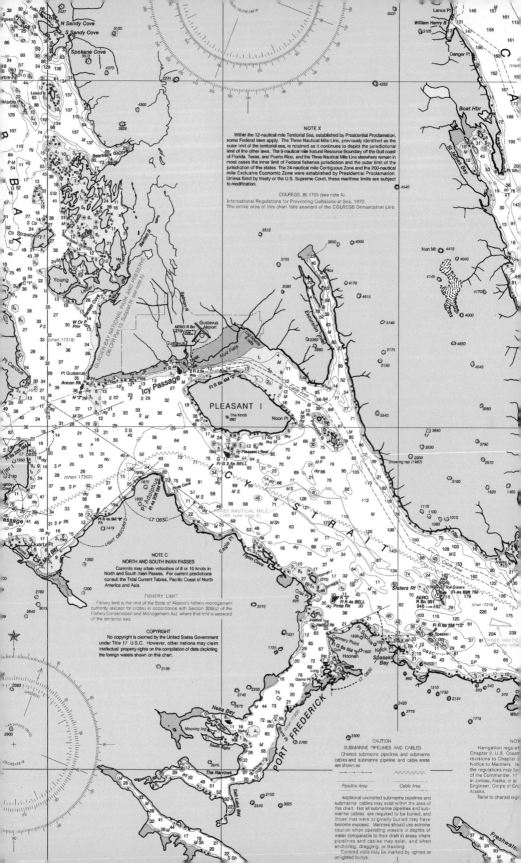

NOTE X

Within the 12-nautical mile Territorial Sea, established by Presidential Proclamation, some Federal laws apply. The Three Nautical Mile Line, previously identified as the outer limit of the territorial sea, is retained as it continues to depict the jurisdictional limit of the other laws. The 9-nautical mile Natural Resource Boundary off the Gulf coast of Florida, Texas, and Puerto Rico, and the Three Nautical Mile Line elsewhere remain in most cases the inner limit of Federal fisheries jurisdiction and the outer limit of the jurisdiction of the states. The 24-nautical mile Contiguous Zone and the 200-nautical mile Exclusive Economic Zone were established by Presidential Proclamation. Unless fixed by treaty or the U.S. Supreme Court, these maritime limits are subject to modification.

COLREGS, 80.1705 (see note A)
International Regulations for Preventing Collisions at Sea, 1972.
The entire area of this chart falls seaward of the COLREGS Demarcation Line.

NOTE C
NORTH AND SOUTH INIAN PASSES
Currents may attain velocities of 8 or 10 knots in North and South Inian Passes. For current predictions consult the Tidal Current Tables, Pacific Coast of North America and Asia.

FISHERY LIMIT
Fishery limit is the limit of the State of Alaska's fishery management authority (except for crabs) in accordance with Section 306(c) of the Fishery Conservation and Management Act, where that limit is seaward of the territorial sea.

COPYRIGHT
No copyright is claimed by the United States Government under Title 17 U.S.C. However, other nations may claim intellectual property rights on the compilation of data depicting the foreign waters shown on this chart.

CAUTION
SUBMARINE PIPELINES AND CABLES
Charted submarine pipelines and submarine cables and submarine pipeline and cable areas are shown as

Pipeline Area   Cable Area

Additional uncharted submarine pipelines and submarine cables may exist within the area of this chart. Not all submarine pipelines and submarine cables are required to be buried, and those that were originally buried may have become exposed. Mariners should use extreme caution when operating vessels in depths of water comparable to their draft in areas where pipelines and cables may exist, and when anchoring, dragging, or trawling.
Covered wells may be marked by lighted or unlighted buoys.

NO
Navigation regula
Chapter 2, U.S. Coast
revisions to Chapter 2
the regulations may be
of the Commander, 17
in Juneau, Alaska, or at
Engineer, Corps of En
Alaska.
Refer to charted reg